TOWARD THE NORTH

STORIES BY CHINESE CANADIAN WRITERS

edited by
Hua Laura Wu
Xueqing Xu
Corinne Bieman Davies

inanna poetry & fiction series

INANNA PUBLICATIONS AND EDUCATION INC.
TORONTO, CANADA

*To new Canadians
and those who support them.*

Table of Contents

Introduction

HUA LAURA WU, XUEQING XU,
CORINNE BIEMAN DAVIES

Originally written in Chinese, these twelve stories have been translated into English to make them available to a general audience, and to scholars and students in Canada and abroad. These are stories of immigrants by immigrants. They reflect how new immigrants struggle to integrate into a new Canadian world; how they cope with gender and class issues, racial bias, cultural differences, and unfamiliar social norms. All the works have been published in Chinese literary magazines in mainland China, Taiwan, and Hong Kong, or in literary columns of Chinese newspapers in North America. Some of the writers have received major literary awards in China; a number of their works have been adapted into movies and TV series in mainland China. The stories included in this anthology were written in Canada between approximately 1990 and 2010. The titles of the original journals in which the stories first appeared have been translated into English.

Toward the North is the first volume of its kind published in Canada. The story writers in this volume approach life quite differently from the second or third generation Chinese-Canadian authors writing in English (who are familiar to us), with their much vaguer sense of distant cultural roots. Having grown up and been educated in China, the new immigrant writers introduced here (in translation) retain strong cultural bonds with their homeland. Their stories about Chinese transplantation into Canadian society are tinged with deep cultural sentiment, fresh feelings of Chinese transnational and cross-cultural experience, and a strong sense of ethnic predicament. The fiction of second or third generation Chinese Canadians tends to be filtered through the focus of the children or the grandchildren of Chinese immigrants.

The title story "Toward the North" by Ling Zhang recounts Zhongyue's one-year teaching experience on a reserve near Sioux Lookout, Northwestern Ontario, as a specialist in child psychology. His pedagogical practice leads him to befriend a Métis boy and his mother; he becomes a witness to tragedy resulting from cultural clashes. It presents its theme of cultural and personal liberation in a famous and remembered song from the time of The Cultural Revolution:

Go toward the north, go toward the north
The children in the south are looking for their liberators.

All of the authors, but one, in this collection lived through The Cultural Revolution in China from 1966 to 1976. The context of this song and the time period lead to further layers of meaning in all of the stories.

Enter, then, into the worlds of wives, lovers, husbands, children, and babies, grandmothers, liars, murderers, immigration scams, vases, cats, and ultimately liberation.

This anthology meets the increasing demand for fiction by Chinese-Canadian writers for study in colleges and universities. More significantly, perhaps, it will entertain general readers, and encourage understanding of contemporary Chinese Canadian life in our multicultural land.

Jia Na Da/Canada

YUANZHI

FENG JIAN STUMBLED OUT of the hospital in a daze. Heading towards the parking lot, he rummaged for the car key in his pocket. Perhaps he had left it in the delivery room. Or he might have left it in his wife's hospital room. He was just about to turn back when he realized the key was in his other hand. He had been holding it so tight that his palm was damp. "Son of a bitch!" He spat out the curse as he opened the car door and quickly got in. He inserted the key into the ignition, turned it to the right, and the engine purred into action. He released the brake, put the shift in drive, and was just about to step on the gas when he realized that he had forgotten all about the seatbelt. So he shifted back into park, fastened the seatbelt, and started all over again. Finally, he drove out of the parking lot, slowly and unsteadily.

When he merged into the westbound traffic on Finch Street, the sun was setting. Driving into the red glare, Feng Jian thought it looked as though someone had smeared the distant horizon with blood from the obstetrics table. As if to escape from the bloodstain, he stepped on the accelerator. Almost at the same moment, a siren sounded, so loudly that it felt like the ground was shaking. He imagined the high-pitched siren puncturing the clear blue sky over his head, leaving it with hundreds of holes.

Instead of the bloody red, Feng Jian now saw a white void. He realized that he had driven through a red light. "Damn it!"

A policeman got out of the patrol car and walked over. He was tall and sturdy, with [add a] receding hair line. He asked, smiling, whether Feng Jian knew the speed limit. Feng Jian murmured, "Sixty kilometres." The policeman then asked what his speed was when he went through the red light. Feng Jian lowered his head and said in a small voice that he did not know.

"One hundred and ten kilometres, sir!" the policeman said, holding his hand out for Feng Jian driver's licence.

"I am sorry, officer. I did not mean to. My wife just gave birth to a baby. I have not slept since yesterday. I took the red light for blood ... no, blood for the sun ... no, no, no, I thought the red light was the sun. I do have a very good driving record. Could you...?"

"Congratulations, your wife had a baby! Boy or girl?"

"A girl," he answered without enthusiasm.

"You are so lucky!" the policeman responded, with what Feng Jian thought was exaggerated zeal. "I have three boys. My God, I envy you!"

You envy me? It is I who should envy you, Feng Jian thought to himself.

"Anyway, you're a father now, and you should be a more responsible and careful driver." His booklet in hand, the policeman started to write out the fine. The smooth movement he made was like that of a knife slicing back and forth, each and every slice cutting into Feng Jian's heart.

"Because your wife just gave birth to a daughter, I will only fine you for failing to stop at a red light. I could give you another one for speeding." He gave Feng Jian the ticket for $140 along with his driver's licence. With a shrug, he walked back to the police car. "Have a nice day!"

Nice day? Are you joking? Getting another daughter and a fine on the same day, Feng Jian felt he was totally out of luck. He threw the ticket on the passenger seat and started the engine with a trembling hand. He had to get to his friends' place fast. Jiajia, his oldest daughter, had been staying with the Tangs' for two days. He must pick her up, get back home, make some chicken soup, and take it to his wife.

On his way home, Feng Jian began to brood. He couldn't understand why he and his brothers were unable to produce a single male child. Because it had so many boys, the Feng family used to be the envy of the neighbourhood in his hometown. What was wrong with his generation? After he had his first daughter, his two younger brothers had daughters in quick succession, as if they were in a competition with him. The Chinese used to believe that the greatest offence against filial piety was failing to produce a grandson. Of course, Feng Jian[1] was not so old fashioned that he would share such a feudalistic and patriarchal attitude. However, his dear mother did not get along with her sister-in-law. His uncle's wife had two sons and a daughter, and they had two boys and a girl, too. She was extremely pleased with her good luck at having two grandsons, and her smug contentment offended Feng Jian's mother, who felt that she could not hold her head high whenever she bumped into a neighbour with a grandson. His mother's sighs could have filled up a large oxygen cylinder.

Feng Jian felt obliged to cure his mother's unhappiness by giving her a grandson. So he began to consider emigrating to Canada.[2] Fortunately he was in the right profession and had earned some good money a few years back when he had worked in Shenzhen. When he went on a seven-day tour of Hong Kong, he consulted an immigration agency there. The consultant estimated that he could score seventy-four points, so he paid six thousand U.S. Adollars there and then. He left Hong Kong and waited back home. Sixteen months later, he and his family arrived in Toronto.

Upon arrival, other new immigrants started English lessons and job hunting right away. Feng Jian, however, immediately went on an information-gathering mission to ensure that the next child he had would be a boy. Someone told him that changing their diet was essential because high protein and high sugar food, supposedly, boosted the chance of having a girl. Consequently, the Feng household stopped purchasing anything sweet, and even stopped adding sugar to pork stew, their favourite dish. Someone else suggested that his wife, Sheng Jiqi, use soda to cleanse her private parts before going to bed. This method was said to be scientifically sound and highly effective, because the Y chromosomes that produce a male child could only survive in a slightly alkaline environment. Since a daily soda rinse could produce such a condition, the probability of producing a boy was as high as ninety-two percent. It was nicknamed "the scientific way to cultivate the land." So the bathroom in the Feng household now contained a box or two of baking soda.

Four months later, Sheng Jiqi calculated that her period was about ten days late. It so happened that their OHIP coverage had gone into effect as well, so she went to see a family doctor who confirmed that she was indeed pregnant. By then, they had been following the new diet for three months, and she had been rinsing with soda for about two months. She also felt different this time compared to her first pregnancy. Feng and Sheng were delighted. When Sheng Jiqi was seven months pregnant, their friends and their landlady told them that the shape of her belly indicated she was having a boy. According to them, if a pregnant woman had a dome-like belly and the tip of the dome leant forward, she was carrying a boy. If she was carrying a girl, her belly would be in a ball shape, bulging out front and back. Sheng Jiqi had a dome-shaped belly. The couple were overcome with joy.

When the doctor said "Congratulations" to him after the baby was born, Feng Jian assumed that it was a boy. "It's a pretty girl!" the doctor continued. Feng was left dumbfounded.

Fortunately, they had not told their relatives back in China that Sheng had been pregnant because they had planned to give them a pleasant surprise. Instead, they had another daughter!

The baby girl was, nevertheless, still their flesh and blood. They'd better get her a birth certificate, the nurse reminded him, when he took the chicken soup to the hospital. Feng Jian had chosen a name for a boy. His Chinese name would be Dawei, his English name Davie, and his diminutive name Dada. The Chinese and English names sounded alike; moreover, the characters were good, their sounds good and their connotations good, too. The names were just like their daughter's: Jiajia in Chinese and Jessica in English, a good match. But now their original choice was useless. What would they call this little girl?

Sheng Jiqi insisted on naming her daughter Liana and giving her the pet name Nana. When Sheng was a girl, she had read a Russian novel whose heroine was called Liana. The character had left such an endearing impression that she had wanted to name her oldest daughter Liana. However, her sisters were strongly against it. They told her there were so many Mannas, Annas, and Lenas around that Liana had lost its exotic nature and become common. Now they were in Canada, and it did not matter if Liana was "common." Feng Jian neither fancied nor hated the name, so he deferred to his wife's preference and put Liana on the form the nurse had asked them to fill out.

"Come on Nana, let Daddy hold you so that Mommy can have some chicken soup." Feng Jian took the baby from her mother and sighed. "Nana, it would be terrific if you were a boy. Then you would not be called Nana, but Dada and Davie. Just like your sister; she is Jiajia and Jessica. Jiajia-Jessica and Dada-Davie are beautiful and resounding names. Now you end up with Nana-Liana. Nana ... Eventually, we'll have Jiajia, Nana, and Dada. Jiajia, Nana, Dada? Hey, Jiqi, what do you think about these names?"

"What?" Sheng Jiqi was taken by surprise.

"Jiajia, Nana, Dada, Jia-Na-Da, don't they sound like Cana-da? Let's have another child and it will be a boy. Let's have Jia-Na-Da! Canada!" Feng Jian warmed increasingly towards the idea. He had been exhausted, but now he felt rejuvenated.

At that moment, having a son seemed as easy as pie.

"Another child? Do you really believe that the sole purpose of my coming to a foreign country is to bear children for your family? Am I a breeding machine to you?" Sheng Jiqi[3] was upset. "Look at you. You have been in Canada more than a year, and you still do not have a permanent job, just part-time jobs or contract work. Your income is as meagre as a labourer's, and we have to use our savings to pay bills. And you still want another child!"

"There is nothing to worry about. We'll have bread and milk, and I'll find a real job. Also, don't forget that you have promised."

"What promise...? Your brothers tricked me." Sheng Jiqi gave him an angry look. But she did recall the farewell banquet Feng Jian's parents and brothers had thrown them on the eve of their departure.

At that banquet, one of Feng Jian's younger brothers was a bit drunk after a few rounds of toasting. Acting upon the moment, he said to Sheng Jiqi, "Dear sister-in-law, please drink up." Then, imitating a character in the Beijing opera *The Red Lantern*, he held up his glass and said, "May the weight of the revolutionary mission now fall on your shoulders!" Sheng Jiqi felt the blood rush to her head and her face burn. She knew what the "revolutionary mission" meant, and she found herself in a very awkward situation. She could not accept, nor could she reject, the toast. Immediately Feng's mother and sisters-in-laws called out, "Yes, yes, drink up, drink up!" Facing all those expectant eyes, Sheng Jiqi simply could not say no, and so after a brief moment's hesitation, she tilted her head backwards and drank up. From that moment on, the toast became a promise to Feng Jian, but to her it was an unbearable weight, especially now after giving birth to Nana.

Feng Jian persisted. "You know, the revolution is yet to succeed, and you and I must keep trying. If we do not have a son, how can we have the courage to face our loved ones in China?

As for our life here, we can manage. Even if we did not work, our savings could still support us for a year or two. Haven't you heard the saying that Canada means 'da-jia-na,' 'na-da-jia,' and 'da-na-jia'? That is, 'everyone dishes out from the big communal pot.' If you have more children, you are entitled to more benefits; if you have fewer, you are entitled to fewer, and if you have none, you are entitled to nothing. So why not have more? If we have another child, we are simply taking a bit more from the big pot! Look at those refugees from all over the world. They all seem to have a brood of kids, and are they poorer than we? No. They can eat and drink until their bellies are full, and they can have whatever fun they fancy. Remember what our Prime Minister Jean Chrétien once said about those people: they just take welfare money and drink beer at home. They felt offended and went out to protest. That is truly "na-da-jia"—everyone is entitled to take what he wants from the communal pot. Admirable!"

"But that 'scientific way to cultivate the land' was said to have a success rate of ninety-two percent; yet, it failed us. Do you still want to try? Just for the sake of arguing, say I was willing to try again—but what if we get another girl?"

"Then we are not destined to have a son, and we'll take it."

"Three daughters! Our family would certainly be like the one in the film *A Sweet Life*."[4]

"Three daughters are not too many. We would still be two short of five golden flowers.[5] Life is a gamble. If you dare to take the risk, there is a chance of success. If you don't, then there is no chance at all. Just now Tang's wife told me she heard of a 'comprehensive scientific way to cultivate the land,' and it's a sure bet."

"Are you kidding me? We tried 'the scientific way,' and it didn't work. Now you want to try a 'comprehensive scientific way?'" Sheng Jiqi snapped.

Feng Jian was really serious. "We did not give the method enough time during last round. You shouldn't take this matter lightly. This method is, scientifically, one hundred percent sound. Your task now is to take good care of yourself." And he couldn't help cracking a joke: "You know, if the land is fertile, the crop will be bountiful."

"Do you mean to say if we do not get the desired harvest, my land is barren?"

"Shut up! You are talking nonsense!" Feng Jian took up Nana's tiny hand and gave Sheng Jiqi's face a couple of gentle pats. They burst into laughter while Nana started wailing.

When the baby was barely a month old, Feng Jian was already pestering Tang and his wife, Tian, for the "comprehensive scientific way to cultivate the land." According to the theory, they had to keep testing Sheng's body temperature to figure out when she ovulated, in addition to continuing with the diet and the soda rinse. They also had to consult a chart that listed the most opportune dates to conceive a boy, taking into account the husband's and wife's birthdays. If one of those days overlapped with the wife's time of ovulation, then the couple would certainly produce a son. Tian took a lot of trouble to get a photocopy of the chart from a colleague of a friend's friend. She passed on the chart to Feng, a map for the treasure trove he had dreamed of so long.

Whenever Feng got a moment, he would unfold the chart on the table and study it just like a soldier studying a military map, murmuring to himself, gesturing with his fingers, and doing mental calculations. He was as serious as a general planning manoeuvres just before a battle of vital importance. To indulge him, Sheng Jiqi did her best: she followed the recommended diet, took her temperature, and kept up with the daily soda rinse. She followed the "comprehensive" method to the last detail.

While the Fengs were trying, Tian gave birth to a boy. Feng Jian was impressed by their successful implementation of the method, and now was even more convinced of its effectiveness.

However, Tang and Tian told him that they hadn't used the "scientific way to cultivate the land," but had just let nature take its own course. Moreover, they pointed out that the chance of having a boy or a girl was fifty-fifty, without the help of science. And they would have preferred a daughter. But no matter how hard they tried to convince him, Feng Jian would not believe them. He simply could not imagine anyone would prefer daughters to sons, as Tang and Tian claimed.

He and Sheng Jiqi sped up their preparation now. On even higher alert, they were like soldiers on a battleground, eyes squarely on the target, body and mind intensely ready. Once the moment came, they would charge forward. Whenever the most opportune day drew near, Feng Jian would become super hyper. He was so eager to do it that he was like an experienced farmer who had the plough and seeds ready and waiting. As soon as the spring came and the cuckoos sang, he would go to the field and plough and sow without delay.

One Sunday, still a week before the special day of that month, Sheng Jiqi sensed something going wrong. Her period was about a week late and she had symptoms of morning sickness. She woke up Feng Jian, who was sleeping in.

He rubbed his eyes, still not fully awake. "Could that be possible?"

Sheng Jiqi was worried. "Why not? Do you remember that classmate of yours who is now a visiting scholar at U of T? A while ago, we invited him over for supper. You drank that evening. I told you that you shouldn't drink because you get drunk from a sip of beer, but you didn't listen to me. You kept saying it was not an everyday event that you would run into an old friend in a foreign city, so you would not mind getting drunk at all. When your friend left, you started to fool around. You insisted that nothing would happen if we did it. Also you refused to use any protection. Have you forgotten?"

Feng Jian put on an innocent air, saying, "Did I do that? I ... I don't remember."

Sheng Jiqi was furious. "You were drunk. I tried to reason with you, but you didn't listen. Now you're trying to blame me. Are you saying that I have been...?"

Feng Jian immediately backed down. He comforted his wife by admitting that he himself was at fault, that the most important thing was not laying blame but figuring out what to do, because he clearly remembered that, according to the chart, that day was for conceiving a girl.

"What should we do? What should we do? Should we...?" He wanted to suggest an abortion but did not know how to tell his wife.

Sheng Jiqi came to his aid. She told him that she would go to see her doctor for a pregnancy test the next day, and they'd decide what to do when they got the result. When the test confirmed that Sheng Jiqi was indeed pregnant, they talked and talked, and eventually Sheng Jiqi agreed to an abortion, though very reluctantly.

However, just before the appointment, Sheng Jiqi changed her mind. As a woman, she felt very badly for her unborn daughter. Why should a boy get the chance to live while a girl would be aborted? Aren't we living in a modern era? Why is a son treasured more than a daughter? Isn't that patriarchal and inhumane? Sheng Jiqi told her husband that if they aborted the fetus, she would never bear a child for him again. Also, if they kept the baby and it happened to be a girl, she would not go through another pregnancy, ever again. She was a human being, not a breeding machine. She had decided that she would no longer act as the means to ensure the continuation of the family line for the Fengs.

Feng Jian was in a dilemma. Sweet talking was not working this time, and he did not even dare to try intimidation. So he had no other option but to wait and hope. The day for the abortion drew closer, but they could not come to an agreement. Sheng Jiqi called her doctor to cancel the appointment, saying that she might have miscalculated the time of her last period and therefore she did not actually know how far along her pregnancy was. She said she would like to figure that out and then make another appointment. Her doctor told her that she could have an ultrasound done before the abortion so that she would know for sure. Sheng Jiqi couldn't say no. Even though her delaying tactic hadn't worked, having an ultrasound was a good option. She remembered Tian once said that a woman could say no to abortion even when she was in the operating room.

The doctor who did the ultrasound was very thorough. He repeated the whole procedure and even asked another doctor to double check. Sheng Jiqi became more and more impatient, recalling that the ultrasound when she was pregnant with Nana was very quick. Why was it taking so long this time? She was just about to ask if something was wrong with the fetus when the doctor told her that she was having twins. He asked her to look at the two shadowy shapes on the monitor and then asked if she intended to go ahead with the abortion. Sheng Jiqi was stunned, and, after a very long while, said she had to consult her husband first.

When Feng Jian was informed, he immediately abandoned his original stance and staunchly objected to the abortion. "There have been no twins in my family, not ever. It's a one- in-a-thousand chance to have twins. Of course we'll keep them."

"What if they're girls?"

"That won't change a thing. I'll then be the father of four golden flowers."

"You set your mind on having 'Jia-Na-Da/Canada', didn't you? What do we do if we have two more girls?"

After a short silence, Feng Jian said, "We'll still have 'Jia-Na-Da/Canada.' There are so many girl names beginning with a D—say, Diana, Debbie, and Daisy. Our third child, no matter if it's a boy or a girl, will have a name with a D, and his or her pet name will still be Dada. And what do we call our fourth child? Well, she can be Jennifer. Remember my classmate in the

States? His daughter is a Jennifer. Her Chinese name is Zhihua, which sounds like Jennifer. Our daughter will be Zhihua—a flower. She can be a flower of Canada. What do you think?"

"Whatever! Four children, all at once. I guess we'll always live a life of poverty."

"Do not worry. Canada will help us raise our children."

"I am done with having babies, son or no son. Can you accept that you might not ever have a son?"

Feng Jian replied very seriously: "I gave it a lot of thought yesterday and got it figured out. There are so many parents who have no son, and there are those who do not even have a daughter. We should be content with our girls. In fact, daughters are closer to their parents. People like to say that you raise a son and he will become someone else's son eventually, while if you bring up a daughter you'll get a son for free. We will have quite a few sons in the future. That's fine by me."

Sheng Jiqi was surprised at Feng Jian's about-face, but this big change was more than welcome. However, she still felt badly for him and really wanted to comfort him. She racked her brains for what to say, and eventually said, "It would be great if we could have a Feng for a son-in-law. Our daughters' sons would then be Fengs."

Feng Jian was overjoyed. He liked the idea and suggested that they should start befriending acquaintances and people from their hometown who had the family name Feng. If they carried out the search while their children were still young, he was sure that one of their four daughters would find a Feng for a husband!

While they were anticipating, happily and excitedly, the prospect of having a Feng as a son-in-law, the telephone rang. It was their family doctor. He wanted Shen Jiqi to have an amniocentesis. He explained that she was already thirty-six, and considered at higher risk of having a baby with defects than a younger woman. If the fetus had a problem, an abortion could be arranged.

So, Sheng Jiqi had the test when she was sixteen weeks pregnant, but didn't hear from her doctor that the baby was fine until the twentieth week of her pregnancy, when an abortion was really no longer an option. The doctor asked her if she wanted to know the sex of her babies. Sheng Jiqi immediately replied: "Aren't they both girls?"

Her doctor asked: "How do you know?"

Sheng Jiqi had no ready answer to that question. After all she couldn't tell her doctor that they had used the "scientific" way. Thanks to her quick wit, she replied: "I just guessed. Could you tell me?"

"Guess again."

Sheng Jiqi became so tense that her heart beat seemed to have stopped. "Two boys?"

"One baby boy and one baby girl," her doctor then replied, one word at a time.

"Really?" Sheng Jiqi's breath was short and her heart was pounding. She had to hit her head and stomp her foot in order to prove that she was not daydreaming. At first, she felt relieved that she could finally unload the weight of the "revolutionary mission." She had managed to produce a real Jia-Na-Da, and had a flower of Canada thrown in for free! Then, she began to feel weighted down again. Feng Jian was still doing contract work, and since he was certainly not a giant with three heads and six arms, how could they manage to raise so many children? She was on such an emotional rollercoaster that quite a long while passed before she remembered to call Feng Jian at his work place to share with him this long overdue happiness.

Feng Jian reacted like a scholar in traditional China who had finally made the breakthrough after many false starts at the civil service examination. He was ecstatic. In a matter of minutes the entire company knew that he would have a son and a daughter. Even his supervisor, who always pulled a long face, let Feng Jian leave early to celebrate with his wife.

There is a Chinese saying that when one has good news, he will be light-headed with happiness. So it was with Feng Jian. He drove like the wind on the 401. He didn't realize that he had hit 140 kilometres per hour. He recited a Chinese couplet, repeatedly, while nodding: "Tend to the flowers with great care but there is no bloom; yet, plant a willow branch unintended and the branch turns into a shady thicket. A willow thicket!" Suddenly a siren screeched, and he knew that he had been caught speeding, again.

When the dark-skinned police officer got out of the patrol car and held out a hand for his licence, Feng Jian recalled the previous incident. He sincerely hoped that this officer would also take into account his soon-to-arrive twins and cut him some slack. Hesitantly he told the police officer: "My wife will be the mother of Jia-Na-Da! Really, she will have a boy and a girl! Two little Canadians!"

Hand still in mid-air, the policeman asked, extremely confused, "What did you say?"

But Feng Jian was also very puzzled. *Why doesn't he envy me?* Feng thought.

Translated by H. Laura Wu and Cory Davies.

"Jia Na Da/Canada" was originally serialized in The World Journal, *March 29-31, 2005.*

[1]The name Feng Jian is a pun on the term "fengjian," which means feudal or feudalistic.
[2]China began to implement the "One Child" policy in early 1980s. The Fengs would have to emigrate to have another child.
[3]Sheng Jiqi could mean "superior to a machine" or "a machine of procreation."
[4]*A Sweet Life* (1979) is a comedy that tells the story of a couple with six daughters. The film was part of the state sponsored

effort to promote the Chinese government's policies of family planning and birth control.

[5]*Five Golden Flowers* (1959) is a well-known romance film. It features five female characters, all having the name Golden Flower, who are model peasants working enthusiastically for the commune.

Grown Up

XI YU

TODAY IS HER DAUGHTER'S fifteenth birthday. Jiang Xue has noticed that many of her colleagues, particularly her Western colleagues, heave a long sigh when their children are growing up because they worry that they will lose control over them. In North America it seems quite common to consider a fifteen-year-old girl to be a woman already. Boys and girls date at younger and younger ages, and so their parents feel that they can no longer influence them. Jiang Xue usually sits there quietly when her colleagues discuss their children growing up; yet every sentence they utter finds its way directly into her mind.

Since early this morning, Jiang Xue had been especially preoccupied with what kind of birthday present she should buy for her daughter, Wenwen. In fact, this gift-giving business for her daughter had been on her mind for a long time. In the past they had been separated from each other for several years, and, as a result, they were not that close. Whenever Jiang Xue thinks about this, she is overcome with regret.

When her husband Liu Lihua went to the United States to study for a master's degree, she accompanied him. But when the day came to leave their seven-year-old daughter behind in Shanghai, both mother and father were heartbroken.

She believed that leaving the child behind in China was for her own good; however, Jiang Xue was on the opposite side of the ocean, and she missed her daughter day and night. And she hadn't realized what the consequences would be.

After three or four years, they eventually migrated to Canada. And as soon as they obtained landed immigrant status, they immediately applied to bring Wenwen over. They didn't expect the daughter who stepped off the plane to be so grown up. She was a slim, graceful, and beautiful young girl with guarded countenance. Jiang Xue intended to hug her daughter warmly and give her many kisses, but to her surprise, there was an unexpected aloofness in her daughter's eyes. Jiang Xue flinched, and then shrank away.

A while ago Jiang Xue had asked Wenwen whether or not she should organize a birthday party for her. *Fifteen is an important birthday,* Jiang Xue thought. Her daughter replied sarcastically, "What kind of birthday party? Get everybody around a table to eat cake? Don't you think that's a little bit childish?"

Jiang Xue was stunned. Even grown-ups celebrate their birthdays. Don't they get together with friends and eat cake?

Lately her daughter has been on the phone a lot, talking to both male and female friends. Since they all spoke with the same Canadian accent, Jiang Xue couldn't make out what sort of people they were—Chinese Canadians or Westerners? Whenever they called, her daughter went straight into her own room, and although Jiang Xue leaned on the door to listen, she could only make out a few isolated words and phrases and couldn't piece anything together.

Jiang Xue and Liu Lihua talked it over and decided that since their daughter didn't want them to throw a party for her, they should let her make her own plans. The child was now grown up. It is only natural that she had her own ideas. Instead, the parents would give her a wonderful birthday present.

Jiang Xue thought about it, and finally a pair of high quality shoes came to mind. Although Wenwen usually wore running shoes to school, on some occasions formal shoes were needed. The pair Wenwen now wore was two years old and was no longer fashionable. Even though these new shoes cost almost one hundred Canadian dollars—even more than that with tax—in Jiang Xue's mind this kind of present was too ordinary. Such a gift wouldn't impress the child or get her to recognize the depth of her parents' love.

And then by chance a few evenings ago, she heard Wenwen mention that digital cameras were very popular nowadays. With a voice full of hope, Wenwen said that you could manipulate and adjust the images yourself. A good digital camera could offer high quality results. On hearing this, Jiang Xue made up her mind. She thought, *If we can make the child happy just by spending a little more money, then buying a digital camera is something worth considering.*

She went to the store and looked around. Digital cameras were really expensive; generally they cost around three or four hundred Canadian dollars. And with the rapid development of digital technology, and despite spending so much money on it, the new camera might soon become out-dated.

Nevertheless, Jiang Xue could not dismiss the idea. If it made Wenwen happy, she definitely would satisfy this one request. Or, should she talk it over with her daughter first?

Jiang Xue took two hours off work to go home early. She was planning to cook a special birthday meal. Her daughter had already made party arrangements, probably for the weekend. Wenwen still hadn't mentioned exactly when. Tonight, though, after dinner, the whole family would take the car to the mall, stroll about, and then decide together what present to get her.

Jiang Xue left the car in the driveway. There was no need to park in the garage since they would be going out again after supper.

She pushed the door open, bent over to change her shoes, and then caught the scent of perfume wafting through the house. She thought this was unusual, and although she felt somewhat absurd, she started to look around the house. Suddenly she noticed that the door to her daughter's bedroom was wide open. She rushed upstairs to take a look. Wenwen was sitting in front of her desk, combing her hair. Lying scattered on the desk were various perfumes, lipsticks, eye liners, and other cosmetics.

Her daughter usually came home from school at four in the afternoon, but it wasn't four o'clock yet, and she was already at home. Although her daughter didn't utter a sound and just stared at her, Jiang Xue immediately felt a sense of panic, as though something unexpected was about to happen. Flustered, she walked over and with a forced smile said, "Wenwen came home early, today, eh?"

Wenwen stared at her mother with a guarded expression then nodded, "Yeah."

Jiang Xue was a little taken aback and suddenly realized that her daughter had something to say to her, but because of her mother's unexpected appearance, she needed time to muster the courage to say it. Jiang Xue herself was even less prepared to continue the conversation, in case the child had something earth-shattering to announce. She quickly turned away and began to retreat to her own room.

"I have plans for tonight," Wenwen announced to her mother's back.

"You...?" Jiang Xue's footsteps slowed, and she was forced to turn back.

Her daughter blinked, but she had no intention of stopping the major announcement that was underway. Suddenly, Wenwen switched to English. "One of my classmates is going to throw a birthday party for me. Afterwards we'll stay at his house for the night...." Her daughter paused.

With thunder rolling in her heart, Jiang Xue was speechless. Perhaps her daughter used English for this difficult announcement to help her mother to accept the situation more easily. After all, an overnight party with both boys and girls belongs to the category of Western culture, it might seem more reasonable in English. However, Wenwen did not realize that by using English to support her argument for going to the party, she also clearly disclosed that the person who would host the party was male![1]

Although her daughter's use of the English word "his" was ringing in her ears, she still did not dare to believe what she had heard. "Your classmate is throwing you a birthday party?" Jiang Xue repeated weakly. She needed to hear the words again. "You are not coming home tonight?"

Continuing in English and without modifying her tone, her daughter answered abruptly, "Yes."

Jiang Xue felt dizzy, and the blood rushed to her head. Her feet were frozen. At the same time, everything became crystal clear. To her astonishment, she realized that her daughter, this mere fifteen-year-old child, had firmly articulated *her* decision. She was not soliciting her mother's advice, much less asking for permission!

For a long time, Jiang Xue had worried about this day coming, and now, suddenly, here it was!

She also realized that her daughter had been secretly planning to do this for a long time, and had already talked over the plans with her friends. While Wenwen was speaking, Jiang Xue recognized an uncompromising expression in her eyes. Her daughter's tone was inflexible, as though she was fully aware that her mother would not approve of her behaviour. That being so, no matter what her mother's opinion or attitude was, wouldn't her daughter still go? Her daughter was the reason for this party. How could she miss it?

Although Jiang Xue felt she had a knife to her throat, she knew she could not retreat. Even if she were told that doing so would be as dangerous as walking through fire, she had no choice but to act.

Seething with fury but seeking reinforcements, Jiang Xue went into her own room and slammed the door with a bang. Then she grabbed the phone and punched in Liu Lihua's work number. Her trembling fingers misdialed the number, and she punched it once more. The phone rang for a while, but no one answered. Unwilling to give up, she dialled again. At last, a Western woman's voice answered. Jiang Xue asked for her husband, and the woman told her that he was in the middle of a meeting.

Still holding the phone in her hand, she sank to the floor like a person paralyzed. A strong sense of frustration and helplessness engulfed her as though the waters of the Huangpu had flooded her heart.

Recently, a sense of ominous foreboding had started to creep into her mind. She knew that her daughter's growing to maturity would come with some problems that would be difficult for them to handle, but she didn't expect that the challenges would be so daunting, so urgent, or so unreasonable. She was caught off guard. To go to a boy's house! And to stay there overnight! To Jiang Xue, this was not negotiable.

She had worried for a long time about this day coming, and now it had happened on her daughter's fifteenth birthday. No wonder Wenwen had complained that her parents' way of celebrating her birthday was childish.

Jiang Xue was eager to find out who this "he" was. Was he Chinese or foreign? Was he a classmate? What did his parents do? How did they get to know each other? Why did he organize a birthday party for Wenwen? And the even more terrifying question, what do they plan to do after dark?

A rapid succession of questions filled her mind, and she felt as though as head would explode.

In her mind, she saw Wenwen's guarded expression and tight lips. If Jiang Xue asked her these questions directly, she wouldn't answer a single one. Even if her mother pressed her, wouldn't she just run out the door? Even though Jiang Xue was her mother, Wenwen obviously felt that she had the right to her privacy and didn't need to explain everything to her parents.

How could her own daughter believe such a thing? Jiang Xue and Liu Lihua had dated for eight years, and in those eight long years, they hadn't even thought about spending a night together. Why, she hadn't let Liu Lihua touch her even once. On the other hand, what relationship did Wenwen have with this boy? How could she just decide to go and stay overnight with another family? And how could she have the nerve to tell her mother?

Jiang Xue's maternal instincts erupted, and, like a lioness burning with flames of fury, she fought the urge to rush back to her daughter's room to scold her. Of course, it was only to protect her, and only for her own good.

Once, long ago, when Jiang Xue's mother had caught Liu Lihua and Jiang Xue hugging behind a door – just that once – her mother told her, "For a girl, the thing that matters most is her reputation. Without a good reputation, such a person is on the road to ruin." They had never even kissed, and yet, the rules were strict.

Jiang Xue's hand was already on the door handle. And if she had gathered her strength, she would have rushed back to Wenwen's room and confronted her. But in the midst of her fury, and just as she was about to pull open her door, the violent and provoking words "shameless hussy" flashed into her mind.

She stopped abruptly. Clearly and unequivocally she saw what would happen. It would be the start of a war between the mother and daughter, with her daughter angrily forcing her way out of the house, leaving her parents, and never looking back. She might move into the boy's home to live. And then, how would she ever get her daughter to come back?

Jiang Xue was distraught at this unbearable thought and overwhelmed by the challenge of the situation. With an anguished heart, she sank to her knees, her hand still grasping the handle. She wanted to cry her heart out.

But she did not allow one tear to escape. She realized that since her daughter would feel that she had already handled the matter with her announcement, at any moment now she might get up and leave. This was no time to cry.

How unfair! To be a mother at this moment, and not even have the right to cry!

Aware that the situation had reached a critical point, she stopped and calmed herself down. She said to herself, *I can't lose this last chance. I must have a talk with my daughter. But, I must use the North American style of thinking.*

This sudden flash of insight came from her everyday reading of books and newspapers as well as from the conversations of the other mothers at work. All these ideas lit up like a bright light. Suddenly she began to see a way out of this stormy situation. Deep in a corner of her heart, her instinct told her that this new approach was the only possible way to approach her daughter. However, she could not stop herself from trembling. It would require both courage and strength.

She hesitated. If she employed this so-called "modern way of thinking," which had been imperceptibly influenced by what her Western colleagues think and do, would it indeed be appropriate in dealing with Wenwen? Would doing so get the desired results? Or would it make things worse by adding fuel to the fire, and instead encourage her daughter to become more and more independent in the future, and more and more reluctant to obey her parents?

With her heart in turmoil, Jiang Xue paced back and forth in her bedroom. Suddenly her legs turned to jelly, her ankle twisted, and she fell headlong onto the cast iron bed frame, bumping her head. Seeing stars, a wave of fear filled her heart. She thought desperately, *Strike me down! Let all this end! I might as well be dead as live such a life as this!* She placed her fingers gingerly on her head where it throbbed and was glad she didn't find any blood.

Jiang Xue thought about those days when her own mother had imposed restrictions on her, and she couldn't bear it. Thinking about her daughter's behaviour today, she knew that simply stopping her was not an option. On top of that, she and her daughter had continued to drift further and further apart, and there was little intimacy between them now. How could she rigidly compel her daughter to obey her?

Thought after thought ran through her mind, and her forehead creased in agony. Then, as if inspired by a mission, she calmed down. In her heart, a single voice was crying out, *This is my last resort.*

With agonizing and contradictory feelings, she arrived at her daughter's door. She was amazed to discover that when Wenwen was all dressed up, she looked so beautiful. Her forehead was smooth and clear; her nose was small and dainty, and gently tilted upward. Her clean and fresh hair was rolled up at the back of her head just like a cloud. She looked as elegant as a jade statue, and she took Jiang Xue's breath away. With a pang, Jiang Xue realized that decades ago she had looked just the same.

Maybe it came from her daughter's confidence, but her own confidence was also strengthened, and as a result she said, "Wait a few minutes for me. I am going out to buy something."

Her daughter was a little surprised, and her eyes widened, but she immediately nodded.

Jiang Xue drove to the nearest pharmacy chain. Without a moment's hesitation, she purchased an item that she had never bought before. Then she immediately drove home. To the store and back had only taken fifteen minutes, a new record for her shopping time.

Wenwen, who was almost ready to leave, watched her mother warily as she entered the bedroom. Jiang Xue began, "When a person grows up and is no longer a child, she will begin to have questions about sex. People also refer to this as sexual relations between men and women."

Perhaps it was Jiang Xue's surprising remarks; perhaps it was her mother's anxiety to hurriedly push on, but from the moment she heard Jiang Xue say these words, Wenwen sat upright at her desk. It seemed as if her mother's complexion was both flushed red from a cold wind and full of the vigour of regained youth. Reappraising her mother, Wenwen listened to her words attentively and without her usual cynical contempt.

She quietly waited.

Encouraged by her daughter's attention, Jiang Xue realized that this new style of speech had had an impact. She could not help but feel a further boost in her confidence. Still, Jiang Xue felt her face burning because when she began to talk about "sex," the word caught in her mouth. Regardless of how unnatural it felt, she instinctively hurried to fill in the space. "Sex is natural, and it is also natural to ask questions about it. Sex is not a simple matter. It has to do with people's feelings and with establishing good family relationships."

Even if she'd had an academic background in science, she never thought she would have been able to openly discuss questions about sex like she was doing in this moment. "Previously, Mom had very few discussions with you about sexual issues," she said calmly. "It was my responsibility to do so. Actually, we Chinese people secretly have a lot of interest in the affairs between men and women, but in public we are not very willing to talk about it. This is a problem."

Jiang Xue's mouth was dry, but she was unable to stop. She had to continue. "But you know, we Asians do not have the same attitudes about sex that Westerners have. They are willing to deal with sex more freely, as though it is just a matter between individuals, while we step back and connect sex and responsibility, and are relatively strict about it. But this is not to say who is right or who is wrong. This is just a difference between cultures."

She could see that the expression on her daughter's face was different from her usual aloofness in the past. With her lips slightly open, Wenwen seemed to be unaware of her amiability and compliance. In her clear eyes was just a hint of anxiety and resistance, but also calmness and understanding.

"Mom doesn't mind that you have a boyfriend." Jiang Xue

said these words almost sincerely, "but I do hope you won't let anything affect your studies...."

She thought that she spoke persuasively, but suddenly she noticed her daughter's face harden. She rushed to fill the pause between them, and, ready to risk everything, held out the gift which she had just bought. Feeling a wave of anxiety in her heart, she said, "This is what Mom is giving to you, a gift for a growh up."

The golden yellow English word "Climax" flashed on the outside of the pink box of condoms. This word meant sexual orgasm. Such a thing had never been seen in the house before. Handing the condoms to her daughter, Jiang Xue could not prevent her hands from trembling. Her face felt scalding hot. She couldn't be sure whether she was being rational, or whether she was being too impulsive. Just the other day, she recalled that one of her Western colleagues, Susan, had given her adult daughter a box of condoms as a birthday present. When she came home, she joked about it with Liu Lihua, never imagining that she herself would so soon become the butt of the same joke.

Wenwen stared silently at the pink box of condoms. Jiang Xue was unable to gauge her daughter's reaction, and so not to embarrass her, she took them back, and deftly placed them in Wenwen's sheepskin purse. Then Jiang Xue said, "How's that? You're all set to go. I'll go get the car."

"What? Mom, why are you getting the car?" asked Wenwen.

"I'm driving you to your friend's house."

Jiang Xue drove the car up Victoria Park Avenue. It was rush hour, and the cars sped along the road. She imagined that everyone else wanted to hurry home as soon as possible. Jiang Xue drove the car, and a smartly dressed Wenwen sat stiffly beside her. As though she were taking a lamb to the slaughter, Jiang Xue felt waves of horror assail her, and she became distracted. She frequently stepped on the brakes, slowing the car down and then lurching forward.

Following the directions provided by Wenwen, they turned down two or three blocks and drove onto a side street called Holms Street. Her male classmate, William Harrison—from the name, it seemed certain that he was a Westerner—lived at number 23. Trying hard to calm herself, Jiang Xue smoothly brought the car to the edge of the curb and stopped.

Just as they arrived, a blonde girl, another student Jiang Xue assumed, was going through the front door of number 23. The girl turned her head at the sound of the car, and glanced at Wenwen who had just gotten out. Jiang Xue watched as the girl checked to see who was sitting in the driver's seat and then looked back at Wenwen and feigned a look of surprise and derision, leading Jiang Xue to suspect that perhaps Wenwen had complained about having an old-fashioned mother. When Wenwen was planning the party with her friends, she may have told them that her mother would never agree to it. *You see,* thought Jiang Xue, *your mother brought you here.*

Jiang Xue glanced at Wenwen. Sure enough, she caught sight of a sheepish expression on Wenwen's face in response to the blonde girl's meaningful smile. Wenwen's smiling expression had a little bit of embarrassment, a little bit of regret, and a little bit of happiness. Suddenly, Wenwen turned around and walked back toward the car. Jiang Xue didn't know what her daughter wanted, but she opened the car door in a panic and leapt out to meet her.

With a lively step, Wenwen walked up to her mother. A warm smile covered her face, and she gently said, "Thank you, Mom." As she spoke, she pulled her mother into her arms and sank her head heavily into her mother's shoulder.

Her daughter used such strength that she almost knocked Jiang Xue off her feet. Staggering, but with a heart bursting with waves of emotion, she quickly regained her balance, and, struggling to hold on to her daughter, she returned the hug just as intensely. She could not stop from gently stroking her child's back. She had waited a long time for her daughter's hug, and she never imagined that this moment would happen.

Now, after all the tension and conflict, her daughter's unexpected embrace filled her with joy. Jiang Xue could not bear to let her go. If this unusual adult gift won her this emotional hug, it was worth it.

"Mom," Wenwen warmly whispered into her ear again, "Thank you ... for not asking." With that, she walked into her classmate's home.

Moved to tears by her daughter's unexpected comfort and praise, Jiang Xue sat in the car for a long time, and watched other parents drop off their children.

When she got home, the moment she pushed open the door, she heard Liu Lihua bellow in a thundering rage, "God dammit! How could this be in our house! Get up here and take a look!" He stood at the entrance of Wenwen's room shaking with fury.

Jiang Xue's heart stopped. Bracing herself, she ran upstairs and walked into their daughter's bedroom and immediately saw the pink box of condoms perched on the spacious and tidy writing desk,.

The box sat there quietly without the least sense of shame.

"Wenwen!" Jiang Xue picked up the condoms and clasping them to her heart made a gulping sound, tears forming in her eyes.

"What's the matter with you?" asked the confused Liu Lihua, who was still overcome with fury. "What happened? Where did it come from? How did it get into Wenwen's room?"

Jiang Xue could no longer control herself. Many times she had held her grief in check. This moment had opened the floodgates of a surging river. Without any grace at all, and without the slightest misgiving, she began to wail. She cried because she understood. She had purposely placed the condoms into Wenwen's purse. Wenwen must have taken them out and put them on the desk.

Jiang Xue thought, *This is our child's unspoken promise that for the time being she doesn't need them. She does understand the distinction between East and West. We have inherited our country's civilization. We are the sons and daughters of China!*

She remembered the daughter who had hugged her mother warmly and joyfully. In that instant, the estranged and indifferent feelings between them had melted away. Jiang Xue's tears were tears of joy. In spite of her husband's angry outburst and panic-stricken questions, and in spite of her complete abandonment of self-control, she cried to her heart's content.

With a long sigh and with infinite love she murmured, "Wen-wen, Mom's good girl. Mom's good girl!"

Translated by John Edward Stowe and Norah Creedon.

"Grown Up" was originally serialized in The World Journal, *February 2-11, 2008.*

[1]In spoken Chinese, the third person pronoun "ta" could refer to he, she, it, or even him or her.

The Abandoned Cat

LING ZHANG

THE ALARM CLOCK RANG madly, startling Xiaokai awake. She jerked up from her bed, heart pounding. As she pulled a corner of the quilt to cover her chest, her heartbeat gradually returned to normal. Stretching her leg out under the quilt, she pressed the clock on the end table with her foot over again and again, but it still jingled. A thought flitted across her mind, and she realized it was Saturday. No work today. It was the door bell ringing, not the clock.

Oh, Shangjie must have brought the cat here, she thought.

Xiaokai jumped out of the bed. Rushing into the washroom, she turned on the tap. There was no time to brush her teeth, so she wet her finger and wiped her teeth instead. Then she smoothed her hair with a little cold water. In the mirror she looked half awake, her cheeks pink. *Not too bad.* She slid her feet into slippers and shuffled toward the door.

As she walked down the hallway, she thought, *Shangjie won't care what I look like. I've been living like a ghost these days so that even I don't care about my miserable face. Why worry now?*

When Xiaokai arrived in Toronto, Shangjie was studying for his PhD degree, with the help of a scholarship and some financial support from Xiaokai, who babysat. Most of the wives of the Chinese students had to commute to their work places daily by the TTC. They worked either as waitresses and dishwashers in Chinese restaurants, or as storekeepers and cashiers in Chinese supermarkets. But, unlike the vast majority of Chinese wives, Xiaokai didn't need to go anywhere. She looked after three children in the apartment building where she lived—a five-year-old, a three-year-old, and an eight-month-old. Her neighbours dropped the kids at her apartment in the morning and picked them up in the evening. Their parents packed everything the children would need: clothes, food, and drinks. Xiaokai only needed to open the door and let the children and their huge bag of daily supplies inside. Since Xiaokai didn't have to go out, she was never concerned about her appearance. She wore no makeup, and she never dressed up. From morning till night, she looked the same. Except for the times when she brushed her teeth, she almost never looked into the mirror and some days she even forgot what she looked like.

Before coming to Canada, she had filled a suitcase with fashionable clothes, but she never used them after she arrived. When she finally thought about those garments, she had gained weight and was unable to fit into them. Those days, Shangjie's was only focused on his dissertation. To him, home was where he ate and slept. She thought he didn't mind her casual appearance. But she was wrong. When she realized the problem, it was too late. She had passed the point of no return.

It had snowed outside.

The fall had passed quickly. Some leaves were still clinging to the trees, but winter soon laid them to waste. Snow flew in the sky, light and dry. When it landed on the ground, it looked like a sticky clump of thick and dirty dust. Even stomping on it wouldn't make it melt and disappear. The wind growled, like a starving wolf, breathless and full of sadness and the trees branches trembled in the bleak wind .

When Xiaokai opened the door, Shangjie stood in front of her. His long neck was hidden under a dark turtleneck. His frost-covered glasses looked like expired plaster, moist and yellowish hiding his two eyes. Something plump was hidden in his coat. That was Timid Huang, their cat.

As soon as Shangjie entered the apartment, the cat jumped out of his coat, ran toward Xiaokai, and sniffed delicately at her toes, one by one. Then she sprawled on the floor, her four legs up and her soft belly exposed. Knowing what the cat wanted, Xiaokai squatted to scratch the little thing up and down. The cat purred loudly, her mouth wide open and her eyes narrow and gleaming. After stroking her for several minutes, Xiaokai noticed the cat's left paw was clenched into a ball and remained closed. She tried to open it gently, but the cat jumped up and retreated a couple of steps back on her three legs.

"She fell down from the stairs last night and was injured. If there's no improvement in the next couple of days, I'll take her to a vet," Shangjie said.

Timid Huang was female, three and a half years old, and adopted from the humane society some time ago. When they got her, Shangjie had needed to go to the university every day to work on his dissertation. Xiaokai had been left home alone. She couldn't understand any of TV programs in English; neither did she have friends to chat with. Loneliness was hard to cope with. She had begged Shangjie to get a dog to keep her company, but he didn't reply, even though she asked several times. Finally he said she should take an English class, or a writing class, or any other class she wished. Xiaokai said she was too tired after babysitting all day long and so it would be hard to learn anything. Frowning, Shangjie asked if she wanted to be illiterate for the rest of her life. He said she had to learn enough English to at least be able to understand doctors, the police, and the weather forecast. With smirk on her face, Xiaokai had replied that she would rely on him. It was enough if one of them understood English. "Anyway, I will depend on you for the rest of my life," she said. Finally, with a sigh he told her that walking a dog was too much trouble. A cat would be better.

The following day, the two went to a pet store. The price startled them. Their mouths opened, but they were speechless.

They never talked about the cat again. Some time later, a friend of theirs told them they could get animals free of charge from a humane society in the east end of the town. They went to the pound, where several halls were packed with row after row of cages filled with a variety of different cats and dogs. Xiaokai instantly liked a pure white cat, but Shangjie preferred one with spots. There were too many choices; they couldn't make up their minds.

A worker took them to a corner at the far end of a hall and pointed to a metal cage. "Look at this one. If nobody takes it, it'll be put to sleep tomorrow," he sighed ruefully.

It was a yellow fox-like cat with a tiny body and huge eyes like large marbles. Her entire face seemed to be occupied by only big round eyes and nothing else. Her hair was scraggly and there was a hairless spot on her back, which looked as though it had been scalded. As they approached, the cat retreated, stepping back to the corner. Finally, she arched her back, her fur standing on its end, looking like the seed head of a dandelion in the wind.

"The litter of four was abandoned on the highway, all injured. They've recovered since we got them. The other three were adopted. With the scar, this one is unwanted," explained the worker. "We don't have much space. We can only keep the animal for two months. We have to put them to sleep afterwards. Her two-month term will end tomorrow."

Xiaokai asked if she had a name. The worker said her name was Yellow. Even with her limited English, Xiaokai understood that the word meant *huang* in Chinese. In a gentle voice, she called the cat by her Chinese name, Ah Huang. No Answer. She called her again; the cat didn't respond, but her arched back gradually returned to normal. Xiaokai pulled out a piece of paper from her pocket, rubbed it into a ball and placed it on her palm. She extended her hand into the cage to tease Ah Huang. The cat hesitated, then walked slowly toward her, her nose nudging the ball-up paper, sniffing. Suddenly her tongue licked Xiaokai's hand. Surprise! The worker told them that Yellow had never showed interest in anyone. Clearly, there was a bond between them. She belonged to Xiaokai. Ah Huang looked at Xiaokai, her eyes blinking slowly. Xiaokai's heart melted. She turned to look at Shangjie and without hesitation, he said, "Okay. She's yours."

The worker thanked them as he prepared the adoption document and a box for the cat. He said that the centre would be responsible for all of Yellow's medical expenses in the future. "You can bring the cat to see our vet anytime," he added.

Shangjie couldn't help but smile. He said she seemed so shy. "Let's call her Timid Huang," he suggested. And officially, that's how Timid Huang got her name.

As soon as Shangjie and Xiaokai brought Timid Huang home, the cat ran under the bed and didn't come out no matter what they did. Shangjie poured some cat food, which they got from the animal center, into a bowl and placed it at the end of the bed, along with a container of water. But Timid Huang ignored the food. The first day passed, and then the second. Timid Huang continued to ignore them. On the third morning, Xiaokai couldn't bear it any more and called the centre for help. The vet explained that dogs always follow their master, but that cats become attached to particular environments. The cat's home had changed and the cat wasn't ready to accept her new home right away. All the vet could suggest was to lure her out with her favourite food. Shangjie and Xiaokai went to the pet store and bought a number of different cat treats. Five plates with different foods sat in a row near the bed, but Timid Huang ate and drank nothing. On the fourth evening, when they couldn't hear anything moving under the bed, the two thought the cat had died. They crawled beneath the bed and carefully pulled her out. Timid Huang lay motionless. An idea dawned on Shangjie. He got some milk from the fridge, heated it and then poured it into a small bottle to feed the cat. Xiaokai held the cat, and he opened her mouth. Reluctantly, the cat took most of the bottle. Eyes narrowing, she fell asleep.

Xiaokai gingerly held the cat in her arms and dared not move, afraid that Timid Huang would wake and run away. She dozed on the couch all night with the cat in her lap. The following morning, when she woke, her hands were numb and Timid Huang was gone. Shangjie was nearby, and he pointed to the end of the bed. The cat had squatted in front of the previous night's bowl and was wolfing down the food. The sunlight poured in, wrapping Timid Huang in soft golden colour, dust motes dancing in the beam of light that caressed her back. Xiaokai felt like a dancing dust mote as well, and she couldn't help but call out, "Timid Huang, how could you do this to me?" Startled, the cat fled under the bed again.

Shangjie and Xiaokai soon realized that Timid Huang must have had many terrifying experiences trying to survive life on the highway. She was nervous about eating in front of them as she was used to sneaking food. The food they offered with their hands must have seemed suspicious. Timid Huang didn't want anybody within earshot when she ate, otherwise she would flee. She would rather starve to death than be around people. But Xiaokai found a way to feed her. She would call her name several times, clanging the bowl of food against the doorframe before she put it down on the floor, and then she would hide in the bathroom. From the gap of the almost closed door, she watched Timid Huang sneak out from a corner. As she ate, the cat's ears perked up and her body shivered. Xiaokai would remain in the washroom until the cat had finished up. About six months later, Timid Huang finally settled down into the routine of a normal house cat.

Timid Huang seemed only to belong to Xiaokai, since Shangjie was seldom at home. Occasionally, when Shangjie watched the cat chase her own tail, he thought she was funny. But other than that, he never paid much attention to her. But, after an argument between the husband and wife, Timid Huang suddenly became Shangjie's cat.

The argument was over a trifle. Shangjie came home and couldn't find any clean underwear after his shower. The hamper was full of dirty laundry. As he threw his dirty clothes into the washing machine, he started to complain. "You were at home. What did you do all day long?" That day Xiaokai had felt exhausted since the children she babysat were sick and restless. As a result, she was moody and she fought back. "I work all day long," she shouted, "and don't do anything but make money to pay the rent."

Shangjie was stung by her words and didn't know what to say. After a moment of silence, he muttered, "Like a peasant, you only think of the instant benefit. You will never change."

Xiaokai had been born to a peasant family, but she went to university, and had been one of the most promising young women in her hometown. Labelling her "peasant" was the most humiliating thing Shangjie could have said. He knew how powerful the word was and where his sword should cut. Xiaokai's her eyes widened and filled with tears. Bang! She pushed all the dishes and bowls off the table and they shattered on the floor. With no meal to eat, Shangjie stormed out.

He didn't return home that night. Xiaokai got worried and called friends and acquaintances, but couldn't find him. She didn't know that Shangjie had gone to the library and had stayed there until it closed. Not wanting to return home and face an angry Xiaokai, he had no place to go, so he bought a ticket for the midnight movie. There were only two people in the audience: himself and another woman, who had also had a quarrel at home. The two complete strangers hit it off right away. They chatted and poured out all their bitterness to each other. Sympathy was like opium. The more they accepted, the more they wanted. The more they offered, the more they had to give. Then they both fell into a large and bottomless black hole.

Shangjie finally came home in the wee hours of the morning. When his steps approached their apartment, Timid Huang heard him first. She woke from sleep, and twitching her ears, she jumped up from her small bed and ran to the door. His key still in the lock, Shangjie opened the door a crack, and Timid Huang squeezed through and climbed up on him. Her legs kicked on his knees; her tongue licked his hand roughly, hurting him. That moment, Timid Huang wasn't like a cat, but like a loyal dog who hadn't seen her master for a long time. Her tongue licked Shangjie, who felt deeply warmed and as though he'd been greeted by a life-long friend. In that instant, Timid Huang wasn't only Xiaokai's, but also his. When Shangjie decided to move out, he insisted on taking the cat with him. The ownership of the cat became a key issue over which they argued incessantly. Like parents fighting for child custody, both Shangjie and Xiaokai wanted to keep Timid Huang. Each owned half of the cat. Every week, they took turns looking after her. Every Saturday one of them brought Timid Huang to the other's place, no exception, and no matter rain or shine.

It was Xiaokai's turn this week. Shangjie was supposed to deliver the cat at nine o'clock. She had been studying for an exam until three in the morning the night before, so she didn't wake until he rang the doorbell.

Now, Timid Huang lay in the corner, her hurt paw clenched tightly. The cat looked like a bag of bones, her eye dull. Xiaokai's heart sank. She broke a cat treat in two and tried to feed her. Unable to avoid it, Timid Huang accepted the morsel, but couldn't swallow. Xiaokai remembered that as a child she had heard people say animals were different from human beings. When they were hurt, they liked to hide somewhere where they could lick their wounds instead of crying for help.

Maybe Timid Huang doesn't want people to see her lick the injury, Xiaokai thought.

"How is your English? Can you follow the course?" Shangjie asked hesitantly.

A moment later, Xiaokai realized the question was not related to the cat, but to her. Not ready for his question, she was momentarily speechless, knowing that if she spoke, she would cry. And, she didn't want to burst into tears in front of him.

The air got heavy in Xiaokai's silence, and it was like rocks were piling up on Shangjie's shoulders. Unable to stand it, he left. At the door, he turned his head. "Call me if Timid Huang doesn't get better." She nodded, still silent. The open door was closed again. He became a grey figure disappearing down the staircase. In fact, had she peeked from the corner of her eye, she would've seen another person waiting for him, but she didn't. She'd had heard a little about his affair, but she had never questioned him about it, not even during their heartbreaking quarrels. In her stubborn viewpoint, if that person was not in her sight, then that person never existed.

Shangjie moved out after his graduation. He had been eager to leave a long time ago, but he hadn't. Instead, he waited until Xiaokai got her landing papers. She knew that he was like a piece of string attached to a kite. Others saw the end of the line in her hand, but only she saw the split threads of the line clearly.

The evening Shangjie officially moved out, he took with him several books, as he had already moved some of his other items at different times. Her head buried under the blanket, Xiaokai lay in bed, listening to his footsteps outside the door. The quilt was her nest, her cocoon, and her protection. The outside world that she didn't want to face was risky. She couldn't leave the safety of her bed. If she did, she would be swallowed up by monsters. The quilt kept her far away from the world, and the inside of the quilt was clean. And safe. Outside she heard him say, "The bank account has been changed into your name. If you have any questions, you could talk to the teller who speaks Chinese," he paused. When there was no response from Xiaokai, he left.

The sound of his footsteps faded as he descended the staircase and Xiaokai felt as though a sharp needle had chiselled a hole in her chest. Her soul squeezed through the hole, floated to the ceiling and then looked down on her body from a high position. It repeated: *run after him! Ask him to come back*! Her body was like a lump of rotting flesh lying on the bed, with no strength at all. Her soul couldn't make her body move. Her soul and body debated all the night. At day daybreak, she got up, but felt as though her legs remained on the bed. Her legless body rolled through the room and into the washroom. She took a cup of water to brush her teeth. Suddenly a dirty yellow stone dropped into the cup. Staring at it, she realized that it was her tooth. One of her teeth had come out.

She took her tooth out of the cup and clenched it tightly in her hand. Dizzily, half awake, she went to the balcony. The sun was strong and burning her skin. The noise from the street, mixed with the heat of the sunlight, almost knocked her down. The street beneath the building looked like a sheet of sun-dried, grey fabric stretching to a very far place. Only a few insects crawled on it—they were cars. Xiaokai pulled a stool over to the railing and climbed onto it. Suddenly she felt a pull.

It was Timid Huang.

The cat bit Xiaokai's pant-leg tightly, hanging from the seam. Xiaokai kicked her so strongly that the cat was thrown back, hitting a corner of the coffee table. Timid Huang lay on the floor, crying her eyes out. *Meow! Meow!* Her tears were red. Blood!

Xiaokai suddenly awoke. Her soul dropped back into her body. She felt her weight again.

She walked toward Timid Huang, and tried to hug her. But the cat didn't want her. As Xiaokai moved one step forward, the cat retreated one step back. The distance between them remained one step apart, neither more nor less. Timid Huang panted, her eyes like knives sharply fixed on Xiaokai. Xiaokai felt as if these eyes had cut through her body, leaving many holes.

Bending her head, Xiaokai looked for something. She found an abandoned flower pot, got her fallen tooth, and buried it. She made a card, just as she used to do as a student at a forestry university, and inserted it into the pot soil:

Planting date: June 7
Plant family: lonicera
Environments: dark
Spacing in the rows: helpless
Flowering date: never
Best fertilizer: fending for itself

The following morning, she called her neighbours and said she could no longer babysit their children. Then she took a streetcar to Chinatown, where she bought an electronic English dictionary. With its help, she searched for information on the internet. A week later, she found a morning job making sandwiches in a café. In the afternoon, she took an English class at an immigration center. Six months later, she enrolled in a horticulture program funded by the government at Seneca College in the evening.

Soon she was in her second year of studies. The following semester, the students in the program had the opportunity to apply for internships. Xiaokai had submitted her resume to a job placement centre, but she still needed to write the exam. So many students were applying for jobs, and the employers would only take the candidates who had the best grades. Knowing its importance, Xiaokai took the exam seriously. She had a slice of bread and a cup of tea for lunch, and then buried herself in books and practise exercises behind the closed door of her room. By suppertime she was so hungry that she decided to cook a meal. Walking to the kitchen, she suddenly remembered that she hadn't fed Timid Huang for a whole day. She looked at the cat, who was stationary and standing in the corner of the apartment, exactly where she had been that morning. Xiaokai picked her up and found her weightless. Her finger in the cat's mouth, she asked Timid Huang if she was on a hunger strike, or if she was being mistreated. The cat bit her finger lightly. She knew the animal wanted to talk to her. *Poor thing, you are sad too, but you can't speak.* Xiaokai released the cat and offered her some dry food. Timid Huang sniffed at it and licked some into her mouth. She chewed for a second and then spit it out. "You picky cat. Okay, don't eat the cookie. You don't want something hard. Okay, if you want to starve. It's your choice." But as she said this, she opened a can of cat food and spooned some of the meat near the dry food. The cat took a few bites, but didn't finish it.

That night Xiaokai was awakened by a strange noise. When she climbed out of bed, she saw Timid Huang squatting on the floor in a puddle of urine, trembling with fear. It seemed that while going to the bathroom, she had fallen and tipped the litter basin so that the litter was scattered everywhere. Xiaokai was about to curse when she suddenly remembered that people in her hometown had always said that cats had an excellent ability to keep their balance, so they seldom fall. *Is something wrong with Timid Huang's balance?* The thought drove her sleep away. Early in the morning, she wanted to call the vet in the emergency room at the animal centre right away, but she couldn't find the phone number. Instead she had to ask Shangjie. He said he would go with her and hung up before she could respond.

The two brought the cat to the animal hospital together. Timid Huang went into the examination room and they waited outside. Xiaokai's mind felt like it was full of cotton balls and she had trouble understanding sentences in the book she held in her hand, even though she recognized each word. She heard Shangjie ask if the cat had eaten something poisonous. Timid Huang had never gone to the bathroom anywhere except the litter box. Xiaokai wanted to say: *Nothing was wrong with the cat during the week she stayed with me. How come she's like this now, after coming to me from your place?* But she held back, squeezing only a neutral *hmm* through her pursed lips.

The vet finally came out of the examination room. He slowly removed his gloves and mask and rubbed his eyes. He looked exhausted, as if he hadn't slept for a couple of nights.

"She has a brain tumour. Huge. Due to the breakdown of her visual and auditory nerves, she's blind and deaf. So that's why she is always falling. In addition, her swallowing nerves are causing her to have difficulty eating. The tumour is slowly killing her, like a blunt knife cutting through flesh. It's painful. Of course, she may die before being killed by pain. But, if you love the cat, you allow her to die peacefully as soon as possible. It's hard for you to imagine what kind of pain she's going through now."

A nurse carried Timid Huang out. The cat shivered and curled into a ball as she sank into Xiaokai's lap. Xiaokai lifted her up, and touched the cat's nose to hers. Cold. She meowed in a whisper. More likely Xiaokai imagined her meow rather than hearing an actual sound.

"If you have made up your mind, you'd better make an appointment as soon as you can. Lots of animals are waiting."

Xiaokai watched the vet's mouth moving. His words, like needles, flew out to her, and her body turned black and blue all over.

On the way home, Xiaokai unbuttoned her coat and wrapped the cat inside. Timid Huang calmed down. She was no longer shivering, but Xiaokai started trembling. From tooth to tooth, muscle to muscle, and joint to joint, she felt each piece of her body falling apart as if she were losing her mind.

She definitely did not want to cry in front of Shangjie. Not crying was the only way to hide her weakness.

Shangjie gave her a ride home. As he parked his car, neither of them spoke. Finally, hesitating, he asked, "Maybe I should make an appointment?"

"Fuck your grandma!" Xiaokai cried out, using the dirty and vicious slang that men from her hometown used. She walked away with Timid Huang still tucked inside her coat.

The appointment was unexpectedly quick. It was on the following Saturday.

Friday night, Xiaokai bathed Timid Huang. The cat's hair

had become thin, and some skin was exposed. Only the hair on the back of her head and neck was still thick. She combed her hair out and braided what was left into two pigtails tied with pink ribbons. Not used to it, the cat rubbed her head against wall and removed the ribbons. She sighed. *Timid Huang, you dislike makeup the same way I do.* "Who will marry you in the future?" she said out loud, even though she knew Timid Huang no longer had a future.

At about nine o'clock, the doorbell rang. Shangjie had come to keep the cat company. He brought his own sleeping bag to stay overnight in the living room. The cat, lightly snoring, had already fallen asleep on Xiaokai's bed. She was hardly eaten anything anymore, and slept most of the time. Xiaokai heard a noise in the living room and knew Shangjie was arranging his sleeping bag. After a while the rustling sound approached the door, but Xiaokai turned the light off. The whole world became dark. All sounds died out. A moment later, the rustling sound rose, but drifted away.

Xiaokai woke at midnight. As she pushed the door open, she immediately noticed a tiny red flash. She turned the light on and discovered Shangjie sitting on the floor, smoking. He quickly butted out the cigarette and coughed. He said he couldn't sleep. Bring Timid Huang out for me, can you?

Xiaokai was wondering when he started to smoke, but she didn't show her surprise. Silently she went back to her room, carried the cat out, and placed her on his lap. He held the cat's head with one hand and gently caressed her bony body with the other, one light stroke, then another one.

"Xiaokai, I didn't move out because of someone else."

She covered her ears tightly with her hands. *I can't hear. I'm not listening! I don't want to!* She repeated these words to herself in her heart, but his words squeezed between her fingers and into her ears.

"Those days were tough, but you didn't want to grow up. You were unwilling to face the hard situation. You didn't want to walk. You wanted me to carry you. I was unable to; you were too heavy."

She heard a bubble break in her heart that made her eyes water. *No. I definitely can't cry in front of him.* She bit her lip tightly, but it did not work this time. Out of her control, the tears erupted and streamed down her face. At the beginning, she felt tears coming from her eyes, but later the tears seemed to be water drops unrelated to her, flowing over her face.

The following morning, when Xiaokai got up, she rummaged through the dresser drawer until she found a cat collar. It was white. Shangjie's name and address was printed on the back. In the middle was a sky blue bow. A pair of little bells dangled beneath the bow. They had bought it after they adopted the cat. But after they separated, the collar was removed. A year later, the collar had become very loose because the cat's neck had gotten so thin.

The cat was still asleep. Xiaokai heated a bottle of milk to feed her. Timid Huang opened her eyes. One sip made her cough, her nose pink and wet, and the milk spilled over. Xiaokai dried her nose and wanted to try and feed her again. But Shangjie said, "Let her have a good sleep."

Throwing the bottle on the floor, Xiaokai asked, "Are you afraid she isn't getting enough time to sleep?"

He said nothing, but bent down to pick up the broken glass. Staring at the bits of glass on the floor, Xiaokai felt a little embarrassed. Shangjie cleaned it up, then placed the cat into a carrying box, and closed the cover. Timid Huang was no longer visible.

He turned and went downstairs. Xiaokai rushed to the window and pulled the curtain open. It was snowing heavily; Shangjie walked alone in the parking lot. She noticed that his back was a little crooked.

"Timid Huang, farewell! You take care of yourself," Xiaokai called out in a low voice. She felt her throat crack, like a piece of dry wood attacked by the wind. Suddenly a sound rose, riding with the wind, across the rows of houses and buildings, ending in her eardrums where the noise echoed for a long time.

It was the sound of Timid Huang's bells.

At lunchtime, Shangjie returned. In his hands, the box was covered by a thin layer of snowflakes. She took the box and opened it. The collar and a strand of golden hair were inside.

"She left peacefully, as though she were asleep," Shangjie said.

"Let me stay by myself," she murmured.

She closed the door and heard his steps recede as he reached the bottom of the staircase. She knelt down, pressing her face to the box. The snowflakes melted; but her face and the box were both wet.

Timid Huang, for three years, you'd tried to escape. Finally, you couldn't escape this box.

Timid Huang, you lived three years longer in order to save me. You taught me how to walk on my own, didn't you?

An echoing sound hummed inside the box, like the one heard from a hollow seashell. Xiaokai felt a warmth flowing softly into her ears and moistening the untouched dry spots on her face. She heard joyful sounds from her dry heart, as if water had kissed the cracked earth after a drought.

The following morning, when Xiaokai went to wash her face, she discovered that a tiny three-leaf plant had sprung up in the flower pot in the corner, where she had buried her fallen tooth.

Translated by Zoë S. Roy.

"The Abandoned Cat, Timid Huang" was originally published in Fiction Monthly, *No. 1, 2007.*

West Nile Virus

HE CHEN

AT THE TIME, we were renting an apartment in a huge building in Toronto, which was home to many people from many different backgrounds. Some were drug dealers. Consequently, there were often inspections in the halls using police dogs. One day, shots were fired in a dispute between two rival gangs, and several people were killed. When we saw that the drops of blood that trailed past our very own door, we decided to move away as soon as possible.

Two years earlier, my wife and I had just immigrated to Toronto and had already decided to buy a house, so we had stacks of Chinese-language newspapers in the apartment. There were numerous real estate brokers in the newspapers, but I finally found a Chinese woman called Lily Liu. I phoned her, and we met that very day. Lily was petite and every bit as cute as her name.

I still recall the day that Lily took us to see the first house. It was a split-level home with a circular arched window. There were two large kitchens, four washrooms, and too many rooms to count. As soon as I saw it, I was strongly attracted to the Italian cantina, where many bottles of thick jam were stored. The backyard, with its fruit trees heavy with cherries and pears, made my heart leap. At that moment, I imagined that this house would soon become my happy home. However, my wife threw cold water on my dreams when she said, "I could never live here! The round arched window of this house looks just like a tomb cave in Southern China."

Then we went to visit another house. The outside wall was covered with ivy, and inside there were two majestic cats. There was a log sauna in the basement. From the living room, you could look out into the backyard and see exotic flowers and rare herbs, and when you lifted your head, you could see all the way to picturesque Lake Ontario in the distance. Cupping her hand to her eyes to avoid the light, my wife looked around and saw the railway tracks for the Scarborough Rapid Transit. She told me that whenever the SRT train passed, the whole house would shake, and the noise of the trains at night would be even more deafening. And to top it off, she didn't like the big lake. "It's easy for water demons to come to the shore," she explained. "And then what would we do?"

Throughout the next few months, Lily took us to see dozens of other houses. We didn't know why, but the more houses we saw, the less interested we became. Soon we could no longer tell one house from another.

One particular afternoon in July, Lily called us to say that a single-family home in North York had just been put on the market. The house was large and the location was excellent, but the price exceeded our original budget. Lily asked if we wanted to take a look. At that time, I was just starting a new business and money was tight, so I refused outright when I heard the price.

Just then my wife asked me, "Who are you talking to?"

I told her, "It's Lily, but the house she is recommending is not suitable." I was starting to feel that whenever I liked a house, my wife always found something about it that she doesn't like. Oddly, now that I had said that this particular house was not suitable, she was suddenly interested.

"I think this house sounds pretty good," she said. "Of course, we must go and have a look."

I drove our second-hand Dodge sedan, while my wife, following Lily's instructions, navigated. Before we reached the house, we realized that the surrounding area was an old neighbourhood. Along the roadside, the mature cedars and green and red maples blotted out the sky. The lawn and garden areas were expansive, and the houses were far from the road. By this time, it was already dusk and the sky was giving off a rosy glow. The rays of sunlight were absorbed by the dense canopy formed by the tall, graceful trees, and the air was touched with a cold, gentle moistness. It felt as though we were in a mountain forest. I drove slowly, trying to make out the house numbers. At last we found the house. The number was 118, and that sounded lucky. I parked the car at the curb, and from there my wife and I looked at the house.

But daylight had faded, and we couldn't make out the details of the house. We could only roughly discern its shape from the silhouette. The house had two floors, and the roof was irregular, somewhat like a trapezoid. It was reminiscent of a traditional house found in the villages of Japan, and it had a profoundly calm atmosphere. A garage was located at the end of a very long driveway, and there was a towering pine tree in the front. Beneath the tree was a wide lawn. Under a large window on the left-hand side was a big clump of shrubs. There was a large covered porch by the front door. There was also an additional structure, a solarium, built with glass walls and doors. My wife and I silently sized up the house. There were no lights on in any of the rooms, but I thought I could see the shadow of someone moving about inside the solarium. Perhaps she (or he) was watching us, as we were watching her (or him).

My wife suggested we approach the house for a closer look. I said that since we were not accompanied by a real estate agent, the people in the house might not welcome strangers. My wife persisted and said, "Since the owners want to sell the house, of course, they would allow buyers to have a look." I couldn't change her mind. All I could do was follow her toward the house. My wife took a few steps along the sidewalk, turned down the driveway, opened a wooden gate, and looked into the backyard. From there, she walked up to that solarium. I thought that the person in the room would certainly open the door and come out. For some unknown reason, all at once, I felt a strong urge to run. But no one came out. My wife pressed her nose against the glass wall and peeked inside. Then she strolled over to the other side of the solarium and looked in. Finally, she came back to where I was standing and said, "There is no one in the solarium. There are only two rattan chairs and a potted plant." That evening she seemed very excited. She had obviously taken a fancy to this house.

The owner of the house was a white man who worked as a senior staff member for the CIBC bank. His name was Doug, which can be read in Chinese as "Dao Ge." I don't know why, but my wife always called him "Mr. Dog." Since in English this name sounds like "dog," I was afraid that Doug would be angry, but he didn't seem to mind. Perhaps in English it is not an insult to be called a dog.

Lily told us that in her experience, an agreement to buy a house is usually reached quite quickly. However, in our case, two cracks were discovered in the basement wall during the formal house inspection. The house inspector warned us that these two cracks might leak when it rained. Doug was adamant that in the twenty years he had been there, the basement had never leaked. This issue became a point of contention between us. So my wife and I added a clause to the offer to buy the house: "Before accepting ownership of the house, the buyer has the right to inspect the cracks in the basement after a heavy rainfall. If a leak is discovered, the buyer can cancel the agreement to buy the house." Unfortunately, that summer we had little rain, and what rain did fall was very light. It was not until September that a big enough downpour occurred. It was a real cloudburst. My wife and I rushed to Doug's house and carefully examined the cracks in the basement. We had bought an infrared scanner from Home Depot, and we used it to search the interior of the wall for moisture. We did not discover any leaks at all. Thus, all the barriers to buying the house had been swept away.

In the middle of October, we were able to move into our new house, which was now enveloped by autumn's beauty. The green maple trees had turned red; the red maple trees had turned purple; and the shrubs were a rainbow of colours. It seemed as though an artist had overturned his painter's palette to create this beautiful scene. With the keys from the real estate lawyer, my wife, my daughter, and I excitedly opened the door of our new house. As we opened the screen door, we discovered a pink card inserted into the front door handle. It was a paragraph written in English in ornate handwriting. At that time, we hadn't been in Canada very long, and I found it difficult to read. It seemed like forever before my middle-school age daughter and I were able to make out that it was a greeting from a neighbour. The neighbour's name was "Swanny," which in Chinese sounded like "Si-wo-ni," so we thought it sounded like a woman's name. She congratulated us on buying this beautiful house and welcomed us as her new neighbour. She said that after we had settled in, she would drop by and visit us. I put the card away for safekeeping, but I felt a little uneasy because my English was not very good, and I didn't know exactly how to be on good terms with a Canadian neighbour.

There was plenty to do in the days following the move. On the one hand, I was busy getting things done, but in the back of my mind I kept thinking about the woman who was called Swanny coming to visit us. But no one came. At the end of October, the United States and Canada have a very important festival called Halloween. The Chinese in Canada call this day "Ghost Festival." On this day, people carve a pumpkin and place a lit candle inside it. They then place the pumpkin outside the door of their house. Both the inside and outside of the houses are decorated with skeletons, vampires, and the like. In the evening, children, as a rule, wear masks and costumes and go begging for candy in their neighbourhoods.

Earlier that day I had bought a lot of candy, but as for the lit pumpkin and other decorations, I didn't know how to go about getting them. I kept on thinking about that neighbour Swanny who had left the card and wondered if she would come and visit. Then I would be able to ask her for some advice about this Halloween festival.

One morning, someone rang our doorbell. I lost no time in opening the door because I thought that Swanny had finally come to visit us. But when I opened the door, I saw an older boy, quite tall, with freckles and dark blond hair. He said his name was Tom and that he was the neighbour who lived next door.

"My mother asked me to give you this cake to welcome you to our neighbourhood," Tom said, as he handed us a box wrapped in paper and tied with ribbon.

"Thank you so much," I said, and then I asked, "Why didn't your mother come with you?"

Tom explained, "Lately my mother hasn't been here. In the spring, she got sick with a disease called the West Nile Virus, and she is still weak. In order to rest and recover, the doctor advised her to stay up north in Huntsville at the family cottage on a lake near Algonquin Park."

"You say your mother has been living at a lake near Algonquin Park," I said, a bit surprised. "Then how did she know that we had moved in?"

"Well, she has lived at the lake now for more than a year, but once in a while she comes home, usually in the evenings, and she mostly only stays a short time."

"What is your mother's name?" I asked.

"Swanny," the young man replied.

"So, that's who it is! We received a greeting card from her, and she said that she would visit us. Now I finally know who Swanny is."

"Yes, I know my mother wanted to visit you, but like I said, she hasn't been feeling very well."

"Please thank her very much and wish her a speedy recovery."

"One more thing." Tom hesitated and then continued, "Tomorrow is Halloween and in the evening my family is having a Halloween party. My mother hopes your family can come and join us."

"You are very kind," I said, smiling broadly. "My family and I would love to join you for the Halloween party."

When Tom left, I asked my daughter how to spell "West Nile." She told me, and then I wrote the letters down on a piece of paper. I understand what "West" means: it is the direction west. I looked for "Nile" in the dictionary and found that it meant the "Nile River." Linking the words together, it became the West Nile River. I had not heard of a disease with this name before, nor was I clear what place West Nile River referred to.

Five years earlier, I had been to the Nile River. At that time, I was still in the Balkan peninsula working in the pharmaceutical business. It was my impression that the part of the Nile within the city of Cairo was covered with modern architecture, and that the river's surface was teeming with both garbage and vessels. During my visit, I took a train along the Nile to the south. In ancient times, Upper and Lower Egypt were connected at Luxor. That section of the Nile River crosses a golden desert with mountainous hills and valleys, and many Egyptian pharaohs' tombs were built there. I remember once I took the wrong boat and arrived at a place where a lot of local residents lived. From the river bank, I was able to see the wharfs, a tourist attraction, which were not very far away. So I took a shortcut along the edge of the river to get there. But midway, I encountered several dogs that chased me and wouldn't leave me alone, causing me to flee in panic.

South of Luxor is the Aswan Governorate. That is the place on the Nile where the famous Aswan Dam was built. The dam caused the water level to rise and flood a great deal of land, leaving behind many small islands. I can still recall a black child singing a verse while paddling my boat. The verse was something like, "Nile, Nile...." Further upstream is the country of Sudan. My impression of the Nile is that it had a north-south axis, so I wasn't exactly sure where the West Nile River was located. I was all mixed up, but still when I think back on that beautiful river, I feel happy.

I also looked up Mrs. Swanny's name in the dictionary. There was no translation for "Swanny," but there was a word that was very similar that meant "swan." And so, in my mind, I began to see a connection between large flying birds and lakes. This was not just because of the word "swan," but also because the boy had said that his mother was living beside a lake to convalesce. I tried to imagine how she would spend her day, all alone by the lake.

The next night, every home was brightly lit with pumpkins. After darkness had fallen, groups of children in masks and costumes began to appear on the street. They went from house to house, knocking at the doors and shouting, "Trick or treat." When the children utter these words, you are meant to reward the child with some candy or you could be punished with a "trick" or prank. The families in each home had prepared some candy to give out to the children. I carried a big pail of candy and stood guard at the door. When I heard the kids knock on the door, I opened it and grabbed a handful of candy for each of them. I think this festival is pretty good. Just give these groups of little ghosts some candy and send them on their way—"by spreading a little wealth, you banish a little evil," as we, in China, say. However, my wife did not like Halloween at all. She said, "This festival is exactly like the Hungry Ghost Festival in mid-July in China. People should hide in their houses and not open their doors to strangers."

After nine o'clock, when the candy was all gone, I went to the doorway and saw that Mrs. Swanny's driveway was full of cars. Under the big tree in the front yard, an eerie wind blew hairy green spider webs, human skulls, and hanging devils. On the lawn, accompanied by the sound of forlorn and bitter howling, grim, shadowy rays of light flickered forebodingly. But then I thought of the invitation that Mrs. Swanny's son had given us, and I don't know why, but I felt that Mrs. Swanny would surely come home from her lakeside cottage to see her family this evening. I told my wife that, as a courtesy, our whole family should accept the invitation and go to the party. Now that we had immigrated to Canada, we should integrate into society and socialize with the local people. My wife insisted that she would definitely not go out during the Ghost Festival or go to a horrifying party. She said that on the night of the Ghost Festival every family should lock their doors to prevent evil spirits from entering the house.

Since I couldn't convince my wife, I persuaded my daughter to go with me. I told her that for a young person like her, joining the local people in this kind of activity is even more necessary. Yet as soon as my daughter went out the door and caught sight of the wailing ghosts and howling wolves in the neighbour's garden, she became frightened and her face turned pale. I coaxed her toward the neighbour's door, but there, from inside the house, we heard the din of even more moaning ghosts, and we saw macabre masks beckoning to us through the window. Suddenly, the door burst open and a skeleton holding a shiny chainsaw in its hands lunged toward us. Panic-stricken, my daughter began to cry uncontrollably, and I had no choice but to take her by the arm and head for home. When my wife saw our daughter's ashen face, she was unable to contain her fury and railed against me, shouting, "What on earth were you thinking? Why are you so interested in the next-door neighbour's business? The child is scared out of her wits. What are we going to do now?"

The argument with my wife put me in a foul mood, so I stormed out the door and ended up on a nearby street, where I walked around and around. Everywhere on the street I saw the lit-up teeth of grinning pumpkins. All sorts of creatures wearing masks and capes were roaming about. I was the only one who still looked like a human being. Many people turned their heads to stare at me.

After walking around in a circle, I gradually calmed down. I was seized with remorse. I should not have forced the child to participate in the Halloween party, especially when she did not want to go. I began to understand that I had been overly concerned with being a part of my neighbour's party. Even my wife had seen that this was peculiar behaviour on my part.

Now I would like to talk a little about another matter.

I had been here for less than six months and it was my first summer in Canada. Because I was in a good financial situation, I did not have to rush into work and so, except for attending some Adult Education classes to learn a little English, my time was mainly my own. Sometimes I would go fishing, and at other times visit the library, museum, or art gallery. At the Art Gallery of Ontario, there would often be exhibitions of famous modern artists, such as the Group of Seven. More than a hundred years ago this group of seven people went far from the city to live among the forest and lakes of Algonquin Park, which is more than three hundred kilometres from Toronto. Their work primarily consists of watercolour or gouache paintings, mostly landscapes, but also some figure paintings. I went to the art gallery a good many times to see these paintings. These works were influenced by the Impressionists, as well as by Chinese and Japanese painters. It wasn't the portrait paintings that attracted me, but rather the scenery and the people within it. The twilight in the far mountains and the sunrise mist blurring the solidity of the lakeshore made my heart yearn to find these places.

One day, while looking at an A. Y. Jackson gouache painting from 1902, I noticed some small print in the lower right-hand corner. It said, *Canal du Loing near Episy.* I knew that this was likely to be a famous scenic spot, but I searched all over the maps and couldn't locate the place until one day, while using

Google's satellite map search, I casually entered the name of that place. As a result, the map of a park suddenly appeared before my eyes. I zoomed in until I could see the lake, the forest, and the rooftops of the homes along the lakeside. Next to the map was a list of directions, showing the route from Toronto to the lake.

I am the kind of person who is very susceptible to temptation. Just as I said before, when I saw that Italian cantina filled with jam, that was it! I wanted to buy the house. The very first time I heard the Canadian singer Celine Dion sing, I had the desire to immigrate to Canada. When I saw the directions on the computer to Algonquin Park, I thought that I could visit the landscape of those paintings, and at the same time go fishing. And so, my passion was aroused.

The next day, I got up before dawn and drove for more than three hours. I came upon a country road and drove with some difficulty until I managed to reach the lakeshore. It was a beautiful lake inside a bay. The road to the shoreline was covered with what appeared to be hyacinths, and the nearby water was thick with clumps of reeds. The area was mostly uninhabited marshland, home to many long-legged wading birds, such as egrets and great blue herons who lived among the reeds. I walked along the shoreline for a long time and was unable to find a suitable place by the water to cast my fishing line, so I kept heading eastward. Eventually, I saw a small pathway leading to the lake where there was a long wooden dock stretching out into the water. It was an ideal place from which to throw a fishing line. I sat down on the dock, but I was uneasy because on the right, about thirty metres away from the dock, there was a house next to the water.

The house was big and had a large deck that also jutted out over the water. I didn't see anyone come out, but I knew that this dock was likely the private property of the house owner. I was a little hesitant, but since I couldn't find another good spot, I threw in my line here and lit up a cigarette. At this time, I smoked like a chimney; I gave up smoking later. Soon I caught my first fish, a perch. It weighed more than one pound. Then suddenly I caught a large mouth bass. The fish there were plentiful and large. They all put up a good fight. There were also a great many white lake birds similar to seagulls. Each time I hooked a fish, my line tightened, and I started to reel the fish in from a distance in the lake. The birds would hover over the area, as though they all wanted to participate in the struggle. Not until I put the fish into the ice bucket would the birds reluctantly disperse.

Then I saw a woman come from the side of the house and step onto the deck. She was quite tall, fair skinned, with brown hair. She was about forty, more or less. White people's skin can age early, and I could see that her neck seemed to be wrinkled. I thought that she also appeared to be lethargic and fragile. She was wearing a long bathrobe and holding a cup of steaming coffee with both hands. At that moment, I was worried that the homeowner would come to tell me that this was private property and fishing was not allowed. But when she saw me, she merely gave me a friendly wave and didn't say anything. I thought her smile was sincere.

This white woman allowed me to fish there, and I felt grateful. She did not disturb me; it was as though I didn't exist. Sitting on a towel and placing her coffee on a table at her side, she attended to her business. With a serene expression, she gazed out over the lake. Initially I came here to enjoy A. Y. Jackson's works of landscape, but now I saw a portrait similar to one by the Impressionist master Renoir. The French beauties in Renoir's style of painting always seem to have a sense of melancholy and fading beauty. I saw in this woman the same beauty and the same melancholy. Just before noon, I suddenly hooked a pike, a ferocious North American freshwater fish. Its body is shaped like a spear; its head resembles a snake; and it swims with incredible speed and formidable power. I exerted all my strength to hold on to the pole. I felt as though that fish wanted to drag me into the water. I strained to control the fishing line, and finally I dragged the fish to the surface. The fish suddenly jumped out of the water, waging a desperate struggle to free itself. The automatic clutch controlling the fishing line suddenly released, and it immediately cut a slit across my fingers. Back and forth, this punishment continued for several rounds until at last I dragged the one-metre-long pike to the shore, only to discover that the fishing line had cut open several painful gashes across my fingers.

After landing this fish, I felt a tremendous sense of achievement. I turned around to look at the woman's deck, convinced that she most likely had witnessed the wrestling match between me and the pike. I noticed that the sun had shifted its angle and was now flooding the deck. The woman was lying on the lounge chair, in repose, with both eyes closed as though nothing had happened. I was a little disappointed. Because I had nothing to do, I started wondering what life was like for this woman who lived beside a lake. I didn't know if there were other people inside the house or not. I thought that she was probably rich and enjoying her cottage, sitting leisurely by the lake and relaxing in the warm sunshine.

After some time, I ate the lunch that I had brought. I noticed that she was still lying on the lounge chair. I thought that she must be asleep. But this time I spotted something unusual. I saw that lying on her white cheek was something that looked like a worm and that she was completely unaware of it. Because the distance between us was not that close, I was unable to see what it was. I thought it might be a piece of coloured thread. However, after some time had passed, I saw that the worm-like thing on her cheek had become two, but she still had her eyes closed and didn't react. I was certain something wrong. I stood up, and in this way I saw that the worm-like thing was streaming down from her face to the ground, and on the ground there was an expanding dark-coloured substance. I walked briskly over to her while at the same time calling out

"Hello!" in a loud voice. She heard me and lifted up her head. The wormlike thing fell off her cheek at once.

Now I could see that her nose was bleeding! I had never seen such a serious nosebleed; the blood flowed down to the ground and had made a large pool. She sat up, and the blood immediately flowed onto her chest. She wiped at the blood and smeared it over her face. I ran over and had her lie down and not move. I immediately grabbed a nearby basin, filled it with cold water, and abruptly splashed it on her face. When I was a child, this is what adults did to me when my nose was bleeding. The unexpected splash of cold water causes the person to be startled, which causes the capillaries to shrink, and then the bleeding usually stops. At the same time, I used some paper towels lying on the table next to her to make a plug to stuff into her nostrils. Her nose stopped bleeding at last. My hands were covered with mud, fish scales, and earthworm mucous; there was also blood from the wound I had from the fishing line that had cut my fingers. My hands were both filthy and unbearably stinky. But I wasn't bothered by any of these things. I used a wet paper towel to clean the blood from the woman's face and neck, and felt the white woman's skin, which was as fine and smooth as cream. At the same time, I inhaled the scent of her body—a mixture of her perfume and her sweat.

After a few minutes, she felt a little better and started talking. She said that she had just fallen asleep and hadn't realized that her nose was bleeding. She thanked me for helping her. I asked her if we should call a doctor, but she said there was no need as she had had nose bleeds before and there was nothing to be done about it. Also, her private nurse would be coming to see her in two hours. Afterwards, she got up and retreated into the house. I was not in the mood for any more fishing, so I gathered up my things and left the lake.

After this incredible experience in this alluring landscape, I did not go to that lake again. But the white woman with scarlet-coloured blood flowing from her nose made a particularly intense impression on me and became embedded in my memory. When I read Nabokov's novel *Lolita*, I learned that the narrator was a pedophile and obsessed with young girls as a source of sexual passion. And now I began to worry that this lake experience might become the source of an unhealthy obsession for me. And then, when I got to my new house and saw the card my new neighbour, a white woman, had given us, I became aware that my heart was unduly excited. And, to go one step further, when I learned that Mrs. Swanny was also convalescing by a lake, I recalled the woman by the lake even more vividly. Even though I knew that these two things were not connected, I was still intensely curious about Mrs. Swanny. The two situations became blended together in my mind. Also, although I had not seen Mrs. Swanny's face, I imagined her possessing the facial features of the women at the lake. I really was an incorrigible.

Halloween was over, and the leaves had started falling. Within a few days, one after the other, the leaves of the maple trees in our family's backyard had dropped off and covered the entire lawn. Every day my wife and I had to collect piles of leaves and pack them into special paper bags in order to recycle them. Then we placed the bags on the side of the road to wait for a leaf collection truck to come and take them away. During this time, other people from the nearby homes also came outside to collect their leaves, and this provided my wife and me with the opportunity to get to know our neighbours.

We quickly became acquainted with Mr. and Mrs. Taylor, our French-speaking neighbours, in the house on the right. They both love to smoke and to tell jokes. As they did not smoke in the house, we would see them run outside from time to time, even when it was windy or rainy, just like whales regularly come to the water's surface to breathe. Still further to the right was a Taiwanese family surnamed Zhen. The roof of their house was particularly large and shaped like a mushroom; it crossed my mind that this house was from a fairy tale. As a matter of fact, Mr. Zhen and his wife actually resembled two little white rabbits. Their driveway was narrow, and their house was smaller than ours.

On the left, across from Mrs. Swanny's house, there was an elderly, Cantonese-speaking man who was always digging holes in his lawn. He was planting tulip bulbs. Tulip bulbs look very much like onions. My wife said that when she saw the old fellow planting the tulip bulbs, he would place some peeled garlic on the surface of the soil. At other times, he would put a few peanuts on the surface of the soil above the tulip bulb, and he even went so far as to put a chicken leg in some of the holes. My wife is not able to speak Cantonese, and she had a hard time talking with the old fellow. He gestured and talked until his meaning became clear. He said squirrels love to dig in the soil and will gnaw on the tulip bulbs, but they were repulsed by the smell of garlic. Putting some peanuts on the top of the soil is another deterrent. When the squirrels bury the peanuts, they are satisfied just knowing they have hidden something underneath the ground. Burying the chicken legs helped to cope with larger animals such as skunks and the like. Once they find the chicken leg, they will not dig any deeper, thus leaving the tulip bulb intact.

Our neighbour on the left is Mrs. Swanny. Her house occupies a lot of land and is not in the same architectural style as my house. It is one of two linked houses, one behind the other. Her front garden is professionally designed with a rock and shrubbery landscape. There is also a large umbrella tree which covers most of the front garden. There is no garage at all, but there are often many vehicles. I discovered that the family's cars were all like SUVs. Some vehicles were high-powered vans, and once I even saw a camper with a bedroom, kitchen, and washroom.

I soon realized that the Swanny family had another member. Mrs. Swanny had another son, and this young man was extremely tall, probably already in high school. Swanny's husband, Mark, was polite and had a moderately firm build, but he looked as though he had already started to age. Their family was energetic; the two sons were particularly robust, and I often saw them leaving the house loaded down with hockey equipment. They also had two black German shepherds, usually quiet, with glossy, polished coats. When they went out, they sometimes took the dogs, too. The dogs are so excited that they usually race out the door and around the yard, but never bark randomly, and they instantly come and jump into the car along with their master when it's time to head out. However, I never caught sight of Mrs. Swanny. Every now and again, I saw several women come out of the house. I didn't know who they were, but I thought none of them could be Mrs. Swanny because when they saw me, they showed no reaction. I believe this would not be the case with Mrs. Swanny. Her son said that sometimes she comes back at night, so when cars go in and out of their driveway at night, I always look out my window. Perhaps I had seen her in the dim light of the night, but I have never been able to identify her.

Then winter came. In Toronto, it snows continually. Before one snowfall has stopped, the second one has already started. As a result, there was already an accumulation of snow in many places. I don't have any special memories of this winter except for a small incident that was difficult to understand. One day when I returned home from work, my daughter told me that someone had knocked at the door that afternoon. Through the latticed window panes of the door and windows, she was able to make out the blurred image of a white man. I had always warned her never to open the door to a stranger, so she hadn't opened the door. In itself, this incident didn't mean anything. I had often met people who came knocking at the door to sell something or to proselytize. But that day, I could see that, in the snow on the ground outside the door, there was a trail of footprints leading from the front door to the backyard's wooden gate. I opened the wooden gate and saw that those footprints went straight in. The snow on the ground in the backyard had never been walked on before, but now there was a big jumble of footprints left there. On top of that, I was surprised that there were several rows of animal tracks that seemed to belong to big animals.

Recently, I had heard people saying that several wild coyotes had turned up in Dufferin Park and even bit a hiker on his calf. I also heard that a Canadian skiing champion disappeared while skiing on Snow Mountain, and it was later discovered that she had been devoured by a cougar. But since my house is located in the city, how could such wild animals get here? Even more suspicious is that these animal tracks didn't come in or go out from the garden gate. So where did they come from? My family's backyard is half an acre in size. There is no way to enter from the outside except by the wooden gate. On the left and right-hand sides there is a closed plank fence. The Taylors' home is on the right, on the left is the Swanny's home. And in the back there is the chain-link fence of my newly-acquainted Armenian neighbour. If this animal came from inside one of these properties, then it would have to jump over a very high wooden fence or deal with the chain-link fence, and then somehow jump back. This was obviously impossible. The next day was the weekend, and I stood guard at the backyard window to watch. Except for few squirrels foraging for food, I didn't see anything. After that, it never happened again, but I kept thinking about it and felt a little uneasy.

Imperceptibly, winter came to an end. One particular night while I was sleeping fitfully, I gradually became aware of a tiny bird twittering outside the house in the dark of the night. I was actually still in a dream at this time, but a part of my consciousness may have been awake. In the dream, I was drawn into another dream. I was back in southern China in my mother's house, asleep in a newly added non-regulation small shed. While asleep and still in the dream, I heard a burst of sweet-sounding bird song, and I felt very satisfied. *Ah!* I thought. *It is only in the remarkable environment of Canada where such birdsong can be heard.* I woke up from the dream, but the song continued. It was my elderly neighbour's caged songbirds that were singing.

These two dreams intertwined and prevented me from sleeping soundly. Then, the next day, high up in a tree in my backyard, I saw a big flock of red-breasted birds playing noisily on the branches. It made me extraordinarily happy. I didn't know what these birds were called. I went to the nearby library and found a book entitled *Distribution of North American Birds.* According to the pictures in the guide, I identified the birds that were perched on my backyard tree as "robins." When I was young, I would kill a lot of birds in the countryside and mountains outside my hometown using an air rifle. There were grey starlings, northern shrikes, orioles, and woodpeckers. But I had never seen this red-breasted robin before.

From that day on, I realized that spring had actually come. I often saw large numbers of birds flying past in the sky, and I noticed that the leaves on the trees had started to grow. Flowers were blooming everywhere; among the earliest was the tulip. The onion-like tubers that the elderly Cantonese neighbour had planted last year had now all blossomed into big wine-glass-shaped flowers. Canada's winter is so long, but almost immediately after the winter season, it is summer; therefore, the plants have learned to grow within a very short period of time.

Except for a large, green lawn, our backyard didn't have any flowers or plants. I used a lawn mower to cut the grass several times. The lawn resembled a green blanket and gave off the cool and refreshing scent of freshly-cut grass. This season we started to plant some flowers. In Canada, the winters are cold, so flower gardens have a mixture of perennial flowers and bushes that can survive the winter, such as roses, supplement-ed by annuals planted in the spring, such as trumpet flowers, fragrant carnations, Chinese flowering crab apples, and so on.

In the back half of my garage there is a space for my garden tools. The former owner, Doug, left behind enough equipment to start a small farm. I immersed myself into the pleasure of working with the soil, the flowers, and the plants. I bought many varieties of flower seedlings and the various components of soil fertilizer. In the backyard, based on the angle of the sunshine, I made several flowerbeds for a number of plants that love sunshine and shade. While gardening, I wore a battered straw hat and stripped to the waist; I was as pleased as Punch with myself. I sweated profusely, and I sometimes attracted mosquitoes that bit me. The mosquitoes are big in Canada, and each slap left a smudge of blood. So I learned to keep a bottle of calamine lotion in my pocket and smeared it on the mosquito bites as soon as I got them.

Spring had just arrived when several weed-like plants sprouted in the middle of the lawn and quickly produced bright yellow flowers. These yellow flowers are called dandelions. In China, we did not understand dandelions. We thought they were lovely flowers. When my daughter was small, she would sing songs like "I am a dandelion seed" and other kinds of nursery rhymes. But when it comes to gardening, is another matter, for dandelions grow and reproduce quickly, taking over the entire lawn in a short period of time. After the dandelion has blossomed, what remains behind is a thick, round stalk with a round fluffy pompom on top. The wind then blows these dry, sallow seeds all around to propagate them. When my daughter saw the dandelions, she would get goose bumps of happiness. My wife saw them as the most abominable of all the weeds.

Usually people in Canada use a chemical herbicide to eliminate the dandelions, but the shop that sells it also sells a tool that can uproot the weeds. My wife insisted on uprooting the dandelions by hand, and she would not wear gloves. That is the sort of person my wife is. For example, she doesn't like to use the washing machine; she would rather scrub the clothes by hand. She doesn't use a mop to wash the floor; she likes to get down on her hands and knees and use a cloth instead. Sometimes, I would try to persuade her not to do that and say, "You should learn to use these tools. Engels distinguished between humans and animals by defining humans as those who can use tools, and animals as those which cannot."

However, my wife continued to weed the lawn in her own way. She would sweat profusely from being in the sun, and her face became very tanned, but she refused to wear a sunhat. When she stooped down and hunched over to weed out the dandelions, her pants and T-shirt would separate at the back, revealing a patch of flesh, sometimes exposing the upper end of her buttocks. In the evening, after pulling out a big pail of weeds, she would complain that her knees were excruciatingly painful. She would use an electric pulse machine and her own hot compress physiotherapy, as well as many bruise plasters.

One weekend afternoon, after I had taken a nap for two hours, I watched my wife through the screen door window. Once again, she was hunched over the grass, weeding a clump of dandelions. By this time, the marigolds and carnations that I had planted were in full blossom. Butterflies were fluttering about the yard, a few squirrels were sitting on the lawn nibbling some food, and the sun was shining in the spaces between the leaves, dusting the mottled ground below. For a moment, I had a sudden sense of detachment. In the yard, right before my eyes, the squirrels, the butterflies, and my wife had all become completely immersed in the act of living. The rainbow-coloured butterflies, the black-tailed squirrels, and even my wife were all in the same joyful mood.

But I was uncertain whether this was merely a comforting but imagined facade. After all, up to now I have been unable to solve the mystery of the winter animal tracks in the snow. The snow in the backyard was able to record the footprints of the animals, but the grass does not reveal any footprints. I couldn't tell whether or not the animals had been coming and going. Perhaps they were wandering about in the night or at other times when I was not aware of it. Perhaps, if I turned my head away for a moment, in that instant the animal might appear. This made me feel uneasy.

At the very moment that I was thinking this, things started to happen. My wife suddenly jumped up and screamed for me. I lost no time in opening the door and running into the backyard. I felt sure that she must have been bitten by something in the grass.

"What is it? What happened?" I asked as I ran over to her.

My wife cried out in horror, flailing her arms about in panic. "Look! A dead bird. In the grass. I touched it!"

"Is that all?" I said. "It's nothing. Who told you not to wear gloves?" I could see a large dead bird in the grass. It was neither a robin nor a starling, but a relatively large black bird. Perhaps it was a North American mountain chickadee or a short-beaked crow. Its eyes were still open, and you could see the clouds in the sky reflected in them. The corpse had already started to decompose and gave off a foul-smelling odour.

I consoled my frightened wife and pulled the hose over to rinse off the hand that had touched the dead bird. After she went back into the house, she locked herself in the bathroom, and I heard the tap running like mad. After about half an hour, she came out of the washroom and said to me, "You make supper tonight. My hand is not clean. It still stinks."

I thought the matter was over and done with, but this was not the case at all. In the morning, the letter carrier arrived. The white man was over forty years old, short in stature, and always very happy and talkative. Every day he had to walk to several hundred homes to deliver all kinds of mail. I was about to leave for work when I bumped into him, and so he handed me the mail. I quickly glanced at the letters and saw a piece of green cardboard among them. There were pictures of birds on the card. Although I can read English, I am very slow and sometimes need to use an electronic dictionary. So

I took the opportunity to ask the letter carrier what this card was all about.

The letter carrier said in English, "This is City Hall." He explained that the card was issued by the municipal government to warn citizens about an infectious disease. I approached him and asked him what kind of infectious disease the card was taking about.

He said, "The West Nile virus. It's a terrible disease transmitted from birds to humans." The virus relied on certain species of birds to spread the disease. The name West Nile sounded familiar. I immediately thought of my neighbour, Mrs. Swanny. She had fallen ill with the West Nile virus.

Listening to what he said, my heart sank. I tucked the card into my pocket and put the other mail in the mailbox. Just then, my wife came out of the house. We have a family import business, and I usually drive my wife to the warehouse with me. This day was no different.

All day I was unable to concentrate. I kept thinking about that green card in my pocket. I kept thinking about the birds that were pictured there. Before my wife learned about this, I wanted to have a complete understanding of the contents of the card. So, taking advantage of the time when my wife was in the back of the warehouse sending out some merchandise, I took out the card, and with the help of the dictionary, carefully read it. The information I gleaned from the card made me a little bit nervous.

The West Nile virus was first isolated in 1937 when it was discovered in a woman's blood in Uganda's West Nile region. It was then confirmed to be one of the most widely spread pathogens—the flavivirus. It is distributed throughout Africa, the Middle East, and the southern temperate and tropical regions of the Eurasian continent. In the 1950s, it was estimated that forty percent of the population in Egypt's Nile River Delta tested positive for this pathogen. Of all the populations, the largest prevalence of the virus occurred in 1974 in Cape Province, South Africa. At that time, nearly three thousand clinical cases were reported.

The West Nile virus is mainly carried by infected birds and then transmitted to humans by mosquito bites. This resulted in the West Nile fever. It can also be transmitted among people through blood transfusions, organ transplants, breastfeeding, and so on. In 1999, the first case of West Nile virus in the United States was discovered in New York. Soon afterwards, the virus spread throughout the whole country with the epidemic becoming ever more virulent. In the same time periods and regions, people began to notice a coincidence between the outbreak of this disease in human populations and the deaths of a large number of birds. By the middle of March, thousands of crows and other birds had evidently died from the virus in New York City and its environs. A large number of dead wild geese in the Canadian prairie provinces of Manitoba and Saskatchewan were also found. The infection of birds and people occurring during the same time period in different regions caused epidemiologists to conclude that infected birds act as hosts for the virus and pass it on to the mosquito. The infected mosquito then spreads the virus to other hosts, ultimately infecting people. Several kinds of birds, mainly migratory, had become the chief medium for the transmission of the virus. According to the United States Center for Disease Control and Prevention's statistics in 2003, forty-five states had more than 9,000 people infected with the West Nile virus, 240 of whom died. Last year there were 2,470 cases with 88 deaths. Canada currently has more than 1,000 cases of infection, of whom 47 have died. And to date, there is no vaccine to prevent the West Nile virus.

I spent more than half an hour deliberating over this flyer, and all the while I had a sinking feeling growing in the pit of my stomach. City Hall was asking its residents to pay close attention to the developments in the West Nile virus situation. In particular, if a dead bird is found, residents should inform the authorities at once. Then someone from the epidemic prevention centre will come and collect a bird's carcass and inspect it to determine whether or not it was infected with the disease. The green card didn't say anything about what they should do after coming into direct contact with the bird carcass. This was what concerned me most. Clearly, the body of the bird found in our backyard had to be reported to City Hall. My concern was, since my wife touched a dead bird, could she be infected? From the information I read about the transmission of the West Nile virus, the disease is spread when a mosquito sucks the blood of an infected bird. Therefore, merely touching a bird should not be a problem. But I know my wife is sensitive and timid, so I had to be careful not to scare her. Just as I was thinking this, I realized my wife had already come into the office and was staring at me.

"What are you reading?" she asked.

"Nothing.... A flyer.... A flyer about birds." I stammered. I had not finished determining how to approach her about this matter.

"What? A flyer about birds?" She came over and looked at the green card on my desk. She snatched it up and quickly glanced at it. Her English is not as good as mine, nor is her basic reading comprehension, but her intuition is sharper than mine by a long shot.

"What does it say?" she asked me, her voice a little too high-pitched.

"It's about an infectious disease. You know about our neighbour, Swanny's disease? This is exactly the same kind of disease that she has."

I had my wife sit down and poured her a glass of water. I explained the contents of the card to her, stressing that, for sure, not all of the dead birds had contracted the West Nile disease virus. And, as far as I could understand it, even if the dead bird were carrying the virus, it still could not spread the disease through contact. The only mode of transmission is through the bite of a blood-sucking mosquito. She listened intently to my explanation. Never before had she listened to what I had to say so earnestly. Our discussion resulted in deciding that the first thing to do was to report the dead bird in our backyard to the authorities. So I called the number that was on the green card and reported the incident. The young woman on the switchboard said that Ministry of Health inspectors would come tomorrow to investigate, and at the same time recommended that we should go to the doctor for an examination. I immediately gave our family doctor a call to make an appointment. The secretary arranged for us to see our doctor the next Monday morning.

During supper that evening, my wife seemed pensive and spoke little. I also noticed that she changed the way we had customarily eaten for the last ten years. Now she put a pair of chopsticks on each dish so that we could pick up the food and place it in our own bowl separately.

I said, "There is no need for this. Why be so sensitive?"

She said, "It would be better to do it this way, just in case there is something wrong."

Before going to bed, I saw that she had taken a quilt from the closet. She had me help spread it on her side of the bed, so that we could sleep under separate quilts. That night she couldn't sleep. She just kept talking, going over and over details as if she were preparing to go on a trip to a place a long distance away.

Thanks to my wife talking until the early hours of the morning, we woke up when the sun was high in the sky. It was the weekend. I got up, opened the door, and looked out to see a strange van parked in the driveway. The van doors were closed and on its side were many pictures of all sorts of birds. It was quite attractive. Over a flock of birds was a line of print: NORTH AMERICAN BIRDMAN. In English, this refers to people who are interested in observing the habits of the birds of North

America. I heard the singing of a sweet-sounding bird outside. I opened the outside glass door, and from the threshold saw a red-beaked bird perched in the crown of our giant pine tree. It was singing with singular excitement. Then, a short string of birdsong broke out from the ground in response to the bird in the tree. After that, a burst of birdsong came from the tree. I couldn't see the bird on the ground because the unfamiliar van obstructed my view. I came out, walked around the van, and saw a man sitting on the lawn. The man was looking toward the top of the pine tree, and the sounds of a bird singing were coming out of his mouth.

"Hello. How are you?" I greeted him.

"Not bad," the man responded, keeping his eyes on the bird at the top of the tree.

"I suppose you are a North American birdman, eh?" I said.

"Yes, you're right," he said and stood up. I could see that this man looked a lot like a bird himself; in fact, he actually resembled a crow. His head was small with two round eyes similar to a bird. His nose was pointed like a crow's beak. I don't know if he possessed these bird characteristics, or if this was just my own fancy. He introduced himself. His name was Youssef, and he was employed as a contractor by the Ministry of Health for the North York municipality. He was specifically responsible for the investigation of dead birds. Before going into the backyard, he asked me some questions about the circumstances, jotting down notes in a huge well-used notebook. I noticed that he had already drawn a pencil sketch of my family's house on the page. Presumably he had drawn it during his conversation with the bird.

Then we went into the backyard to find the dead bird. After my wife stumbled upon the bird the day before yesterday, I used a shovel to move it to the secluded west corner of the backyard and covered it with some leaves. I brushed the leaves off lightly and found the thing with no effort. It was very strange; the day before yesterday, the bird appeared to be decayed, but after being buried in the leaves for two days, it seemed to have a fresh appearance. The birdman, Youssef, wearing a pair of latex gloves, picked up the bird and moved it from hand to hand to get a good look at it. The bird looked as though if you blew one breath into it, it could fly away. He said that the bird was a raven, about four years old. After that, he placed the bird in a transparent, hermetically sealed plastic bag, and, using a marker, wrote on the bag the collection site, an identification number, and so on.

"Do you think that this bird has the West Nile virus?" I asked him tentatively.

"I don't know," he said. "The laboratory at the Ministry of Health will discover the cause of death."

"What might have caused this bird to die?" I asked.

"Birds die for many reasons; just as people die for many reasons. But birds die for straightforward reasons—at least not from murder. I come into contact with dead birds all the time; you can see all kinds of them in my van. The freezer at the top has dead swans, wild geese, quail, black-headed gulls, and grey herons."

"Can you tell me how birds usually die?" I asked. "When I was young I saw so many birds in the trees and in the hills, but I never saw a single dead bird apart from those killed by people."

"That's a good question. Birds usually die in a place that is not accessible to people. For example, I know a seagull graveyard in a bay in Rice Lake that is more than two hundred kilometres from Toronto, and where there is a large forest that few people visit. I have seen many old seagulls flying in a fixed direction toward that lake and forest where they go to die. Most birds will fly into the deep woods when they are ready to die. After they die, their dead bodies will be eaten by other animals or insects. The bird dying in your garden is not a normal death."

"If this bird had the West Nile virus disease, will touching it cause infection?" I asked.

"I don't know. Maybe it will; maybe it won't. I am not a virologist. I'm just a birdman," he said.

"Have you met anyone suffering from West Nile virus ?" I asked.

"What did you say?" He turned his head and stared at me with his wide-open eyes and pointed face, really looking like a bird. Then he responded, "I have seen too many. In my hometown, which is on the bank of the Nile River, there are many people who have been infected with the West Nile virus. Once when I was young and still in Egypt, a British research team gave all the people in my village a blood test. The results showed that half of the people had contracted the West Nile virus, including me. However, we are still alive and in perfect health.

After Youssef had collected the dead bird, he didn't seem inclined to leave. He asked me if he could sit and eat his lunch in the backyard. Although I was not very pleased, I was too embarrassed to refuse. He took an engraved tin lunchbox out of the van. There were several pieces of round flat bread in it, the same kind that I had seen on the streets in Cairo. Youssef continued to talk about the Nile while he tore the round bread into pieces. "The ancient Egyptians believed that after death the soul would turn into a bird and fly up to heaven," he said. "Therefore, we believe that when we see so many birds flying, we are seeing people's souls. Since the birds have the West Nile virus disease, then, it is not strange that people are infected as well."

"The Nile River people and the West Nile virus have always coexisted peacefully. But this is not the case for outsiders. The most notable example occurred in 323 BCE, when Alexander the Great, the king of the ancient kingdom of Macedonia, died while in the prime of his life after coming to Babylon. At that time, he was only thirty-two years old. In the city of Babylon, a large number of crows had died a mysterious death, just as it happened last year in New York State where a great many crows died. From the day it started, Alexander the Great's persistent high fever would not subside. Finally, he succumbed to mental confusion and died in agony. Nowadays, many people believe Alexander the Great died of the West Nile virus."

I only half believed what he had said, but I felt there might be some truth to it. Perhaps the Indigenous people along the Nile have antibodies and are infected with the virus without getting the disease. But there was one thing that I still didn't understand: since this was an ancient disease, what caused the outbreak within the last few years?

Youssef could not answer this question. However, he mentioned something else. He said that in the winter before last, North America had hardly any significant snow falls, and the weather was unseasonably warm. As a result, the brown bears in the northern forests could not hibernate; since the temperatures were too high, they woke up. When they crawled out of their dens, they were unable to find something to eat, and so broke into people's residences and injured several people. Higher winter temperatures allowed many insects that would have usually been frozen to death to survive, and this gave rise to increased numbers of insects everywhere, harming the forest trees. More insects attracted more birds, and as the birds spread, so did the West Nile virus. Youssef pointed to a big tree in my yard and said, "Look, this tree is covered with green caterpillars."

I looked up but couldn't see anything because the tree branches were rather high. Youssef handed me the binoculars that he used for bird watching. I took a look and saw many long, hairy, green caterpillars crawling along the tree branches. Their density was utterly astonishing.

"How can this be? This is extraordinary. How could I not have noticed this?" I gasped.

"Isn't it on the local TV every day? And in the newspaper?" Youssef said. I was embarrassed. Since I am not able to understand English programs very well, I nearly always watch channel 4, a Chinese TV station on satellite TV. Every day I watch the familiar faces of Li Ruiying and Luo Jing.[1] I only watch the local channels once in a while for the local weather forecast and, of course, the NBA basketball games.

"Your region is a good deal better than some. In Mississauga, the caterpillar situation is an absolute mess. Those caterpillars have already started to spin silk and drop down to the ground. Many people's roofs and driveways are covered with caterpillars. Each step results in a thick gooey juice. If this continues, probably fifty percent of the trees in the city will be killed by these caterpillars."

"Are you saying that the caterpillars in the trees will come down and crawl on the ground?" I paled with fear.

"This will certainly happen. However, I know that city hall is preparing a plan and getting ready to spray pesticides using planes. The members of city council are now debating whether or not to ask the federal government to pay the five-million-dollar cost to exterminate the caterpillars."

"This is unthinkable. How can they use planes to spray pesticides in a residential neighbourhood? The insects may not be the only ones killed; perhaps even people will die."

Youssef was ready to climb into the tree to lay out traps to capture a few live bird specimens to use for laboratory testing. He climbed very high; soon he disappeared from sight, hidden by the dense foliage. I sat under the tree, peered through the spaces between the branches, and watched the sometimes hidden, and sometimes visible Youssef.

By now I had learned the birdman's life story. When he was young, he was a Nile River fowler. His family had been earning their living this way for generations. Later, he came to North America and was employed by the New York airport to keep the birds off the runways by using a group of wooden decoy hawks. Eventually, the airport replaced him by using a machine that emitted ultra-high frequency sound waves to drive the birds away, and so he became an independent bird catcher once again.

That day, Youssef stayed up in the tree in our backyard for a long time. At first, I felt he was working very conscientiously, but later I realized that he was probably amusing himself with the birds that were flying back and forth. He prolonged his stay in the crown of the tree, becoming almost one with the birds who were flying in the sky above.

All this time, my wife had been standing behind the window, watching Youssef's every move.

Recently I have noticed that my wife is often standing at the window, silently staring outside. I can't figure out what she is paying attention to. Ever since the day before yesterday, after she had touched that dead black bird, she seems to have acquired a peculiar bird-like stance. That night when I was fast asleep, I was suddenly awakened by her nudge. She said, "Wake up. I saw our next-door neighbour, Mrs. Swanny!"

Still groggy from sleep, I asked her, "What are you yelling about? It's the middle of the night. Are you dreaming?" She pulled me up to the window and had me peer out into the dim light of the night. From this angle, I was looking out over Mrs. Swanny's front yard. During the day, you could see that the gigantic umbrella-shaped tree in their garden was covered with crimson blossoms. These blossoms look a little like Japanese cherry blossoms, but are even more vivid. The plants that grow beneath the tree are unique, and those who pass by will frequently take pictures of the display. Lately I had been a bit puzzled, for during this period of time our neighbour's home had become quiet. It seemed as though no one lived there. I didn't know who was caring for those plants and flowers. I rubbed the sleep from my eyes and carefully scrutinized the outside.

This time I noticed the silhouette of someone moving about in the flower garden. Gradually, I could see that it was a woman with clipped, short hair. She was using a small rake to loosen the soil in a sunken garden bed and was watering it at the same time. I saw her very clearly. It could not have been a dream. She was facing the street, and there were streetlights illuminating her body with lemon yellow rays. I don't know why, but I could not see her face.. I was not sure that she was Mrs. Swanny, as I had never actually met her before and even now could not see her well. One thing that I am sure of: in the past I had noticed quite a number of middle-aged women going in and out of her house, but she wasn't one of them because, in contrast, the movement of her silhouette seemed so graceful and so mysterious.

I found myself becoming a bit stirred up and anxious to see her face, so much so that I even had an impulse to run outside into the night and help her with the watering. That way I could finally determine whether or not she was the woman from the lake. I watched her from the window for about two minutes. She wandered about in the garden, now appearing, now disappearing, as illusory and unreal as a shadow on a photograph negative. And then she suddenly disappeared.

I felt a little lost and disappointed because I didn't get a good look at her. But I thought, if she really has come home, perhaps she will come and call on us. If she doesn't, in that case, I should still be able to see her, at least the same way I had seen her tonight. I told my wife that Mrs. Swanny returning home must be a good thing, indicating that even though she is infected with the West Nile disease, it is nothing to be afraid of. Didn't she return home to recover? My wife said that she didn't think that way at all. Why would the neighbour water the flowers in the middle of the night? When she was young her grandmother had warned her that people must not water the flowers after dark because if they do, it will cause the person to waste away.

The next day was Monday. In the morning, I accompanied my wife to the doctor for her check-up. Our family doctor's office was in a neighbourhood near the rental apartment where we had lived a year ago. Because Dr. Xu is from Taiwan, he is able to speak Mandarin. Even though we had made an appointment in advance, we still had to wait a long time. Among the other people waiting, there were several Chinese people as well as Eastern Europeans, Iranians, East Indians, and Black people. The secretary is a Hong Kong emigrant, and we were familiar with her. Sometimes she is very warm to us, and at other times she is chilly. The back of her head is noticeably flat, and since we don't know her name, behind her back my wife and I call her "Flat Head." Our appointment time had passed some time ago, but Flat Head told us that there were still five patients ahead of us.

Canada employs a universal free health care system. For minor illnesses you go to see the family doctor. If your family doctor believes you need to see a specialist, then you are referred for an appointment.

At ten o'clock we finally met with Dr. Xu and told him our situation. Dr. Xu was very familiar with us, and he wanted to take some of my wife's blood and give it a complete laboratory analysis. He took five or six vials of blood, and in the meantime he asked me if I was willing to get my blood tested, too. It had been quite a long time since I had had a physical check-up, and I thought his suggestion was a good one. So I went back to the reception area to get my medical records from "Flat Head." I rolled up my sleeve to let the doctor take a few vials of my blood. When he finished, the doctor ordered a list of routine tests: x-rays, ultrasound, ECG, etc. and he sent us to a nearby medical testing centre.

After we had finished our tests, we asked when we would get the results. The nurse said it would take two weeks: one week to process the tests, and after that one week to send the report to the family doctor's office. We asked whether or not we could come back and pick up the report ourselves, so that we could find out the results sooner. The testing clerk looked at me with consternation and said, "Absolutely not. You can only hear about the results at the doctor's office."

When the tests were finished, it was already noon. Without having to go too far away, we found a McDonald's for a quick bite. I noticed my wife beginning to look a little strange. She said, "To have to wait for two weeks is too long. Won't it be too late for the treatment?"

Trying to comfort her I said, "You definitely will not get the disease. So many people have told you that the West Nile virus is blood-borne and is not contagious. And besides, you look very healthy. Look, you easily ate a hamburger and fries. How can you be sick?"

She said, "Actually, I didn't want to eat, but I ate in order to do all I can to increase my strength. If I couldn't keep anything down then the situation would really be serious."

From that day on, I told her not to go to work but stay at home and rest. I made a big mistake in doing this. I should not have let her linger at home by herself, giving her ample time to let her imagination run wild.

After eating supper on Wednesday evening, I prepared to go out for a walk with my wife. Just as we were leaving the house, we watched a number of vehicles arriving one after the other at our neighbour Swanny's house. The first was a large GMC Safari station wagon, carrying two canoes on the roof. Then there were several cars towing jet skis and a truck towing a large boat. By this time, I wouldn't have been surprised if I had seen a car dragging a seaplane. Last fall, I had also seen a number of cars in the driveway carrying canoes and a boat, but I had never seen so many vehicles and water sports equipment as this. These vehicles were not in the driveway, but were all parked by the side of the road. A great many people had gone into the house. It seemed as though, for a long time, there had been no one going in or out of their house. I hadn't seen Swanny's husband and two sons for a long time. So, it was unusual to see so many people there that evening. I told my wife, "Perhaps Swanny's whole family stayed up at the cottage at the lakeside to keep her company and help her recover. Now that her illness is cured, the whole family has returned home, even bringing back the boat and canoes."

My wife said, "Then why are there so many people?"

I answered, "Perhaps this is a recovery and coming home celebration party for Mrs. Swanny."

At that moment, I noticed something unusual. A black sedan decorated with white lilies drove up. The black sedan drove directly into Swanny's driveway and came to a stop. I was startled to see Swanny's husband and two sons get out. They were all wearing black suits. I had seen them many times, but each time they had been dressed in loose and comfortable everyday clothes. They were never dressed as formally as today. Their expressions were sombre, but when they saw us they still greeted us politely.

"It's been a long time since we saw you. How are you?" I said as we walked past.

"Yeah, we haven't been back for a long time. We were all at the lakeside, keeping my mother company," Swanny's son Tom said.

"How is Mrs. Swanny? Did she return, too?" I asked.

"No. My mother passed away," said Tom.

"What? Is this true?" I said in disbelief.

Mark, Mrs. Swanny's husband said, "Yes, she passed away a week ago. Since last summer her condition seemed to be slowly improving, but recently her health suddenly worsened. She has been fighting the West Nile virus for a long time, but in the end she was not able to defeat it. After she died, we took her back to her hometown in New Jersey. She was an American, you know."

"I am very sad to hear about Swanny. She was a good person," I said. My heart suddenly felt empty. It was very strange. A few nights ago, my wife and I saw a woman tending the flowers in her garden, and we had thought she was Mrs. Swanny. But by that time Swanny had already passed away.

That night I kept thinking about Swanny. In my mind, as soon as I closed my eyes, she appeared in that lethargic slumber with blackish red blood dripping from her nose. I could no longer distinguish between Swanny and the woman by the lake. A thought began to form in my mind: "I have to go back up to that Algonquin Lake to take a look at the woman one more time. Is she still there? Is her nose still bleeding?"

We were told that we had to wait for two weeks to get the test results. At first, I thought that the time would pass by quickly, but those two weeks dragged by extremely slowly. By now my wife was in a very bad state. Mrs. Swanny's death deepened her fear and panic. Many symptoms began to appear on her body. First, she felt an aching and burning sensation in her finger joints. Then, there was a choking and breathless feeling in her chest, which was accompanied by severe pain. She was restless now and unable to stop moving. The first few days she would only stay inside the house, then she felt unable to breathe in the house and would run out into the street.

At first, I still went to work and let my wife rest at home by herself. In fact, it would have been much better if I had taken her to work with me and allowed her to do a little business to distract her. At work, I was always ill at ease, and from time to time would phone home to ask her how she was doing. Sometimes when I phoned there was no answer, and I knew she had probably gone out into the street. She told me that when she walked outdoors, she felt more relaxed. A few days later, when I had not been at work long, she phoned me and said that she could not bear the thumping of her heart and asked me to hurry home right away. I realized that my wife's condition was getting worse. Her hair had lost its lustre and within a few days had become flat and dry, even white in many places. Her complexion was dark and her eyes dull. She told me that when she was walking back and forth on the street the neighbour, the old man who had planted the tulips, was continually staring at her. Even when she walked to the end of the block, he still watched her. I said, "Your appearance is not right. Your hair is not combed. Your clothes are buttoned all wrong. Whoever caught sight of you would think it very strange."

I told her not to be nervous because it was impossible for her to have the disease. In order to convince her, my daughter and I spent the whole day on the internet getting information on what might be wrong. We entered her symptoms into the computer. The results essentially showed that her symptoms were not those of the West Nile virus, but were rather symptoms of menopause. Another possibility was a kind of anxiety disorder caused by a shock that had given rise to an autonomic nerve disorder. However, she did not believe what we said. If we persisted in our claims, she just got angry and her symptoms worsened.

In order to weather this storm, I didn't go to work. I hung a "Gone on vacation—Temporarily closed" sign on the company door, even though this meant that I would lose thousands of dollars in revenue every day. I kept her company all day long. When she felt the chest tightness, I gave her a back massage. When she was nervous, I soothed her with calm words to get her to relax. Her temperament became like that of a four-year-old child—sometimes good, sometimes bad. I went with her for walks outside. This was the most important method she used to calm down. When she and I walked around the tree-lined road, she would seem very happy, and many of her symptoms were alleviated.

We've been married for more than ten years. In all these years, except for the period of time before we got married, we have almost never been as close as we were when we went together on these walks. While she was walking she would speak about many things without pausing. She said that the previous day she had bumped into the Taiwanese neighbour, Zhen. She had never spoken with him before. Yesterday he was weeding near his gate and, taking the initiative, greeted her. He said that the night before, someone had thrown a lot of fish into his yard, and he asked her if she had met with the same experience. She said, "Taiwanese people certainly talk a lot of nonsense. How could fish be thrown helter-skelter like that? What a joke!"

She also said that the garden on the corner, which was surrounded by a carved cast-iron railing fence, was owned by a person from India. She was annoyed because the many flowers in his garden grew in a wild and disorderly mess, and the garden was covered in dandelions. The day before yesterday when she passed by the Indian's garden, he was pulling up weeds by hand just like my wife herself does. The Indian said that they were in the restaurant business and were usually very busy. They liked the flowers but had no time to care for them, so the garden was unkempt. My wife said that she could forgive him now.

She also brought me to a back lane to see a newly renovated house. After expanding the house, the front wall was resurfaced with patterned granite. It was her favourite stone. She said that in the future we should tear down the house and rebuild it—she had the blueprints in her mind—so that the square footage of our house could be doubled. We passed by another house that had also been rebuilt. The walls of that house had been plastered with mortar, and the added second floor resembled a little hat. My wife turned up her nose at this house.

Every day we would walk for a distance of three blocks to Godstone Park, where there is a large expanse of grass and woodland. The park is home to two soccer fields. Toward the evening there are often a lot of people playing soccer. There is a team of young Koreans with their own uniforms accompanied by a group of pretty girls who cheer them on. They play against a group of Black children. We would sit on a park bench and watch them play. Sometimes we would watch people walking their dogs, or join a group of elderly Chinese people who come to watch their children do *tai chi* under the trees.

My wife developed a routine of exercises for herself. In her first set, she interlaced the fingers of her hands together, then raised them with palms upward, and then, taking a deep breath, she sunk to a squat and then stood up. Her second set was a yoga routine. She spread out her arms horizontally in the shape of an airplane and raised one leg towards the back. In her third set, she walked backwards slowly, and, after a few steps, her left hand and left foot were in unison. She was very earnest in her efforts. The hot afternoon sun shone on her face, turning it a bronze colour and causing the appearance of butterfly freckles. Sweat covered her face, yet she gave no thought to any of it. Her intensity moved me. Sometimes women are very strong. I knew she was doing everything in her power to battle the disease, even though the disease does not necessarily exist.

Everything had changed. Before, staying home was her favourite thing. Now I had to be doubly careful, because during this time her mood often shifted. She used to watch reruns on TV and never tired of them. She was able to watch late into the night but now, as soon as we started watching a show, she immediately told me to change the channel.

One day at the end of our walk, she became utterly dispirited. She said that she was afraid to go home. But we had to return home. On the way home, the sky clouded over. I had to keep talking to make her happy. When we crossed an intersection, I spotted a branch overhanging a wooden fence that surrounded a family garden. There was red fruit growing on the top of the branch that looked like Hawthorn fruit. I reached out my hand and plucked a few berries to give her to look at, and while taking a bite I asked, "What is this fruit? I wonder what it tastes like." The fruit was extremely sour, causing me to grimace.

My wife's countenance changed at once, and she scolded me,

asking me why I took a bite so thoughtlessly. What if it was poisonous? Normally, she would scold me with a few sentences and let it go at that. But now I noticed that the expression in her eyes was unduly animated, and saliva had collected at the corners of her mouth. I grabbed her by the shoulders and made her calm down. I felt the muscles of her back tense up like iron. A feeling of fear suddenly overwhelmed me. The situation was becoming critical.

Youssef, the birdman, had come back. I went out and saw his bird-painted van parked in my driveway. He greeted me from a distance and told me that the last time he was in my backyard, a blue jay and a cardinal that had been captured in his cages had tested positive for the West Nile virus.

Moreover, the Ministry of Health had already been informed about our neighbour Swanny's death. This year she was North America's fifty-first casualty of the disease. The Ministry of Health had designated this area as high risk. And, starting tomorrow, a program of mosquito extermination would be underway over an extensive area.

Youssef was holding a big bundle of printed material, which he attached to a lamp post at the curb. On it were pictures of birds, and the poster informed people that if they find a dead bird, they must report it to the Ministry of Health so that it can be tracked and investigated. Other instructions included: Don't secretly dispose of the bird. To protect against mosquito bites, don't stay outdoors at dusk with uncovered skin. If you do go outdoors for an activity, apply mosquito repellent.

The birdman led me into the backyard. He pointed to some things that could hold water, like old flower pots, and told me that these things will breed mosquito larvae. I held up a flower pot and examined it carefully. I could see several red thread-like larvae wriggling in the water. He also had me take a look at the tree branch with the green caterpillars. Their bodies seemed much bigger than before. The birdman told me that city hall had already leased the plane. Tomorrow, they would begin the aerial spraying of insecticide.

The next day, I told my wife to stay in the house and not to go outdoors for exercise. At about nine o'clock the next morning, I heard a plane flying at a low altitude in our vicinity, probably spraying the insecticide to kill the green caterpillars. At noon, a large contingent of people wearing white protective clothing entered our neighbourhood. It looked as frightening as a scene in the movies with Ku Klux Klan members. I saw two fumigation personnel enter the backyard carrying two electric sprayers on their backs. They squirted a mist of white spray everywhere. One of them saw me standing inside the window and raised two fingers toward me in a "V" sign. I had closed the windows and doors tightly and only used the air conditioner for ventilation, but still the house was filled with the strong smell of chemicals.

In the evening, the family doctor's secretary "Flat Head" phoned to say that tomorrow morning Dr. Xu wanted to see me. I asked her whether or not the test results had come in. She said yes, but to leave specific questions for Dr. Xu. She declined to comment further and just hung up.

The phone call from "Flat Head" was definitely not a good sign. When the family doctor notifies you halfway through the waiting period, then the test results may show there is a problem. It had only been seven days since the blood test, so that confirmed that there was something wrong. My heart sank. I really did not understand how my wife's luck could be so bad, to merely touch a dead bird and be infected with the virus. But now there was no way I could tell her that everything was all right. My wife became very quiet, her complexion paled, and her body seemed to shrink noticeably. I comforted her by telling her not to be too nervous. We still didn't know all the facts. We should wait until tomorrow to find out what Dr. Xu had to say. Even if there was a problem, she should not be afraid. Fear would only make the problem worse.

Thinking back, that night was the most uncomfortable that I can ever remember. I lay in bed with my mind racing and a splitting headache. I imagined my roof and eaves outside were covered with birds whispering in secretive voices. The birds seemed jubilant. They were flying around inside my room, worming their way into my quilt, and drilling into my brain. I was sleeping inside a foul-smelling nest. Later, I dreamed about animal footprints in the snow in the backyard. I dreamed that there was an animal pacing back and forth in the middle of the yard. It was an animal in the cat family—its whole body was pitch-black and it bared ferocious fangs.

I heard my wife crying. It was not a dream. She was actually crying. She said she was so afraid that she wanted to return to China. I said, "Okay, we'll go and buy a plane ticket back home tomorrow." But she said no to this because China doesn't have the West Nile disease and they wouldn't be able to treat that kind of illness. Then I said, "Let's not even think about these things ahead of time. We can sort it out tomorrow after we see Dr. Xu."

The next morning, my wife and I arrived at the doctor's office. We had to register first with "Flat Head," who was extremely busy. She was wearing a telephone headset, but owing to the flatness of her head, the two sides were too narrow, and the earphones kept sliding to one side. Finally, "Flat Head" said to me, "Dr. Xu wants to see you, not your wife." At that moment, my head exploded. I thought that my wife's condition must be so serious that the doctor was afraid she would not be able to handle the strain, so, first he would speak to a family member about the problem. My wife was thinking the same thing, and said to me that under the circumstances, she was not afraid, and it would be better to know the details as soon as possible. Then my wife held my hand tightly and walked into Dr. Xu's examination room as if entering an execution chamber. Dr. Xu looked at my wife and said, "Your blood test reports are in, and there are no problems. Everything is normal, and you are in good health." Then Dr. Xu turned to me and said, "Your blood has tested positive for the West Nile virus. To stop the infection, you must have specialized treatment at once."

When I heard Dr. Xu say this, my first reaction was to roar with laughter. How is this possible? So now it is me that is infected with the West Nile disease. I am glad my wife is not sick. If her blood tests had been positive, she would have fallen apart for sure.

In this muddled way, I learned that I was the one infected with the West Nile virus. Since I was the first instance of an Asian immigrant to be infected, the Ministry of Health treated my case with special attention. After being placed in the North York General Hospital and given rigorous monitoring, I became a research subject. Every three hours a nurse would come and take my temperature, blood pressure, blood sugar content, pulse, and so on. And every morning the head doctor, wearing a white gauze mask along with a group of similarly clad people, would come to see me. They asked me many questions and then started to draw blood for tests. I remember that nearly every morning I would have several vials of blood drawn. As a result, after a few days, as soon as I saw the nurses who took the blood, I wanted to run away. This made me think back to thirty or so more years ago, to my family's pitiful chicken.

At that time, it was common for people in China to get injections of chicken blood. My mother suffered from many illnesses. Every day, she had me go and catch our only chicken and draw its blood to inject into her. I remember that when I went to catch it, that chicken would struggle desperately to escape. By the time I caught it, its fear was so intense that I remember the scene to this day. And now, when the nurses come to draw my blood, I felt myself behaving in the same way as that terrified chicken of years gone by.

I probably became infected with the West Nile virus when I was bitten by a mosquito while I was planting flowers in the garden. This type of mosquito is called a bird-biting mosquito. They prefer to suck bird blood, but if they see a human body stripped to the waist and covered with smelly sweat, it is only natural that they would also want to take a few bites. Before sucking the blood out, the mosquito will first discharge anti-coagulant serums into the body of the person whose blood is being sucked. It was in this way that bird blood was injected into my body.

When you come to think about this, it is really a remarkable thing—in my body there was actually bird blood! I didn't know what sort of bird the blood comes from. I hoped it wasn't from a noisy sparrow or from an ugly and inauspicious crow. An owl or an American vulture wouldn't be nice, either. If it were a swan's or a grey-faced goose's or a flamingo's or an albatross' blood, I would have felt a little bit better. For the past few days I had been thinking about this puzzle continuously. My skin had a strange itchiness, and it felt like many fine down-like feathers were about to emerge. I didn't know whether this illusion was a symptom produced by the West Nile virus disease or not.

However, a week later, the doctors overturned my theory about getting the virus from a mosquito. Altogether, there were three virology specialists who participated in the analysis of my case. From the results produced by cultivating my blood serum, they discovered that the genetic variations of the virus found in my blood stream differed from the current mutation. The virus had been dormant in my body for more than two years; therefore, I could not have been infected by a mosquito bite this summer.

Since the doctors were deeply concerned about tracing the source of my body's viral infection, they made an extremely detailed inquiry into my activities during that summer two years ago. The doctors wanted me to look back to this time period to the people I had come into contact with and to the places I had been. This investigation might reveal the conditions under which I had contracted the viral infection. I explained to the doctors that that summer, other than studying at English Classes for Adults, I just walked around, played ball, went fishing and visited the library and the museum. I inevitably started talking about how the Group of Seven's landscape painting triggered an interest in going to fish and to sightsee in the Northern Great Lakes area. I told them that there were many water fowl, forests, and reed marshes in those places. My mind flooded with the intense memory of the woman beside the lake, but I intentionally did not say anything about her. I could not help myself and asked this one question, "Do West Nile virus sufferers have nosebleeds?"

The doctor answered my question saying, "This is a possibility. Sometimes, in certain West Nile patients with a low white blood cell count, the capillaries will rupture over large areas, causing nasal bleeding." Immediately the doctor followed up his explanation and asked me, "During that period of time, did you come into contact with a person who had a bleeding nose? Or do you, yourself, have any unusual conditions to tell us?"

I said, "Nothing ... just a casual question ... nothing more." For some reason, I just didn't want to tell other people about this experience.

But the doctor could evidently see from my body language that I was hiding something. He said, "A patient has an obligation to give a frank, honest, and detailed medical history to the doctor. This is particularly important if it related to a contagious disease that may cause death. This kind of circumstance is similar to an eyewitness in a law case. There is a duty toward the administration of justice to give objective testimony. To refuse to give evidence or to give false testimony will lead to serious consequences." But I still hemmed and hawed, reluctant to talk about this matter. This was a very personal question. It also occurred to me that if my medical history were somehow connected to the woman by the lake, I would not be able to explain this matter to my wife.

Two days later, the nurses told me that I was going to have a Holographic Brain Memory Scan. I had never heard of this sort of test. I had already had an ultrasound, a CAT scan, an MRI and so on, which were all available at the North York Hospital. Later I realized that this test was not going to be at the hospital. We had to go to the University of Toronto's newly built Medical Science and Psychology Laboratory. I went by ambulance, sirens blaring, escorted by uniformed ambulance personnel and a doctor.

One hour later, the ambulance entered a courtyard with an elegant and quiet garden, and stopped in front of an enormous building. I went into the laboratory. It was a futuristic room, and I felt like I was in the middle of an interstellar spaceship station in the Milky Way. The nurses here must be specially selected to be young and beautiful in order to put the patient completely at ease. I was taken to a machine, and many electrodes were placed over my whole body, with a number of electrodes especially concentrated on my head. Then, I was given an injection of medicine. A metallic taste started to ripple through my whole body like a wave. Together with a lot of buzzing sounds, my chair was pushed forward. All at once I became very sleepy. And then everything went black.

When I regained consciousness, I felt like I was soaring in the air and surrounded by many large birds that were flying with me. But I couldn't make out what was in front of me because of the thick clouds and mist. I flew for a long time, and then I followed the flock of birds out of the clouds. I saw the lake and the forest. Suddenly wheeling, I thought I caught a glimpse of the cottage on the lakeside and the long, wooden dock. I seemed to be under some kind of spell and was being pulled toward the house. I saw the woman who had been beside the lake. She looked so touchingly weak and beautiful with blood dripping from the usual place. When I was with her, I was overcome with delight. I only recall a slight vestige of that joy now, and am not able to repeat the particular details because the doctor dimmed those memories. It was not until after this test was over that I realized its purpose.

During the course of the experiment, my dream was, in fact, controlled by the laboratory doctor and shown on a computer monitor. The doctor had me fly into a dream world panorama where he could see my dream's desires. Circling from a high-altitude position, when the computer mouse pointed a little, I would fly toward the lakeside cottage just like a guided missile. This was really a frightening experiment. The doctor could clearly see my entire fantasy world! I believe that that type of pleasurable meeting with the woman by the lake would make one's face blush. And every image had been recorded on disc. On top of that, when he had finished the experiment, he had wiped away my memory of the dream, leaving behind only a trace as a prompt.

Sure enough, when the doctor had a chat with me after the experiment, he put his finger right on the unusual events that happened to me two summers ago when I was fishing at Algonquin Park. After undergoing the test, I felt no need to continue to conceal this affair. I told him all I remembered. And I also spoke out about my own feelings and ideas concerning the transmission of the West Nile virus. Since my fingers that had been cut open by the fishing line, perhaps I got infected with the virus when I stopped the woman's bleeding beside the lake. The doctor did not say anything at all. He just kept writing things down. Then the doctor said that they would look for the women at the lake and investigate whether or not she was the source of my body's West Nile virus. I felt agitated and said to the doctor, "I hope that when they find the woman by the lake, they will not disturb her."

Two weeks later, I left North York Hospital. It was arranged for me to be placed in a convalescent centre in the Algonquin region to recuperate. This place is situated in the forest, facing a misty bay. The doctors told me that I belonged to the group of latent West Nile virus cases and at present had no symptoms.

In the future, perhaps the disease would surface, but perhaps it would not. I didn't need to take medicine or have any injections because there wasn't any medicine to deal with this virus. It mainly depended on one's own immunity and ability to resist the disease. Of course, the fresh, pure air of the forest, the abundant sunshine, and the suitable physical exercise would be a great help in restoring my health. The doctors didn't reveal to me whether or not they found the woman at the lake, but I felt that they made arrangements to allow me to return to the place that was the source of this event. It seems this was a kind of psychological therapy.

I didn't feel sick. Other than a slightly raised temperature, no other clinical symptoms were evident. Every day I would work out in the gym, read books in the library, or take walks in the forest. My favourite thing to do was to paddle a canoe by myself on the lake. The lakes in Algonquin Park cover a huge area, with a circumference of several hundred kilometres and thousands of small islands. They say the lakes appeared during the late glacial geological period. I spent all day long paddling the canoe on the nearby lake, gradually getting to know the surrounding geographic area. I went along the shore to try and look for that cottage, but couldn't remember the exact location.

One day, I finally caught sight of a house that actually matched the cottage in my memory, but I didn't see the dock that I had been fishing from. This lakeside cottage seemed as though it were abandoned. Many white water birds were perched on the house, and many more birds were just landing. That day the lake was shrouded in a dense white fog. The birds looked like sheets of paper in the mist, or like snowflakes drifting down to land on the cottage. And at that moment I felt an inconsolable sorrow in my heart. I continued paddling the canoe closer to the shore by the house. One after the other, the birds continued to drift down. Some landed on my canoe. A few settled on my shoulders.

Translated by John Edward Stowe and Norah Creedon.

"The West Nile Virus" was originally published in People's Literature, *No. 6, 2008.*

[1]Li Ruiying and Luo Jing are well known news anchors of the Chinese Central TV.

Hana no Maru

SHIHENG

ON MONDAY MORNING, before Tao Ran left for her job interview at the seafood restaurant Hana no Maru, her friend called and said, "If the lady owner asks if you are married, just say no."

"Why?"

"Don't you see? A married woman will not be that attractive to men. That's all. Besides, in the view of most Japanese people, a married woman stays at home for her husband. That is, she would hardly be out at night. Once the lady owner knows the truth about you and is uncertain whether you will be able to do your best for the customers, she won't put you on the evening shift. But evenings yield the best tips."

Tao Ran responded abruptly, "I won't work as a bargirl. You know that."

"Relax. That restaurant is legit. The lady owner herself caters to her customers by eating and drinking with them now and then. But the young female employee she is looking for will only be for washing dishes and serving tables."

Hana no Maru is located on Akasaka Street. Not as famous as Ueno Street, Akasaka marks a quasi-red-light district of Tokyo. During the day, dwarfed by the modern and flamboyant high rises, Akasaka appears to be a street from the past—both narrow and long. Many shops flanking the street hang posters made of rough cloth, on which there are Japanese patterns painted in blue. There are also shop signs in *kanji* and lanterns used as sign-boards. All these decorations retain and display the long tradition of Japanese culture.

The sign with the image of a carp in the window told Tao Ran that she had reached her destination. The lady owner, Hanako, surprised Tao Ran with her casual clothes and appearance. She did not ask about Tao Ran's marital status but only, "When can you start working?"

Tao Ran answered as if she was reciting from a book: "I have classes in afternoons and assignments in evenings. During weekends, I have experiments to do. Generally, I am available in the morning and at noon."

The lady owner's tone showed a little surprise: "Is that so! But you must work Friday evenings. Otherwise I won't be able to handle it." Since it had not been easy for Tao Ran to find a job, she did not want to lose this opportunity, so she said yes.

In the next few days, the owner said almost nothing to Tao Ran. She showed up in the restaurant around eleven o'clock every morning to repeat the same ritual: she sat quietly in a corner, ate a sashimi meal, and had a bowl of miso soup. Her face looked half awake and half asleep. Tao Ran never heard her discuss the restaurant's operation with the two chefs, nor bark orders to Sato San. Usually she'd vanish without a trace after her meal. However, it was clear that the three smitten male workers strove to please her. With or without the presence of the female boss, business in the restaurant always proceeded in an orderly way. Hanako routinely appeared in the restaurant, becoming the focus of the three men, and generating certain tensions in the otherwise relaxed atmosphere in the restaurant. The forty-something chef worked more dexterously with the tuna chunks, while stealing quick glances at Hanako eating her food, just to see if she was happy with his dish. The assistant chef, a white-faced young man, appeared to be shy and awkward when he brought her tea and soup. During this time, Sato would look for this and that to order

Tao Ran to do. His intention and effort to impress his boss were clearly written all over his face.

Sato asked Tao Ran to clean the washroom. On her way there, as she turned the corner, she almost bumped into a man just coming out. As she was about to apologize, the man, holding a garbage bag in his hand, began to speak to her in Chinese: "You don't need to do anything in this washroom. I have just cleaned it."

Seeing her confusion, he went on: "My name is Husheng.[1] I also work here. But I have been mostly on night and morning shifts. That's why we have not met. But we will get to know each other as time goes on." When he finished speaking, he hurried out to dump the garbage. He was not seen again in the restaurant that day.

Busy as she was all the time, Tao Ran still tried to figure out what kind of a person the owner was. Hanako did not possess the flexibility and liveliness of a young girl, nor the sternness and tendency to nag of a middle-aged woman. Her actions demonstrated the maturity of a woman in her thirties, while her pale face and her swollen eyelids showed that she missed her sleep. She was a little taller than most Japanese women. She wore something most women in Japan dared not put on—a pair of flowery-print pants that were fairly tight for her strong legs. The white crewneck t-shirt and dark blue cardigan made her look both casual and elegant at the same time. Her facial features suggested mystery: she had light brown eyes, a high nose, and full lips. At the same time, the shape of her face, her skin tone, and hair colour were absolutely Asian.[2] But what struck Tao Ran as most difficult to comprehend was the facial expression Hanako often wore, a look as airy and soft as a cloud, too far away and ambiguous for anyone to be sure about.

On Thursday afternoon, after she finished washing all the bowls, plates, and chopsticks, Tao Ran took off her work clothes, the kimono of blue rough cloth, and rushed to the railway stop on Akasaka. It was her bad luck to run into Sato, who was also running to the train. This male *yenta*[3] asked countless questions of Tao Ran, including her age and marital status.

Tao Ran responded with her own question: "You look over forty—are you married?"

Sato raised a finger. "I am a one-time-crossed-out."[4] Because Tao Ran couldn't follow him, he continued, "That means I divorced once, and am now single."

Seeing the expectation on his face, Tao Ran put away any further inquiries and changed the topic: "Oh, Hanako, our boss, is fairly pretty, isn't she?"

Sato became elated immediately. "I got to know Hanako long ago. She and I are old friends. When a trading company was ready to offer me a position, Hanako happened to telephone me about her need for help in her restaurant. So I gave up a more prestigious and lucrative job, and ended up working here to help her out."

Sato continued, remarking mysteriously to Tao Ran, "Don't you think that Hanako looks *half*? She is from Okinawa. You know Okinawa, right? The southernmost part of Japan. Have you heard of the Ryukyu Islands? There are U.S. military bases, where many U.S. soldiers are stationed all year long." He winked slyly. "Hanako came to Tokyo from Okinawa when she was still a teenager to learn *kabuki*, and she became good at playing music, chess, and dancing. She then worked as a bargirl at a bar in Ginza. That was where and when I got to know her. All the waitresses in that bar were very attractive. The admission was 50,000 *yen*.[5] There were even some Chinese girls like you. In their close-fitting Chinese dresses, which emphasized their breasts, waists, hips, and legs, they...." He began to look as if he were intoxicated with too much *sake*. He said, "Now Hanako owns a restaurant, while I have become an employee working for her."

Tao Ran responded, "She is so smart. I thought she inherited this restaurant from her family. Now I know she started it herself."

"Eh, started it herself?" Sato was quite indignant. "Have you seen Kawasaki San, the *Oji San*,[6] who is often in our restaurant to help out? He is the actual owner! Kawasaki is also an old customer of Hanako's and the president of a big company."

Continuing their conversation, they came to a crossroads where they had to part ways. Sato said with all eagerness, "Tao San, let me treat you to dinner this Saturday."

Tao Ran smiled and said mischievously, "I have to eat with my husband that day. Sato San, be careful. Try not to pick the wrong person again to avoid being crossed out for the second time."

On Friday evening, when Tao Ran arrived at work as usual, there was indeed an *Oji San* over sixty working busily in the restaurant. Sato winked, indicating this old man was Kawasaki. Tao Ran said hello to everyone and went straight to work.

After dark, Akasaka came to life with all the noises of the night. Customers filed into Hana no Maru. Hanako had knotted her hair on top of her head and put on a pair of wooden clogs. She wore thick powder on her face and a light purple kimono. Matching the coolness and chill of the autumn, purple-coloured maple leaves, in various shades, spread from the collar to the very bottom of her kimono.

With her sleeves swinging in the fall wind, Hanako stood at the entrance greeting every customer with a bow and words of welcome. She then served the tea that Tao Ran had prepared. Sporting a charming smile, Hanako chatted quietly with the customers, old and new.

She had memorized the name of every old customer. "Ah, President Watanabe, you weren't here in the past few days? How's your health? I will get them to bring the half bottle of Scotch you did not finish the last time. They will have dry plums and ice cubes for you as well." To customers coming for the first time, she was instantly familiar as if they were family members. "You, sir, you look so much like Toyokawa Etuji San.[7] Are you sure you are not his brother?" Or "You are just so handsome!" Taking small, quick steps, she moved between tables to light customers' cigarettes, pour tea, or serve wine while chatting and laughing with everyone. She also yielded to the request of a customer to pick up a wine cup for a sip. With her skill, she manipulated all these male customers so that in no time the twenty or so seats in the restaurant were all occupied. After a few rounds of wine, both the customers and the owner had flushed faces. Then Hanako would turn on the karaoke machine. Holding the microphone, she would sing, in a shaking voice, a song popular at the time. As the half-drunk customers, rocking left and right with the rhythm, sang along with her, the atmosphere in Hana no Maru would reach its climax for the night.

Like her boss, Tao Ran kept herself busy. She poured tea, jotted down orders, brought cigarettes, filled wine cups, served soups and dishes, and removed empty utensils while she took time to wash piles of dishes and bowls. Her clothes were wet with sweat. As soon as it struck eleven o'clock, without even saying goodbye to Hanako, she punched her card and ran like a shot out of the restaurant, shutting out the noises of songs and laughter inside the restaurant.

As usual, October in Tokyo brought cool breezes. With neon lights flashing, Akasaka at midnight radiated charm and glamour. Like Hanako, Akasaka was doing its best to attract visitors. Rows of bars and restaurants satisfied countless working men with good food and beautiful women, squeezing their wallets empty, and then spat them onto the street one by one, leaving the autumn wind to take them home to their wives. Tao Ran was amazed to see that Hanako operated as a totally different person at night. She played her male customers with such ease, seducing them for their money. She was not into the marriage business, but she certainly did not have any qualms sharing these men's salaries with their wives.

When a drunk blocked her way one evening as she left the restaurant, murmuring inarticulately, "I would like to treat you to a cup of coffee," Tao Ran jumped aside, and tried to continue on her journey.

"Tao Ran, it is me, Husheng. It is still early, and I would like to buy you a cup of coffee." He repeated his invitation.

There was no doubt at all in Tao's mind what this coffee invitation meant. The man's next question would be "Can I come to your apartment tonight?" He would not take her to a Love Hotel, for it would not be worth wasting money on a one-night stand like this. If it was mutual, neither person needed to spend any money, which would be fair to both sides. Tao Ran had sternly rejected numerous such fools. But, as time went by, she learned that these lonely and hardworking men had their good manners and courtesy. They too had rules they would follow. They would not get angry when turned down. On the contrary, looking sorry, they would apologize and look elsewhere for their next target, someone either emerging from a metro entrance or walking along the street. To be sure, with so many women in this world, a man can find one who is a match for him.

Standing before Tao Ran, Husheng said quietly, "I just want to chat with someone, someone from China."

"It would be even better if this someone is a woman from China, right?" Tao Ran said sarcastically.

"I have not spoken Chinese for a long time. I really just want to chat with you for a little while."

Seeing the timid and begging look in his eyes, Tao Ran agreed and followed him into a café called Dream Waking. The café, dark and crowded, was no more than twenty square feet. The space was so tight, a person could easily walk into a table or chair. In the hall, Teresa Teng's song "Lover" filled the space. Ever since she died in Thailand, Teng's fans in Japan have been playing this song in her memory.

Each sitting before a cup of coffee, the two were silent, simply adding sugar and cream into the cups and stirring with small silver spoons. The spoons hitting the thin and fine porcelain cups broke, just a little, the silence between them.

Husheng finally spoke. "Do you know that Hanako is Chinese?" Tao Ran was so shocked that she almost spit out the coffee she had just taken into her mouth.

"It is true; her mother was a Chinese living in the Philippines. After the war, an old Japanese soldier took her to his hometown Okinawa, and he became Hanako's father. But later on, as Hanako became more and more pretty and began to look like a mixed-race child, he started beating the mother. Unable to find out who the real father was, the old solider threw the mother and daughter out of the house. That was why Hanako and her mother came to Tokyo."

"Is it true that Hanako's real father was a U.S. soldier?"

"Nobody knows. Her mother died a long time ago without ever telling her anything. But she was a woman who grew up in the Philippines and was fluent in English. The old Japanese soldier was good for nothing else but gulping down *sake* and using Hanako's mother to satisfy his sexual desire."

"How did you get to know Hanako?"

"Well, that is another sad story." With a sip of his coffee, Husheng began. "I came to Japan as a student. I was in school for the entire first year, while at the same time I worked to make money for my tuition in order to keep my immigration status. Every day was the same. This made me feel fettered, and I often woke up suddenly in the middle of the night. One day, I returned home after work only to find that my wife had disappeared. She took all her jewels and our entire savings. I knew that, disappointed in me, she could not stand the loneliness and poverty any more. I did not hate her for taking away our money, but I was upset because she was already two months pregnant with my baby. To look for her, I quit my language school, became an illegal immigrant and worked all day long to make money. In my spare time, I went one by one to the bars to look for her. It was at Cherry Bloom, a high-end bar, where I got to know Hanako."

"But did you find your wife?" Tao Ran was eager to know what happened to this couple.

"Yes," he answered. "But she told me that she was not pregnant with my child. The father was actually Kawasaki Syacho, head of the Big River Electronic Corporation."

"Kawasaki! Which Kawasaki?"

"The same old man whom you saw helping Hanako in our restaurant this evening." Seeing that Tao Ran had nearly finished her coffee, he asked if she would like to have something else. She ordered a plum wine. The plum soaked in the amber-coloured wine looked greener than usual in contrast to the shiny ice cubes. And it left a faint but soothing fragrance in the mouth.

Husheng got himself another coffee, to which he added only one lump of sugar. Tao Ran noticed that his fingers trembled slighting as he held the silver spoon to stir his coffee. Sinking into memories of his past, he continued with his story.

"A fellow townsman of mine used to work as a bartender at Cherry Bloom. From him I learned that Hanako was also Kawasaki's lover. So I began to frequent that bar. Somehow, during the first evening, when I was sitting there alone and bored, she left two oily-faced Japanese men to come over to talk to me. She asked me if I was Chinese. Telling her I was, I asked if she thought Chinese people were too poor to be looking for women in a bar like this one. She smiled and did not seem to mind. She told me that she was half Chinese, and said she had not seen any Chinese people in the bar before. On a hunch, she knew I was not Japanese.

"We began to see each other. When I went to that bar in Ginza, except for the fifty thousand *yen* I spent as my entrance fee, the rest of the costs for tea and sweets and whatnot were all taken care of by her. She is very good-hearted, though she does not have much education, unlike a Beijing woman like you who keeps studying and earning different degrees. She is not like my ex-wife, either. A Shanghai woman like my ex would do anything for money." He seemed to be still filled with anger.

"Once I asked Hanako what she would do when she became too old to drink with her customers. She did not know. I told her that, of the many women who came from the countryside to Tokyo to make a living, lots of them would first drink with the customers, and then eventually have someone buy a shop or bar to become owners themselves. Hanako approached Kawasaki, who in turn agreed to help her. The result is the Hana no Maru restaurant. Of course, Kawasaki is no fool. He is the sole owner of the restaurant, but he gives Hanako sixty percent of profit."

Tao Ran said, "With so many customers, business at Hana no Maru seems to be going quite well."

"That's true, owing largely to Kawasaki. Having many director friends from big companies, he brought them all, one after another, to our restaurant. His friends were happy to spend their money here after having a good time with marvelous food and beautiful women."

Tao Ran immediately saw the pride in his eyes and at the corners of his mouth as he smiled. He turned around and ordered his third cup of coffee. Tao Ran asked, "Will you be able to sleep tonight after so much coffee?"

He said, "I have another job working as a janitor during the day. So far, I have worked twelve hours today. And I will have to stay here till dawn so that I can, when Hanako closes up, take her home." His eyes were bloodshot, and a lock of his hair hung limply on his forehead.

"Take her home? Whose home? Do you two live together?"

"Tomorrow, Kawasaki will go on a business trip to Osaka. So Hanako does not have to stay the night with him tonight. I will take her to my place since we have not been together for quite a few months."

"So you don't mind sneaking in on a woman belonging to someone else for the rest of your life?"

"Tao San, as far as I can see, you are as lovely and kind as Hanako. I will marry Hanako as soon as we have saved enough money, and, after I marry her, I will get Japanese nationality. Hanako and I will then move to Hawaii to open a restaurant with both Chinese and Japanese cuisine. We will make tons of money, and then ... have many babies.... Kawasaki the old fool will go to hell...!"

He continued to mumble, off and on, until his lips as well as his eyes slowly closed. After his head fell on to the small table, he began snoring. Even three cups of coffee were not enough to keep him awake. The song "Lover" still played in the background. And, a deep sadness and the sharp pain caused by endless longing and waiting hovered in the air.

The coffee and plum wine made Tao Ran numb. She could not distinguish tipsiness from exhaustion; she only knew that her head was heavy in a nameless way. She dragged herself outside, taking much longer than usual to walk through the well-lighted streets and lanes. By this time, the tall buildings in and around Akasaka looked like huge lifeless black cubes standing behind the grey curtain of the night. Jealously, these buildings peered down at the men and women moving on the streets below, waiting quietly for tomorrow to come.

Translated by Dongfeng Xu.

"Hana no Maru" was originally published in The Sojourners: Stories by Chinese-Canadian Writers *in 2004.*

[1]"Husheng" means "born in Shanghai." So Husheng was originally a Shanghai native.
[2]Hanako's facial features indicate that she was a child of an interracial relationship.
[3]The Chinese original is *changshe fu*, literally "a man with a long tongue," or a gossipmonger.

[4]Original in Japanese, *batsu ichi* (巴次).

[5]50,000 *yen* equals $535 Canadian nowadays.

[6]Original in Japanese, *Oji San* (叔父さん).

[7]Toyokawa Etuji (豊川悦司) is the name of a famous Japanese film star.

Vase

YAFANG

THE VASE'S DISCOURSE: MY FIRST EXISTENCE

BANG! I, a white, fine china vase, fall to the floor and break into pieces. My fall is unexpectedly fast; the three people who witness it—a man, a woman, and their daughter—are all stunned.

The moment I am out of the man's hand, his eyes fire up with instant gratification from the outburst of anger, then a forced composure replaces his extreme rage, and eventually an emptiness that is impossible to disguise.

Emotions in the woman's eyes are much more complex: disbelief, apprehension, despair, numbness immediately after being ambushed by an emotional tempest, and the resultant yet lasting pain deep in the bottom of her heart.

In the daughter's eyes are hurt and fury.

The speed of my fall is as fast as lightning, while the process of my breakdown seen by the three pairs of eyes is, as if in slow motion in a movie, painfully slow. The numerous small pieces of my body unhurriedly relive every day and every moment of those seventeen years my human companions and I have shared.

I was born in the famed Chinese city, the capital of Chinese porcelain. An encyclopaedia describes my birthplace as follows: "the fire of the kilns keeps burning for thousands of years. Chinaware produced there is pure as translucent jade, as shiny as a mirror, thin as fine paper, and when struck, resounding as chime stone. The fame of its porcelain, because of its unique characteristics, reaches afar, both within and outside China." Elegant colour, minimalist design, and fine texture define my style, unpretentious yet refined. After I was wrapped up by a woman's skilful hands, I left my hometown and arrived in the biggest city in China, where countless events had taken place and numerous legends were germinating. I resided in a display case of gorgeous artworks in a magnificent shopping centre. I was the plainest in the midst of my flamboyant and multicoloured neighbours, but I firmly believed that I possessed a unique beauty that was timeless. I was waiting for a connoisseur who would recognize my true value.

The day I had waited for eventually came.

A young couple stood in front of me. To be accurate, it was the young woman whom I attracted. Gently she took the man's hand and led him to me. She was tall and graceful, her complexion ivory and fine as mine. Her dress was white with light blue patterns, simple and elegant, just like my design.

"I love this vase. The design has a timeless charm. Let's put it in our new home," she said to the man in a soft voice.

So the apartment of that newlywed couple became my home.

The woman loved beautiful things. Therefore, I had flowers in my mouth quite often. Lilies of various colours were her favourite, so were pretty and passionate birds of paradise. Flowers were smiling, and so was I, watching the young couple's blissful life. The woman was an accountant, and her man was a network engineer at a foreign company. Their life as a newlywed couple was sweet and affectionate. She believed that life was as beautiful as the lilies I held.

However, notes of disharmony intruded into the melody of their life that was charming as the lilies. He fell silent sometimes; out of concern she tried to have him confide in her, but he became impatient, his words and tone rude, sometimes even nasty. She felt hurt but tended to see things from his angle: perhaps he was under pressure from work but wanted to tough it out all by himself in order to spare her the worry.

Life went on.

One day, a year later, she sported a smile as radiant as the flowers I held. She told him they would have a daughter. She leaned against him, eyes glowing with fond anticipation. She stared at the birds of paradise in me, picturing their little girl: a pretty, carefree, little bird.

Their baby girl was born. She was, in her mother's eyes, a beautiful bird of paradise. Nursing a baby was blissful but very demanding. The mother's sleep was being cut into small pieces. Yet her daughter's cry was a command to her; as soon as she heard the cry, the woman rushed over to tend to the baby.

The man was busy with the company's projects. He left home early and came back late. His tightly knit eyebrows and sullen expression hinted at pressure from work. One night he was woken up by the baby's cry.

"I have a deadline to make. I cannot rest when the baby cries like this. I'd better move into my parents' place for a few days," he informed her the next day.

"Why do you leave us when we need you the most?" She, always gentle and compliant, looked at him with a forlorn expression while she was breastfeeding the baby.

"Do you really want me to lose my job?" he snapped back.

As days dragged on, rude words and even verbal abuse occurred more frequently. Once the easily agitated man raised his hand and it fell on the woman.

The shadow of that hand darkened the lilies I held, and it also gnawed at her wounded heart. She held the baby to her heart and stared at me, tears falling down her cheeks. What to do? Leave him? Looking at her sleeping daughter's little face, she told herself, *my baby needs a father, not a broken family.*

Flowers placed in me bloomed and wilted, wilted and bloomed. The baby grew into a teenage girl.

Then a letter from the Canadian embassy in China came. She pointed at a body of blue water on a globe, telling her daughter: "Mom came across the Five Great Lakes at a geography class years ago. I could not even dream then that one day we would go and live in Toronto, by Lake Ontario."

Her daughter asked, "Why do we have to go and live in a place where we know no one?"

She replied, "I want you to grow up in a place where life is less stressful."

Their possessions were grouped into two categories: things that would be left behind on this side of the earth and things that would travel to the other side of the globe. The fate of my neighbours had been decided: some were put in suitcases or boxes that would stay behind, and others went into cases or boxes that would travel across the ocean. However, I stood where I had been, on top of a side table (which had been given to the new owner of the apartment). I had no clue what would happen to me, and I felt sad and perplexed.

It was on the eve of their departure that she carefully wrapped me up in soft paper and put me in a handbag that she carried with her. Now I knew: she wanted to take me personally when flying over the ocean to Toronto. I realized how important I was in her mind and was deeply moved.

On the airplane, she attended to me just as if she were guarding her dream.

When arriving in Toronto, they were taken by a friend to their new residence, which the friend had rented for them. With the help of the friend, they went down a flight of narrow stairs, carrying their belongings to a basement apartment. It was sparsely furnished. The bigger bedroom had only a bed, a desk, and a chair. In the other bedroom was a single bed. The third room was an open-concept space, serving as living room, family room, and kitchen. In it stood a dining table and four chairs. There and then, it struck her that the staircase was a rather cruel metaphor: their trip from the other side of the earth was actually a descent to the bottom of the social ladder.

She took me out of her handbag, unwrapped me, and put me on the desk in their bedroom.

That night, they all went to bed for their first night in Canada. She was just about to turn off the light when she caught some rustling noise and then her daughter's scream. She and her husband went out to investigate and saw a mouse sauntering across the sink.

She said to him, "You go and sleep. I'd better stay with her for a while."

When her daughter fell asleep, she went back to their bedroom. He was sound asleep, overcome by the long and tiring journey.

There was a small window in the basement. She wanted to have a look at the Canadian moon, but the window was so tiny that she could not even catch a glimpse of it; what she saw was the bright but cold moonlight.

She walked to the desk and caressed my smooth surface. She picked me up and put her face on me, as if she were hugging a dream.

How could I foresee that in two years' time and in this very basement, I would be thrown to the floor and broken into pieces?

That day he got some bad news: he had failed the examination again, and his hope to obtain an engineer's license was dashed like a bubble being popped. Upon arriving in Canada, he had set his mind to passing the exam so that he could find an engineer's job. The process was long and gruelling. He took several courses and sat for the test a few times, but he failed all of them.

He was exasperated and flew into a red-hot rage. He raised his hand again, as he used to. However, this time, his hand was held there but did not hit the target, because their daughter shouted out, "You are breaking the law if you hit her!"

He was stunned and enraged. He had lost control of his professional life, and home was the last domain where he thought he still had control. Now his daughter was telling him that he no longer had absolute authority at home, either.

He had to find an outlet for his anger. His eyes swept the entire room and eventually fell on me. He grasped me and threw me to the floor with great ferocity.

I felt so much pain, physical pain that came and went in a blink of eye.

She was also hurt, but her pain was in her heart, and it lasted.

Two years later...

E-mail message from the daughter:

Happy birthday, Mom!

Sorry that being away from home, I can't light the candles for you and celebrate your birthday by your side.

But I have couriered a gift to you, and it should arrive today. What is it? It will be a surprise, and I won't spoil the pleasure right now.

Mom, I want to tell you on your birthday that you are my hero. I still remember that on the eighth day after our arrival in Toronto, you walked for over an hour to apply for a job at a restaurant that specialized in handmade *jiaozi* dumplings. To me you were so brave. Your work there was to make dumplings, which had nothing to do with your professional training, but you took that labourer's work so that dad could focus on taking courses and applying for a licence to work as an engineer, and so that you could feed the entire family. I also remember that on the Chinese New Year eve that year, when we were making *jiaozi*, I noticed you could not lift your thumb because you had worked so hard at the restaurant making *jiaozi*. It saddened me, but it also made me admire you and your perseverance.

Mom, you have made so many sacrifices for us.

I am now a university student. I've got scholarships from different sources, and I've also saved money from the part-time jobs I've had for the last two years. You do not need to worry about my tuition and living expenses. I sincerely hope that you will take some accounting courses in order to return to the profession you were trained for.

I enjoy studying social work, the discipline I have chosen. I am especially interested in a course I am taking right now, Gender. Even at high school, I was engaged in setting up a student club, Study Group on Women's Issues. At its activities, fellow members and I raised and discussed many social problems concerning women and gender. This Gender course gives me the opportunity to continue exploring a topic I am passionate about. Plus, it provides me with new perspectives through which to examine women's collective experiences and gender relations. I believe this course will lay a solid foundation for my future career as a social worker and for my personal growth.

Mom, I am looking forward to my trip home so that I can share what I've learned with you.

With love, Daughter

Mother's reply:

My dear daughter,

Many thanks for your gift! When I opened the box and saw the light blue porcelain vase, I wept tears of happiness and surprise. The colour reminds me of the blue water of Lake Ontario.

You must have known that two years ago, when the white vase was smashed, so was my heart. But that moment turned out to be a turning point in my life, too.

I had suffered silently for so many years because I had always wanted to keep our family together. However, when you said, "Mom, I want to protect you," I woke up. I had been trying to mend a dream, an unrealistic dream. My child, what you said gave me the courage and strength to leave my broken marriage.

My child, you tell me that I am your hero. Actually, you are my guardian angel, and you have led me out of the dark tunnel.

In these last two years of your high school life, you worked part-time so that you could save money for college and lessen the financial burden on me. Your decision worried me tremendously. I am afraid it will affect your studies. Yet you made it: you are a good worker and an excellent student. What makes me so proud is your love and compassion: you have been helping children of new immigrants and your fellow students who have difficulties in their studies. You have decided on majoring in social work and are prepared to serve the vulnerable in society, the underprivileged groups. Good for you!

I have enrolled in an accounting program. You are right, I should prepare to re-enter my own profession.

A Toronto Chinese community organization plans to run a training program for "women ambassadors." After training, those ambassadors will work with their own community, informing women about how to prevent family violence and where to turn for help when being abused. I have decided to participate in the program. I suffered from abuse, and I do hope that people will see the impact of domestic violence so that they will fight against it. I also hope women who are being abused and living in pain and fear can break free. To me, this will be a process of healing.

My child, our immigrant experiences have brought us hardship, but I take pride in your healthy growth and in my new life.

With love, Mom.

THE VASE'S DISCOURSE: MY NEW EXISTENCE

I, a light blue vase, am the reincarnation of the white, fine china vase, a phoenix rising from the ashes of its former existence.

Blue is the colour of a clear lake, as deep and pure as the eyes of the woman because they have been purified by her tears. They hold the agony of her previous life and the smile of her new life.

I am a vase of life, a vase full of life.

I hold a bouquet of flowers in my mouth. Among them is a bird of paradise, red as a burning fire.

Translated by H. Laura Wu and Cory Davies.

"Vase" originally appeared in Migrating Birds: Contemporary Chinese-Canadian Women's Writings *in 2009.*

The Smell

XIAOWEN ZENG

A T 98 AUDREY STREET, in an upper-class neighbour-hood on the outskirts of Toronto, sits a two-storey house. With three bedrooms, four bathrooms, a front door facing east, and favourable *fengshui*, it meets all Chinese middle-class standards.

On Friday night, as was her custom, Minmin cleaned all the rooms in the house. Then she prepared supper for herself and lit two candles in the dining room, one vanilla and the other lily. The mixture of the two smells quieted her. This was just what she needed at this moment, like an injured female wolf needing herbal medicine or a thirsty lamb needing water from a stream. After bathing and changing her clothes, she sat down at the dining room table and began to eat supper: a plate of shrimp and another of Chinese broccoli with two kinds of mushrooms. The table was made of premium mahogany, and it was glossy enough to see one's reflection in. With six chairs surrounding it on four sides, it looked like it belonged at the centre of a happy family.

Two years ago, she had risen at three in the morning on Boxing Day, while her husband Zhong Li, ensconced in bed, refused to get up. Minmin had braved the cold, hard wind alone to line up in front of Leon's, a local furniture store. Consequently, she was able to buy this set of table and chairs at half the regular price. Buying such pleasing furniture inexpensively had made freezing herself worthwhile.

It was almost as if Minmin had digital memory in her head that retained the history of every piece of furniture: when it was purchased, the location of the store, and the price. Each item came as a result of careful comparison shopping and it had to match with the rest of the furnishings in the house. More than once Minmin had told Zhong Li that she had put her blood, sweat, and tears into their home.

Zhong Li's place across the dinner table was empty.

Minmin had signed the divorce agreement the day before. For the sake of their former feelings for one another, Zhong Li had left Minmin some time alone to say goodbye to the house. Their daughter Maggie had just been sent to Minmin's mother's place in China for the summer holidays. Minmin would be less sad with her daughter gone. Zhong Li had arranged everything well—hiring a lawyer, the divorce, sending their daughter back to China, letting Minmin move out. He was good at planning.

"Because I plan, I am successful," were Zhong Li's words.

And Minmin had once been the woman behind the successful man.

"Goodbye." Minmin pondered these two words as she carefully peeled shells from the shrimp. Moving out from under Zhong Li's shadow and leaving the house was a form of goodbye. From this point on she would not have him to shelter her from the wind and rain, but, of course, neither would he be there to block the sun; this too was a form of goodbye.

Actually, Minmin and Zhong Li had not been apart very often; the longest was five years ago. After Zhong Li immigrated to Canada, he had tried his hand at various occupations, but eventually he could not make ends meet, so he decided to return home to blaze a new trail. By then China had become a paradise for risk takers. Unexpectedly, Maggie contracted a kidney infection. Medical treatment was free in Canada, so the wisest thing for Minmin to do was to stay behind with her.

The night before Zhong Li was to embark, Minmin cried.

"What is there to cry about? It's not like I'm abandoning the two of you in some remote and desolate place," Zhong Li said.

Minmin could not stop crying. She was to Zhong Li like an apple to the earth: she had no way of resisting the force of his gravity. Now the earth was moving; how could she not feel the chilly fear of desperation?

Two years ago, Zhong Li had returned to Toronto, much to Minmin's relief. Their reunion had marked a satisfactory resolution to their previous parting; the suffering that had occurred between goodbye and reunion could be put aside. However, this time saying goodbye was completely different.

The taste of the shrimp wasn't bad. Minmin cooked shrimp in hot oil with fried garlic and dried chilli peppers; then she added a few drops of vinegar before putting them on the plate. Zhong Li had always liked this dish. He had an unwavering love of shrimp. However, after eating a few, Minmin had no more appetite. She proceeded to collect the dishes and attentively wiped the table. She was unwilling to allow her rival, that woman called Tan Chang, the opportunity to criticize her for being sloppy.

Tan Chang had been waiting to move into this house for a long time. More than once, she had declared that she had given her virginity to Zhong Li and then had to wait with bitterness for more than four years before the fog lifted and she finally saw the sun. "Her virginity!" Minmin snorted. "If she had tried to catch a Western man with that line, it would have become the subject of jokes in bars." In Tan Chang's mind, Minmin and Zhong Li's twelve-year marriage was of little significance. When comparing their love versus another's, how many women under the sun wouldn't believe the scales were tipped in their own favour?

Just as she did each time she left the house, Minmin checked each window in each room, upstairs and downstairs, and straightened the curtains. Returning to the dining room, she blew out the candles. Two wisps of white smoke floated up; their fragrance seemed a little stronger.

Minmin bit her lip, and left her dream home....

The next day Zhong Li helped Tan Chang move into 98 Audrey Street. Zhong Li carried Tan Chang through the front door and directly up to the second-floor bedroom. Like peeling an onion, he hurriedly pulled off her clothes.... Tan Chang screamed as she rolled on the big, soft bed. She didn't need to suppress her voice as she did in the apartment. She shouted out her happiness.

When Zhong Li had returned to Beijing five years earlier, as soon as he disembarked from the plane, he discovered that the world had changed. The first thing his old friend Wang Shengming asked when he saw him was, "Are you still with the same old lady?" Zhong Li noticed afterwards that all the similar-aged men around him, whether or not they were divorced, were surrounded by a bevy of seductive girls almost a generation younger. He decided then that he was out of date.

Zhong Li and Wang Shengming opened a consultancy together for those wanting to emigrate to or study in Canada and named it "China-Canada Bridge." At the same time, Zhong Li and Minmin bought their first house near Toronto's Chinatown. Minmin turned the house into a transfer station for new immigrants, and received China-Canada Bridge's clients. Husband and wife working together—one at home, the other abroad—quickly built a thriving business.

As a dishevelled Minmin drove a van all day, rushing between her own house and the airport and the hospital to look after Maggie, Tan Chang appeared in Zhong Li's sights. She was a recent university graduate: fashionable, sexy, and with no inhibitions. Like a tornado, she drew Zhong Li into a vortex of passion. After only a few months, Tan Chang had started to plan for a future with Zhong Li, clearly indicating that she was hoping to live permanently in Toronto. The path to the future is never smooth; there are always a few roadblocks. Of course, the two biggest roadblocks in her path were Minmin and Maggie.

Zhong Li returned to Toronto and sold the house in Chinatown. Then he and Minmin purchased the house at 98 Audrey Street, beginning a family life that seemed too perfect to be real. Zhong Li encouraged Minmin to stay at home to care for Maggie's health and studies, and to give up her heavy responsibilities; Zhong Li would manage the business. Needless to say, Minmin was overcome with gratitude.

One year later, Tan Chang quietly arrived in Toronto and began working at China-Canada Bridge. Zhong Li juggled his lover and wife for two years. Then he got tired and wanted to stop. He told Minmin that the competition was fierce; China-Canada Bridge had lost many customers and was facing bankruptcy. The only option was to mortgage their property to the daughter of a rich businessperson, Tan Chang. The loan would be used to support the company's business operations. In reality, Tan Chang's father was a shoe repairman who did not know where his next meal was coming from. Not long after, Zhong Li told Minmin that he wanted a divorce. Minmin discovered that their debts had surpassed the amount that they had invested in the house. She had no other alternative but to sign the house over to Tan Chang. Minmin hired an accountant to check the company books. The business showed losses for the past two years, but there were no suspicious items. Zhong Li and Minmin's other property, such as the car, furniture, and appliances were worth seventy or eighty thousand dollars. Minmin did not want any of the household property, asking for only fifty thousand dollars in cash instead. Eventually the two sides reached an agreement.

For men in Canada, there is probably nothing more expensive than a divorce; however, Zhong Li was fortunate that he was able to regain his freedom for so little a price.

Tan Chang finally finished screaming and said, "Minmin really knows how to indulge herself; this bed is so comfortable."

Zhong Li, trying hard to catch his breath, haltingly asked, "Don't mention her now, all right?"

"Do you feel guilty?"

Zhong Li shook his head. "It wasn't her who made the mortgage payments these past two years."

"Still, she earned the money for the first payment. Plus, you lived together for so many years; she was entitled to at least half your property...."

"Let it go, it's finished; don't mention it again. If you're going to feel guilty, don't move in."

"Ha!" Tan Chang let out a laugh that was neither warm nor angry. She extended her long leg and admired her newly pedicured, bright red toenails for a second. "Who has any greater right to move in than me?" Having said this, she jumped off the bed and toured every room in the house naked, like a victorious queen inspecting her war booty.

She picked up the two candle remnants from the dining room windowsill and threw them into the garbage pail. Then she sat down in front of the dining table and saw her lovely face reflected in its surface. With defiance and determination she stated, "A new life is beginning."

After she returned from China, Maggie didn't seem disappointed with the one-room bachelor apartment that Minmin had rented. Even Zhong Li's disappearance did not seem to surprise her. Maggie was a child with a developmental disorder. She was slow in reacting to changes that took place around her and her ability to understand adult relationships didn't match that of other eleven- or twelve-year-olds. Maggie lived in her own reality.

Their one desk and bed took up most of the space in the apartment. Minmin cooked in a kitchen so small and narrow that she could barely turn around, and she and Maggie ate on a small round table. They had little contact with the outside world, and eventually the apartment became like a prison in a foreign land. Minmin felt guilty for having dragged Maggie there. And upon seeing Maggie's accepting look, Minmin's heart and even her breathing became heavy.

Minmin finally found a job as a filing clerk in a non-profit organization helping developmentally disabled children. Although the salary was small, it was ideal for someone who did not have Canadian working experience and could not speak fluent English.

The Friday of the Victoria Day weekend, many of Minmin's colleagues left early to start enjoying the long weekend. She had one or two hours to herself, so she borrowed a copy of a book on the psychological counselling of children with developmental disabilities from the office library. She used an electronic English-Chinese dictionary to look up new words.

"Is that book difficult to read?" A man's mild voice came from behind her.

Minmin turned to face a thirty-something white man. His appearance and clothes were nothing out of the ordinary: chestnut-coloured hair, brown eyes, a blue shirt, and matching blue jeans. His body gave off the fragrance of Palmolive soap. *Could one know a man by his smell?* Minmin used the same soap.

Minmin nodded, a little bit embarrassed.

The man continued, "How is it that you are interested in this book?"

"Because my daughter...."

"Oh." The man nodded as if he understood clearly.

"I am a mother. Do you know...?" Minmin stammered. Immediately she realized that she was stating the obvious, so she felt even more awkward.

The man took a business card from his pocket and handed it to Minmin. "I am a child psychologist; I provide free counselling every Thursday here. If you need help, come look for me."

Minmin carefully read the name on the business card: "Ian Brown." She waved the book in surprise. "You are the author." This time it was Ian's turn to be embarrassed. He nodded. "I should have made the book a little easier to understand, so you wouldn't have to consult a dictionary. I didn't consider immigrant readers...."

"I am reading it slowly; I can understand it." Minmin's tone seemed to comfort Ian. He laughed casually, and without any hard feelings.

After Minmin helped Ian find the file that he wanted, he said goodbye.

"I nearly forgot to ask your name," Ian said.

"Minmin."

"What does it mean? I know that Chinese people's names all have a meaning."

"Stone that contains jade." Minmin shrugged her shoulders. "I probably will always be a piece of stone, a hard stone to crack."

"If one doesn't crack open the stone, how does one find the jade?"

As she watched Ian's back, Minmin wondered if psychologists talked to all their clients like that or was he hinting at something else, something more personal?

The house at 98 Audrey Street experienced an almost imperceptible change in the hands of the new mistress. In the beginning, it was just a faint fishy smell in the kitchen. Surprisingly, the smell progressed quickly from fishy to stinky, even though Tan Chang didn't cook. She placed the garbage bin in the garage to try and get rid of the smell. But, the stink turned up in the dining room; then like a virus it spread to the living room, master bedroom, and the bathrooms.

Zhong Li and Tan Chang turned the house upside down cleaning and rearranging things; no corner of the basement and garage escaped their attention. In spite of the cost, they had the sewer cleaned out and hired a specialty cleaning company to thoroughly wash the rugs.

Whatever they did, it was of no use. There was no way to pin down where the smell came from, even though it was everywhere.

The notoriety of this stinky house spread. Every time Zhong Li and Tan Chang invited someone over, they declined tactfully. Even the plumbers were unwilling to re-enter the house. It was like they had placed themselves inside a castle isolated from the rest of the world and were fighting a never-ending war with the smell. They could not see their enemy; they could only smell it. It was as if that smell was a shadow puppet master driving them from pillar to post, even torturing them to the point of exhaustion.

In the evening, the stink was like a pack of invisible flies swarming above their heads, driving them insane. Compared to the other rooms, the stink in the living room seemed slightly less, so Tan Chang moved there to sleep and Zhong Li followed her.

"Don't follow me, all right?" Tan Chang said.

"How can I bear to let you sleep alone?"

"Don't sweet talk me. It was you who destroyed me by moving me into this stinky house."

Zhong Li was angered. "Do you think you are a princess? Wasn't the apartment that you lived in before stinky?"

"Correct me if I am wrong, but the reason that I lived there was to wait for you to get a divorce."

"Who asked you to wait?"

"It was you, down on your knees crying, that made me wait!" Tan Chang howled.

"You seduced me in the beginning!"

Tan Chang sat up and stared at Zhong Li for a long time. Finally, she squeezed out a sentence through the cracks in her teeth: "Get out of here!"

As if words were knives, they each searched for the sharpest to stab the other.

Zhong Li thought that he and Tan Chang had been cursed. He got up and left the living room in bare feet. He went into the kitchen, wanting a bottle of beer, but only found an empty refrigerator. The stink in the kitchen was becoming more difficult to bear by the day. The days when the kitchen was full of food and fragrance had gone and would never return.

At Minmin's request, Maggie agreed to accept Ian's psychological counselling. Minmin was a little nervous the first time she took Maggie into Ian's office, almost as if she was the one receiving counselling. She glanced at the reflection of her waistline in the window. Time is like a demonic mirror; as soon as one turns around, a willowy waist becomes a pot belly. If she had known that she would be returning to the singles market at nearly forty years of age, she would have found a way to preserve her figure earlier.

A stick of incense on his desk gave off a wisp of smoke. A small island in southern China vaguely appeared to Minmin through the mist; there was a temple on the island. One year, on a quiet afternoon under the white glare of the sun, she had pushed open the temple's door. She had lighted a stick of incense and selected a bamboo slip. On the slip were two lines of poetry: "The sound of quiet sobbing underneath the Chinese Goldthread tree; fortunately, a soul mate awaits over the wall."

"Your name is 'Maggie?'" Ian asked.

Maggie nodded.

"Did you pick the name?" Ian turned and asked Minmin.

Minmin said, "I read an American short story when I was in China called 'The Gift of the Maggie.'" The look in Ian's eyes told her that he had read the story too. "I was deeply moved by it."

"Why did you pick that name?"

"Because the story was similar to mine and Zhong Li's, except that the girl in the story had blonde hair...."

"Who is Zhong Li?"

"My ex-husband."

"Oh...." Ian's tone seemed both sympathetic and suddenly enlightened.

"Upon graduating from university, Zhong Li and I became Beijing 'floaters.' Do you know what Beijing floaters are?"

Ian shook his head, bewildered.

"Floaters in Beijing do not have Beijing household registration...." Minmin struggled to explain, but then could not help but laugh. "You probably don't know what household registration is; it is one of China's distinctive features."

Maggie also laughed; it seemed teaching this white uncle was an amusing matter.

Ian immediately sensed a few threads of warmth, trust, even intimacy floating over to him from Minmin and her daughter. Charmingly, he said, "I am extremely interested in China's culture; however, you must be patient with me."

In the next half hour, Minmin related her and Zhong Li's story. After graduating from university, they grew weary of their hand-to-mouth existence and the monotony of small town living. They left for Beijing to seek better opportunities. Because they couldn't find jobs, the only thing they could do was sell lamb kebabs on the street. Even today, when she encountered the smell of lamb, she wanted to vomit. She even pedaled a flatbed tricycle to pick up supplies when she was pregnant, and once, during a rainstorm, she fell into a gutter. Maggie was saved, but her brain was damaged.... They had saved a bit of money, so they started a business reproducing artwork. Later, they immigrated to Canada....

Minmin finished by saying, "Once I awoke from the dream, my husband had become my ex." She heaved a great sigh of relief; using English to tell a story was a very heavy burden.

"Does your ex-husband love Maggie?" Ian asked.

"He should love her. What do you think?" Minmin asked Maggie.

Maggie nodded, and then shook her head.

"Zhong Li was always envious when he saw other people with bright and active boys," Minmin said. She did not understand why she trusted Ian enough to tell him all about her private life.

All three were silent for a moment.

The incense had burned out, but the smell still lingered in the room. *Smells don't have wings; they can never fly far away*, Minmin thought.

Standing up to get ready to leave, Minmin said, "I am sorry. I monopolized the time that you and Maggie had to talk."

"Actually, it is important for me to begin Maggie's counselling with a conversation with you," Ian said.

"My English is poor."

"You speak very well! I understood everything you said. Also, I know that you have a kind heart."

Minmin quickly averted her eyes. Having a kind heart was big pair of shoes to fill; she didn't know if she could fit those shoes.

Ian politely bade Minin and Maggie goodbye and he extended his hand to shake Minin's. Minin thought his hand was warm and comforting, and she felt strangely aroused.

One month later Zhong Li and Tan Chang had reached their limit. They couldn't bear the smell anymore; if they stayed, they were going to have an emotional breakdown. They finally decided to sell the house. Many people came to see it; however, they seldom made it past the kitchen. Even though Zhong Li and Tan Chang installed deodorizers in every room, they couldn't cover up the smell. They bit their tongues and dropped the price on the house, then dropped it again, but still could not find a buyer. After trying everything, they decided the only thing they could do was to sell most of their shares in the company to Wang Shengming and apply for a high interest loan from the bank in order to buy a new house. They knew that to repay their debts they would have to scrimp to get by. However, they were at the point where the price didn't matter as long as they could escape this reeking hellhole.

On Maggie's birthday, Zhong Li took a present over to Minmin's apartment, the newest *Harry Potter* video.

Maggie asked Zhong Li to stay for supper, but he shook his head saying that there was something at home that he had to take care of.

Minmin asked him, "How are things going?"

"Don't ask. The house smells to high heavens. We tried to sell it, but nobody wants it."

"That house is very nice; those people don't know value!" Minmin seemed to be incensed for Zhong Li's sake.

"You've lived there before; you know its value. I reduced the price by one half, and still nobody wants to buy it."

"If I had the money, I would be the first to buy it," Minmin said sentimentally. "Actually, I miss the old home very much...."

Zhong Li sensed the weakness in Minmin's voice and said immediately, "I could still lower the price a bit if you want to buy it...."

"You know I only have fifty thousand dollars. The most I could offer is seventy-five thousand...."

"Couldn't you get a loan from the bank?"

"They wouldn't give me one; I've only worked a short while, my income is too low, and my credit rating isn't high enough."

"All right, I will talk it over with Tan Chang."

Zhong Li informed Tan Chang of Minmin's offer when he returned home. Tan Chang responded feebly, "Sell her the stinking house. She just has to pay cash up front. Phone the realtor to draw up a contract."

The next day Minmin bought back her dream home at fifteen percent of its market value.

One week later, Minmin returned to 98 Audrey Street as its owner. Zhong Li and Tan Chang had rented a truck to move their furniture. Tan Chang had become haggard from having her life turned upside down by the house. Her hair was in disarray, and dark circles had formed around her eyes. She complained incessantly, like an abandoned wife. Minmin, in contrast, was like a breath of fresh air—calm, cool, and collected as if she had recently received love's nourishment. After Minmin exchanged a few words with Tan Chang, she went into the kitchen, and, from her handbag, pulled out two candles and placed them on the window sill, one vanilla and the other lily.

Minmin looked through the window to see that Tan Chang had loaded all the curtain rods onto the truck. She couldn't help but let out a few light laughs. The night she had moved out, Minmin had taken that half plate of shrimp and stuffed some down every one of the tubes of the curtain rods, allowing the stench to take over the whole house. Now those shrimp were going to follow their owners to their new abode.

At that moment, Minmin noticed that Tan Chang's abdomen was swollen; the smile on her face slowly disappeared....

Translated by Lloyd Sciban and Shu-ning Sciban.

"The Smell" was originally serialized in The World Journal *in the U.S., March 3-5, 2008.*

Little Weeping Millie

DAISY CHANG

D EAR MILLIE, do not weep! Grandma didn't decide to move into a seniors' home because she was angry with you. If that were the case, Grandma would be very spiteful. To tell you the truth, I've had the idea of living by myself for a long time now, but I struggled with the decision. Basically, I've been nurtured by traditional Chinese culture. I am not learned, but I did graduate from a teacher's college. Although the ideal of three generations, even five, living in the same household was considered a blessing in our ancient agricultural society, many people paid a steep price because of it. Thus, in China today it is gradually becoming more common to live in small families.

My movements have slowed over this past year, and my hearing isn't as good as it used to be. That morning, I thought that you had already left for work at McDonald's. I didn't know that you had switched from the morning to the evening shift, so I used the washroom first. I was in there a little longer than usual, which meant you had to restrain yourself by pacing up and down outside. So you became angry and yelled at your mother, threatening that if Grandma did not move out, you were going to leave home! Your mother and father are very filial. They immediately reacted, not only to make you stop, but also insist that you kneel in front of me to apologize.

Once you explained, as you sobbed convulsively without stopping, "Grandma, I was angry when I said...," I knew that you loved me. Afterwards your mother and father, during their lunch break no less, hurried home from work just to take me to my favourite restaurant, House of Countless Blessings near Chinatown. As you know, Grandma has a weakness for Jiangsu-Zhejiang food.

When Mr. Wu, the restaurant owner, saw us, he immediately ushered us in. He took the cane from my hand and said politely, "Most respected elder, at last I have the pleasure of seeing you. By coincidence, I have some good news to report. Do you remember the newly constructed Chinese seniors' home behind the restaurant? It has opened! The furnishings and equipment are new and high quality, and the staff are Chinese. Furthermore, there are still openings. This location is convenient; everything is here. You don't have to trouble your illustrious son and daughter-in-law to drive you; you can visit anytime you want. You will not only find a beauty parlour in the vicinity, but there is also a ladies' wear store, a Chinese supermarket, and a doctor from Taiwan. As well, they speak more Mandarin than English, so, there's no problem with communicating wherever you go."

His reasoning persuaded me. Of course, it is nice to live in your house; however, you live in the suburbs. If I want to go anywhere, I have to impose on others. I can't drive, speak English, or take a bus. Living in the suburbs is like not having legs. In addition, no one is home in the daytime, so it is difficult to find someone to talk to. I can only watch videos, but after you've watched soap operas for a while, your eyes start to go blurry. Longer than this and you get bored to death. However, living in a seniors' home is different. Everyone is old; you needn't worry about finding someone to talk to, no matter what the topic. There is also a nurse on duty twenty-four hours a day; if something happens, there is help available.

After we were seated that day, I deliberately joked, "Boss Wu, you forgot one benefit: that you will prepare good quality *Jinmen sorghum* spirits to let an old lady enjoy herself to her heart's content." Mr. Wu laughed so hard that his eyes squinted into a single line and replied, "Naturally! If that is what this respected elder likes, how could she be denied?"

Grandma likes to drink; my wet nurse, who also liked to drink, taught me. Each time she raised a glass, she would always wet a chopstick with a little bit of liquor for me to try. Tasting became my habit. Even my father and mother did not know. Later on, I married into your grandfather's family and there was no liquor to drink—what could I do? The only thing to do was to ask my wet nurse to help! She would sneak the liquor over, and I would hide it in the kitchen. Then I would wait until my mother-in-law wasn't paying attention, and I would take a drink, enjoying myself to the fullest. One day I returned to my room and was found out by your grandfather when he smelled the liquor on my breath. "Were you drinking?" he asked. Of course, I lied and said no. He laughed and did not pursue it; otherwise, it would have been difficult for me, a new daughter-in-law!

If it hadn't been for your grandfather dying so early and your mother feeling sorry for an old person like me living alone—it didn't matter what I said, she wasn't willing to let your grandmother live alone in Taiwan—I wouldn't have thought of infringing on my son and daughter-in-law by moving in to live with you. These past few years, your mother has been managing affairs both in and outside the home—what a burden! Add to that, Grandma had been running her own home for dozens of years; being this old I know the importance of self-respect. I don't want to trouble anyone. If I can avoid going out, I don't go out. Nevertheless, for me, sitting at home every day makes me feel like an eagle that is used to soaring freely through the skies that suddenly has its wings clipped and is locked in a bird's cage; there is no limit to how depressed one can get. Look how good things are now. Living in the seniors' home, I not only have nurses and doctors at my beck and call, but I also have a brand-new home of my own. I can move freely and comfortably shop and visit friends—what happiness! You should be happy for Grandmother; what is there to cry about?

Admittedly you haven't reached seventeen yet; however, you are always complaining that you want to quit school and move out to live independently. You also believe that the little money you make working at McDonald's can pay for your clothing, accommodation, and transportation. This is a little unrealistic. If a young person does not study hard, does not strive to make a better future, what will become of them? Grandma should be the one anxious and weeping for you!

You grew up abroad, so you know little of Chinese culture. Furthermore, your parents are first generation immigrants; they are busy every day making ends meet. Not only do they not have the time to teach you about these things, but also, as a single child, you get everything you ask for, which soothes their guilt for not being able to take care of you very well. This explains why they do not scold you for living a life of shallow pleasure and befriending a few young "foreigners" who love to play and have no ambition.

A little while ago Grandma read a wise saying in the newspaper: "A father and mother's home will always be a son's or daughter's home, but a son's or daughter's home will not always be a father and mother's home." I cannot agree more. Even though you are all filial, I cannot forget that I am a guest in my son and daughter-in-law's home. I can only watch with a sore heart as the young granddaughter that I love so much gradually succumbs to Western culture. I cannot issue a word of warning.

Now I have my own home, I have the courage to ask you a question: "Why don't you like to study?" Grandma was different from you when she was young. With all my heart, I wanted to study. It was only because I was a girl that I was held back by our backward tradition of regarding men as superior to women. In those times, we studied for seven years in elementary school. After I finished these seven years, my family did not permit me to register for the middle school entrance exam and thereby continue on. To top it all off, our family was from a long line of scholars, but as a woman, I was still denied the opportunity to continue my studies.

Grandma's ancestors were very well known in their old home of Salt City, Jiangsu. About nine hundred years ago, during the Northern Song Dynasty, when the Jurchens invaded, my family fled south from their ancestral home in Shanxi in order to avoid the turmoil. After fleeing several times, they finally settled in Suzhou. Surviving the Southern Song and Yuan Dynasties, they moved to Salt City more than six hundred years ago. From that point in time to my own, there have already been twenty generations. Grandma still remembers the ancient temple of Mount Tai that was close to our old home. The temple, over a century old, was thronged with worshippers burning incense. I still remember the large gold-lettered plaque hung high inside your great-grandmother's house that was inscribed with the title "Top Classic Scholar." The imperial court had conferred it on your great-grandfather because he was one of the top five students in Salt City's "Top Classic Scholar" provincial civil service exam.

It was only because I was a strong student that some rich relatives wanted to hire me to tutor their son who did not know how to study. However, because that boy was older than I and considered one of my elders, they were too embarrassed to talk about it out loud. Later on, when they learned that I loved to eat watermelon, they used the excuse of inviting me over to eat some watermelon so that I could tutor that boy on his lessons. At home, whenever we had watermelon, I was only ever allowed one piece. They would let me eat half a watermelon. Sometimes, when I yearned for watermelon, I would find an excuse to visit them. Under the pretext of checking his homework, I would arrive without invitation and eat watermelon to my heart's delight.

At that time, studying hard guaranteed both watermelon to eat and the attention of one's relatives. It was like winning a big prize and I loved the feeling of accomplishment. But my family was old-fashioned and they insisted that I couldn't continue my studies. I decided then to spread the word that if a family was willing to support me in my studies, I would marry into that family as a daughter-in-law.

When my teacher found out, he asked to see me and gave me a dollar to pay for the exams to enter middle school. To this day, I hold a grudge against my father who was willing to spend any amount of money outside the home, so why was he so stingy with his daughter? If my teacher hadn't helped, I would have many regrets now. At that time, I swore to my teacher that I would return the money once I had found work. However, my teacher shook his head and said, "As long as you pass the entrance exams, you needn't return the money." I immediately fell to the ground crying and kowtowing in thanks to him. That scene will be etched into my heart for the rest of my life.

When the exam period arrived, I had to take the exam out of town. In those times, transportation was inconvenient, and the road was long. There was no way I could return home on the same day that I took the exam. Therefore, I decided to lie. I told my father and mother that I was going to play at Auntie's house, and that I wouldn't be returning until the next evening. They agreed. Later I was accepted into Nanjing Middle School. However, it just so happened that a girl from our village who had gone to Nanjing to study was sent home because she was pregnant, which shamed the whole village. From that point on, nobody was willing to send their daughters to Nanjing, no matter which middle school they attended. Moreover, Father said, "Other people see it when your trousseau is large, but who can see it when your learning is deep?"

Fortunately, my teacher told me that it was free to study at the women's teacher's college; however, one had to teach after graduating. This is the reason I became a teacher. As a teacher, I put all my heart and soul into developing the younger generation, and the students all liked me.

After graduating from teacher's college, a teacher called me into her office one day. A young man was already there. His family had sought out a matchmaker and he was sent to meet me. I only met with him for a short time, nevertheless, it was perfect that he also liked to study. We married quickly. After we married, he left for the United States to study aeronautical engineering. He not only assisted his country in developing aeronautical technology, but he also taught in university and eventually became the dean of engineering at a famous university.

Although your grandfather was intelligent and had an illustrious career, he had a bad temper and could not be called a good husband. Grandmother isn't telling you these things because she wants to create a bad impression of your grandfather in your mind. Rather, Grandmother wants to share with you the lessons that she has learned in her marriage. A happy marriage and rich knowledge are not obtained at the drop of a hat. Many white girls believe that after they fall in love and get married, their marriage will be like a fairy tale and that the prince and princess will live a blissful and happy life. When they encounter adversity and the dream gives way to disillusionment, they never recover from the setback. Rather, they give up in despair. They truly are pitiable.

I remember when we left the Chinese mainland and first arrived in Taiwan. We lived in a residence assigned by the government. Another family lived just above us. Therefore, when we quarrelled, I was never able to out argue him. His voice was loud, and I alone was afraid of the ridicule if somebody heard us arguing. The only thing I could do was learn to tolerate everything he did, always yielding to him.

One day he got a cramp in his leg, and I knelt down to massage it. Who would have thought that he would kick me away? In contrast, once when we were going out and I lost my balance climbing the stairs, I fell and rolled back down the steps. I moaned on the ground, unable to lift myself. He, however, did not come to help me up. Although your grand-father received a modern education, his thinking was that of an ancient Chinese male: dictatorial and authoritarian. He didn't know what love was. He only spoke nicely when he wanted me to make love with him. Actually, it doesn't matter if you marry a dictatorial and authoritarian man, as long as he is reasonable. Unfortunately, your grandfather was not that reasonable, which made my life very miserable.

There was one time your grandfather became angry, blaming me for not preparing supper on time. He threw dishes at me and loudly insulted me in front of our children. He made me completely lose face; my self-respect was shot to pieces. In a moment of anger, I walked out the door and left home. I walked and walked until I noticed an advertisement for a babysitter on a local power pole. I immediately went to apply. The employer hired me and even gave me a bowl of rice; however, they didn't give me any chopsticks, vegetables, or meat. I looked at the rice and cried. Later on, your uncle asked around and found out where I was working; he came to take me home. I apologized to my employers and admitted that I had run away in anger. They said it was no wonder I had been useless to them, I just wasn't the servant type.

On the way home, I could see your grandfather from far away; he was already standing in the street. He welcomed me, all smiles. Once I had returned, I wanted him to apologize. And he did. He lowered his voice and said he was sorry. But I didn't accept it. I asked him to apologize in a loud voice, as loud as when he had insulted me, so that the neighbours could hear. Instead, he replied, "I'm not crazy! Why do I want to let the neighbours hear me apologize?" I asked him, "Why did you let the neighbours hear you insult me?"

Your grandfather was like all men. Although he was married,

he still liked to have girlfriends. Plus, he was brazen about it. Once he realized that I was afraid of the neighbours making fun of me, he didn't restrain himself in any way. There was a time when he had two girlfriends. Once, when he wrote to both of them, he even wanted me to prepare the ink for him. When he finished the letters, he ordered me to take them to the post office. The more I thought about it the angrier I became, so I switched the letters, putting one girlfriend's letter in the other girlfriend's envelope, and then sent them. By doing this, I caused him to lose them both.

Oh, Little Millie, you and I both know that it is wrong to lie, but I had no choice. The first time I lied in order to be able to participate in the entrance exam and have the chance to continue my education. I had to deceive my father and mother by saying that I was going to Auntie's house to spend the night. Only by doing this did I have the opportunity to receive a teacher's education and to marry your grandfather. If I had only had an elementary school education, he definitely would not have married me, and you wouldn't be here.

Since then, I've had a different view of lying than most people. I emphasized two things: the first was motive, and the other was result. If I was forced to lie, and had no evil thoughts, and no intention of hurting someone, when I had no control, then I could be forgiven for occasionally telling a white lie in order to get through a difficult situation.

For example, for the sake of the children and our marriage, I completely subjected myself to your grandfather. This was my decision; I couldn't blame anyone else. When he told me to run the errand of sending the letters to his girlfriends, if I had refused, wouldn't we have fought? People laugh at a couple who always argue; they have no face whatsoever! The best thing for me to do was to deceive him, allow my petty planning to cause him to lose two lovers at the same time. I have forgiven myself for this transgression, and I believe that God will forgive me as well.

Afterwards, whenever your grandfather rebuked me, I would address your uncle who was still in high school then: "Mama will take you to a movie, whichever one you want." Your uncle would agree. But who knew that he would buy a ticket for me then leave, saying that he would pick me up when the movie was over? Because he didn't like to watch movies, my son tricked me in this way. I had only just arrived in Taiwan and I was feeling bad. I didn't know anybody, I didn't know where to go, and I was afraid of going to a movie by myself. For the sake of relieving the pressure, I invited your uncle to accompany me, but I didn't anticipate that I couldn't count on my son to stay with me through the movie.

Mothers are all brave, and Grandmother is no exception. We were in Sichuan during World War Two. The Japanese bombed us repeatedly. Every time we heard the moaning and whining of the air raid alert, each family, young and old, evacuated to the air raid shelter. At that time, I only had one child, your uncle. When we were fleeing from the air raid, I would always hold your uncle tightly against my chest inside my shirt. It didn't matter how cold the wind was; I only feared that he would be killed by a bomb. Grandmother would have preferred to die herself in order that his small life be saved. There were some unfortunate mothers who carried their children on their backs, and when they reached the air raid shelter, discovered that their children had already been killed by stray shards. Those mothers cried their hearts out, but it didn't help. That traitor, Wang Jingwei,[1] can't be forgiven. He placed red signs on the trenches around the air raid shelter, so that the Japanese planes could bomb them. So many people were killed by bombing, and so many were smothered to death in the air raid shelters.

Grandmother is telling you these things for no other reason than to let you know that friends, husband, sons, and daughters, none can be relied upon. You can only rely upon yourself. However, if you don't have any learning, or money, how can you support yourself? In Grandmother's opinion, a job can be lost, and money can be stolen or robbed; only learning can never be thrown or snatched away. Besides, if you lose your job, learning can help you rise from the ashes. If you are robbed of your money, you can earn it back.

Next time you raise a fuss and say you want to quit school, please think carefully about what Grandmother has said. Grandmother does not want YOU to be a Little Weeping Millie all your life.

Translated by Lloyd Sciban and Shu-ning Sciban[1]

[1]Wang was the head of a Japanese controlled government during their occupation of China.

Surrogate Father

BO SUN

M Y FRIENDS CALL ME Qiao the Genius or Master
Qiao. My name is actually Qiao Guangzong, a name
given to me by my grandfather, who did not know
how to read or write a single character. If I'd had a younger
brother, he would have been named Yaozu. Guangzong and
Yaozu. What vulgar names![1] I was born in the Year of the
Rabbit, and now I am thirty-six years old. I graduated with
distinction from a well-known Chinese university and am
now a doctoral student of computer science at the University
of Toronto. Please do not think of me as a nerd. I have many
interests and hobbies. I can sing and dance. I can discuss literature or sports. As a matter of fact, I am a sharp shooter
on the basketball court, though I cannot claim I am as good
a player as Michael Jordan. My classmates at university gave
me the nickname "Old Hand in Romance." Although it was
not meant as a compliment, I found the "romance" part
rather endearing. No matter how you dissect it, romance is
pretty romantic.

Who could have foreseen that a clever guy like me could
ever be snared? How could I have known that that woman
from Taiwan would cause me so much trouble? Could it be
that I, Qiao the Genius, have exhausted all my good fortune?
I'd rather be writing thousands and thousands of computer
programs of extreme complexity than deal with the mess I find
myself in right now.

My wife, Lu Xiaodan, is a beautiful woman from Shanghai. We bumped into each other at the foot of the Great Wall, and two years later we tied the knot on the banks of the Huangpu River. Soon after, I got a full scholarship from U of T and flew, by myself, to a snow-covered Canada. A year later, Dan joined me. She was a Chinese literature major in Shanghai, so she could read English but could not speak it. When she was settled in Toronto, she enrolled in English language classes.

Barely six months had passed when Dan began to want a child. She was almost too eager, perhaps because she was almost thirty. Nothing could be easier. All I had to do was simply stop using that nuisance of a condom. Very soon, she was pregnant. We celebrated the happy event with much joyfulness. And I used that opportunity to have a whisky or two.

Unfortunately, Dan miscarried two months later. We were both very sad, but we tried again about six months later. That effort ended in miscarriage, too. Dan was devastated. Her days were spent in deep sorrow. I tried to comfort her, but my efforts were in vain. I was also afraid that because of her profound depression she might be suicidal so, I sought high and low for a psychiatrist for professional help.

During that crucial time, Situ Jianye and his wife became our neighbours. We lived in an apartment building owned by the university that had all the necessary facilities and very low rent.

Situ was a PhD student in the Department of Sociology. He was from Hong Kong, so his Mandarin was rusty. He was rather short and far from handsome. However, his wife Chen Yaping was tall and pretty. She was also very sexy. Moreover, she knew how to befriend people. In the opinion of all the people they met, she was a beautiful flower stuck on a pile of cow dung. What a waste!

When she was told that Ping used to be a nurse, Dan's pretty face, which was clouded with grief, broke into a smile. As it happened, Dan and Ping were both born in the Year of the Ram and they were both Scorpios. Pretty soon they became chummy and started thinking of each other as sisters. They went to classes together and visited each other often. Sometimes I found Ping at our place when I got home from the university. But her husband and I seldom met. Situ was busy job hunting while I was focused on finishing my dissertation, spending most of my time in the computer lab.

Several times after being intimate with Dan, I'd lie beside her, spent, and listen to her babble about Ping's family affairs. Situ had passed his thesis defence. He had sent out hundreds of application letters but had yet to receive an offer. They were both frustrated. Dan seemed to be really concerned for them. I told her not to worry herself silly about someone else's troubles. She, however, blamed me for not being a good friend. Then she would lick at my moustache and say to me: "Who could be as lucky as you are? IBM is interested in you even before you graduate."

Yes, luck certainly smiles at me! But I am Qiao the Genius, with an IQ of 140. Who the heck is Situ? He should count himself extremely lucky to have a wife as attractive as Ping. The worst mistake a woman can make is to marry the wrong man, and a man's worst mistake is to pick the wrong profession. It was Situ's own fault that he chose the wrong academic discipline. After all, this world favours the fittest. The more I thought about his misfortune and my good luck, the more pleased I was with myself. But I did not say anything to Dan because she thought of Ping as a sister. Also, it was awkward since we were both stark naked.

Believing that she would not be deemed a real woman if she were not a mother, Dan struggled with her self-esteem and was still determined to have a child. By July, she had gotten her confidence back and ordered me to stop wearing that thing.

To draw on the lessons we learned from the previous two miscarriages, Dan issued three rules as soon as we learned the test results: she would not do household chores, she would not drive, and she would not have sex. She would do whatever it took to keep the baby safe. And she said that Ping prescribed the last rule and repeatedly emphasized its importance. I knew that my wife could be easily provoked and that total obedience was the best strategy to appease her, so I pledged compliance. But privately, I thought the first two rules would be easy to follow because all they required was that I'd work harder at home. However, the last commandment was, for me, simply unacceptable. It meant that I would not be able to enjoy conjugal bliss for over a year, which would certainly make me sick. Even our family doctor had never written a prescription as harsh as that. What was Ping thinking?

With the arrival of September, a new school year began. Dan and Ping started their accounting courses at a community college. They were inseparable. I was extremely grateful to Ping since she gave Dan a ride to school every day and they went on shopping trips together. When shopping, Ping carried all the groceries and other things, too. Sometimes she even came over to do chores like mopping the floor, tidying up the kitchen, and so on. As time passed, I gradually began to think of her as one of the family, too. Together we had meals and watched TV, and on weekends we would have her husband over for supper once in a while. Situ, when he joined us, seldom spoke. Perhaps it was because of his poor Mandarin, but I believed it was more because he was feeling low due to the fact that he had failed to find a job. But his appetite was not affected; he never put down his chopsticks at a meal, not even once.

Then a miracle occurred. Just when Situ had given up all hope of locating a job and was ready to return to Hong Kong, he received an e-mail message from the University of Chicago, offering him a two-year contract position to teach sociological statistics. The university wanted an immediate response. Although it was a mere contract job, it was better than nothing. Moreover, U of C was a first-class university, and the contract could be renewed. So we were all very happy for him. Situ wanted Ping to move to Chicago with him, but she refused.

She pointed out that she had just started her program, that she could not leave Dan behind, and that Chicago was not that far away for him to travel. Situ, thus, had to leave her behind.

The evening before Situ left, the four of us had a farewell dinner at a Chinese restaurant on Spadina. I had never seen Situ so happy and so talkative. He even snatched up the bill when it came. Tightly he held my hands in his, urging me to take good care of Ping.

Naturally, after Situ left, Ping became a fixture at our home. Every two or three days she would have supper with us. Quite a few times, she slept in our conjugal bed, while I had to make do on the couch in the living room. If that had become known, people would have started to think that those two were lesbian lovers.

Pretty soon Dan was four months pregnant, and all was well. Ping apparently was an old hand. Dan was so grateful that she seemed almost to worship Ping, as though without Ping she would have no hope of keeping her baby. So one day at supper I said that Ping should be a godmother to our child. They laughed and said in unison what a superb idea it was.

This also meant that I had been celibate for four long months. This was unusual for me. Since my second year at university, I had never been without a sexual partner for more than three months. During my first year in Canada, I had three women, all Caucasians. And we had enjoyed our casual sexual relations. My affair with my last partner, Lucy, did not end until a week before Dan's arrival. Of course, Dan would never learn about those women—never—but she was fully aware that I was as strong as a horse.

Those four months were truly a time of horror. I was full of sexual energy, but I had no outlet. So I threw myself into swimming and playing basketball. Exercises increased my appetite. At one supper, I wolfed down half a chicken, two chunks of steak, and a plateful of beef and broccoli stir-fry, as well as a bottle of French red wine. Dan, assuming I was experiencing setbacks in my studies, was too scared to comment, while Ping simply smiled.

What was more troubling was that I started to dream of pits, caves, and doors of all sizes—all symbols of female sexuality. Sometimes my dreams were very graphic. I remembered dreaming of Ping's plump breasts and fleshy buttocks. I had no clue why I fantasized about her. Perhaps it was because we were seeing each other frequently. To be frank, her body could easily inspire any male's fantasies. However, Dan never appeared in my dreams, which, I admitted ashamedly, was a betrayal of my dear wife. I thought about having sex with some other women on certain nights, but I was afraid that Dan might find out and make a big scene out of it. It would not be worth the trouble, especially when she was pregnant with my child. So I toughed it out, for the sake of my unborn child.

One wintry evening, with a cold wind blowing and snowflakes dancing all around, Ping was at our place to keep Dan company. They were watching the news when I left for my office after supper. I was revising a paper that was to appear in *Nature*. Around eleven o'clock the phone rang, breaking my concentration. It was Ping. "Hi, Qiao the Genius. Could you do me a favour? My computer just died on me. My project is due tomorrow. I would have asked Dan, but she has gone to bed."

I drove home, and twenty minutes later, I was in Ping's apartment. I checked her computer and found a virus. Then I went back to our apartment to fetch some anti-virus software. Dan was fast sleep, so I quietly closed the door. When I got back to Ping's apartment, I found that she had changed into pyjamas. She handed me a glass of brandy, sat down beside me, and leaned towards me, watching me fix her computer. My, the sweet fragrance from her body and that pair of sparkling eyes! They were simply irresistible. I hurried, intending to leave as soon as possible in order to escape temptation. However, she filled my glass a second time and then had one herself. I had never seen her drink strong liquor before.

It was past midnight when her computer was fixed. Before I could leave, Ping pulled me into her bedroom. She shut the door, stripped off her pyjamas and stood in front of me without a stitch on. Staring at her huge and firm breasts, I was bursting with desire and completely lost control.

We were in each other's arms. It was as if everything had frozen in place, and even the air seemed to stand still. After our lovemaking, we were both soaked. "We are sick," Ping whispered. "Otherwise how could we have managed without sex for so many months?"

"Aren't you afraid that Situ will find out?" I asked. She shook her head. "This is strictly between you and me. That bookworm husband of mine won't ever know." Then it suddenly dawned on me that I had not used a condom. She assured me that she was not ovulating and so there was no need to worry. We began to make love again.

When I got back home, pretty light-headed, it was already four o'clock. I went to bed, and when I caught a glimpse of Dan sleeping sweetly, the guilt crept up on me. However, fatigue quickly overcame guilt, and I was soon fast asleep.

After that night, Ping did not come to our place as often, but I became a frequent visitor to her apartment. She regularly called me at my office late at night to invite me over. When I arrived, she would feed me a big bowl of soup. She claimed that her soup was nutritious and could boost the *yang* in a man. Then we would have sex without any further delay. I had to admit that she was the best partner I'd ever had. Probably as a result of being a nurse, she had a superb knowledge of the human body, and I admired her for her expertise. I love women who are graceful hostesses in the living room, excellent cooks in the kitchen, and lustful partners in bed. Dan could not compete with Ping in bed. Very soon I was as addicted to her love-making as an opium user is to the drug. I had to visit her bedroom every night, and, every time we were together in bed, I was inexhaustible and insatiable.

I was still worried, so I asked her again if she was concerned about her betrayal of her husband. She smiled and said, "How about you? We're just having sex, and the affair won't last. So it will not have any real impact on our respective harmonious family lives. Situ is a good husband to me. I agreed to be his wife in the first place because I liked his honesty and kindness. Also, he is from a family with money. So I will not give him up, not without good reason. Just as you will not divorce Dan. But Situ is burying himself in his studies. He got his PhD, but he is rather slow. Believe it or not, his IQ is only one hundred, even lower than mine. It is a shame that modern science can only clone sheep. If human beings could be cloned, I'd choose someone like you, both handsome and intelligent."

I did not expect that Ping would put forward such a self-serving "theory" to justify our actions. But if she was not worried, why should I be? As long as no one got wind of what we were doing, all was fine. However, I cautioned her a number of times that we could not risk a pregnancy. She assured me that she was taking birth control pills. A couple of times she took them in front of me.

Things did not go as smoothly as I had hoped. One night in early February, Ping showed up at my office door. She was holding a test result and told me, with abundant joy, that she was pregnant. I felt dizzy and broke into a cold sweat. "You have been on the pill, haven't you?"

"Of course, but you must have very active semen."

"What do we do now?"

"I want to have the baby."

"What? I'll become the father of two children in the same year?"

"Whatever you say, I want to keep this baby. I will be a mother sooner or later; and I've got you, a top-notch semen provider."

"What am I, then, a semen-spitting machine?"

"What's wrong with that? You have made a huge contribution to the human race. There are not that many geniuses in this world, you know."

"Are you sure this child will be intelligent?"

"Of course! I have complete confidence in you."

"Be honest. Did you do this intentionally?"

"How do I put it? It was somewhere between subconsciously and intentionally. But I did forget to take the pill a few times."

"Is your husband unable to have children?"

"No. But I do not want his semen. He is stupid and ugly, unlike you. You are clever and handsome."

"You could have gone to a semen bank. You can even get the semen of a Nobel Prize winner."

"I thought about it, but it could hurt Situ's ego. Also, it would feel weird to have the semen from a total stranger put into my body. I could not tolerate that psychologically."

I didn't answer.

Doubtlessly, Ping used me as a surrogate father. I bet she never bothered to take the pills. I felt cheated. Had I really been fooled by that woman? But she eventually talked me into accepting her plan of keeping the baby. Everything went as she had planned. That weekend, she drove to Chicago.

In early March, Situ came back with Ping. They happily announced that Ping was pregnant. Dan, who was heavy with her baby, gave Ping her blessing, while I shook Situ's hand and offered congratulations. Dan even joked that our baby now had a buddy even before it was born. If our babies were a boy and a girl, they could be husband and wife in the future. That remark made Ping laugh like crazy but sent chills up to my spine. Wouldn't that be incest?

A few days later Ping came to my office in the evening to say goodbye. She would go back to Chicago with Situ and be an accommodating, good wife. She said that Situ was such a fool that he believed the baby was his. He was so pleased that he had even shed tears. Suddenly, she began to weep. A crying woman was what I feared the most. So I held her in my arms, wiping away her endless tears. She, on her part, urged me to treasure Dan and also asked me to visit her if I got the chance. We were like two lovers parting forever. I was even moved to tears. Just before she took her leave, she lifted her wool skirt and leaned on my desk, invitingly. I could not help but throw myself onto her.

When we were in the heat of the act, somebody knocked at the door. I stole a glance at my watch, which indicated eleven o'clock. It was the time for the housekeeping staff to clean the offices. We had to wrap it up in a hurry. Ping was tidying her long hair as I went over to open the door. It was Situ who was at the door. Ping and I were stunned.

Ping reacted first and accosted her husband, who pushed her aside and yelled: "An adulterer and a whore! I listened in and heard you, clearly! I could not believe my ears but now look at you! What a sight! Somebody e-mailed me some time ago. It said you two had been up to some hanky-panky. Don't kid yourselves into thinking you were so clever that you would never be caught. Even walls have ears, and you cannot pull the wool over everyone's eyes. That thing in your belly, it might be his...."

Neither Ping nor I said a word. We just let him talk and talk, to let out his pent-up anger. Then I pleaded with him that Dan should not be told about the affair, not until she gave birth. It was not the time to stir up unnecessary trouble. If Dan was enraged, she would kill a cheating husband like me.

The final round of negotiations took place in my office, but Situ had the upper hand. He insisted on a DNA test to decide the paternity of the child. If he was the father, all was well. If I was the father, he would consider the option of divorce. Or he would require me to pay support until the child reached sixteen in the amount of five hundred Canadian dollars each month, totalling one hundred thousand dollars. He would also hire a lawyer to draft the document. Eventually, he promised that he would leave Dan out of this messy affair. To avoid further complications, I agreed to all his demands. Ping just bent her head and kept silent throughout the negotiation.

The next day at noon, they left for Chicago. Before their departure, Ping cried until her eyes were red and swollen. Dan was in tears. I gave Situ's hand a squeeze and said, "Take care" to Ping. Then they were gone, but trouble was looming. This was my year, the Year of the Rabbit. Could it be that my own year would be my unlucky year, and that I would not be able to escape the coming disaster?

The frozen soil thawed, and soon the earth was covered with tender green grass that had an intoxicating fragrance. Our son was born during that early spring. Dan's smiling face told all our friends that she had forgotten the pain she had suffered when in labour. Our eight-pound boy was, to her, a sun that never set.

As a new father, I experienced a happiness that could not be described. But when I recalled that a woman in Chicago was pregnant with another child of mine, I was deeply disturbed. I had no clue how to deal with the birth of a second child in six months. As it turned out, Situ was quite a handful. I had been contemplating the possible outcomes, but all seemed to end in tragedy.

To my great surprise, three days after my son's birth I received an anonymous by email. It read:

Dear Mr. Qiao the Genius,

Congratulations on your precious son! There is no need for you to worry. Situ Jianye is sterile, but his wife does not know. So your affair was predestined. Even God cannot judge who of the three of you is right and who is wrong. Perhaps you did someone a big favour, even if it was unintended.

Yours truly, Anonymous

This was certainly a poison-pen letter, but who had sent it?

Was it a bag of lies or was it the truth? I would have to play the part of the detective. The investigation was by no means easy. The email came from a yahoo address. Anyone can get a yahoo address, so as a clue the e-mail was like the needle in the proverbial haystack. All of a sudden, I became conscious that time was passing far too quickly and Ping's child would come into this world in no time. Then Situ would conduct the paternity test. Catastrophe would descend on me because I could not deny the child was mine. My guilt was eating away at my conscience day in and day out, and I could not endure the torture. I wanted it to end, no matter what the outcome. What was the worst-case scenario? Dan kicking me out?

At last, October came and Ping gave birth to a seven-pound baby girl. Hearing the news, Dan laughed heartily, so much so that she almost dropped our son. She said that Ping gave us a daughter-in-law. Then she told me that the three of us should drive to Chicago to visit our relatives.

Ping, meanwhile, called me at my office to inform me that she had reached an agreement with Situ Jianye. She had admitted that the child was mine, but said she had used me merely as a surrogate father, or a semen donor. Consequently, there was no need for a paternity test nor should I have to pay child support. If he failed to honour this agreement, she would divorce him.

I had to let her know about the anonymous letter I got months before. She was speechless for a moment and then said very calmly: "No wonder he accepted my ultimatum without much fuss. The message you got seems to have come from a highly reliable source. Since he has kept me in the dark on such an important matter, we do not need to feel guilty for what we did. Life will go on just as the earth revolves and the sun rises and sets."

It does not matter if Situ is sterile. Nor does it really matter who of the three of us is at fault, Situ, Ping, or I. However, I can never be as guilt-free as Ping is whenever I face Dan and our son. I will always be afraid that Situ might someday decide to confess to Dan. My carefree days are gone forever, and I am laden with a heavy burden of uncertainty. Having slept with Ping is indeed the source of all my troubles!

Translated by H. Laura Wu and Cory Davies.

"Surrogate Father" was originally published in Fiction Star Monthly, *No. 7, 2000.*

[1]The phrase "Guangzong yaozu" means "bringing glory to one's ancestors." So Guangzong and Yaozu used to be popular names for boys in traditional China.

An Elegant But Stiff Neck

TAO YANG

THE RAINBOW BRIDGE International Airport is enveloped in a light mist. While waving at Zhou Bu, Xue is not sure whether she means to say "Farewell" or "Wait for my call." The sticky sweat under her armpits refuses to dry. Pressed against the hard railing, she senses a stinging pain on her round arms and curvy bust. She wraps herself in a black silk scarf to cover up her bare back, clamps an amber-coloured purse under her arm, and walks towards the overpass leading to the departure level. Her drifting thoughts seem to settle down as she threads her way through the noisy crowd.

During the Shanghai-Tokyo leg of her flight to Toronto, Xue has kept quiet and managed to blend into the mass of excited passengers. Now she is sitting in the economy section of the airplane heading to Toronto. She is acutely aware that finally she has left behind the robust yet maddening Shanghai she knows so well. She is surprised by the mature age of the healthy-looking, blue-eyed, blonde stewardesses working for Air Canada. One of the stewardesses offers her, with ample kindness and composure, a choice of food and drinks. Xue doesn't give it much thought and asks for a drink. The stewardess babbles something she fails to understand. A hand beside her takes a pack from the tray, and its master interprets for her.

"Good for you," the stewardess says. The way she speaks tells Xue that she considers Xue fortunate to have a gentleman companion. Xue turns her head and notices that the young

157

Japanese man sitting beside her has somehow become a Shanghai native in a dress shirt and a tie. "It's a sandwich, a snack recently added to the menu of Air Canada flights. Air China does not have this. Just the right amount for you."

Xue gives him a standoffish nod. "Thank you but I am not hungry."

"It must be your first flight. You are still not used to it. When you adjust, you'll be hungry. This is not enough for me. But it's not a problem; we can ask for more."

Xue smiles at him out of politeness.

"We all experience this for first time. Enjoy your sandwich. I'll be back in a moment." He gets up and walks to the back of the airplane.

Xue thinks, *It might be my first time, but it won't be with you.* She gives another glance at the retreating back, taking note of his high-quality white shirt, carefully cut short hair, and English that she cannot fully understand. Another self-assured immigrant in the technical category.[1] *Don't assume that I'll throw myself onto your lap the moment I find myself on an airplane.* She then examines the multi-coloured sandwich: green lettuce, yellow cheese, and reddish cold cuts bookended by two pieces of brown bread. She takes a hesitant bite and puts the sandwich down. Mixed feelings well up inside her, and she finds the dizziness and persistent unease suffocating.

Outside the window, the sky foggy and leaden. Xue cannot tell if it is dawn or dusk. She used to lead a carefree life, but the past twelve months have been filled with ups and downs, satisfaction and frustration. This fluctuation of emotions has transformed her formerly full body into a slimmer, more inviting figure. Zhou Bu said that she looked thin and weary, but Yihai assured her that she was even more willowy and graceful. Xue knows that Yihai is obsessed with her breasts, which are firm and high, yet soft to touch. He saw them just once. It was during one of their trysts, and, by pure chance, her breasts were bared. The nipples, softly pink, suddenly stood out. He tried to fondle them with his mouth, but she deftly slipped away. After that encounter, he could never say no to her. She knows that she owes him a lot. Money is not a concern for Yihai, who is willing to do anything to win her smile; however, thirty-five thousand U.S. dollars is by no means a trifle. At the very least, the amount exceeds his annual salary as a departmental manager in a foreign company. He laments the brevity of life, and meeting her when he was already forty. She tells him that there are many more happy days ahead, if he is not afraid to be decisive.

"If you really want me, get a divorce." She watched him intensely, with a bewitching air of hurt and displeasure. His silence reminded her of their favourite song:

If you love me, then give me a sip of water;
If you love me, then give me a kiss so tender.

That night, at his wife's dressing table, she struggled in his embrace with unyielding determination. He persisted but eventually stopped. Then he said he understood. He swore to heaven and earth that he would win her over, persuade her to lie willingly in his arms. So he gave her all the money she asked for, and now she is living her dream—to emigrate. The route she has chosen is unconventional and even somewhat absurd, and she herself is not sure if the risk is worthwhile. She has yet to give herself to him, avoiding it even at the last moment. The day before yesterday, Yihai paged her persistently the entire evening. She did not call back. She was with Zhou Bu, who was helping her pack. He gave her tiny room a thorough search, and the only thing he could add to her packed suitcases was a reference book on medicine and pharmacy. She took it out, complaining that the cases were too heavy.

He said, "It is handy to have your own reference books. You will not need to go to the library whenever you want to check some information. If you find the suitcases too heavy, I can sort them out one more time."

He did that, but he only took out a bottle of perfume. He

knew very well what was in those suitcases, since he had bought most of the things himself the last few days. Xue sighed but did not stop him. She just wiped the sweat and dirt from his hands. She had told him that she was going to a medical school to study pharmacology. It was better to feed him a white lie than tell him the truth.

"Please go home. It's almost dawn, and you have to work today."

"No, I don't. I've got a half-day leave."

He caressed her soft hands, looking intently at her. "After I send you off, I'll start to inquire if I can visit you as your fiancé. Canadian universities might have different rules and regulations than the American ones." She stared at the shadows cast by the light and inhaled deep and long. If her sham marriage had been with him, at least he would not have wasted all those years of courtship.

It was quiet in the other room. Apparently her parents were too tired to stay up. They were both in their late fifties. Certainly, they would have wanted to be with their daughter and talk, but they did not want to intrude. She thought, *I have married myself off in such an underhanded manner, even had a picture taken of the wedding party as proof. The parents were hired and the groom was bought. This is a horrid betrayal of my own parents.*

Her pager kept vibrating. She could imagine the desperation Yihai was suffering. Zhou Bu said: "Call back. It might be something very urgent."

Xue did not respond to his remark but simply said: "If you do not want to go home, you'd better rest here. I'll go out to be with my parents."

The airplane flies through sleepy clouds. Xue's heart sinks. She also feels exhausted. The stewardess pushes a loaded cart along the aisle, and when she reaches Xue's seat, she says something in a gentle, low voice. Xue does not understand her.

She thinks that the stewardess is telling her that she is wanted at the back of the plane, for some reason. She stands up and searches around for her seatmate, the fellow Shanghai native who has been sucking up to her. The stewardess realizes that Xue has no idea what she has said, so she gestures to her to sit down. Standing up and sitting down right now is arduous because something very hard and stiff is wrapped around her slender waist and round buttocks. As her anxiety increases, she begins to anticipate problems. Xue is hiding fifteen thousand U.S dollars, but the money is not hers. When she lands at Toronto's Pearson International Airport, she must give it to the man who is to be her husband in her arranged marriage, Canadian citizen George Zhang.

"I asked the stewardess to fetch you. I have changed my seat to the back. There are two seats there now. If you want, you can lie down. You look really tired," her fellow Shanghai native whispers into her ear.

Xue is relieved. "Thank you. I am not tired. Sorry, but I have not asked your name."

"No problem. I am Liang Zhengjun." He wants to continue, but Xue turns her head and goes back to her seat.

Xue is worn out. It is quiet inside the plane, and the night-lights give out a milky yellow glow. This is not an illusion. She is indeed flying to Canada as a new immigrant. No one can stop her now. But still she cannot enjoy food or sleep in peace; she has been living in fear and anxiety for too long. She still owes the money she borrowed when she tried to immigrate as a skilled professional, and she spent another twenty thousand U.S. dollars on this marriage scam. A small mistake in the documents she submitted or any misstep during the interview could jeopardize her application. If she cannot secure a visa, all the money she has spent will have been wasted. George Zhang has informed her that even if he did not take a single penny, an appeal would cost double what she has spent so far, and it would take a long time. The Canadian bureaucracy is as slow as the Chinese one. Her monthly salary is only about three thousand RMB. If she tries to pay off the debts with her salary, it will take years. Yihai may have the money, but he is married with a son. Even if she were content to be his second wife, which would bring shame to her parents, she would still have to wait a very long time for his divorce.

At night, with all the lights on, Pearson International Airport, is shining. It doesn't have the dazzling beauty that Shanghai Rainbow Bridge Airport does, but it has a grandeur that Rainbow Bridge lacks. Xue meanders, along with the crowd, through long corridors. Air Canada, American Air, Northwest…. Endless glamorous advertisements adorn the walls. Many white women walk past her, their smooth necks bare and unornamented. There is a young woman; her flat back is fully exposed, and around her bare arm is a piece of bright blue scarf decorated with sparkling beads. She is gorgeous but not coquettish. Five or six minutes and quite a few corners later, the crowd thins out. Only Xue and a number of her compatriots from Shenyang remain. She suspects that they will probably take the same exit, but she dares not ask. So she pretends that she knows the way.

Xue has already made up her mind that she will perform a disappearing act at the airport, escaping before encountering her "husband," who is waiting for her at the exit. Her aim is to save the fifteen thousand U.S. dollars she carries. George Zhang has it so easy. All he has done is fly to China, go to a banquet, have a couple of pictures taken, and make a few long-distance calls, and he has already earned three hundred thousand dollars in Chinese currency. Why should he get so much money for so little effort?

Yet sneaking away under so many pairs of eyes at the arrival level in a huge and unfamiliar airport is not going to be easy. Even if she covers her face, George Zhang will still be able to pick her out, because her above-average height always attracts attention. On their "wedding" night in the Wuxi village, George Zhang indicated, with a thick-skinned grin, that if she agreed to make the sham marriage real, he would not mind at all giving up the second instalment of the payment. Reckless because she was slightly drunk, she squinted her eyes in order to bring him into focus, and told him bluntly that even if he paid her twice the amount, she would not consider his marriage proposal. George Zhang is an independent immigrant and a bona fide professional, but nevertheless he is selling himself to make money. Of course, he knows that to have Xue means he would have to give up some of that money.

Xue takes her suitcases from the conveyor belt and watches the other passengers depart one after another. She feels edgy. At that moment, she catches sight of Zhengjun, who is about to walk out of the sliding door. She reacts immediately, rushing towards him and waving. "Liang Zhengjun!"

Zhengjun spins around, surprised to see her. It is a pleasant surprise, but he is at a bit of loss, completely unlike his former self on the airplane when he tried repeatedly to strike up a conversation with her, ignoring her constant rebuffs. Xue hesitates. Then she catches a glimpse of the crowd anxiously waiting beyond the automatic doors. George Zhang is there, waiting to ensnare her.

"Do you want my address? If you need my help, you can contact me." Zhengjun tries to get out a pen.

"Are you in a hurry? I want to ask you a favour. If you have to leave immediately, I won't bother you."

Zhengjun really does want to leave immediately. The minivan he has arranged to pick him up is waiting outside. If he misses it, he'll have to spend at least fifty or even sixty dollars on a taxi ride. Still her soft voice and weary but still disarming beauty are too much to resist. "I'm not in a hurry. What do you want me to do?"

Xue knows that she doesn't have the luxury of being anything but honest, so she looks directly into his eyes and says: "I can't go out through that exit. I don't want to see the person waiting for me there. Would you help me? I must leave through a different exit, and I'll need a place to stay. Just for one night. I can explain why later on."

Zhengjun is astonished at her request. Xue senses his reluctance so she assures him: "Don't worry. I won't cause you any further trouble. And I can pay."

Zhengjun thinks to himself that the very act of confiding in him is trouble enough. *No wonder people say that women who succeed in coming to Canada, except students, all have hidden motives. To get involved with them is inviting trouble. Even if I wanted to, where would I find the time for an affair?* But he cannot say no to her expectant eyes, even though it is already midnight and he is not sure where he can take her.

"We are both from Shanghai, so I'll help you. Give me your suitcases. You go upstairs. There you can go to Hilton Hotel on the other side. Then you go down and find Section 12, and I'll wait for you there." He bends over to take her suitcases as he is speaking. Xue intuitively recoils, and the silver necklace with tiny drumstick charms around her neck trembles. *Am I making a mistake now because I'm desperate?* she wonders

Zhengjun guesses what is going through her mind and hands her the leather bag he carries. "My passport is in it. Don't be afraid. Go upstairs. I will wait for you."

His words put her at ease, and she is almost touched. This is, undoubtedly, the crucial moment that makes their emotional involvement later on possible. Xue grabs his bag, and without a moment of delay turns and runs towards the staircase. She is afraid that George Zhang might see her through the automatic doors that are sliding open and shut constantly.

After rushing through the hall and the overpass connecting the airport and the hotel, Xue comes out in the Hilton lobby. She finds a place where she can hide beside the revolving door but still be able to watch the busy lanes of traffic. She opens Zhengjun's bag and takes out a booklet with a blue cover. It is a Canadian passport issued to Liang Zhengjun. The place of birth is listed as Shanghai. She does not have the time to give it a thorough examination, but she is sure that it is not a fake. After he has picked her up, the minivan travels at high speed on Highway 401, through twinkling urban lights. Xue and Zhengjun keep quiet most of the time, apparently deep in their own thoughts. Mr. Yang, the driver, rambles on: "I am lucky today. Yesterday I had a long wait. My customers didn't clear customs until one-thirty in the morning…. No matter how many passengers there are, I can only pick up those from one flight…. Pretty girls from Shanghai like you should not do labourers' work, no matter what. When a girl, young and tender goes into a factory, she comes out a wrinkled old hag no one wants to look at. Any work beats a factory job…. I have long ago stopped dreaming of finding an engineer's position. I'll stick to this job as long as I can. Whatever changes they make to the immigration rules, Chinese will always be coming to Canada, legit or not…. If they ask me, I'll tell them they'd be better to stay in China. Why give up a good life back home and come here to swallow bitterness and endure hardship?"

As the minivan jolts and bumps, Xue's round, curved knee keeps knocking against Zhengjun's. She does not move away, but she is not sure why. Does she feel grateful or is she still frightened? Anyway, she holds out her hand, seeking his. Holding his big hand in her own, the air in the van becomes still while their breath becomes short and laboured.

Xue gets a basement room in the guesthouse run by their driver, Mr. Yang. It is a single-family house with a front lawn and a back garden. The Yangs live upstairs, and downstairs is the guest house, their family business. The main floor and basement are divided into seven or eight rooms, all for paying guests. In Shanghai, you can find houses like this one only along Huashan Street or Kangping Road. Here houses of similar size and design line both sides of the street. On their front lawn, tiny lamps flash like fireflies. Xue assumes that she has been taken to a neighbourhood where rich people live. Zhengjun informs her that her room is paid for. He will come the next day to help her find permanent accommodation. He gives her the telephone number of the computer company where he works and then leaves in a hurry. Xue stares at his shadow as it slowly disappears, and she feels a sense of total loss.

Xue checks each and every corner of the room carefully. Only after she is certain that no one is spying on her, does she take out all the U.S. dollars hidden around the sensitive parts of her body. She spreads them on the bed and counts them. Every single note is here. She has counted them so many times that she remembers clearly all the creases and folds in the few worn notes among them. She gathers the notes together, puts them in a plastic bag, and takes the bag with her to the bathroom. After a shower, she returns to her room, spreads a sheet she has brought along, and stretches out on the bed. Her entire body is relaxed. Even her usually high breasts, though still softly pink, now droop languidly. She smiles coquettishly because she knows a gentle touch will make them pop up. Xue feels drained, and a moment later she is fast asleep, her hand tightly holding the bag full of money.

Totally unaware of the mayhem that her disappearance has set off, Xue is enjoying a sweet sleep during her first night in Canada. George Zhang has been waiting anxiously for her the whole night at the airport. Even the security guards take notice of him and find his presence suspicious. George has to approach them, asking, "My wife is missing. What should I do?"

The security guards don't care about his missing wife. They are concerned only with what he is doing at the airport, and are not of much help to him. Eventually, with help from Air Canada staff at the information desk at the airport, he gets in touch with the Shanghai office of Air China. He is told that nothing untoward has occurred during the flight and the airlines cannot disclose any information about individual passengers. Neither can immigration and customs at the Vancouver Airport. He doesn't want to, but he finally has to admit that Xue has vanished right before his eyes, and that her disappearance is premeditated. He has rented a room for Xue and paid the deposit. He is waiting for the second instalment of the agreed payment, which he plans to spend on tuition and expenses for a degree from the University of Windsor. After he gets his degree, he may have a chance to find a job in the States. He has given up any hope of finding a decent job in Canada, and now realizes that his hope to make this sham marriage a real one was wishful thinking. He recalls how Xue behaved back in Shanghai, bossing people around, and guesses that she must have some influential friends. Also, Zhou Bu kept a close eye on both of them. Obviously, Zhou has his plan, too: when Xue has settled in Canada, he will follow her. Eventually they will pick an auspicious day and get married. George Zhang did not anticipate that this woman could strike so quickly and so ruthlessly. She has robbed him and left him penniless! He calls Xue's parents, Zhou Bu, and even some of those who attended their "wedding" banquet in the Wuxi village and from whom he had managed to get a telephone number. No one, except for Xue's parents and Zhou Bu, gives a damn. It is crystal clear what has happened, and he should have known better. He is enraged and exasperated. He paces back and forth beside the row of telephones at the arrival level.

When Xue gets up the next day it is already noon. Actually, she is woken up by Zhengjun's knocking on her door. The first thing she plans to do is to send the money back home. Only after she has her things sorted and packed does it occur to her that she forgot to make that important call to inform her parents of her safe arrival. She asks Zhengjun how to call Shanghai, and he uses his calling card and dials the number for her. Her mother cries once she hears Xue's voice: "Where are you? We have been worried sick. Do not hang up, your dad wants to talk to you."

Her father urges her to put her own safety first. She is in a foreign land and she should use extreme caution, especially when dealing with strangers. Xue takes the hint: her father is not simply urging her to be careful; something must have happened after she left. She wants to ask but is afraid to cause more trouble than she has already. She now regrets having given George Zhang her home number when they first met. Not surprisingly, George Zhang searched for her when he failed to see her at the airport and could not collect the money she owes him. Her mother takes over the phone, but she is choosing her words carefully and hinting at something that Xue cannot quite grasp. Zhengjun is busy loading her luggage and ready to go, so Xue ends her call and hurriedly grasps her purse.

Here in Scarborough, house after house is flanked by an expanse of green lawn and tall trees. The roads are wide, and there are no bicycles in sight. *China should be like this,* Xue thinks. "But how can I find work if I can't ride a bike," she wonders aloud.

"By bus. We have twenty-four-hour service here." Zhengjun points at a bus running beside them while steering his car with one hand. Then he steps on the accelerator, and the car overtakes the bus. His hair, though not really long, blows in the breeze. Shanghai in July is so hot and humid that life is hell without air conditioning, but here the breeze makes the air crisp and fresh. Xue wears a bright pink dress and a pair of off-white sandals with silver straps and high heels. Her clothes, except for winter wear, are all new. Zhengjun stretches out a tentative hand to touch her, but Xue dodges it by leaning toward the door, her head turned away slightly, stiffly expressionless.

The affectionate intimacy she showered on him during the ride from the airport vanishes. Zhengjun is puzzled. There are more and more Chinese faces in this city, but Zhengjun has yet to experience any romantic involvement. Now this pretty woman from Shanghai, who just walks into his life, gives him boundless pleasure and surprise. The titillating warmth left by the caress of her slender and soft fingers still lingers. He is aware that new immigrants from his home country are all very capable. Those who adjust well live comfortably, like fish in water, while those who struggle, like fish out of water. But not a single person is idle. Even those who come with loads of money and can afford not to work for six months or more are still active, mentally if not physically. They surf the net to look for desirable jobs or strike up leisurely conversations in chat rooms. Zhengjun cannot figure out why this beautiful woman from Shanghai has come to Canada. She is too old to attend high school. She seems unattached, so she is not here to be reunited with a husband. Also, she has an unfathomable expression of secrecy that nevertheless fails to conceal a troubled heart. Zhengjun cannot suppress his burgeoning curiosity about this mysterious woman.

Zhengjun takes Xue to an old, two-storey house in a neighbourhood near Chinatown. He talks briefly with the landlady and then goes to work, leaving Xue behind. He is supposed to accompany his manager to a meeting with a client regarding a software project. Xue doesn't want him to leave, so he promises to come back in the evening and urges her to have a good rest to get rid of her jetlag.

In her room are a single bed and a shabby table. The dull grey walls are spattered with spots and stains. Only the houses with pitched roofs across the street offer some comfort to offset her self-pity. Xue puts aside her suitcases and hurriedly leaves to explore Chinatown. There are all kinds of Chinese goods in the stores and a multitude of Chinese people on the street. They even have ear-picks.[2] If she had known, she would not have spent an entire afternoon searching for them in the small shops along Yuyuan Street back in Shanghai. She asks two pedestrians for directions to a bank and both reply enthusiastically: "To open an account? Go to a Bank of China branch." Even the shop assistants seem to know that she has just landed in the city. She is baffled. Her outfit is as fashionable as everyone else's, if not more so. Why is she singled out as soon as they see her? What if they also notice the money she carries on her? When she finds the bank, it is already four o'clock, and the bank is closed. She peers through the window and looks around uneasily in order to remember its location. Then she beats a hasty retreat, fearing that she may be followed.

Daylight still lingers at nine-thirty in the evening. Xue wants to cook a simple meal, some congee and a stir-fry, but she discovers when stepping into the kitchen that the entire room is cluttered. She pulls open the fridge, but there is no room there, either. She is trying to figure out what to do when a man, with only a blanket thrown over his shoulder, walks out of the bathroom. She is shocked and rushes downstairs to talk to the woman from Sichuan, whom she met earlier. The Sichuan woman gives her a rough idea who her neighbours are. The two men on her floor work in restaurants. They usually leave early and return late. Xue is horrified. She has cleaned brownish stains off the toilet, which must have been left by those men. She feels so sick that she almost throws up. In Shanghai, she used to run back home to relieve herself no matter where she was because she could not do it anywhere else. Now she is cleaning a toilet for men. How can she stay here? How can Canada allow unrelated men and women to live under the same roof?

Her appetite spoiled, Xue shuts herself in the tiny room she rents and finishes some food she brought from home. Shanghai is an overcrowded city, but she still had her own space, small as it was. She might have found her work less than satisfying, but hers was a middle-level position in a company that distributed medicine and medical equipment. She routinely got a bonus, just like everyone else in the company. If she had wanted to, she could have found herself a husband and got her own place with a mortgage. This wouldn't have taken too much to achieve. She did not do those things simply because she did not find the right man. The more she reflects on her current state of affairs, the more convinced she becomes that she was right to sever all ties with George Zhang. She is also doing the right thing not to give him the money, which she borrowed from Yihai. Although Yihai is more than happy to give her the money, she intends to pay him back, sooner or later. He is not a family member, and the chance of them getting married is very slim. Still she can always count on his helping hand. Recalling how dependable he is, she has an urge to call him there and then. She takes out her calling card but remembers the landlady's instruction: she should have her own telephone if she wants to make phone calls. She feels so disheartened that she wants to cry.

There is a knock on the door. Just to be careful, she kicks her cases deeper under the bed. It is the landlady, informing her in broken Mandarin that her boyfriend has paid only a fifty-dollar deposit. She must pay her rent right away, first and last month. Xue patiently explains to the older woman that she will pay the next day after she changes her money into Canadian funds. The landlady says that she is willing to accept U.S. money. Xue tells her that she does not know the exchange rate, but the landlady says that she knows and can give Xue a better deal. Xue is sceptical and eventually she convinces the landlady that she has sufficient money to pay the rent and manages to get her out of the room.

As soon as she wakes up the next morning, Xue decides that she will move out. She hurries to the bank and opens an account. After some thought, she does not put all her money in the account, which proves to be a fatal mistake. She is worried that when Immigration Canada gets wind of her disappearance, they may search for her and, when they find her, confiscate her money. She does not dare send the money back to her parents, either, because she knows that they will be suspicious when they see so much money. She has to keep the money at hand, just in case she fails to find a job, and she needs it to survive.

Xue stands on the sidewalk, looking at the streetcars running along the rails in the middle of the street. They are longer than a bus but shorter than a train car. They are also very frequent. Streetcars are something refreshingly new to her. They must be like the tramcars of old Shanghai, Xue thinks. She inquires about the fare and is told that a ride costs two dollars and twenty-five cents, no matter how long it is. That is more than ten Chinese dollars. Better walk back. However, a short while later, she finds her legs are stiff and sore. She should have put on her walking shoes. Then she sees a reflection of her graceful figure in the window of a shop and notices the attention she attracts from people on the street, men and women alike. She realizes that the high-heeled sandals are a perfect match for her fashionable dress. It would be great if Zhengjun were with her and could drive her around in the city! He is a software engineer, drives a Japanese car, and speaks good English. He must have made it in Canada. Is there a woman in his life? The eager and solicitous attention he paid her indicates that he is attracted to her. But she is already in rough waters and should not invite more trouble. She finds a phone booth and inserts a couple of coins. The coins fall through, and the line remains silent. She stops a Chinese-looking passerby for help. He tries but does not get through, so he tells her to try another phone. "Use a Bell phone, not this kind. This is operated by a private phone company."

Xue nods at him with gratitude. She tries again at a different booth and finally gets connected to the company Zhengjun works for. There is noisy confusion in the background. Xue is still contemplating how to sound natural when a voice with a strong Cantonese accent tells her, impatiently, that Zhengjun has not come to work. Xue is disappointed. Without thinking, she dials a Shanghai number and leaves Yihai a terse message: "I am unhappy. I want to go home. Come and fetch me."

Real trouble is waiting for her when she returns to the rooming house. The landlady is sitting in a chair right at her door, blocking her way. She demands the rent be paid immediately. Xue says: "It is dingy and rowdy. I have to share the bathroom and kitchen with men. I can't stand it. I'll move out."

"For a rent as low as this, of course you share. If you want your own space, nice and quiet, you pay money. I had women tenants before. They didn't complain. We've settled on how much you pay and how long you stay. You can't move out."

Xue forces her way towards the door. The landlady realizes that Xue is not intimidated, so she backs down. "You pay the first month and you can go."

"Why should I? I've been here only two days; the fifty-dollar deposit is more than enough."

"One day or one month, they are the same. Your boyfriend booked the room for you. I turned away other tenants."

The argument becomes raucous. The Sichuan woman downstairs pokes her head out and draws back after one peek. Xue insists on fetching her luggage and leaving while the landlady firmly refuses to let her into the room. Xue steels herself and gives the older woman a push. The landlady falls off the chair, tumbling to the floor. Xue rushes into the room and starts packing. The other woman struggles to get up and goes downstairs, groaning angrily.

Xue gets her things packed and squeezes the bag of money safely into a suitcase. She is ready to go. Then a police car, lights flashing and siren sounding, appears at the front door. Xue looks down from the window in terror. Two police officers, a black man and a Caucasian woman, walk upstairs slowly and calmly, with the landlady at their heels. They stop Xue. The landlady complains in broken English, and the officers listen patiently. Then the male officer turns to Xue. He may be asking her if the landlady is telling the truth. Xue feels something is pounding in her head. She racks her brain, trying to search for English words from her memory and from the English lessons she took, but she cannot put a coherent sentence together. She knows very well that she is not making any sense. At that moment, Zhengjun appears. Xue rushes to him, asking him to explain on her behalf. The landlady also holds him tight, wanting him to testify for her. Zhengjun figures out what the problem is, and he advises that Xue pay the three-hundred-dollar rent to avoid further complications. Xue also becomes afraid that this encounter with the law may have more serious consequences if not settled right away. The only trouble is that she does not have Canadian money and her U.S. funds may arouse suspicion, giving her secret away. Zhengjun takes the landlady aside, telling her that he will go and get money from a bank to pay the rent. The landlady leaves with him, without further ado. The two police officers find this turn of events rather anticlimactic. They lecture Xue that under no circumstances should she use force; if she feels threatened, she should call 911. They also inform her that a landlady has no right to deny a tenant access to her room, no matter what. Xue nods nervously yet gratefully. She hopes that they will go away quickly so that she can get her things ready and leave this damned place. They leave the room. Xue puts her head close to the window, listening. Her heart pounds loudly. The wait is as nerve-racking as time she spent at the Vancouver airport when she was waiting for the immigration agent to stamp her landing papers. She is on edge, anticipating imminent danger. Heavy steps climb up the stairs again. This time the officers come straight to the point, asking Xue to show them her ID, passport, and immigration documents.

On her immigration form, her husband's name, George Zhang, looms large. The police officers ask her why she hasn't joined her husband since she arrived in Toronto. Does she know that her husband is looking for her all over the place?

Xue realizes that she understands every single word the officers utter. Subconsciously, she uses her fingertips to push up the sliding strap of the black silk bra she is wearing. The white policewoman waits for her reply, her stony face expressionless. Xue finds herself in the same embarrassing situation as when the visa officer at the Beijing embassy questioned her about which kind of contraceptive measures she and her husband used. She cannot evade the question, nor can she hide herself. She gets some control over herself and answers, "My husband and I got separated at the airport."

The officers state that they can take her to her husband. Xue does not respond immediately and then says, with words and gestures, that she is scared of having sex with her husband. The policewoman is obviously shocked by her reply. She does not comprehend and so follows up with another question: does she mean that she dislikes having sex with her husband? Xue lowers her head. Tears of hurt and humiliation swell up. The two officers are now really at a loss, unsure what to do next. However, they tell her, before they take off, that they are obliged to inform her husband that she has been located. Xue takes their statement as a hint that she should make a quick departure.

Zhengjun returns from the bank. Xue feels that she is about to faint and longs to lean on him. But he has not completely recovered from the shock he had, so he asks angrily: "Why did the police stop me and check my ID? You must tell me what this is all about!"

"Don't ask questions now. Take me away. I'll tell you later." Xue shakes her head, vulnerably.

Zhengjun has no choice, so he takes her back to the guesthouse where she stayed the first night. Their driver, Mr. Yang, has gone to the airport to meet more newcomers from China. Zhengjun insists on an upstairs room, but Xue gives him a gentle nudge. "The basement will be fine." Courteously Mrs. Yang shows them a room, takes the money for the night, and leaves.

Left alone with Xue in a small room, Zhengjun feels an indescribable discomfort, an apprehension that he has not experienced before. This mysterious woman is not someone he wants to deal with, nor someone whom he can handle. He may have flirted a bit, but he's never had an affair before. What if she has gang connections? If that is the case, his future in Canada could be ruined. He should get as far away from this hornet's nest as he can. The most sensible thing to do is surely to get back the money he has spent on her and leave. Also, he has to go to work tomorrow. One has to have the time and means to get romantically involved.

But things have already spun out of control.

Xue, as soft and yielding as a cloud, quietly glides into the room. Her hand is massaging her fluffy and velvety hair, and she is holding a horn comb under her arm. Her slim neck is lustrous, and her bare back smooth. Her pair of high-heeled slippers draw attention to her long and shapely legs. Under the lamplight, her body exudes sensuality. Zhengjun pants laboriously.

"Help me dry my hair at the back. I somehow can't lift my arm."

Xue issues the order while examining her reflection closely in the mirror. Fatigue of the past few days renders the fine lines along the wings of her nose more conspicuous and the bridge of her nose higher. Yihai once remarked that she could use those little vibrations of her slightly up-turned nose to express a variety of mood changes. At this moment, her unadorned face lacks some of her usual sensual charm but radiates innocent purity. In the mirror, Xue catches sight of the dumbfounded Zhengjun gawking at her. He seems hesitant, wanting but not daring to make a move. She waves at the image in the mirror. "Hurry up. My hair is still wet. If it dries, I can't style it."

Zhengjun watches her put a hand into her thick hair and give it a shake. Tiny sparkling droplets fall on his face. They are moist but not tender at all. Intuitively, he stands up and inches his closer to her. The room is small, but the distance he has to cover is huge. She shoves a hair dryer into his hand. He holds it tightly but cannot find the switch. His eyes are glued to Xue's exquisite white shoulder. Xue twirls and turns on the dryer for him. He holds it up stiffly as if on automatic pilot and mutters: "Why dry it? When you sleep with wet hair, you won't have nightmare." He is fully aware that his joke is clumsy.

"What did you say? What are you hinting at?"

"Xue, I really want to stroke your hair."

"Why? But if you want to, just do it."

His raging desire explodes. His hand becomes numb as it touches her forehead and caresses her hair. The hair dryer clanks and falls. Xue bends over and picks it up. "Be careful. It's a gift." Zhengjun stares at her, noticing that she curls up her lips. But apparently she is not annoyed. Without realizing, he slips down to his knees, wraps his arms around her sexy legs, and gasps, "Xue, I'll buy you a new one, a better one. Xue...."

Xue stops him. She feels heat travelling up her legs, a sensation she has never experienced before. Unexpectedly, she loses her balance and collapses onto the bed. Zhengjun falls on top of her.

Afterwards, Xue covers her naked body with a light cotton sheet. She does not sense anything extraordinary. It feels like a sharp sting by some kind of insect. She regrets that her first time had not been with Yihai or Zhou Bu and that she treated them with such cruelty. They followed her around loyally, but she held up her last defence and denied them sex. She then looks at Zhengjun lying beside her with mixed feelings. Zhengjun is embarrassed. He realizes that his rushed act disappointed Xue. It should not have been like this. In the beginning, he was impulsive but determined, nervous but excited; however, he had not expected that Xue was still a virgin and so he had ejaculated prematurely and hastily. He sits there now, speechless. A prolonged and heavy silence hangs in the room. Time, Eastern Standard Time, flies away. Zhengjun knows very well how important time is to him. Explanation is useless. He should leave. But perhaps there won't be a second chance for him if he runs away now. There is no hope of recovering the money he has spent. How can he ask her? He puts on his clothes and is ready to leave, though unhappily. Xue turns to face him, and the sheet around her plump buttocks also moves. "Are you going?"

"Xue, I didn't plan this. I didn't know this was your first time."

Shaking her head, she says: "It's not your fault. It's mine." She then picks up her purse, counts out a few notes, and hands them over. "That's for the money you lent me. Thanks."

"Xue, I can't take the money. You'll need it. You have just arrived and have no clue how hard it is to find work."

She grabs his hand and puts the money in it. "I won't bother you. I can take care of myself. I should have done this long ago. I was stupid. I'm grateful to you anyway. You do not know who I am, but you've helped me. You'd better take the money because I need you to do me another favour."

"Tell me and I'll do it for you, Xue."

"When I tell you, you may despise me. I have come to Canada through marriage fraud. I don't want to meet him because I don't want to give him the rest of the money. He has already got more than his fair share. Also, he wants to take advantage of me." While speaking, she takes out all the money and shows it to him.

Zhengjun has speculated about her, but he is still stunned by the fact that for the past few days she has gone around carrying so much cash. Xue continues: "Here are fourteen thousand U.S. dollars in total. I want you to put them in a bank. This money is for my parents, but I dare not send it back right now. I don't dare to put it in my bank account, either. I fear that he will report me to Immigration Canada and that the authorities will freeze my account."

Zhengjun hesitates. This is a lot of money, more than his net annual income. He takes it, but regrets it right away. "You are not worried about giving me all your money, are you?"

"Why should I worry? How many lovers do you have? Not many, I guess. I suspected that you might still be single. Judging by the first glance you threw at me, I knew you harboured some ideas."

Zhengjun turns the whole matter over several times in his head. He does not want to confide in her about his current difficulties. The very thought that he will lose her right after he got her is painful. Her curvaceous body, partially revealed, is even fairer and softer than her smooth neck. Xue is waiting for his reply, and she smiles a very delicate smile. He cannot say no to her, so he takes her money and writes her a receipt.

During the next couple of days, Xue becomes more and more agitated. Zhengjun makes a few calls but fails to show up in person. She senses that he is avoiding her. This time, she feels, is different from her previous involvements with men in Shanghai. If she had settled down with either Yihai or Zhou Bu, she would have been reconciled with her lot and been at peace. She certainly would not fool around. But Canada is different. Here she has no idea how to play the game. Actually, not knowing how to play is not the real problem since she will figure out the rules of the game eventually; what really bothers her is her own body. She often experiences tingling sensations inside her, and she longs to cling to, to lean on, to hang onto someone. Ever since she entered university, she was a desired object and was courted by men, but she has never found herself in a situation where she has no control at all, until now. She starts to hate Yihai and Zhou Bu. It is their fault that they are weak-hearted. If one of them had been bold enough, she would have been his. Then she would not have ended up here, suffering alone. She calls Yihai, who tells her that he has made up his mind during the few days when he lost touch with her. He will be happy only when he is with her. If he loses her, his life becomes meaningless. He deeply regrets that he has let her go. He then pleads with her, asking her to return and be his wife.

"What about her?" Xue asks out of habit.

"I have talked to her. As a matter of fact, she knew all along that I loved you. She has given up on me, and we are getting a divorce. I am waiting for you, Xue. I love you, Xue!"

Xue clutches the phone but does not say anything for a long time. Tears run down her face. She does not hang up but walks out of the booth as if in a trance. Yihai's words drift away with the breeze.

Xue decides to go and visit Zhengjun at the address he has given her. She cannot afford to wait another minute. She knows that when a man enters a woman's body, he does not necessarily pledge himself, just as a woman is not giving the man any promise when she gives herself to him. Sexual intimacy is not an unbreakable link that ties a man and a woman together, not in Canada or elsewhere.

She begins to sense that her survival may be in jeopardy. After that night, she found herself a place and settled down, but her money is running out. Now she is fully aware that the money she entrusted to Zhengjun was not just pennies. She also found out that the place he works at is not a computer company but a factory that manufactures car seats. She becomes increasingly frightened by these ominous developments.

Zhengjun's address leads Xue to a three-storey detached house. She stands in front of the building, sizing it up for a long while. She doesn't have the courage to face the possibility that the address he has given her may turn out to be a lie, too. Now she knows that many independent immigrants are cannier and more skilled liars than she could ever be.

A middle-aged Chinese man answers the door. Even before she finishes explaining why she is here, he points at a side door. There is no doorbell on the side door. She knocks timidly; no one answers. She pushes open the door and finds a flight of stairs leading to the basement. She goes down the stairs, calling out Zhengjun's name.

A woman, heavy with pregnancy, appears, and a boy of eight or nine trails after her. "You are here to see Zhengjun. Please wait. He is in the kitchen."

The boy runs away to fetch his father while Xue steals a few glances at the woman. She is thirty-something, withered and weary-looking, in a very loose outfit, but apparently extremely content. Xue feels hot and blushes. Fortunately, the light is dim so that she can hide her embarrassment. Another married man with children! Xue feels sorry for herself, once again rushing into a relationship so heedlessly. What a mess she has gotten herself into!

Zhengjun comes out and seems composed when he sees Xue. He doesn't find fault with her but leads her to a maple tree outside the building where he begins to tell her what he has lived through. George Zhang found him and came to ask about her. He even followed Zhengjun, warning him not to get involved and threatening that if he did, he might endanger himself and everyone else concerned. Zhengjun tells Xue that George Zhang has lost his mind and urges her to use extra caution.

Then he gives her back all her money. He has not put it into his account. His wife takes care of their money, and she knows he couldn't get hold of so much money all of a sudden. With such a big amount of money in his care, he is extremely worried. Even when he goes to work, he is afraid something awful may happen. Xue nods and doesn't even count the money because she knows that Zhengjun dare not embezzle it. She smiles, her elegant but stiff neck turning a tiny bit. Then she turns, walking away in the direction from which she came. Zhengjun fixes his eyes on her disappearing figure, feeling self-pity and relief all at once.

That day at dusk, a robbery and killing takes place on a lawn not far from the York University campus. A Chinese woman is stabbed to death and robbed of all the money she has on her. The case shocks the local Chinese community. Some of the media speculate that it is a racially motived hate crime. The police plead with the public for eyewitnesses and information.

But the case grows cold, and the killer is still out there. The victim's name, as you have probably guessed, is Yang Xue.

Translated by H. Laura Wu and Cory Davies.

"An Elegant but Stiff Neck" originally appeared in The Sojourners: Stories by Chinese-Canadian Writers *in 2004.*

[1]Immigrants to Canada generally fall into three groups: 1) Investors, entrepreneurs, and self-employed people; 2) Skilled workers and professionals, often referred to by the Chinese as independent immigrants; 3) Family members and relatives sponsored by Canadian citizens or immigrants. Most new immigrants from China are young professionals in the technology sector. They are referred to, by the Chinese, as *"jishu yimin"* or "immigrants in the technical category."
[2]An ear-pick is a small gadget that the Chinese use to pick ear wax.

The Kilt and Clover

XIAOWEN ZENG

IT BEGAN AS A SOFT, gentle mist, as if someone had carelessly scattered a handful of droplets from the sky. Soon, however, rain moved in, quietly covering my face with what felt like a cold, wet layer of loneliness and despair.

Yet, I knew, water also brings life. The Welland Canal crosses St. Catharines, drawing water from Lake Erie on the south and emptying into Lake Ontario on the north. Day and night, its traffic brings life to the small city.

I watched as a huge steel vessel prepared to set sail on the canal. Its hull was reddish brown and its cabin snowy white. A Canadian flag flew on the mast, a red maple leaf in bold relief against the white background. On the deck, several sailors in bright orange raincoats were busy doing their chores. Seeing the colours in the grey misty rain comforted me, and I almost felt cheerful.

In the two years since I had landed in Toronto, I had failed to find a stable job. I had taught psychology back in China, but I could not work as a psychologist in Canada because my spoken English was not good enough. So I worked in a food-processing factory earning a measly eight dollars an hour. My mother would often email me, telling me that they were in urgent need of money and I should not sit idly by while they were struggling. While she never studied psychology, my mom certainly knew my soft spot and was always ready to poke at it.

For months, I had been searching high and low for a better paying job. One day I found an online ad that said a newly opened retirement home in St. Catharines was hiring cleaning staff. It paid fifteen dollars an hour, nearly twice my current wage. A week after I applied, I went for an interview and they hired me on the spot.

Before I left Toronto, fellow workers at the factory told me, "You will die of loneliness in St. Catharines!"

Can loneliness really kill? Perhaps it could get to some, but not me. I have never been in the limelight. Maybe social butterflies cannot stand being left alone, but I have been alone ever since I came into this world. When I weigh loneliness against survival, survival always wins.

I watched the vessel sailing away on the canal, heading for Lake Erie. This was just another day in its life. Some came ashore, while others boarded and sailed away; it didn't matter whether it was foggy and raining or if it was fine and sunny.

I moved into an old apartment building in downtown St. Catharines. The building was as plain as a matchbox. Not even the fog and rain could cover up its shabbiness. The corridors were dim and gloomy. There were announcements on the wall about fumigating for cockroaches.

My apartment was small and empty. Before I was able to buy a bed, I had to put my bedding on the carpet. Lying down, I felt an icy stiffness. Light from the street poured unhindered through the window, throwing some strange images on the pallid walls. I earnestly wished for tomorrow to arrive.

The next day I reported to work at the retirement home. In the corridor, I ran across a teenage girl, a blonde with clear blue eyes. She wore a pink tank top and a pink mini skirt. She also had two pink pompoms. A walking Barbie doll dressed as a cheerleader. Just like in a film, the surroundings seemed to fade into a pale background as if to set off her dazzling beauty.

"Do you happen to know where the housekeeping office is?" I asked.

"The last room at the south end, on the first floor." The girl smiled, revealing a mouthful of neat white teeth, enviably perfect.

"Thank you!"

"*Buyong xie* (You are welcome)!" Unexpectedly, she answered in Chinese.

I was pleasantly surprised. "You can speak Chinese?!"

The girl giggled and switched to English. "I learned a couple of phrases from my Chinese classmates. Are you new here?"

I nodded. "I moved to St. Catharines yesterday."

"I hope you'll love St. Catharines." Her voice was so sweet that it made St. Catharines sound like some holiday destination on a Caribbean island, a paradise on earth.

"Do you work here, too?"

"No, I'm a volunteer. I read newspapers to the residents. I'm Angela," she smiled and extended her hand. "If you have any questions later on, just ask me. Right now I have to leave for my cheerleader practice at school."

Angela waved goodbye and headed out the door. I stared at her retreating back and thought that the phrase "Miss Sunshine" was most likely invented for a girl like her.

The housekeeping manager, a heavyset middle-aged woman of African descent, gave me a uniform, a set of cleaning tools, and detergents. Fully equipped, I began to work.

I met Angela in the staff lounge often, and I gradually got to know her. She was on a diet and usually had only a yogurt and an apple for lunch. She wanted to become a model so gaining weight would mean the end of her chosen career.

"You do volunteer work here. That's very noble," I told her.

"Not really, lots of my classmates volunteer. And helping others is very rewarding, too."

"The old people here must love you."

Angela nodded in agreement and giggled. "They say I have a superstar's voice." Then she asked about my work here.

"It's not bad. But I can only work five days a week, and I make just enough to get by. My family needs money, so I would like to find some odd jobs on the side."

"You can't babysit because you don't have the experience. But you can clean, can't you?"

"Of course!"

"My cousin Sean is looking for a cleaning lady, I think. I'll ask him," Angela said.

A week later, Angela, quite excited, told me, "My cousin wants you to do some cleaning at his place. A bit of lawn mowing and gardening, too."

"Great! Thank you so much."

Angela shrugged, saying, "Don't be too excited! You should know my cousin is a bit weird. He's over forty and single. But you won't see him that often. He is a sailor on The Miller. When he's on the ship, he'll be away for months at a time."

A sailor steering a ship on the clear water, under the blue sky. The image set me dreaming. I recalled the huge vessel in red and white on the canal, and the sailors in their bright orange raincoats. Does Sean have an orange raincoat, too? I wondered.

The early summer sun had passionate lips. All the grasses and leaves it kissed grew fat and green, no matter how dull and wilted they had been.

At ten o'clock sharp on a Saturday morning, the time Angela had arranged for me, I was at Sean's door in Port Dalhousie. His was a three-storey house of grey brick. The front garden had two trees: a red maple and a white lilac. There were flowers and plants under the trees, but the garden was not properly cared for.

Sean was far from the image of a sailor that I had been imagining. He was not tall and slim, with blue eyes and blond hair. Rather, he had brown hair and brown eyes. The arms sticking out of his blue-grey T-shirt were not really sinewy. His skin was not tanned a radiant bronze; it was just dark because of

his olive complexion. For whatever reason, he avoided looking squarely into my eyes. His expression was hard to read, a
mixture of humility and shyness.

Right away I smelled the loneliness inside him. Perhaps
loneliness transcended borders and cultures.

"What's your name?" he asked

"Grace."

"Your Chinese name, please."

"Lei."

"Lei..." Sean tried hard to imitate my pronunciation.

"It's not easy to say, so I don't mind you using my English
name."

"I'll learn to say it properly." Sean became quite serious.
"When you're here, you're trying your best to adapt. We Canadians should do the same; at least we should learn how to
say your name."

Sean showed me the house: a living room, a study, a kitchen,
a powder room, and a laundry room on the first floor. And
right there, hanging on the laundry room door, was indeed an
orange raincoat! I wondered if this was a sign that Sean might
bring some colour to the dull routine of my life,

There were three tall bookshelves in the study, all reaching
the ceiling, and all laden with books. On the second floor I
noticed a guest room and a bathroom. Sean pointed at the door
of a third room. "That's my bedroom," he said. "You don't
need to clean it. I'll lock it up when I'm away."

I nodded. He is the boss, and I'm the hired help. I just follow
orders.

The third floor, the attic, was also full of books. Sean explained, "Wherever I go, I'll buy a book or two, so my place
has become something like a second-hand bookstore."

Sean and I agreed that I'd come every Saturday to clean the
house, mow the lawn, and take care of the garden. He'd pay
me eighty dollars a week. He would leave a key underneath
the mat outside the front door so that I could unlock the door.

"Is it safe?" I was a bit worried.

Sean shrugged it off. "There hasn't been a single case of breaking and entering in Port Dalhousie for over ten years. Anyway, who reads books in this age of the internet?"

"I enjoy holding an actual book in my hand," I said. "Somehow, it puts me at ease."

Sean looked directly at me for the first time and said, "There aren't that many people like you around."

In a mere two weeks, I transformed Sean's front yard into a real garden. The newly planted forget-me-nots, morning glories, impatiens, and daisies swung gracefully and charmingly, as if they believed the summer sun were their lover.

One day a blonde woman passed by as I tended the garden. She pointed at the golden daisies. "Such lovely flowers!" The praise sounded exaggerated, disingenuous.

The woman reminded me of Angela, even though she was at least twenty years older. She wore a bright red silk top that barely covered her breasts, which stuck out straight and upright, , as if they were not affected by gravity. Implants, undoubtedly. Her fingers and toes were painted a gaudy scarlet.

"Thanks," I replied.

"I haven't seen you before. You must have moved in recently." I nodded.

"Sean should've had a woman a long time ago."

"I am not Sean's woman," I immediately told her.

Her blue eyes swept over me daringly, then she shook her head and said, "No, you aren't his type."

I lowered my head and continued weeding. I was very much accustomed to the arrogant and condescending air put on by beautiful women. Silence always seemed the best way to deal with them. The woman sighed pityingly and left. I was very much accustomed to pity, too. But I never paid any heed to it.

The following Saturday, when I arrived at Sean's place, he was sitting in a wicker chair in the front garden, waiting for me. At his feet was a brand new lawn mower. "I just bought a new mower. Doing the lawn will be easier for you." For a brief moment our eyes locked.

"The old one still has some life left."

"I've been promoted to first mate on The Miller!" he said.

"Congratulations! Your family must be pride of you!"

He smiled and corrected me: "It's 'proud,' not 'pride.'"

I was embarrassed and said in a very low voice, "My English is really poor."

"No, no." Sean seemed genuinely dismayed to have hurt my feelings and hurriedly added, "Your English is not bad. If you keep practising, you'll improve. If I spoke Chinese, I am afraid I'd bite off my own tongue."

I gave him a quick glance, grateful for his comforting words.

"I'd like to give you a raise, to one hundred dollars a week," Sean continued.

"But I am doing the same work."

"You're doing a terrific job. My neighbours have started complimenting me on my beautiful garden. Before they'd just complain about how unkempt it was, saying it was dragging down the property values in the entire neighbourhood."

"You're away most of the time; of course you don't have the time to take care of your garden."

"Thank you for your kindness." And then he pointed at a plant in the garden bed, full of joy. "Look what I found. There are quite a few clovers. I love clovers, always have!"

Clover is a darker green than the other leaves and grasses. There are deep green patterns on the leaves. The flowers are purple and small, usually the size of a fingernail. They look reserved and timid to me.

"I found a poem about the clover online. Let me print it out for you." Sean rushed back to his study. A few minutes later, he handed me a piece of paper with the poem on it. It was called "Four-Leaf Clovers:

I know a place where the sun is like gold,

And the cherry blooms burst with snow,
And down underneath is the loveliest nook,
Where the four-leaf clovers grow.
One leaf is for HOPE, and one is for FAITH,
And one is for LOVE, you know,
And GOD put another in for LUCK—
If you search, you will find where they grow.
But you must have HOPE, and you must have FAITH.
You must LOVE and be strong—and so—
If you work, if you wait, you will find the place
Where the four-leaf clovers grow.[1]

The new mower was terrific and I finished my work an hour earlier than usual. Before I left, Sean gave me two books from C.S. Lewis' *The Chronicles of Narnia* series: *The Lion, the Witch and the Wardrobe* and *Prince Caspian: The Return to Narnia*.

"C.S. Lewis' books are easy to read," Sean said. "I hope you like them."

I left Sean and his place, holding the books in my hand. My palms felt much warmer than they used to. The two books were like magic charms, linking Sean's world to mine.

Winter rushed in uninvited and unexpectedly. After one or two cold snaps in early December, the Welland Canal froze over. All ships, big and small, stood docked at the Port Dalhousie piers. Without tourists' presence and sailors' laughter, the port became deserted and silent.

Christmas Eve happened to be my cleaning day at Sean's. I called him to ask if he wanted to cancel it. He asked me to come.

When I walked into his house, Sean was sitting beside the fireplace flipping through a photo album. "It's very cold. Do you want to warm up a bit first?" he asked.

The fire burned briskly, radiating an enticing warmth that I found hard to resist. I hesitated for just an instant and then declined with a shake of my head.

When I finished working, Sean asked me, "Do you have any plans for tonight?"

Again, I shook my head.

"I've decided not to join my family for Christmas. I want to have a quiet evening," Sean said.

Isn't his life too quiet? I thought. "What about your parents?" I asked. "Won't they be disappointed?"

He snorted. "My parents have been divorced for ten years. They couldn't care less. Especially my mother."

I was shocked by his bitterness. "Don't say things like that."

"In her eyes, I will always be a loser, a pathetic drowning dog...."

"How can that be?"

"She wanted me to go to university to become a lawyer or a doctor, just like my older brother and sister, but I never enjoyed school, even when I was a little kid. I skipped classes all the time...."

"But you love reading. You have so many books!"

"But they're all 'useless' books."

"I thought Canadians didn't place as much weight on education as we Chinese."

"Education and social status go hand in hand, and no one in the world thinks lightly of social status," he replied with a grim look on his face.

I could not reply.

Fortunately, Sean changed the topic. "Can you cook Chinese food?"

"Sure."

"How about," he suggested timidly, "we cook dinner together? I've never had Chinese food on Christmas Eve."

"No problem."

"Can you make sweet-and-sour chicken?" he asked with eager expectation.

I started to laugh. "I've never made that dish. Sweet-and-sour chicken is American Chinese food; it's not authentic."

"Then make whatever you're good at. Give me a list, and I'll do the shopping." Sean gave the clock on the wall a quick look. "I hope the supermarket is still open."

An hour later, I was busy deep-frying and stir-frying. Sean fussed about, but he was of little help. I made a vegetable soup and four dishes: shrimp and mango salad, chicken braised in Coke sauce, snow peas with minced garlic, and *Gong Bao* fish filet with hot peppers and peanuts.

Sean and I sat down at the dining room table facing each other. He opened an aged French red wine and poured us each a glass. It swirled quietly, a suggestive scarlet red. "It's snowing," he whispered as he raised his glass.

I turned and saw snowflakes dancing among the trees. Although the TV weatherman predicted no snow for today, we were having a white Christmas after all.

Sean loved my dishes. He poured the *Gong Bao* fish sauce on his rice and finished the last mouthful. We talked, on and off, about our respective families. Despite my faulty English, I managed to tell my story.

I came from a very ordinary family. My father was the taciturn type, and my mother was the real head of the household. My mother always said that the greatest achievement of her life was giving birth to two children, a daughter and a son. But her greatest disappointment was giving birth to a homely girl. I was that homely girl. To use my younger brother Yang's words, I would have scared the audience if I were an actress. I have long and narrow eyes, a low and flat nose, and thick lips—not a single feature meet the conventional Chinese idea of beauty.

My mom asserted repeatedly that Yang and I should have had a "face swap." It was a total waste for a boy to have a pretty face. But heaven did not attend to my mom's bid. Consequently, both my brother and I had trouble: Yang was spoiled by women who found him attractive, and he dumped girlfriends so frequently that he was still single when he was thirty. As for me, no man noticed me even when I was eighteen, and at thirty, I was also unspoken for.

When I graduated from university, I was given a teaching job at Donghai College. Because my mom was in poor health, I lived at home and did all the household chores. My parents had a two-bedroom apartment. They lived in one bedroom, and I had the other. Yang had to sleep in the living room. Later on, Yang carelessly got his girlfriend of the day pregnant, so he had to marry her. I gave up my room to them and moved into a dorm room for young and single faculty members at my school.

I had done nothing spectacular in my career or in my personal life. There is an old saying: "When transplanted, a tree will die but a human will flourish." Perhaps if I moved to a different country, I might have some hope. So I immigrated to Canada. But I have since learned that the flourishing part of the transplanting process can take years.

Yang was laid off recently, and then my mom called me asking for money. I had to send back all the money I had saved over the past six months, and I had to start from scratch once again. "When I save money, I save one dollar at a time," I explained. "But, when I send money back home, I send by the hundred."

"But you aren't obliged to do it," Sean said.

"In every family, there is one child who has to sacrifice. Also, I owe my mom. She gave me life and raised me, and no matter what I have a duty to her, and to my family."

"You don't owe anybody anything. When she chose to bring you into this world and bring you up, she should not have expected you to pay her back."

"But how could I not repay her?"

"You feel guilty, don't you? And your family takes advantage of your guilt!"

"Sean, this is too complicated. I … I am different from you."

"You are wrong again. You and I are the same. You must get rid of your guilt, and then you'll be at ease and can relax."

"It's not that easy. I can't do it. You see, I escaped to Canada, but I am still under my mother's thumb."

"Did you come to Canada just to be a cleaning lady?"

I lowered my head and said, "No, actually I wanted to go to school."

After dinner, Sean asked me to sit by the fireplace, and this time I accepted his invitation.

"You have really sexy lips!" he said.

This was the first time in my life that someone praised my lips. I could not believe my ears. Back in China I had heard many disheartening comments about my looks. Yet, now I was being admired. It was true that there was no accounting for taste and that "if you lose on the swings, you may win on the roundabouts."

"I once saw a Japanese supermodel, and she looked just like you."

"She is really lucky if she can make it with looks like mine!" I laughed.

Sean chuckled, squinting at me. "I like your sense of humour." Then he reached out and embraced me. When his lips looked for mine, I, out of character, met them willingly. If they were sexy, why not put them to good use? Like two snowflakes falling into the fireplace, my lips quickly melted in his kiss. On this snowy, despondent Christmas Eve, I felt my hunger for loving caresses rise up from the very marrow of my bones.

Sean climbed up the stairs, leading me by the hand. My hands were trembling. I saw a smear of dim light before me, a dimness that was full of evocation and temptation.... I blamed that bottle of old French wine for whatever was about to happen .

Sean did not turn on the light. He sat me down, gently, on the bed. Soon I felt like a small sailboat gently bobbing on a lake. His caresses were tender, like warm breezes and gentle raindrops He steered me through a winding passage between soaring mountains and rugged cliffs. And, finally, he brought me to rough water and rode me to the crest of a huge powerful wave. The scream that came up from deep inside me could have been heard over the sound of crashing ocean surf.... When the waves subsided into calm ripples, I heard his laboured breathing. Then the ripples calmed down, the water became as tranquil as the surface of a mirror, and everything fell into a peaceful silence.

Waking up the next morning, I found myself on the bed in the guest room. Sean did not take me to his bedroom, the room that was always locked. I put on my clothes and went downstairs. Sean was making coffee in the kitchen. We said good morning to each other rather awkwardly. He did not look at me; his eyes were fixed on the coffee maker.

I said goodbye quietly.

He turned and asked, "Would you like to have some coffee before you go?"

I shook my head and left.

It was unexpectedly cold outside. The streets were so quiet that I could almost hear the snowflakes fall. After a night of revelry, tiny St. Catharines was sound asleep. But Sean's kisses were still on my lips, burning.

To me, a man was a tome filled with mysterious writings. Back in China, relatives and colleagues had tried to match me up a couple of times, mostly with men who studied science or applied science. However, in the game of love, I was like a poor writer: I often started the story, and then it went nowhere. Only once did the courtship proceed beyond the first date. The man was a chemist with a lanky figure. Even though I was over thirty, I was still very green, and I did not know how to flirt and be coy. I also tried my best to keep my feelings of being a complete failure buried deep inside. So when he showed just a tiny bit affection, I gave myself up to him eagerly. Soon afterwards, he was informed that his mother had cancer. Being an extremely dutiful son, he decided to return to his hometown in Shanxi to care for her. So he did not turn out to be my Mr. Right. He did not plead for my hand in marriage, and I did not pledge my eternal love for him. Our romantic interlude ended quickly.

"Sean ... Sean...." I practised saying his name out loud while driving home. Will he be the protagonist's name in a story that will become my new life?

On New Year's Eve, Angela disappeared. She didn't come home after work, and when her parents did not see her the next morning, they called the police. Sean and I searched for her everywhere, but could not find her. How could "Miss Sunshine" evaporate like a droplet of water?

"She must have run away and didn't want to tell us why," Sean whispered repeatedly.

Angela's absence from the staff lounge robbed it of the sweet breath of youth, and the room was left with a stale, sour odour. My heart felt like a puppet controlled by numerous invisible but pitiless strings: it hurt.

The next Saturday, I went to Sean's place to do the cleaning as usual. He wasn't there. He returned when I was about to leave. He gave me a gentle kiss and asked, "How about a walk along the canal?" A stroll along the canal in the coldest days of the winter? This was perhaps Sean's idea of romance.

The canal had turned from the clear blue water of the fall into a wintery grey ice that merged into the grey, overcast sky. There was literally no one around, just a chilly wind blowing that accompanied us as we walked. I shivered. Sean held out a hand and pulled me closer.

"Winter is the worst season of the year," he said. "I can't sail and have to stay home. It bores me to death. Married sailors can stay at home with their wives and children. Single ones like me have to tough it out."

"But ... why don't you marry?" I could not help but blurt out the question. I was invading his privacy, but I felt compelled to ask, even if it offended him. I didn't want to admit to myself that his answer to the question was very important.

"I...." Sean spoke haltingly. "No woman would be willing to wait for me. I am away for so many months."

"But many of your colleagues are married." I didn't want to give up.

Sean let go of my shoulder and replied with some awkwardness: "Probably my damn personality is to blame."

"There's nothing wrong with your personality," I said lightly.

"When you're married, you have to deal with the endless little things in life. I'm afraid I'm not cut out for it."

"Perhaps those little things are not as hard to handle as you think."

"Let's not talk about this," he said with a sigh.

I fell silent. Perhaps like many men and women in this world, he and I were like two porcupines in winter time: they want to cuddle up against each other, but at the same time they are afraid of being hurt by the quills. Sean and I were two porcupines born and raised on opposite sides of the globe, and this made things even more difficult.

That evening, Sean invited me to a restaurant. On the walls, among the usual pub décor, were a dozen tartan kilts in bright red, dark green, and greyish-blue. A white tag bearing a girl's name was attached to each of the kilts.

A polite middle-aged man greeted us. When he recognized Sean, he smiled and said, "Good evening, Sean!"

"Evening, my old buddy!" Sean introduced us: "This is Lei and this is Jim. He's the manager here."

"Welcome!" Jim cupped my hand with his and placed a kiss on the back, very much the gentleman. Then he turned to Sean and asked, "The usual place?"

Sean nodded and Jim led us to a corner booth with padded seats.

"Why the kilts on the wall?" I asked out of curiosity.

"Those are the kilts of our former waitresses. When they left, they gave us their kilts as a souvenir."

What a great idea to use the kilts as markers of the past! This restaurant certainly was unique. Sean's cell rang, and for some reason he walked outside to answer it. Did he do it out of politeness, or did he have something to hide? Through the window, I could see him shivering in the cold wind.

Jim asked me what I'd like to drink. I answered, "A cup of English tea, but I don't know what Sean wants."

"Rum. For years he has been drinking nothing but rum here."

"Do you know him well?"

"Of course. His ex worked here for three years."

I looked at Jim, shocked by what he had said.

"That was already more than twenty years ago," he added. "Time sure does fly! It was here that Sean got to know Sharon. What a shame their marriage didn't last. See, Sharon's kilt is right there, behind you."

I turned and saw a bright red kilt with black checks. A small white cloth tag was affixed to it by two tiny clips in the shape of a clover. The name on the tag was Sharon. I recalled Sean's expression of happiness when he saw the clovers in his garden. *Was that just a coincidence?* I wondered. I also noticed a couple of photos beside the kilt. "Is Sharon in those pictures?" I asked.

"This one." Jim pointed at one picture over our table.

I suddenly felt Sharon's presence! In that picture were two waitresses, one brunette and one blonde. They stood in front of the restaurant holding a huge burger, laughing innocently yet provocatively. All of a sudden I recognized the waitress wearing the red kilt with black checks. She was the blonde woman who had chatted with me in Sean's garden the other day.

I pointed at the blonde and asked, "Is this Sharon?"

Jim nodded. "You got it."

"She's beautiful."

"It's very easy for a pretty woman to make a man lose his head, but beauty is not the fountain of happiness." Jim excused himself and went to fetch my order.

Sean apparently came to this restaurant often. But why would he bring me here? Why would we sit beneath Sharon's photo where, with a mere lift of head, we could see her kilt? I felt as if Sean had locked me in the dark cellar of his memory. It left me confused and suffocated.

Sean returned to his seat, his brows knitted tightly.

"Something bothering you?" I asked.

"My mom called. She gave me another lecture, complained that I'm not living a so-called 'normal' life."

Our dinner went on in silence. I wanted to comfort him, but I wasn't good at expressing myself in English. I also wanted to talk about Sharon, but I was afraid of upsetting him.

That night Sean and I lay in bed in the guest room. We were in complete darkness, and lost in thought, as if we were two deep ponds of still water, worlds apart. The poem about the clover lingered in my memory: "One leaf is for HOPE, and one is for FAITH, and one is for LOVE." How I longed for an evergreen leaf of love!

Spring arrived, reluctantly. Flowers and plants in Sean's garden began to appear in cheerful colours. Sean set out on his voyages and was seldom at home. I anxiously waited for his call, but at the same time I was trying my best to smother my hopes. I suddenly felt very lonely. I realized that if you cherish hope, you start to understand where loneliness comes from.

Sean called me on Victoria Day and told me that he was back in St. Catharines. He also invited me to go to the Lakeside Park with him. I had not seen him for two or three months, and he seemed to have changed, but I couldn't pinpoint what the changes were. He seemed to be a familiar stranger to me, always and forever.

We stopped at the Lakeside Park Carousel. Sean told me that there were sixty-eight animals in total on the carousel. They were antiques made in New York over a hundred years ago. The carousel was bought by some Canadians who brought it here. People had taken good care of it, maintaining and painting it regularly and so it was always bright and colourful.

"Let's take a ride," he suggested.

I was somewhat hesitant. "But the carousel is for small kids."

"Look around. Lots of grown-ups are riding it. Besides, it's only five cents. It's the cheapest entertainment you can find in Canada!"

I was persuaded. He purchased the tickets and held my hand. We jumped onto the carousel.

"What colour do you like?" he asked mischievously.

"Bright ones," I replied

He helped me onto a light blue horse. "This colour is a perfect match for you!"

A little boy, seven or eight years old, walked up to Sean and asked, "Could you put me on a horse?" The boy had curly hair and a lovely face with fat cheeks, like Cupid in a painting.

Sean smiled, and his eyes narrowed into slits. "Of course! But you cannot ride beside this lady," he pointed at me and continued, "because she's mine."

The boy nodded his agreement. Sean put him on a red horse. "This one runs so fast!"

"You're a liar. All the horses run the same—all fast!"

They both burst into loud laughter. I saw an expression of fatherly affection in Sean's eyes that I had never seen before. Afterwards he climbed onto a brown horse beside mine. The carousel began to turn, and children started to laugh. The carousel turned round and round slowly, as if it meant to coax us into a daydream. Blue sky, the clear lake, and Sean's smiling face revolved before my eyes. When he laughed, he was almost handsome.

"Even when I was a kid, I believed that riding the carousel was romantic," Sean said.

"Thank you!"

"For what?"

"For sharing a romantic experience with me."

Sean gave my hand a gentle pat. "Even the best things in the world become meaningless if you don't share them with someone."

The next Saturday at Sean's place, I found a pile of wrinkled shirts thrown on the counter in the laundry room. So after the cleaning, I took out the iron and ironing board and began to iron Sean's shirts. The shirts had been washed, but the smell of Sean still wafted out amidst the steam.

You get a very special sensation when you iron a man's shirts, I thought.

Sean came back. He stood at the laundry room door and looked at me with such a startled expression. His eyes spoke not only of surprise but also fear, the fear of an intruder. He stuttered, "You ... you aren't supposed to do this."

"I just wanted to help out."

He looked awkward and displeased. "I'm not used to this kind of help."

He and I stared at each other, silently, for almost a minute. What is he not used to? A real woman or a real relationship? I hurriedly put the iron and board away and left. No kisses.

A woman ironing his shirts in wafting hot steam and with apparent enthusiasm: the image frightened Sean. *Intimacy could be very threatening,* I thought.

For a couple of days a strong wind and high waves ravaged Lake Ontario. Sean and the sailors piloted The Miller, entering the lake from the canal. They spotted a body floating in the water. Police were called in. A DNA test confirmed that it was Angela's body.

Immediately the discovery became the top news story in all forms of media in St. Catharines. I saw a picture of Angela's remains on TV. I was so terrified that my hair stood on end. I could not imagine that the body I had seen on the television was Angela's. Angela, as pretty and perfect as a Barbie doll.

A news reporter interviewed Sean. He looked dead tired. His voice was hoarse, and he broke into tears. He uttered one sentence: "My heart is completely broken."

The next day the police confirmed that Angela had been murdered. St. Catharines was shrouded in fear and sadness. Many residents did not dare to walk their dogs in the parks, fearing that the killer might be hiding in the bushes or woods.

I called Sean several times, but he never answered. I guessed he turned off his cell. Three days later, he finally returned my call. He told me that he had planned to ask for a leave, but since the second mate on the ship had fallen ill, he had to go back to work. He was on his way to Montreal.

A week later, I read in a local newspaper that The Miller had had an accident and was stranded in a narrow section of the St. Lawrence. That accident cost the shipping company tremendously. Even though Sean was not at the helm, as the first mate, he should have kept a closer watch over the steersman. So he was demoted to the rank of an ordinary sailor.

When I went to Sean's place the following week on my regular cleaning day, he wasn't there. Another week went by, and again he wasn't there. But this time I found a note and one hundred dollars on the dining table in the kitchen. His note had two short sentences:

Dear Lei,

    For personal reasons, I've decided to no longer make use of your services. Thank you for your help and I wish you good luck!

    Sean

For a moment, I went completely blank. With a mere note, no regret and no apology, he had shut me out of his life. I gave the entire house, except that locked bedroom, a thorough cleaning. I polished every piece of the silverware sparkling clean even though that was not in my job description. The last thing I did that day was water the flowers and the lawn. When I saw they were thriving under the sun, I left, feeling good about my work.

Later on, I made a detour and drove by Sean's house a couple of times, hoping to see him or to catch a glimpse of him sitting under the tree. But what I saw instead was the garden taken over by weeds.

Eventually I ran into Sean in front of The Kilt and Clover. He was in the middle of a fistfight with a blond man. The man had hit Sean over the head with a baseball bat on the head, and Sean was bleeding. But then Sean somehow twisted his opponent's arm, almost to the point of breaking it.

"Stop it!" I pleaded. They just ignored me.

Jim was there and he called 911. Police officers rushed over and took both men away. Jim watched the police cruiser driving away and sighed, "Oh, those two!"

"Why did they fight?" I asked.

"That man with blond hair, Fred, used to be Sean's best friend. Until Sean dropped by Fred's apartment one day and caught him and Sharon, Sean's ex wife, in bed."

"Oh my god!" I cried out, my voice hoarse.

"Then Sharon divorced Sean and married Fred. So, Sharon and Fred have always been an open wound in Sean's heart."

"When did this happen?'

"Some eighteen or nineteen years ago."

"But why can't Sean let it go?"

"Well," Jim sighed again, "many men push themselves into a corner and refuse to leave."

At midnight, Sean called me from the police station, asking me to bail him out. I agreed. I paid the five-hundred-dollar bail and Sean became a free man. No hugs, no kisses, and no grateful tears. We left the station, as if nothing out of the ordinary had taken place.

"Sorry to have bothered you," he murmured.

"No big deal. I just hope this won't happen again."

Sean fell silent. *He had never and would never make me any promises,* I thought.

"I'll write you a cheque for the five hundred dollars tomorrow," he said, changing the topic.

I drove him to his place and stopped the car at the gate. I stared squarely ahead, not wanting him to see the expectations in my eyes. He did not get out of the car right away; instead he gave my right hand, which was gripping the wheel tightly, a light pat and said, "Sorry."

"No need to say you're sorry," I replied, on the point of bursting into tears.

"You know I'm a loser...."

"But you don't need to be a loser. We can change our own fate, you told me so."

"Yes, and I wish so hard that I could have...." He paused and then climbed out of the car.

I turned my head and watched his back as he walked away. I noticed he now had a slight stoop. When had that happened?

Sean's heart and mine had tried to reach out for one another but we had failed.

Another week went by. Another TV news report shocked the entire city: the police had broken open the case of Angela's murder, and the murderer was Fred! Actually it was Sean's fight with Fred that provided the detectives with the crucial clue. When they detained the two men, the arresting officer happened to notice a scar in the shape of a crescent on Fred's arm when they took his prints. Out of curiosity, the officer asked Fred how he got it, and Fred tried to dodge the question, which piqued the officer's interest. Tests proved that the scar was a perfect match of Angela's teeth; she must have bitten him when he assaulted her.

St. Catharines' angry residents followed Angela's murder case closely. One month later, the final piece of the puzzle came out.

Fred had an accomplice: Sharon, Sean's ex-wife!

It seemed that after their marriage, Fred kept complaining that Sharon was not a virgin. Sharon was so afraid Fred would dump her that she promised to find virgins to satisfy his perverse need. Sharon was a sales person, and she had plenty of opportunities to meet teenage girls. So she befriended them intentionally and threw parties for them at her place. At those parties, she would offer the teenage girls alcoholic drinks, show them adult films, and then give them to Fred, who would then rape them. Fred did this three times. The poor girls thought that they had gotten drunk and that that they had somehow consented to sex with Fred. They also believed that they didn't have sufficient evidence to have Fred and Sharon charged. Consequently, they could do nothing but silently bear the shame and humiliation.

Fred had at some point set his eyes on Angela. At first Sharon hesitated. After all, Angela was Sean's cousin. But she gave in when Fred threatened her with divorce. So she offered to help Angela fix her dress for her graduation ceremony. She picked Angela up at the retirement home when Angela finished her shift. From there, Sharon drove Angela directly to her place under the pretext that Angela could try on the dress.

Sharon put sleeping pills in Angela's soft drink, and the girl quickly passed out. However, as Fred was raping Angela, she awoke and put up a tenacious fight. She screamed loudly and managed to bite him on the arm. She shouted that she would call the police. Fred was enraged and, with Sharon's assistance, suffocated Angela with a pillow. Then they put her body in a sleeping bag and threw it into Lake Ontario in the darkness of night.

I covered my face with my hands and started to cry. The beautiful blonde girl who had aspired to be a model, "Miss Sunshine," who had always sincere and innocent smiles for everyone, had been brutally killed.

On numerous subsequent nights, I tried repeatedly to imagine how Sean felt, speculating about how he felt about the cruel fact that Sharon had killed his own cousin.

The door and windows of Sean's house stood tightly closed. Fall had arrived and the autumn leaves piled up, layer upon layer, on the ground of the front garden. They covered up the delicate clovers. There was no trace of Sean's presence on the path in the garden. The complete silence frightened me.

Eventually I gathered up enough courage and decided I needed to talk to Sean. Sean's neighbour, a man wearing gold-framed glasses, told me that Sean had pancreatic cancer and was in the hospital.

I went to the hospital and asked a nurse to tell Sean that I wanted to see him. He refused. His message was, "Please do not give me any reason to care for this world." Could he really leave the world, carefree? I left without seeing him.

Two months later, out of the blue, I received a call from Sean's mother Marcia. She told me that she had gotten my number from Sean.

"Sean passed away last Saturday," she said.

I fell silent on my end of the telephone line. I still cherished a warm feeling for Sean deep in my heart, but that warmth was now swept away by the cold autumn wind of death. Marcia asked me if I was willing to help her clean up Sean's house for the last time. She was in poor health, and her other children lived outside St. Catharines. I agreed without hesitation.

The next day, when I arrived at the house, Marcia was having coffee in the kitchen, sitting in the very chair Sean would always use. Marcia was rather stout, and she looked very sad. Actually the entire house was depressing.

"I'm Grace," I introduced myself.

Marcia replied, "Thank you so much for helping me out."

"Actually I am also helping myself."

I looked all around. The house remained the same, even though the man was dead. The man who had held me in his arms, the only man who had ever told me that I had sexy lips. Now he was on the long journey of no return....

Marcia told me that she was the executor of Sean's will. She wanted to sell the house, but, before she could, she had to have the house cleaned and get rid of all the garbage.

"But there's not really much garbage." I was rather puzzled.

"Go to his bedroom and you'll see," Marcia sighed. She then stood up, and said, "I have a huge headache. Please excuse me. I have to lie down on the couch."

The door to Sean's bedroom was wide open. I walked into it and was stunned by what I saw: there were pornographic magazines everywhere—*Playboy, Gallery, Club*—on the shelves and on the night tables, on the carpet and on the windowsills. Sean must have collected every porn magazine published in the last twenty years or so. And there were piles of adult videos too, all of them featuring beautiful women with blonde hair and blue eyes, with huge breasts and wide hips.

So Sean had been living in a sexual fantasy world. He had tried to reproduce in his imagination the sick love that he and Sharon had shared. Did love only exist as a hallucination? Did obsession really offer him any comfort?

Love can save, but it can destroy, too. But when in love, who can see the thin line separating salvation and destruction? Real relationships are always complicated and demanding. Sean could not deal with that. I wondered if, except for Sharon, he had ever loved another person, a human being of flesh and blood. That thought infuriated me, and I felt blood rushing into my head. I madly turned the bedroom upside down. I was desperate to find any sign of my existence in Sean's life among those hundreds and hundreds of semi-nude and even completely naked blonde beauties. Just one tiny sign!

About an hour later, I found a collection of poems in the drawer of a night table. Between the pages were two admission receipts. I looked at the date and realized that they were the stubs for the carousel—Sean's and mine! I sat down on the carpeted floor, grabbed the two pieces of thin paper, and breathed laboriously. I was drenched in sweat. I did not know how much time had elapsed before I put the two pieces in my purse, very carefully. Then I went downstairs and fetched a box of large black garbage bags from the kitchen. I started to stuff the magazines and videotapes in different bags.

The magazines smelled rotten, and I became so sick that I had to rush to the bathroom to throw up. I vomited so hard that I felt as if my heart were being heaved out....

One after another, I moved all the bags downstairs and put them outside on the curb. I counted meticulously: twenty-seven in total. Under the cold and desolate autumn sun, those bags stood in a row, black and pathetic. They contained Sean's world of fantasy and emotion, his entire world. Now his world was squeezed into them, waiting for the garbage collectors and disposal in a far away landfill.

I tended to Sean's garden one more time, the final time. To my great surprise, I saw a four-leaf clover, and, with great care, I put it in my purse too. "One leaf is for HOPE, and one is for FAITH, and one is for LOVE." But the last one is for LUCK.

Marcia and I went to the bank of the Welland Canal after we left Sean's house. A little while later, The Miller sailed by. Marcia and I waved to the ship. The crew blew the whistle three times and lowered Sean's bicycle into the lake.

"Sean used to take his bike on board the ship. Wherever it docked, he would go on shore and tour the place. He would buy a book or two and enjoy the city scenery," Marcia explained.

The bike drifted slowly towards the distant horizon, where the water and the sky met. Marcia sighed and said, "Perhaps I was too harsh on Sean all along. Only when I was in his house today did I realize I knew so little about him."

I did not say anything. Is it true that understanding, forgiving, and even love always come too late?

The day before I was to leave St. Catharines, I got a call from a man who claimed he was Sean's lawyer. He asked me to meet him in a little café owned by a Puerto Rican. When I arrived at the café, the lawyer was already there, sitting in a corner booth and waiting for me.

"In Sean's will, there is one provision that concerns you," the lawyer informed me.

"Concerns me?" I did not expect that.

"He required that from the proceedings of the sale of his house, fifty thousand dollars, be given to you. It is designated for your tuition at a Canadian university and your living expenses when you are a student."

I looked at him, completely astounded. "How ... how could this be possible?"

"I am certainly not misrepresenting him."

"But I didn't do very much for him, really...."

"You appeared in his life, as a real person. That's more than enough."

"I know so little about him."

"There are additional provisions for his monetary gift."

"What provisions?"

"You must be accepted by a university. I will send the tuition money directly to the university. You provide me with the address of your landlord, and I will mail the rent on your behalf."

I knew why Sean made these provisions: he was afraid that I might not go to university at all.

When I told my family the news, both my mother and my brother demanded that I take out the money and give it to them so that they could invest it in the stock market.

"That's impossible. I cannot take one penny out. The only way I can use the money is to go to university," I told them. When I hung up, to my surprise, I laughed quietly. It was the first time in my entire life that I said no to my family.

I went to the Kilt and Clover one more time to say goodbye to Jim. Sharon's kilt was replaced by a new one, one with blue-and-green checks. Her picture had also disappeared. Jim told me that when the TV station had reported the news about Fred and Sharon committing the murder together, Sean had charged into the restaurant and forcefully torn Sharon's kilt and photograph from the wall. He had then poured gasoline on them and set them on fire right in front of the door. He had squatted beside the burning pile and stared at it. While the kilt and picture burned into ashes, his eyes had dimmed, as if, bit by bit, they were sinking into a bottomless darkness. He had set fire to his love right where his love had started.

Three years later I got my Master's degree in psychology from the University of Toronto. I opened a clinic in the business section of the downtown core. My advertisement in the newspapers said that my specialty was treating patients with obsessions.

On the third day that my clinic was open for business, I had my very first client, Kane, forty-five years of age. On the form he had checked "Obsession with internet pornography." Because of his obsession, he had lost his job, his health was deteriorating, and he was suffering from loneliness. With his brown eyes, thinning hair, dark complexion, and mixture of humility and shyness, he immediately reminded me of Sean.

Kane sat down in my office, and right away he saw the four-leaf clover that was framed and hanging on the wall.

"A four-leaf clover? Really rare. You found it?" Kane asked. I nodded.

"You're lucky." I detected a trace of envy in his voice.

Like a magic key, that clover leaf unlocked the heavy door of my memory: Sean's garden, the fireplace on that Christmas Eve, the revolving antique carousel, the clear blue water of the Welland Canal....

Perhaps I had loved, though in my own unique way, I thought. If I could exchange luck to get love, I would be more than willing to do it. Tears began to well up.

"I am so sorry. Have I said something to upset you?" Kane asked apologetically in a low voice.

I realized that I was sitting before my first client in my professional life. So I wiped away the tears, a bit embarrassed, and then I said in a very calm and soothing voice, "Let's begin, Kane. Tell me your story."

Translated by H. Laura Wu and Cory Davies.

"The Kilt and Clover" was originally published in Literature, *No. 6, 2009.*

[1]"Four-Leaf Clovers" was written by American poet Ella Higginson.

Toward the North

LING ZHANG

X IAOYUE,
   *I, your dad, am going away for a while.
You'll understand the reason I'm leaving when you
grow a little older. The place I'm going to is in the north
of Toronto, far north. But no matter where I live, my heart
is always with you.*

SIOUX LOOKOUT

Zhongyue Chen bent over a table, holding a magnifying glass
and pouring over the newly bought map of Canada, searching
for that strange name. Like tadpoles with various tails, lakes
and rivers were swimming beneath his magnifying glass. Finally
he got rid of the tadpoles and located a sesame-seed sized black
spot in the northern part of Ontario. Turning on the computer,
he found a dozen indexes on Google.

  Town's population: 3,400. External population: 1,800. Latitude: 52 degrees north. Main inhabitants: The Ojibwa. Area:
a reserve land according to Indian treaties....

  The description page gradually blurred. A few words that
looked like mountains rising up from the ground blocked all
his vision.

  Latitude: 52 degrees north.

  Zhongyue pulled out a map of China with worn-out edges.
Searching for 52-53 degrees along the north latitude, he found

a lonely spot: Mohe. He had heard this name. His high school geography teacher had told him that it was the northernmost county in China.

In other words, Sioux Lookout and Mohe were almost at the same latitude.

Zhongyue felt as if warmth from his feet had moved up to heat his whole body. He could hear his heartbeat. He left the webpage and started to type a message: "I accept all the terms of the contract and will take over the position within two weeks." As he finished, his finger tapped on the Send key, and the email went out. Then he felt his finger shiver slightly. Closing his eyes, he seemed to see transparent wings all over sky; they were carrying him, filled with eagerness, to the little town with a strange name in northern Canada.

The following day, Zhongyue started to pack his luggage. He gave all his large pieces of furniture and electronic appliances to Xiaoxiao Fan, his wife. All his necessities were in four suitcases. Two in the trunk and the other two on the back seats would fill up the car. He closed his bank account; had the car checked; bought an insurance policy for the trip; took his daughter, Xiaoyue, to his family doctor for a general exam; and said goodbye to his supervisor, colleagues, and friends. Unexpectedly, everything went smoothly and easily.

A week later, Zhongyue started his long journey by car to Sioux Lookout.

He departed in the morning. Before his car reached the highway he pulled it over and made a call to Xiaoxiao with his cell phone. The phone rang for a long time before someone answered. "Is Xiaoyue in?" he asked.

The response was a question with a smirk: "How long has it been since you took Xiaoyue to school? Don't you know her school bus for the summer class comes at seven thirty in the morning?"

After a pause, he answered, "Okay, Xiaoxiao. I'm leaving now."

But no answer came from the other end, so he had to hang up. Remaining momentarily at the side of the road, he realized he had hoped she'd say something. But what did he expect from Xiaoxiao? He knew, as a matter of fact, no matter what she said, that he had his mind set. She had known this about him and, so, she said nothing.

Driving out of Toronto, he saw fewer houses and buildings. Fields appeared along the roadside. The corn stalks shook their yellow tassels in the wind. As he drove farther north, there were no more houses, and then even the crops disappeared. Weeds were scarce. Only large expanses of wild land remained. Occasionally brooks and ponds came into his view, but they were blanketed by quietness. They seemed to have been there for a thousand years and were too lazy to ripple on the water's surface. Summer insects kept crashing onto the windshield, their bodily fluids splashing against the glass, scattering green splotches. With no cars or human beings around, the road ahead loomed like a huge grey cloth, unfolding smoothly toward the ends of the earth. Zhongyue couldn't help but roll down the window, stretch out his free hand out, and wave it in the wind. The blood seemed to storm though his body, roaring: *go toward the north; go toward the north; go toward the north!*

Zhongyue's expectations for the north were rooted in unsure concepts formed in his earliest years.

He was born the year that the Vietnam War broke out. Three-year-old Zhongyue, along with the children in the neighbourhood, had watched a Vietnamese movie. The content of the film was unclear. He only vaguely remembered that a group of South Vietnamese children, starving and skinny, quickly sharpened bamboo sticks. However, he clearly remembered the song in the movie. The lyrics were repetitious and rhymed and it was very catchy.

Go toward the North! Go toward the North!
The children in the South are expecting their liberators.

Go toward the North! Go toward the North!
The children in the South are expecting their liberators.
Go toward the North! Go toward the North!
The children in the South are expecting their liberators....

That was the first song Zhongyue had ever learned. It was buried in the bottom of his memories. During his growth, more things piled up. The surface memories were forgotten, but the memory of the song at the bottom still remained; having melted into his flesh and bones, it was hard to forget. He didn't know what the difference between the south and the north was, but that song had inspired his initial longing for the north.

Later, his uncle and aunt were dispatched to the military farms in Northeast China as re-educated youth. They wrote letters home often. At that time, Zhongyue's father was still alive, and his mother read their letters to his father at the dinner table. All of those letters contained complaints about hardship in life. Not totally understanding the letters, Zhongyue just remembered what he wanted to remember: the endless fields that no combines could reach; the cloudless horizon; and the winter snow, thicker than a quilt, which covered the land completely. Those letters had sparked his imagination about the beauty and expanse of north.

He had grown up fast, like dough mixed with yeast. As a ninth grader, he'd already reached six feet. His pants were forever too short; his shoes, forever too tight; the door, too low; and his voice, too coarse. The comments about his personality in his school reports always said that "this student needs to get along with others." When the students were paired up at the beginning of each term, nobody was willing to sit with him at the same table. When the students went camping, no one wanted to sleep next to him. There was no place for him to feel comfortable with his own body except in the playground. He was like a tall, clumsy bear walking on a crowded lane in an exquisite southern town. He had trouble dealing with sophisticated human relations. In every situation, he would either hurt people or people would hurt him. The small southern town in which he lived was like a small-sized gown embroidered with gold threads. Wearing it became a burden. Whenever he moved, he could easily break those delicate stitches. His young heart felt the restrictions of the southern town where he lived.

He'd begun to dream of the north, the place he had never been, but to which he felt drawn. He longed for the north because of its breadth, simplicity, informality, and boldness.

After high school, there had been a chance for him to flee from the south, but he'd missed it. His scores for the entrance exams weren't very good and he was only accepted by a local teachers' college.

When he had graduated from the college, he missed another chance to flee from the south. He fell in love with a girl named Xiaoxiao Fan and yielded to her wishes. They both went to graduate programs at the university in the provincial capital.

Surely, life had gone along its natural path. After his graduate studies, he'd taught at the same university. Then marriage, the birth of a child, the decision to study abroad, and immigration to another country became new responsibilities that life threw at him, one by one, every few years. Like an iron man, he carried out all those tasks. With his mind set on each target, his feelings gradually became semi-numb. The song "Toward the North" occasionally resounded at unguarded moments. That melody was weak, like an interval murmur between heartbeats. He almost believed that his dream for the north had slipped away with his youth and died in his old memories. Nothing in this world would stir up his peace and quiet again.

But he'd been wrong.

One night, at midnight, he woke up from a confusing dream. As usual, he touched the empty side of the bed before he remembered that Xiaoxiao had moved out. Sitting up, sounds filled his ears. He thought it was tinnitus—he had developed it recently. After a while, he finally recognized it was the melody that had long been buried in his heart. It resounded in his ears so loudly that he couldn't sleep. He got up and went out, jogging on the empty street for a whole hour. Back home he took a cold shower, but he still couldn't fall back to sleep. *Go toward the North. Go toward the North. Go toward the North.*

The drumbeats became stronger and stronger, as if they were striking his eardrums, so that he could hardly bear it. Like the gusts of dark wind and fierce storms, the sounds of the drumbeats invaded his blood and coursed through his body. He was in pain, and he stumbled. The drumbeats made his heart swell to many times its size. He felt as if his heart had changed into a balloon, risen to his throat, and then stuck there. It couldn't go up or come down. His breathing became erratic.

He knew that some part of his life had been slowly dying, but that other parts were gradually recovering.

He also understood that he couldn't resist that call; he had to obey it.

So he quit his job and scoured the internet, looking for a chance to go north.

That was how he stumbled onto Sioux Lookout.

Xiaoyue,
Most First Nations children are living under very poor conditions. During long winter, many contract otitis, which is caused by an upper respiratory tract infection. Because there is no immediate medical treatment available, many of these children lose their hearing permanently. The ratio of deaf children to hearing children is several times higher than that in Toronto. All urban children are very lucky to be born in the city.

Zhongyue had majored in education and specialized in Educational and Child Psychology in a graduate program. In Canada, he'd obtained another master's degree, majoring in Hearing Rehabilitation Science with a minor in Education of Children with disabilities. After graduation, he'd gotten a position in a hearing rehabilitation programme with the Toronto District School Board. Now he was on his way to Sioux Lookout for a one-year contract job to replace a teacher on maternity leave. He was to care for the hearing impaired children at six schools, train them in sign language, and teach them some knowledge of hearing aids and maintenance.

He arrived during the summer break, when the students were on holidays. With the help of a map, Zhongyue drove to the different schools. After his tour of the six schools, he understood the concept of "nearby." The shortest distance between two of those schools was about an hour's drive. Sioux Lookout was the middle point between the six schools, so he settled down there.

The local school board arranged accommodations for him in the western corner of the town. He moved in that night. He fell asleep right away after driving for three days. The next morning, he was awakened by sharp bird cries, and he discovered that he was surrounded by woods. The entire house was made out of logs; there were no exceptions, from the beam to the wall, and from the floor to the furniture. The logs were coated with varnish. The grains of the wood, annual rings, and even insect holes were visible and countable. The surface of the logs were carved with designs, such as plants, birds, animals and human figures. All these carved images had simple and clear lines, as well as three-dimensional, sharp cuts. They looked alive, like they were moving and flying. Sunlight like a broad, white band flowed down through the two skylights in the roof and brightened the whole room. Dust looked like a silvery powder slowly falling through the light. It reminded him of a fairy tale picture book that he had bought for Xiaoyue. The illustration of a cabin in the forest in that book matched the scene he awoke to that morning.

As he left the log house, the startling blue sky seemed to sweep him off his feet. He closed his eyes for a while before getting used to the clear and sunny light that bathed the woods around him. Turning around, he noticed that he was on a slope. As he walked down the slope, a smear of grey light emerged a few steps ahead. That light grey stretched out into the distance. The further away, the narrower it became, and eventually it turned into a fine line that merged with the horizon. The wind picked up and something shining in the smear of grey caught his attention. *Oh, there is a lake there*, Zhongyue thought. Not a single person was in the woods, and not a single boat was on the lake. Zhongyue couldn't help but cry out to the sky. Several water birds whooshed through the air, their wings spread wide and strong. He plucked a handful of green grass, squeezed it into a lump, and threw it into the thick water, but the clump didn't even make a ripple. His palm felt the cool green pulp, but his heart felt hot and unsettled. He felt like shouting wildly.

So he walked up to the top of the mound, and, with his hands around his mouth, he yelled crazily. "*Ah ... yu ... hum ... yah...!*"

The wind tore his voice away and then carried it back. The echoes bounced among the trees. He continued crying loudly until his voice became husky. Then he fell onto the grass, feeling like his guts had been emptied but his mind had become clear.

At that moment, the cell phone in his pocket rang. A social worker from Whitefish Elementary School was calling him to say that a student had broken his hearing aid during a fight. He asked if Zhongyue could go test the student's hearing and order a new one before school was scheduled to start. The social worker said he knew it was still the summer break, but the parents were worried, and the family needed special care. Zhongyue said that it would be noon when he got there. The social worker said he'd already taken the student to Zhongyue's office.

When Zhongyue got to his office, the social worker was waiting at the door. Zhongyue quickly flipped through the student's file, which the social worker had brought with him. The boy was Neil Maas, and he was six years and ten months old. He suffered from an extremely severe congenital sensorineural hearing loss. His speech discrimination was almost zero. Zhongyue asked about the child's language ability. The social worker said he could only speak a few simple words and use some basic sign language. The boy would go to a rehabilitation class as soon as the school started. This was why the parents were anxious to have a new hearing aid. Zhongyue asked why the child's parents had not come. The social worker answered that the boy's father was rarely at home; his mother worked in a fish processing plant and was unable to come right then. Before Zhongyue entered his office, the social worker tugged at his sleeve. "This child is a little bit different," he said with hesitation. Zhongyue smiled and told him that he'd seen all kinds of children, and not to worry.

They entered the room, but it was empty. Zhongyue called Neil, but no one answered. The social worker placed his finger on his lips, making an earthshaking whistle. In an instance, Zhongyue heard an answering whistle from somewhere above. Looking up, Zhongyue saw a boy, like a monkey, sitting on a ladder in the corner and frowning; the child's dark eyes stared down at him. Face to face, Zhongyue made a sign: "Good morning." The boy returned some ambiguous words. Zhongyue didn't understand it and wondered if it was Ojibwa. Stifling a laugh, the social worker said it was actually foul language, insulting the other's mother. Ignore him, he suggested. Zhongyue disregarded the boy. Sitting down, he pulled a deck of cards out of his pocket. He placed them on the table one by one, purposely showing the cover of each. They were photographs of NBA stars; each of them included the athlete's signature.

A rustling noise came from behind him. Zhongyue knew that Neil had come down, but he didn't turn his head. Calmly he shuffled the cards and displayed all the cover pictures on the table. Then he mixed them up and showed the pictures again. Soon Zhongyue felt a warm breath on the nape of his neck. It was Neil. Zhongyue collected the cards and put them back in his pocket. Turning his head, he looked directly at Neil, face to face.

Neil was a little short with bandy legs and a large head. When he looked at others, his eyes rolled up, and wrinkles formed on his forehead, making him look like a wizened old man. He had big ears; according to a Chinese saying, big ears brought fortune, but in his case they only decorated his head.

Zhongyue asked Neil one word at a time, "What is the number of Michael Jordan's jersey?"

Neil didn't answer. Zhongyue repeated the signs. Still, no answer came from Neil, but his eyes fixed on Zhongyue's pocket. Zhongyue felt as if his pocket had several holes punched through it. "If you let me check your ears, this deck of cards is yours."

Neil's poker face remained intact, but his body gradually lowered and finally, he sat on a stool. Zhongyue changed into his white lab coat, and, holding an otoscope, he pinched Neil's ear. Then what happened was just like in a Hollywood action film, but only in slow motion. After a long while, Zhongyue began to understand. At first, he thought he saw a reddish-brown leopard leap from the stool. Both the stool and leopard arched into the air in a beautiful curve. The stool fell onto the floor, but the leopard didn't.

The animal jumped straight onto him. Zhongyue wanted to duck, but it was too late. The leopard's eyes were only two inches away from his. He saw its eyes split open; the whites of the eyes flowed out, drop by drop. The leopard was pressing down on Zhongyue. He wanted to push it away, but he couldn't move—his hand had suddenly gone numb.

When he finally sat up, the leopard was gone and the stool was in pieces. The social worker held his wrist tightly and asked where the first-aid kit was. Zhongyue pointed to the top cabinet. The social worker let go of Zhongyue's hand in order to find a bandage. It was then that Zhongyue noticed a row of pod-like petals, red, on his white lab coat sleeve. He knew they were tooth marks.

Zhongyue said to the social worker, "Go find Neil. If you can't, call 911."

He bandaged his own wrist and drove to the clinic in town. He touched his pocket and found no cards. The pain in his wrist became more intense, like needles pricking his veins. His heart pounding, he ground his teeth, thinking about many ways he could punish that little boy.

Xiaoyue,

I've finally learned how Sioux Lookout got its name. In fact, I should've guessed. This is a war-related name. Three or four hundred years ago, the Sioux tribe often attacked the Ojibwa tribe. To defend themselves, the Ojibwa people built a lookout here. Doesn't it sound like the story of China's Great Wall beacon towers? These two tribes in the northern wilderness killed each other for a long time, until the Europeans entered their territories. I'm thinking about the history and the people who were buried here. Their lives were totally different from those who live in our cities. I always feel my heart throb, as if I am disturbing unsettled souls.

Zhongyue reached the clinic and had his wound treated. When he got back, it was afternoon. The pain killer and anti-inflammation injection made him drowsy. He fell asleep on the couch. In his sleep, he suddenly heard someone push open the door. As he sat up, he saw Xiaoxiao in her bright blue, down-filled coat, a snow-white cashmere scarf wrapped around her neck. All he could see of her face were her two black eyes and her bangs. Surprised, he asked Xiaoxiao why she didn't call beforehand. Xiaoxiao didn't speak, but turned her face away. Zhongyue asked, "Don't you feel warm? You are wearing so much."

Xiaoxiao turned around, took a look at him, and said, "I'm cold. My heart feels cold actually."

He tried to hold her hands, but she didn't allow him. Then he woke up knowing it was a good dream, but a dream nonetheless.

It was completely dark. Looking out the skylight, he saw that the night was clear. A crescent moon was surrounded by some torches. Zhongyue looked out the skylight again and realized that the stars he could see were larger and brighter than those you could see in the city. Out the window, he could see Penguin Lake, which had changed and now had fierce, dark waves madly crashing against the shore. The rocks on both sides were swallowed by the dark lake. Forest sounds rumbled as though rocks were falling down from the mountains. He shook from head to toe. The log house seemed to be as fragile as a paper cage, as though a finger could break through it. Startled, he got up and turned the light on. From the kitchen, he found an ice chisel and steak knife, and placed them at a handy distance.

He thought about going to the municipal government and inquiring about the registration for a gun. In this wild and barbaric place, only a gun made a person brave; everything else was bullshit.

At that moment, his stomach growled so wildly that he remembered he hadn't even eaten lunch. The refrigerator was empty since he hadn't had time to do any grocery shopping. Perhaps the store on the street corner was already closed. He picked up a packet of instant noodles left over from his trip and mixed them in a bowl of hot water. He wolfed down the tasteless food, but he still felt hungry. *No matter how lofty my ideals, I'm still vulnerable to hunger,* he sighed.

He began to sweat and he remembered his dream in which Xiaoxiao looked the same as she had when they first started dating. They both were sophomores, but in different departments. He studied liberal arts, but she was in science. He didn't understand her courses, and she didn't understand his, but they had things to say to one another since they had other common interests. They didn't know where or when they had first crossed each other's paths, and now he didn't know how they had gotten so far from one another. They no longer had anything to say to each other. She didn't share her ideas with him, and he didn't share his with her. Remembering that, in his dream, Xiaoxiao had said her heart was cold, Zhongyue felt disheartened. He couldn't help but make a phone call to Toronto.

It was his daughter, Xiaoyue, who answered the phone.

They only spoke a little before Xiaoyue got impatient. She said she wanted to watch *Nim's Island*. The tape needed to be returned to the library the next day. Zhongyue asked if her mother was in. Xiaoyue said with hesitation that her mother was upstairs, and that a male friend named Xiang was keeping her company. "Do you want me to ask her to come down?" Xiaoyue asked. After a pause, Zhongyue said that there was no need to do that—he had nothing important to say.

After he hung up, he sat motionless on the couch, realizing that Xiaoxiao's heart had become completely cold toward him. How could she have gotten together with Xiang so quickly? Xiaoxiao had been slow to act in the past. It had been two years from their initial handshake to the first time they made love. She was different now, experienced. He had helped her gain the experience that had matured her. And in the end, he wouldn't be able to enjoy her maturity.

That thought made him sick. His head throbbed, and he felt as if his temples had been pinched by the two large pincers of a mantis. He laid a thick layer of Tiger Balm on his temples, making his tears stream down. His headache eased off, but the pain in his wrist worsened. The pain was stronger now than it had been in the daytime. It was like a knife cutting rather than a needle pricking. It was a kind of slow torture, in and then out, but not cutting through. Zhongyue thought that perhaps the medicinal effect of the painkillers had expired, so he got up and took two more painkillers. But they didn't work and he felt colder and colder.

He took off his coat and went to bed, covering himself with a quilt. Then a sticky sweat spread over his body. Kicking off the quilt and partially exposing his body, he felt cold again. On and off, he struggled with the quilt. He tossed and turned all night without sleep. As he was about to finally fall asleep in the wee hours of the morning, he heard something move outside.

His eyes were closed, but suddenly he was all ears. He had adapted to the dark environment, and as soon as the suspicious rustling noise began again, he knew right away that it was not wind, water, leaves, or birds. It was a person approaching his door, making him edgy. The nearest neighbour was five minutes away by car.

He got up quietly, switched on his cell phone, and, by the light from the screen, dialled 911. One press on the button would do the job. Then he picked up the ice chisel on the end table. Bending over slightly, he moved to the door, his eyes firmly on the peephole. The sight through the hole made each piece of his hairs stand up like porcupine's quills. He saw a huge glass, bead-like eye, an eye against his own. He heard his teeth chattering.

Zhongyue pulled the door open suddenly. Unexpectedly, the person outside the door fell into the house and was thrown toward him. His ice chisel dropped onto the floor, making a loud noise. In the dim light, he saw a big woman who wore a scarf and a blouse over a long gown. Turning on the light, he noticed that she had a straw basket on her back. After she put it down, she looked smaller immediately. "Who are you?" Zhongyue asked warily.

Before speaking, the woman bent down so that her head reached her knees, and coughed violently. The dry cough made her body shake in her black clothes, like a woodpecker pecking at the old, hard trunk of a tree. *Bang, bang.* Finally Zhongyue couldn't stand it and handed her a cup of water. She drank it up, and her cough calmed down.

The woman took off her scarf and gently tossed it aside. Some water droplets splashed onto Zhongyue's face. It was dew. The woman's face revealed that she worked outdoors all year around. He immediately noticed her cheekbones and hair. Her cheekbones were high and looked like they had been carved from wood, with sunspots on each side. Her hair was very long, like withered grass, and was coiled around on her head twice in a thick braid. The end of her braid was tucked behind her ears, and a small yellow daisy decorated her hair. As the woman spoke, the pink gums in her mouth showed. Her face looked friendly.

"Dr. Chen, I'm Neil's mother. I'm here so early disturbing you because I have to hurry to work."

Her English was not good. She tried to say a few sentences, but it seemed as if she were trying to climb a mountain and cross an ocean. Zhongyue only understood the three words — doctor, Neil, and mother—but these three words were enough to help him decipher her message. The First Nations people in the area called all those associated with the hospital Doctor—it was more or less the same in China. Zhongyue didn't bother to correct her. His hand on his mouth, he yawned, and wondered how long it would have taken her to write an apology letter in English.

The woman didn't wait for Zhongyue to respond, but walked up to him and rolled up his sleeve to check the bite. She removed the thin gauze. The flesh looked pink, and it was swollen with a yellow liquid. The woman also placed her hand on Zhongyue's forehead and uttered: "Bullshit." He did not know if the woman was swearing at his wound or at her son because of what he'd done.

Pulling a small bag out of her pocket, the woman fished into it and took out some herbal leaves. As she crumpled the leaves in her palm, a pulpy liquid oozed from them. She coated his wound with the mashed herb. It stung! Zhongyue cried out and pushed the woman away. It was as if she had rubbed salt into a wound. When the burning sensation faded, a cool feeling took its place, and he felt his cloudy mind suddenly clear.

"This is an Indigenous herbal medicine called 'squirrel tail.' It can stop bleeding. It is also an anti-inflammatory. And it works fine."

Zhongyue listened with surprise. After a while, he realized she was speaking to him in Chinese.

"You ... have you been to China?" he stammered.

The women laughed, her gums glistening. "I came from China. I'm a Tibetan. I can't speak good Chinese."

Zhongyue was surprised yet again. After some minutes, he asked, "How long have you been here? How did you come?"

The woman didn't answer, but instead removed a few things from her straw backpack and placed them in the refrigerator. "These are vegetable and meat dishes. They go well together. You can cook the rice yourself. One container a day. It's enough for a week."

The woman stacked them carefully and then wiped her face with her scarf. "Doctor Chen, Neil was born prematurely, only one pound ten ounces. Converted into the Chinese measurement, that's three quarters of a kilogram. He spent his childhood in the hospital. He suffered so much, and he is afraid of people in medical uniforms. Unfortunately, you wore a white coat."

As the woman spoke, the freckles on her face gradually darkened, and she looked sad. "I'd like to ask you for help, Dr. Chen. Can you also teach me sign language? Neil will be in the rehabilitation language class. Teachers will use sign language in their instruction. Neil will learn it. If I don't, he won't be able to use it at home. Only for two weeks. When school starts, I won't disturb you. I can cook for you, and do laundry for you in exchange. I start work at nine in the morning. but I can come here at seven. One and a half hours should be plenty for me to do what needs to be done."

Zhongyue sighed. He said that no one could learn sign language overnight. Even if she could learn it quickly, she would forget it easily if she didn't practise often. In two weeks, one could only learn the very basic signs. If she really wanted to learn, it would be better if the whole family came, so they could practise together.

The woman nodded, saying that she would bring Neil and start the following day.

"Is Neil's father coming?"

She shook her head, saying that only she and Neil would come. She sounded determined. Zhongyue couldn't find a reason to refuse her.

The woman wrapped her scarf around her head and picked up the basket. As she stepped outside, she turned and added, "My name is Dawa. It has the same sound in both Chinese and English."

Leaning against the door, Zhongyue watched the woman walk away, leaving soft wet footprints on the weeds covered with morning dew. The sun in the north, thick and heavy, blanketed the woman and the trees with its golden rays.

Xiaoyue,

   Dad has always felt that sign language can show a person's personality and emotions the best. The spoken language is polluted by the choice of vocabulary and intonation. The true meaning can be disguised. But sign language flows directly from the heart, it cannot be disguised as something else. I often see colours and hear sounds from the sign language.

Mother: right palm open; place the thumb of the right hand against the chin. Wiggle the other four fingers while signing. All the things related to women use this action, a little bit like the left side in a Chinese character.

Father: right hand open; place the thumb of the right hand

against the forehead. All the things related to men use this action. Sitting in the doorway, Dawa was learning sign language from Zhongyue. Zhongyue was squatting on the stone steps just below her. All he could see were Dawa's feet. Her toes were open and webbed, like a duck's. The smell of sweat drifted from her toes and made Zhongyue's nose itch. The summer had left its mark on Dawa's feet. They were dark, and the parts that were outside the shoes were even darker and shinier.

When the heat reached the fifty-two degrees north, it lost its energy. The wind brought some coolness with it in both the morning and the evening. Dawa wrapped her head with a headdress all year round, protecting herself from heat in summer or cold in winter. His eyes gradually looking up, Zhongyue noticed the sunflower design on Dawa's headscarf. The flower's yellow petals were tightly squeezed together, as if they were desperately escaping from an invisible disaster. It was the only colourful garment she wore. Out of the corner of his eye, he also saw Neil standing in the meadow only ten steps away., He was making a rope with sweet grass.

Neil hadn't spoken to Zhongyue. Dawa had waved at him a couple of times, but he had refused to come closer. But they had communicated in other ways. As matter of fact, Neil and Zhongyue had been engaged in a kind of dialogue, in their own way. From the corners of their eyes, they sought each other, looked away, and then returned the look, in the same way a radar tracks signals.

Morning: raise the left arm horizontally. It stands for the land. Have the right thumb open and the other four fingers close together. Slowly raise the hand. It means the sun rises from the ground.

Spring: raise the left arm horizontally. It stands for the land. Form a circle with the left fingers. Pass the right hand through the left hand circle; then spread open the right hand fingers. It means the plant comes out from the ground.

Dawa's gestures were awkward, but gradually her hands

gained confidence. When she held her fingers tightly together, they looked like they were holding soil after a downpour, like the rich soil was being squeezed between her fingers. When she opened her fingers, it looked like her fingers had flicked away soil, as though green droplets of water had splashed from her hand.

Neil was still braiding the rope. The sweet grass passed nimbly through his fingers, and the rope gradually grew longer, like a blue-grey snake coiling in his lap. Finally Neil tied a knot to hold both ends together. It became a loop.

From the corner of his eye, Zhongyue saw Neil pull the grass loop over his head and slowly walk toward Dawa. After a few steps, he hesitated.

Zhongyue made a wrong gesture intentionally. Dawa also made a wrong sign. And Neil took a few more steps and finally stood behind Dawa.

Zhongyue gestured wrongly again. Dawa followed suit. Neil cried out and grabbed Dawa's fingers from behind her. He pressed them down and then re-opened them. Dawa turned her head and pushed Neil toward Zhongyue. Winking at Zhongyue, she told Neil to tell Dr. Chen that he was wrong.

Neil glanced at Zhongyue. Suddenly he bent down and pounced on him. Since he had prepared for this, Zhongyue grabbed Neil's collar and pushed him back down to ground. Then he placed his knee firmly on Neil's chest. Neil was like a huge bug nailed on a board; his limbs were flailing helplessly, and his voice was whining, but his body was stuck. Hearing Dawa's footsteps behind him, Zhongyue shouted, "Dawa, stop there! You can't report this fight. It's no use. No one else is here. You have to let me do it my way, like we discussed."

Both Dawa and Neil became quiet.

Zhongyue pressed his knee harder. Neil was like a fish in a pot. His mouth opened to cry, but no tears came. Lowering his face close to Neil, Zhongyue said, half in English and half in sign language, "If you dare to bite me again, I will keep you like this for five days." Then Zhongyue removed his knee from Neil's chest.

Neil stood up, walked hesitatingly to Dawa, and sat down. He eyed Dawa, but Dawa ignored him and bent down to dig into her straw basket. She took out a packet of cigarettes. Tearing it open, she drew out a cigarette, but her hand was trembling so much that she couldn't light it. Zhongyue couldn't help but laugh, and told her she shouldn't be upset. If she kept spoiling her boy, he would never grow up. Zhongyue said he had done something good for everybody.

Dawa finally lit her cigarette. After a puff, she started to cough. The cough made her eyes fill with tears. Zhongyue grabbed Dawa's cigarette and threw it away, saying it was not good to smoke in front of children. Dawa pulled off her scarf, dried her eyes, and retrieved the cigarette from a clump of weeds. She didn't even bother to rub the soil off, but immediately lit it again and took another puff. "Even if I don't smoke, Joy will," she sighed. "If Joy doesn't, someone else will. Winter is deadly long. How can we survive if we don't smoke?"

Zhongyue guessed that Joy was probably Dawa's husband. He asked Dawa to bring Joy the following day. *Mother is too soft for this naughty boy. Father should make rules.*

Dawa laughed loudly. Her laugh was like the sound of a hungry crow whose flapping wings could shake the leaves off a tree. "You should ask people in town who the naughty boy in our family is," she croaked.

Xiaoyue,
> *Dad met a stubborn boy here. He's not even seven years old, but he has spent most of his life struggling. In fact, he is only trying to survive in this world. That's all.*

Although Dawa had carried Neil for five months, her belly only looked a little bigger. Then her belly stopped growing. When she got up one morning, Dawa noticed that her pants were looser then when she had put them on. When she touched her abdomen, it seemed flat. Realizing that her baby was too quiet and wasn't kicking, Dawa was afraid, and her heart sank. There was no time to call Joy, so she drove to the hospital by herself. Once in the hospital, she had to stay there. The test results showed something abnormal about the foetus' umbilical cord and placenta. They weren't sending enough nutrients to the foetus; instead, they were absorbing the nutrients themselves. Because of that, the baby grew smaller and might die at any moment. The doctor decided to induce labour immediately. Dawa went into the delivery room. She did not even have a change of clothes with her.

After the birth, the baby was washed and wrapped. He skin was the colour of meat, a reddish-black. When Dawa held in the infant in her hands, she could almost cover him with her palm. She only dared look at her baby after she had uttered the words, "Buddha bless you." Fortunately, he had all four limbs and all of his organs. His face was the size of an egg, but it was covered in wrinkles that exposed two pea-sized eyes. His eyes barely opened and then closed. His mouth opened, and he made a humming noise that sounded like a swarm of mosquitoes—he was crying. Before Dawa had time to comfort him, the doctor had carried him away. The baby had to be put into an incubator where the air was infused with oxygen.

At birth, her son weighed one pound and ten ounces, which broke the hospital's twenty-five-year-old record.

The doctors told her that he might have pulmonary hypoplasia, brain damage, impaired vision and hearing, bone deformities, and motor nerve damage. It would take a while to define the symptoms. The primary question now was how to help him breathe and prevent any possible infection. "Do you understand?" they asked. "Do you need an interpreter?"

Dawa shook her head, her mind blank. The doctor's English was not in fact clear. She didn't understand much of it, but she didn't need to completely understand it. It was enough for her to understand one of those sentences.

That same night, Dawa signed the treatment plan at the hospital and boarded a helicopter with her infant in the incubator. They flew to the Thunder Bay General Hospital, the nearest one equipped with neonatal facilities. Once on the aircraft, she fell asleep under a thick blanket, snoring loudly. With the sky so close overhead, she was nervous, and her muscles tensed. But now her sky had fallen; she didn't need to worry any more. *Dear heavens, do whatever you like.* This was her last clear thought before she fell into a dark dream.

Neil lived in the most advanced incubator at Thunder Bay General Hospital for five months. His first medical problem was jaundice. Then he developed pneumonia followed by persistent eczema. After his recovery, pneumonia attacked him again. One by one, each illness, like a mountain between them, separated Dawa from Neil. Wanting to hold her son close, Dawa had to climb those mountains one after another. Finally, one day, she was too tired to move.

That day the doctor came to give Neil new medicine. The veins on Neil's hands and feet were too small. The nurse could only insert needles into his head, where there were already two intravenous lines—one for liquid transfusion and the other for blood transfusion. She selected the finest needle, but barely found a vein. Her first try failed. Then she poked a couple of places. Each time she inserted the needle, Neil opened his mouth. Dawa knew that that was Neil's cry—he didn't have the energy to make sounds. Dawa felt as if the needle were pricking her heart over and over and chiselling a hole there. It was her flesh and blood at the end of the needle. She couldn't breathe. Darkness suddenly covered her eyes; she saw nothing.

A moment later, her sight came back, and the nurse said she could hold her baby. Neil could leave the incubator once a day for half an hour. Dawa took Neil and asked the nurse gently, "Can I be alone with him for a couple of minutes?"

The nurse nodded and walked away, gently closing the door behind her.

Dawa lay Neil flat on her lap. She gazed at the needles attached to the veins in his head, which glinted dark blue under the dim light. She saw her son's body filled with intravenous injections, shivering like a jellyfish floating in the water. She stared at his peapod-sized palms, and his hands which formed loose fists, and she knew each of his breaths was a battle; she knew every bone and every bit of flesh in his body cried in pain. Nobody could hear his cries; only she heard them clearly. That day, the third needle in Neil's head was the last straw on the camel's back. Suddenly it all became too much of a burden. She no longer wanted to climb the mountains between them. Not because she couldn't, but because Neil couldn't, and she knew she was the only one who could find a solution.

If the oxygen mask was removed, after five or ten minutes he would no longer have to climb those mountains.

Dawa placed her mouth at Neil's ear. "Maybe you should go, eh?" she whispered.

Dawa's voice was very light, like the early morning breeze coming out of the woods. The tree don't feel it; only the leaves sense its presence. Dawa was negotiating with her baby.

Suddenly, the infant opened his eyes fully. A turbid yellow tear dropped from the corner of his left eye. She wiped it with the back of her hand, but then another cloudy yellow tear came out of the corner of his right eye. She suddenly understood his words. He said, "Climb the mountain. Climb it. No matter how high it is, we should try." Dawa bent over her son, and began to cry.

When he was discharged, Neil weighed barely five pounds. Dawa wrapped the infant in a woollen blanket, placed him in a basket, and brought her son back to town. Many people stood along the street. The basket was passed from the first person to the last. Neil's appearance made the most ambiguous blessing sound insincere and Dawa could see the sorrow in everybody's eyes. *What a pity! Pour old Joy!* And she guessed what they were thinking.

At the time, Joy was at a bar that opened just before suppertime. Joy only had time to sit on a tall stool and drink his first glass of draft beer. When he heard the news, he grabbed the lemon slice on the glass rim, placed it in his mouth, and hurried onto the street. When the basket was handed to him, he had a moment of surprise. The Thunder Bay General Hospital wasn't far, but it wasn't close by either. It took a few hours to get there on a Greyhound bus. He'd been there twice during Dawa's hospitalization; the first time was when Neil was born, and the other time was two months ago. Even after so much time, he still felt his paternity. The infant's eyelids shivered under the strong afternoon sun. Although the baby was ugly, he still softened Joy's heart. In fact, at that moment, Joy sincerely wanted to be a good father. It was later that he couldn't control himself.

Since then, Dawa and Neil had continued to climb their mountains, high or low; they had gradually gotten over them. Only the last mountain, rising steep into the sky, blocked them completely. They seemed unable to climb over it. That mountain was called deafness.

Xiaoyue,

I just heard today why that deaf child was called Neil. His surname was Maas. Neil Maas was the name his mother gave him in order to humour Canadians; only she knew the real significance of it. If you omit some sounds when speaking it fast, it becomes Nima. It's a common Tibetan name, meaning the sun. Neil's mother was born and raised in a small town in Qinghai where both Han Chinese and Tibetans live. How she came to live in this remote town in Canada, I believe, is a mysterious and interesting story, but she didn't want to tell me. Her name is Dawa, meaning blue moon in Chinese. A mother named Moon calls her

son Sun. I think she holds a lot of hope for him. However,
such a name, given to such a child, seems somewhat cruel.

September arrived. It was like summer at noon, but like fall in
the early morning and evening. It was the last weekend before
school started. Sioux Lookout was the largest town within several hundred square kilometres. Its department store was in the
largest shopping mall in the area. The mall was a bit crowded
on this particular day—parents from everywhere around had
come to shop for school supplies for their children. With no
need to rush to work, Dawa dropped Neil at Zhongyue's place,
and then drove to the mall to get things for Neil.

Watching the dust dancing after Dawa's car as it vanished at
the end of the dirt road, Zhongyue squatted near Neil. "The
person who controls you has gone. Do you want to learn or
play?"

Neil didn't speak, but his clay-like face moved, exposing two
rows of grey teeth. Guessing this was probably Neil's smile,
Zhongyue sat the boy in his car and drove to the corner store.

The woman storeowner, who knew Zhongyue, shouted at
him: "Ah Ningning!" Zhongyue knew this meant "Greetings"
in Ojibwa, so he said the same. The owner asked what he
wanted. Zhongyue said he needed a can of skim milk and a
roll of hemp string. The woman filled a bag quickly. Hesitating
for a second, Zhongyue asked for a pack of locally produced
cigarettes. Stifling her laugh, the woman said, "You've learned
fast. Tobacco made here is soothing and also much cheaper
than that in Toronto." When the purchases were bagged, the
owner got Zhongyue's change and asked him if he was still
teaching old Joy's wife. Zhongyue said that she didn't know
how to read, but that she had learned how to use sign language
and gestures. He asked how the storeowner knew Joy, since
he lived in Whitefish. The woman smiled ambivalently, saying
that everybody in the area knew Joy and his family. Zhongyue
placed his finger on his lips and shushed. Noticing Neil in the

corner, the owner sighed, "He's deaf, ha. He can't hear." She took a small packet of jelly beans from the counter and put it in Neil's hand.

Zhongyue led Neil to the door, but was called back by the woman. Looking at him, she shook her head. After hesitating for a while she said, "That old Joy is a jerk after a few drinks. You should be careful."

Neil got into the car and opened the packet of jelly beans. He chewed the first one, but then spit it out. Then he rolled down the window, and threw out the whole pack. Zhongyue watched him and thought that the kid was not stupid.

Zhongyue bought the hemp string to fly a kite. He had a kite that he had bought from a fair before he left China. It was very old. The kite, in the shape of a swallow, had a black body with a red beak and eyes. Its tail was tied with long festoons of coloured paper. The line was broken and hadn't been fixed. A few years earlier, he had taken his daughter to participate in the Kite Festival on Toronto Centre Island. The kite had gotten stuck in a tree, and with a great effort, he had managed to get it down. Xiaoyue had had a good cry, and Zhongyue could still remember his daughter's weight on his back, her tears hot on the nape of his neck. *Does Xiaoyue still fly kites? Does she go with Xiang, her potential stepfather?*

Xiang had been Xiaoxiao's colleague. He had a wife in China. He was supposedly in the middle of a divorce. Xiaoxiao must've been in his heart for a long time, but Xiaoxiao hadn't been sure about him. But that was a while ago, of course. His daughter mentioned Xiang often in her emails. Maybe Xiang also tried to please Xiaoyue, for Xiaoxiao's sake, of course. Zhongyue felt that his daughter was like that kite, stuck on that remote tree—Xiang. With the string still in his hand, he was unsure whether he should pull. If he pulled too hard, the line would break, and Xiaoyue would spend her whole life with Xiang. If he didn't pull, he would watch his daughter drift farther and farther away from him. He thought of calling Xiaoxiao that evening to talk about bringing his daughter to Sioux Lookout for the Christmas break. Whenever he had mentioned this idea before, Xiaoxiao had always had a vague answer—perhaps Xiang had already made plans for the holiday. Zhongyue would only mention it one more time—the last time. If she consented or not, he would drive to Toronto and bring his daughter here.

The weather was good. When he looked into the sky from the slope, he found it different from when he was on the ground. That clear sky, like a huge blue cloth, wrapped the slope, the land, and the lake tightly and thoroughly; no air could escape from it. Only occasionally drifting clouds would make narrow gaps in that blue fabric. If the wind blew in from the gap, the kite would fly away. The hemp string in his hand would get shorter, and his swallow would seem to be riding on a cloud.

Neil ran after Zhongyue. Huffing and puffing, he called, "Bird! Bird!" Zhongyue stopped suddenly—this was the first time that Neil had talked to him. Getting out a piece of paper from his pocket, he wrote down a large word—"KITE"—and held it in front of Neil. Zhongyue told him that it wasn't a bird, but a kite. "Say 'kite.'" Neil looked down at his shoes and said nothing. Zhongyue held up Neil's chin and asked, "Neil, would you like to fly the bird?" Neil hesitated and then nodded. Zhongyue shook the line. "If you say the word 'kite' ten times, I'll let you hold it."

Before hearing Neil's answer, Zhongyue pulled the kite in and walked away without looking back, knowing that Neil was stumbling after him.

When he finally stopped, Zhongyue knelt down, coiled the string around Neil's index finger, and then lifted him onto his shoulders. Then he ran with the boy along Penguin Lake. The wind whistled past his ears as startled flocks of wild geese hovered over the lake. Zhongyue was all ears. The sounds of the wind and geese gradually faded, and he only heard Neil's cries.

"Kite! Kite! Kite! Kite! Kite! Kite! Kite…!"

That day, Neil shouted "kite" several dozens of times. The

sound of the word beat against Zhongyue's eardrums. He put Neil down and told him that he could stop shouting. Neil's voice was hoarse. Suddenly, Neil left the kite to Zhongyue and he bolted toward the woods.

Neil stopped under a tree, unzipped his pants and urinated against the trunk. Hearing Neil doing his business, Zhongyue felt an urgent need to relieve himself as well. He tied the kite to a stone, opened his zipper, and urinated just like Neil had. The urine from the long night came out, one high and one low; one thick and one thin. The buzzing sound in the wind accompanied its warm odour, and then the sound got quieter. Zhongyue felt his depression melt away with all the smelly urine, and each pore of his body opened to the clear breeze and sunlight. Incredible pleasure rose in him.

They zipped their pants up and walked out of the woods. The kite bumped along on the ground. At the end of the sandy road, away from the slope, a yellow dot moved toward them slowly. Neil said that his mother was coming. Zhongyue asked what he would say when he saw his mom. Thinking for a while, Neil suddenly pointed to Zhongyue's crotch and then his own. "You, big. I, small." It took a moment, but when Zhongyue understood what he had heard, he burst into laughter. Seeing Zhongyue laugh, Neil followed suit. They laughed so hard they couldn't walk. They lay down on the grass in the sunshine, stretching their arms and legs.

Zhongyue closed his eyes for a while, and then became aware of a dark cloud settling over his face. He opened his eyes and spotted the shadow of a black skirt nearby. Dawa was sitting on the tree stump next to him. She wore a pair of oversized sunglasses that covered nearly half of her face. He could see part of a bruise and a trace of tears. Shocked, Zhongyue jerked up. "What happened to you?"

Dawa said she fell.

Zhongyue pondered that for a while and then shouted, "He hit you, didn't he? Don't lie to me."

Dawa pulled a corner of her scarf to wipe her face. After a while she said, "Don't make a fuss. Things here aren't the same as in the city. You should mind your own business, not other people's."

Zhongyue's face darkened, and he said, "I'm not in charge, but the social services are."

Dawa's face paled. When she spoke again, her voice cracked with emotion. "If they take Neil away, I'll chop you up. I swear!"

Zhongyue said with a sigh, "You're talking nonsense. If people from the social services came, they would take Joy away. Why would they take Neil?"

Calming down gradually, Dawa said, "Dr. Chen, don't worry about me. I'm happy. I've never seen Neil laugh like this. I thought it wasn't in his nature to laugh."

Zhongyue asked, "Is it worth your tears? If you love to see him laugh, you must find a way to make him laugh all the time."

Dawa hesitated for a second and said, "If Neil had met you earlier, he'd have been much better. Dr. Chen, do you have a child?" Dawa asked.

Zhongyue thought he had left his worries behind in Toronto, and he hadn't expected that one question to bring them back. His sunny mood suddenly became cloudy. "My daughter," he sighed. "I'm not going to talk about her."

Neil got up from the ground and climbed on top of Dawa like a monkey. He rummaged through Dawa's backpack to see what she'd bought. He found a lunchbox that sported a picture of Harry Potter, a pair of new sneakers, and several pencils with rubber heads in the shape of a basketball—they all were for school. Neil tried on the new shoes with joy and then handed them back reluctantly. Dawa's eyes fixed on her child and asked him, "What did you learn from Dr. Chen?"

Neil looked at Zhongyue, who said, "The kid will go to school tomorrow. He'll be stressed out for a whole semester. It'd be better to let him play today. When school starts, I'll go to Whitefish School every Monday afternoon to train the teachers there. After that I can stay to help Neil. Let him have fun today."

Neil seemed to understand, so he uttered some odd words to Zhongyue. He didn't catch them, so he asked Neil to repeat what he'd said. Again, Zhongyue didn't understand. Dawa laughed, saying that only she knew what her son's words meant and she explained that Neil wanted to show Zhongyue some herbs.

"Neil's grandpa was a medicine man in the tribe—not a Western doctor, but an herbalist. First Nations people believe in using herbs for healing, except in the case of accidents or emergencies. The family were healers from generation to generation. When Neil was a baby, his grandpa took him to pick herbs."

"So Neil's father is also a medicine man, too?"

Dawa didn't answer, but urged Neil to go ahead. After a few steps, Neil stopped and looked at Dawa. Whining and muttering, he refused to go further. Dawa scolded him as she ran to the car to get the new sneakers. After the boy put them on, the three started walking again.

Down the slope, wild geese were flocked along the shores of Penguin Lake. Neil snapped a branch and whipped it left and right, playfully poking at all the creatures they walked by. Zhongyue laughed, saying that a benefit of being deaf was being unafraid of noise.

The surface of the lake looked grey under the midday sun. Wherever the wind had blown past, there were fallen leaves. Some leaves flew in the soft wind and refused to land on the ground. Bending over, Dawa picked up what looked like a stone and put it in Zhongyue's hand. He took a look at it, and it turned out to be a goose egg, much bigger than a chicken egg. The shell looked pinkish, and the egg felt warm to the touch—maybe it had just been laid. He asked if it was edible. Dawa said it tasted better than chicken eggs. Zhongyue said that he'd pick up a few. Dawa put her fingers between her lips and whistled loudly, calling Neil. She pulled off her scarf

and knotted the four corners together to make an instant bag
for Neil to hold the goose eggs.

Soon, Neil had filled half of the pouch. Zhongyue said it
was enough. He wanted to carry it himself. Dawa found a
tree trunk that had a hole in it—perhaps birds had built a nest
there. Dawa put the egg bag into the hole and surrounded
the tree with some large pebbles. "We'll take the same route
back. We only need to remember this tree. Why should we
carry such a heavy thing? There's still a long way to walk."
Zhongyue laughed. *I've lived in the city far too long, he
thought.*

The road came to a fork. One branch ran along the lake;
the other turned towards the woods. Dawa chose the one that
angled towards the trees.

"Herbs near the main road aren't very good. The area is
polluted by people and cars."

The road narrowed, gradually becoming a trail that snaked
through the trees. Their steps on the fallen leaves from the
previous year made hollow echoes. The trees became tall and
dense. The branches crossed over each other and wrapped everything up. The sunlight looked like ribbons coming through
the trees, hanging down between the branches and dappling
the ground with yellow flecks. It seemed more like dusk than
noon. Deep in the woods, a woodpecker pecked on a tree. A
bird fluttered in the tree; the leaves rustled and fell onto the
ground.

Dawa and Neil stopped almost at the same time. They had
found a fingernail-sized pink flower between two big fir trees.
Its petals were short, but it's stamen was large and dark brown
with tiny thorns on it. Neil knelt down and pushed the surrounding weeds aside. The tall stem was revealed, and Neil
found even more flowers.

"These are dog rose berries, rich in vitamins. They can be
made into tea and heal constipation. You must get rid of all
the thorns though. Otherwise...." Dawa paused. Zhongyue

asked her to continue. Dawa hesitated and said that it would be hard to remove them from the other end.

Neil raised his bottom, pointed at it, and muttered, "Ass, block."

Dawa chuckled and said, "You little bug. You don't hear what you ought to, but only what you shouldn't listen to."

"He didn't hear—he saw." Zhongyue said. "Neil's good at lip-reading. We should try to speak in front of his face and use fewer gestures."

Pinching a flower, Neil tried to pluck it, but Dawa stopped him. From her backpack, she removed a small pouch, took out a handful of tobacco shreds, and respectfully scattered them on the ground. Eyes closed and palms together, she quietly prayed. After opening her eyes, Dawa waved her hand and let Neil pick the flower.

"The First Nations people respect Mother Earth and never desecrate the land. They only take a plant or a tree from the woods for a good reason. And they always offer some thank-you tobacco beforehand."

Zhongyue also took some tobacco shreds from Dawa's pouch and scattered them. He murmured, "Earth Mother, you know everything. I can't lie to you. I, a Han Chinese from a faraway place, am plucking a flower because of curiosity. I am not constipated now, but should I become constipated in the future, I'll know what to do."

Dawa laughed and said, "Dr. Chen, you're funny. Your wife must always be amused."

Neil collected a handful of dog rose berries. After throwing them into Dawa's backpack, he walked ahead. Fifteen minutes or so later, he came back with a bunch of maiden ferns clutched in his hand. Dawa shook the soil off the roots and displayed them in her palm to show Zhongyue. The fern looked delicate and soft, its stem pinkish, trembling slightly in the wind. "This is called virgin hair. It is used to treat a cold and also kidney stones."

Zhongyue jumped back a bit. He said, "The name makes me nervous. It reminds me of corruption among government officials." Both of them burst into laughter.

The three found more herbs and eventually reached an open field. The midday sunlight poured down on aged tree trunks that stood one by one, numerous charred scars crawling like serpents from the bottom to the top. The land was bumpy, and the exposed roots looked like dark blood vessels on a lifeless breast. Zhongyue guessed that the land had either been burned by lightning, or by a forest fire, some time earlier. From the green woods to the scorched earth, there was only one step, no transition. One step forward was green life, and one step back was barren death. Both shocked him.

Looking up, Zhongyue thought that the blue sky was large and open well, a well so deep that it was out of reach. He seemed unable to reach the world beyond the well even if he tried all his life plus two more afterlives. He formed a trumpet with his hands and shouted into the sky, "Oh ... Oh ... Oh ...!"

After shouting, Zhongyue was embarrassed. He said, "My hometown is in the crowded south where people live close to one another. When we eat, we try to make less noise because we don't want our neighbours to know what we're eating. When we go to the toilet, we don't want the next-door neighbours to be aware of what we're doing. When we speak, we lower our voices, afraid that the neighbours might overhear. I suffered from this closeness during childhood. So when I'm here in this less populated north, I want to roar."

Dawa said, "You can roar as much as you want. It won't harm deaf Neil. We Tibetans are fond of yelling. Let's see who roars louder."

Zhongyue rounded his mouth again, but he couldn't make sounds. It was as if he were a deflated tire. Dawa laughed until tears came. Zhongyue asked, "Why are you laughing? You should roar. Or sing a song. The song about the Tibetan Plateau sung by Li something is damn good."

Her mouth twisted, Dawa told him that Li sang in the style of Han Chinese. Real Tibetans didn't sing that way. Zhongyue asked her to sing a song in the genuine Tibetan style.

Dawa declined, saying that she hadn't sung for a long time, but finally he persuaded her and she reluctantly agreed.

Zhongyue didn't understand Dawa's song, since it was in Tibetan. He felt the tune, light and gentle like the water under small bridges in South China, instead of the loud Tibetan music that spoke of strong emotions. It was a stretch to say that Dawa was singing. In fact, she hummed, half through her throat and half through her nose. Zhongyue asked if it was a love song and if Dawa could translate it. Her face flushed, Dawa said it was hard to translate, but Zhongyue insisted that she at least give him a general idea.

Dawa thought about it for awhile and then translated a few lines:

If you don't scoop the water right way,
the stream will flow away.
If you don't pick the flower in time,
the spring will be over
If you don't sing songs again, you'll be old.1

Zhongyue clapped his hands excitedly. If Dawa didn't want to get old, she should sing another one using her loud, enjoyable voice, he said, just like the Tibetan singer Tseten Dolma.

Dawa covered her face with her hands for a long while. Then she stood up suddenly and sang, shocking Zhongyue. The song was in Chinese, and its tune was as sharp as knives that seemed to pierce his eardrum and stab his heart. He felt as if his heart had been cut through and was suddenly full of holes.

The eagle flies around the hilltop,
Because it can't find a cliff to land on.
The cloud flows in the sky,
Because it can't find a place to drop its rain.

The person rides on the back of a horse,
Because he can't find a way back home.
It's hard and bitter....

Neil was standing motionless, staring at Dawa's lips. The flowers in his hands dropped onto the ground. His eyes, on his clay-like face, looked like melting water from a thousand-year-old snow, clear and shiny, reflecting the sun, moon, and stars. Zhongyue knew that something had moved Neil for the first time.

That thing was the soul.

That night, after saying goodbye to Dawa and her son, Zhongyue couldn't sleep. Moonlight, through the gaps of the bamboo blinds, caressed his eyelids, leaving a dappled white light over everything in the room. Closing his eyes, he saw the blue flagstone road in front of his childhood home, like a snake meandering toward the river. In his small southern town, the river was shallow and the water was brownish yellow. When motor boats passed by, bits of leaves, soil, and dead animals rolled in on the currents. During the summer, Zhongyue and his brothers, half-naked and in wooden slippers, ran into the river, climbed into any of the boats parked along the bank, and then jumped into the water. The water opened a hole and immediately swallowed up their bodies, which looked dark and smooth like the skin of a loach. Decades later, he clearly remembered the pattern and colour of the blue flagstone path, and the pounding sounds made by their wooden slippers.

He knew that the horse in Dawa's song had brought him back to his hometown, step by step.

At dawn, a rustling sound on the roof woke Zhongyue up. He realized that he'd fallen asleep. He took an extra large flashlight and turned it toward the skylights. A dark shadow flashed by. He knew that it was a raccoon, which had a den on the roof. *Before the winter I must get rid of that den,* he thought.

Xiaoyue,

Neil has a great feeling for music. People with normal hearing rely on musical forms and patterns to access the core content, but Neil, skipping those things, directly enters the bone marrow of music—rhythm. I think Neil could be an outstanding drummer. The Aboriginal powwow *drum follows the rhythm completely. But for the First Nations people, a person's occupation is based on the family tradition. If Neil grows up and stays on the reserve, unlike many young people who leave for big cities, he will most likely become an herbalist, like his ancestors.*

Old Joy wasn't old. He was only thirty-eight, but his name was already more than a decade old. Old Joy got his name for two reasons. First, it was because of his looks. Old Joy had started to go bald at the age of twenty-eight. When he was thirty-five, he was completely bald, with only a thin circle of yellow hair on his head.

Second, it was because he had seniority when it came to prison terms. Old Joy had been imprisoned three times in total. The first time was for fighting, the second was for smashing a car window, and the third was for stealing a newspaper from a grocery store. Each time he had been released from probation after being in jail for a few days. He had a thick criminal records. In the words of a popular Chinese slang, Old Joy had been to the dark mountain.

In fact, Old Joy had also been of course many other minor transgressions, mostly theft, but he was fortunate enough not to be caught. Occasionally he was involved in one or two shocking offences, each of which happened after he drank too much alcohol.

More than a decade earlier, when Old Joy hadn't been called Old Joy, he had been an ordinary and obedient young person, a little shy. At that time, he had seriously followed in the footsteps of his father, exploring the world of herbs. He had been ready to take over his father's practice as the town herbalist. He would have trailed after his father, his grandfather, and his great grandfather, step by step, in the family tradition. But, as it happened, he missed one step and fell into a bottomless wine cellar. From that moment, his future had to be rewritten.

Old Joy was born to a mixed-race family. Old Joy had ancestors of Irish, French, British, and Dutch derivation. So when Old Joy had still had hair, it was light brown. He had sharp features, pale blue eyes, and a straight nose. So when a Tibetan woman named Dawa first met him at Taer Temple in Qinghai Province, she was sure he was white. As for his slightly dark skin, she thought it was simply a tan.

Dawa had been to Taer Temple countless times, and she was familiar with each building, each Buddha sculpture, even every stone step and threshold. Like a doe, she could scamper through the pebbled paths between temples and monasteries. She always found her way into the main hall; she would push open a side door at random and go through the narrow channels with the help of the light from the butter lamps.

At the time, she had already been working as a tour guide for a couple of years after her graduation from tourism school. Taer Temple was the main attraction that she lead her tourists to. But on that autumn afternoon, she went as a visitor instead of a guide. Standing outside of a huge building with a gold-tiled roof, she looked up at the last warm sunshine before the advent of winter snow.

From all appearance, she looked the same as any other Tibetan women her age. She had slightly high cheekbones and skin the colour of the sun on the plateau. She had a sprinkling of freckles on both sides of her nose. As she smiled, her pink gums were exposed. She wore a colourful Tibetan robe, and her long braid was decorated with silver jewellery that clanked when she moved. Only when she lifted the hem of her robe, crossed the high threshold of the gold-tiled hall, and knelt

down before a statue of the Buddha, did she appear sorrow-
ful—overcome by sadness that seemed much older than her.
Dawa prostrated herself on the floor in a dark corner, instead
of on the mat in the centre for tourists. The light from the
butter lamps shone dimly and outlined her vague shadow on
the wall, which looked like ancient dust. The hem of her robe
stuck to a thin layer of dust and broken spider webs. Looking
up at the Buddha, she couldn't see his face, only his gold-coated
plump toes. She counted Buddha's toes and murmured two
names over and over again:

Khetsun Wangdue. Wang Zheren.
Khetsun Wangdue. Wang Zheren.
Khetsun Wangdue. Wang Zheren.

Khetsun Wangdue was Dawa's first husband, her former
classmate at the tourism school and colleague at the travel
company. They worked on the same route—from Taer Temple
to the Sun and Moon Mountain and to Qinghai Lake, and vice
versa. Wangdue went on the route one week, and Dawa went
the alternate week. Their wedding had taken place on October
1st, the National Day, the third year after their graduation.
Unfortunately, the bright red marriage certificate lying in Dawa's drawer was useless since Wangdue never had the chance
to be a groom. The coach he rode in had an accident on the
way to the Sun and Moon Mountain. Wangdue wasn't found
in the wreckage of the bus. A few days later, people found his
body on the riverbank. The Public Security Bureau conducted
several investigations but found no good reason to explain why
his body was so far away from the coach. Dawa was a bride
for eleven days on paper before she became a widow.

Dawa's second husband, whose name was Wang Zheren, was
a Han Chinese teaching at Qinghai University who was interested in minority customs. Wang Zheren had been in Dawa's
tour group once. He had followed Dawa and visited Qinghai

Lake. Dawa had sung all the way, and he had listened to all her songs. He fell in love with Dawa, and he was persistent in courting her. Having gone to school with Tibetans and Han Chinese, Dawa had friends in mixed relationships and marriages, so she wasn't afraid of marrying a Han Chinese. Because of her previous experience, she was frightened by the word marriage. She never mentioned Wangdue, her first husband, to Wang Zheren. But at the wedding, someone got drunk and called Wang Zheren by her first husband's name. Wang Zheren didn't lose his temper, but, back in their bedroom, he was very upset. As an educated Han, even though he was angry, his voice was still gentle. "I don't care about your past, but I do care about your dishonesty." After he said this, Wang Zheren slept in his clothes at the end of their bed. At dawn, Dawa woke up to the strong smell of urine and found the sheet wet. Wang Zheren's body was cold. Later, a forensic doctor identified the cause of death as a heart attack.

As a result, Dawa, at the age of twenty-six, became a widow for the second time.

One, two, three....

Dawa counted the Buddha's toes ten times, and, knowing she'd rolled her tongue over those names over a hundred times, she lowered her head onto the floor and whispered, "Buddha, I beg you to lead them to the safe and peaceful land of light."

She smelled the stale dust on her nose and lips; she felt her eyes hurt, but not because of tears. The tears lay in the shallow riverbed of her rocky life and they had dried out before they could flow down. Without looking into a mirror, she already knew that those tears had left cracks on her forehead. That day, she clearly heard the noise of her youth wilting in her body.

Slowly she stood up and walked outside. Dust fell from her dress and danced in the mottled sunshine between the buildings. The autumn sun was strong like a knife, forcing her to close her eyes. Dark golden stars danced in front of her eyes, and she almost fell. Then someone suddenly held her waist. After a while, she felt warmth and strength from an arm, a man's arm.

That arm supported her and led her out of the threshold of the gold-tiled temple. Slowly she walked to the roadside and sat down.

Dawa noticed the head with brown curly hair and the face with a healthy complexion—a face like that of the people from the plateau. "I'm sorry. I ... too long."

Dawa had learned some English for a few weeks in the tourism school, but since her work was with domestic tour groups, the limited English she knew became rusty. The young foreigner finally spoke. "How do you do? My name is Joy. I'm a Canadian."

The foreigner spoke Chinese, but his tone was strange and didn't sound Chinese.

"Do you like Taer?" Dawa asked. She knew the questions was trivial, but those were the only English words she could say. She had no choice.

The man named Joy nodded and then shook his head. He had so much to say. His eyes were filled with two oceans of questions, but he could only smile. His Chinese and her English were both stuck in the bottleneck; Joy and Dawa sat on the roadside, desperately looking forward to a breakthrough.

The afternoon sun became strong, gradually thickening the outline of the monastery and the mountains. A group of women in rags knelt down at one step and then moved on to another step along the path leading to Taer Temple. Looked at from a distance, they were like a group of ants carrying bits of mud. In a corner of the temple, a small monk was relieving himself against the wall. His robe was red, and it looked as if blood had been splashed on the rugged, yellow, muddy walls.

Joy pulled a dictionary from his backpack and gave it to Dawa. In a small notebook, he neatly wrote a sentence in English and then tore the page off for Dawa. Dawa checked the dictionary to decipher the words.

"I didn't come for sightseeing. I came to learn Tibetan medicine."

In reply, Dawa wrote some words in Chinese and tore the page off for Joy, who then looked through the dictionary and guessed their meaning.

"Why do you want to learn Tibetan medicine?"

"Tibetan medicine and our herbs have something in common." The bottleneck cracked, and the water flowed out with difficulty. They both were excited about this strange form of communication. Their faces flushed. Page by page, the notebook got thinner and thinner.

"I've been here looking for a doctor for three days, but I can't find him."

"Who?"

This time, Joy scribbled the name in Chinese—the name he'd memorized.

"Living Buddha Muchi."

Dawa laughed aloud. Living Buddha Muchi was a doctor in the Taer Temple Hospital. She'd led groups from medical organizations to the hospital many times. After several visits, she had become friends with the living Buddha.

Dawa grabbed Joy's book and wrote down in Chinese, "Buddha Muchi is a busy man. You can't see him without an appointment."

Disappointment, like clouds, gradually covered Joy's face. She ignored him, got out her cellphone, and made a few calls. She put down the phone and extended four fingers of her hand in front of Joy's face. She said, "Meet Living Buddha Muchi at four this afternoon"

Joy suddenly understood. Hesitating for a moment, he hugged Dawa tightly. Dawa felt as if everybody were looking at her. Her head spun and her face flushed. She wasn't sure if she should push him away. She felt her body become tense, inch by inch.

That afternoon, Dawa took Joy to Living Buddha's Muchi's dwelling place. The boy server took them in and said that the living Buddha was meditating and reading the scripture. Dawa gestured for Joy to leave his backpack for the boy to take care of. Joy waited outside the room holding a white-yellow-and-blue *khata*—a traditional ceremonial scarf used in Tibet. The compound was extremely quiet. The wind was silent; even the fallen leaves seemed to roll over the ground with caution. After a while, some movement was heard, and the boy opened the door to invite them in. They entered the meeting room. In the centre of the room, a middle-aged man sat under a huge butter lamp. His traditional red-and-yellow habit made the place look brilliant. With his palms held together, the man looked peaceful and wise. His face looked like a lotus flower, as though he'd lived in paradise.

Joy bowed deeply to present the silk *khata*. The living Buddha stretched out his hand to touch Joy's head for the blessing. Removing a copper bracelet from his wrist, Joy held it in his hand in front of the living Buddha and begged him for opening light —that is, a blessing. Of course, this was at Dawa's instruction. After a very brief greeting, the two immediately engaged in conversation. The living Buddha spoke fluent English, which Dawa didn't understand. Every nerve in her body was wide awake and excited, as if numerous tentacles had gently stroked the wonderful door. She felt that the low-pitched voices of the two men were like two quiet streams joining under the pine trees and occasionally splashing bubbles. Or they were like bees flapping over a field full of rape blossoms. In her vision, it looked as if the entire landscape were covered with golden honey.

At that moment, Dawa completely forgot Wangdue and Wang Zheren.

It was dusk when they left the residence of the living Buddha. The sunset was heavy, as if mountains had pushed the gold-tiled building down. Visitors gradually dispersed. The fall wind carried sand and gravel through the woods. The air felt wet with a trace of frost.

Joy took off the copper bracelet that had been blessed by the living Buddha and put it on Dawa's wrist. It was very old. The image of a bald eagle was engraved on the clasp. She wore a small personal possession—a Tibetan dagger with an eagle etched on the handle. At that moment her heart warmed. He, like her, was also fond of eagles. But she couldn't express herself in English, so she took her dagger out and placed his eagle next to hers, trying her best to show her enjoyment by nodding and smiling. Later, when she finally learned his family background, she understood that both her people and his had a deep bond with the eagle.

"Can you tell me your address?"

This was what Joy wrote on the last page of his notebook. After the sheet was torn off, he and she would part. As a tour guide, she met a lot of tour groups and often gave her address to people as they were leaving. It was a touching moment, but she knew that their brief connection could not become a lifelong bond. She didn't expect anything from him and vice versa.

She watched him gallop down the mountain to catch the last bus. His tall and lanky figure went up and down like an ostrich and gradually disappeared in the thickening darkness. She thought their meeting was like a story, an interesting story. Stories were the background of life, but not life itself. Stories happened every day. They were like clouds floating across the canopy of her life. Her life wouldn't change because of them.

However, she still looked forward to hearing from him. And two months later, when she'd almost given up, his letter finally arrived.

The letter wasn't long. It was about his journey and some new pharmacological prescriptions he'd learned. Her answering letter was very brief, not only because of her English, but because she felt like her life was boring and empty. Gradually their letters became longer and more frequent. Besides work and studies, they touched on a number of other areas and Dawa started to consult English dictionaries and the world atlas.

Later, in one of his letters, Joy carefully asked if she was willing to come to Canada and live with him. She guessed that this was his proposal. She was glad he didn't use the word marriage, and she felt lucky that she could avoid explaining her past due to her poor English. Years later, the truth gradually emerged. Recalling that period of time, she finally understood that she had married Joy because she was tired of struggling in life. But she didn't realize that, in so doing, she had messed up her whole life.

When she wrote the letter with the words "I do" and dropped it—stamped with overseas postage—into a mailbox, she suddenly remembered something. A year earlier, she had taken a group of government officials on a tour around Qinghai Lake. By the time her tourists had reached the lake, a heavy downpour began. Without any shelter nearby, most of the tourists ran back to the coach. She was behind and had to take shelter from the storm in a gift shop. Only one monk was in the store, also sheltering from the rain. As the monk turned to her, her legs became weak, and her heart jumped in her throat—the monk looked like Wangdue. Looking at her, the monk was also frightened. His eyes closed, and he kept silent for a long time before he breathed a sigh. He said, "Poor woman, you should go. Go as far as your horse can take you."

A year later she finally flew over half the globe and joined Joy in northern Canada. When she saw him again, she was shocked by two facts. First, Whitefish, where he lived, was such a small town— in fact, the entire town was made up of three streets. Second, Joy had changed significantly; he had become quiet, and he looked much older. She didn't know that alcohol, like a worm, was chewing through Joy's guts. She couldn't see what was inside him; she only saw his skinny outer body. His body was like a tree without roots and its wilting would come sooner or later.

By then, Joy had already developed a reputation as a drunkard in the town. Whenever the bar was open, he drank there. Whenever the bar was closed, he drank at home. At the beginning, he picked on others when he was drunk, and Dawa helped to clean up the mess. Later, Joy began to find faults with Dawa. When he wasn't drinking, Joy was quiet and even behaved like a gentleman. But alcohol could change everything. There was a very thin line dividing heaven from hell, and Joy couldn't balance. He either fell down one side or the other.

The first time he was brutal to Dawa was when she was pregnant with Neil. That day, Dawa came home from work and decided to go to the corner store to get a jar of pickled cucumbers. She had a surprisingly good appetite, but she threw up what she ate. Her stomach couldn't keep any food down; only pickled cucumbers satisfied her empty stomach for a short while. In the closet, she found her ceramic piggy bank, in which she stashed away her pocket money. But when she turned it over, it was empty.

"Where's my money?" she asked Joy. He didn't answer. Like a wall, Joy blocked her from going anywhere.

"Who gave you a ride home?" Joy asked, tugging at her hair. Dawa wanted to say that it was her colleague who had driven her home because she was unable to drive after vomiting. But Joy's fist firmly closed her mouth. He pushed her down the stairs. Like a sack of flour, she fell to the floor. She still could walk afterwards even though her foot was sprained. But later at midnight, she bled profusely and had to go to the hospital. When the doctor saw the bruises on her, he became suspicious, but she insisted she fell down accidentally.

Neil was a really tough baby who had survived his mother's injured body for five months. Dawa had hoped their child could bring Joy back, but she failed. Neil's birth softened Joy's heart, but the change didn't last. And Joy chose hell.

Everyone in Whitefish knew why Joy's wife had those injuries, but Dawa remained silent about them and never reported Joy to the police. People guessed the reason for her silence: Dawa hadn't received her landing papers yet. Separation might lead to her repatriation. But they were only half right. The other reason was that Dawa had a secret, down deep in her heart, and no one knew about it.

Xiaoyue,
A powwow is an Aboriginal outdoor gathering that usually takes place in the summer. Sometimes the powwow season extends into the fall if it isn't too cold. It's a bit like Chinese temple fairs, but not exactly the same. Powwows also contains some aspects of prayers to the ancestors and thanks for blessings. When I arrived, the summer was almost over. So I only caught the final powwow at the end of September, which took place at Sioux Lookout. When there is a powwow, people from nearby all come. This usually less-populated northern area suddenly became bustling. I bought you a fan made of eagle feathers, dyed peacock blue, from the market. A wooden sculpture of an eagle head—a very special ornament—hangs from the handle. The eagle has a very special place in the Aboriginal culture because they believe that the eagle in the sky is closest to the creator. Tibetan culture includes a similar belief: the eagle symbolizes bravery. All the traditional battle costumes of Aboriginal men are always decorated with eagle feathers. Many powwow ceremonies start with an eagle feather dance. This dance is performed by four of the strongest men selected from the tribe. When eagle feathers slowly drop from the sky onto the land, the dancers pick them up in different ways to commemorate all their fallen fighters. When they perform the eagle feather dance, everyone in the audience must stand and salute them.

Zhongyue had never heard such sounds. The six or seven drummers were strong men, and their faces were painted in striped patterns. They sat around a huge *powwow* drum. Nobody was a leader or a follower. They beat the drum and paused at the same time. The drumbeat was slow. The drumstick hitting on the drum was only a prelude—the resulting tremor was the climax. That tremor didn't come from the drums. Instead, it seemed like it muffled thunder rolling over the ground. The sound shook Zhongyue's heart and made it beat wildly. "Blood-stirring" was an overused word in a certain era in China, but that day Zhongyue thought of that word again and again. His blood had run coldly in his body for half of his life, but on that day his blood was stirred up, like flood water eager to burst the dam.

Their songs were also sung in a way that Zhongyue found haunting. He wasn't even sure he could call them songs. No lyrics, only a melody of up-or-down cries. The pitch was high, as if it had reached the mountain peak, only one step away from the sky. Then the tune became low, as if it had dropped into a bottomless pit, only one step from the centre of the earth. Like the strong gusts of wind, the sounds travelled between sky and earth, jumping from one water drop to another, from one tuft of grass to another, and from one cloud to another. No musical notations could record this complicated melody; music theory could not sustain its power and freedom. This sound broke the rules of logic. It had nothing to do with the vocal chords, nothing to do with the throat, and nothing to do with the brain. It bounced to the world directly from the heart, without any touch or contamination from any intermediate links. Zhongyue felt an itch on his face. Touching his face, he felt his tears; he knew that this voice and his soul had collided somewhere outside of his body.

Men started to dance. They wore costumes decorated with eagle feathers, their hands holding various weapons and tools. Their dance was a narrative, describing practices carried out by the men of the tribe since time immemorial: worship, expeditions, hunting, burials, and questions about heaven. The movements of the dancing men were strong and wild. The movements of their feet and hands were their words.

The women wore colourful cloaks, embroidered skirts, and jangling bells on their skirts and dresses. The women didn't like to tell stories. Their dance was related to emotion. Their cloaks spun around like butterflies that swirled all over the place, and their steps teased the dust. The women's smiles reminded people of harvest, children, of nature, and the beauty of the world.

It was already fall. The people who had arrived in the early morning wore thick jackets and caps. But it felt like summer when the sun shone at noon. Both the performers and the audience were sweaty. The people on stage were hot because of their active movements and thick costumes. The audience was also hot because they shouted excitedly. Zhongyue walked around but couldn't find a shaded seat. People kept offering him cigarettes and tobacco, saying *"meegwetch"*—he knew it meant thanks in Ojibwa. He guessed that they were the parents of his students.

Then it was the children's turn to perform.

Though the children's clothes and accessories were simple, all of them had eagle feathers, and the girls had bells on their skirts. The age of the children was also uneven. The oldest ones were teenagers who tried to imitate the adults' expressions. The younger ones had only gone through a couple of *powwow* parties; their steps were not steady yet. The youngest ones were toddlers learning to walk. They cried when they stepped onto the stage. The audience burst into laughter and couldn't stand straight.

Zhongyue finally found a shady corner and sat down, but the music suddenly stopped. Someone took the microphone and coughed gently. The crowd became quiet. The person next to Zhongyue said he was the chief. The speech the chief gave was extremely modern. The first time was in English, and the second time in Ojibwa. He spoke about world affairs and then local business. After giving thanks to heaven and to the four seasons, he said that he appreciated the rain and sunshine.

He was also grateful for birds in the sky and animals on the earth. He gave thanks for the harvest and for kind neighbours. It was a lengthy speech filled with big words, Zhongyue felt sleepy as he listened.

As Zhongyue was about to close his eyes, his neighbour nudged him awake. The voice from the microphone had gotten much louder.

"You can see how lovely our children are, but don't forget to thank those who help our children: schoolteachers, volunteers, and school bus drivers. Don't forget that there's a father among us who helps our children, but who has left his own child."

As all the audience turned to look at Zhongyue, he flushed, sweat spreading all over his face. Before he could wipe his sweat, several large men came and picked him up. They ran around the audience and placed him on the podium. Someone passed a microphone to him. Feeling nervous, Zhongyue forgot how to speak English. He stammered, "I ... I'm not...." He couldn't find any more words to say; he only saw hands in the audience clap like trees waving in the wind.

Returning to his seat, he felt as though his body had been scattered and he couldn't get the pieces back into place. His hands and feet kept trembling; he didn't know whether it was because of a panic attack or because he was so touched by the gesture from the community.

Drumbeats resounded, but the tempo had changed and become very fast.

Then a small and skinny boy came to the stage and stood still. He began to spin quickly, following the rhythm of the drumbeat. He wore head gear made of fur and a black-and-yellow mirror hung between his eyebrows to protect his forehead. He was dressed in green. A breastplate made of porcupine quills was on his chest, and a huge shield of eagle feathers on his back. Brass ankle bells were tied on each of his legs. His clothes were embroidered with the designs of animal feet and geometric patterns, which were blurred because of his movement. No matter how fast the drumbeat was, the boy never missed one step. His steps started with the drum and finished when it stopped. His ankle bells jingled like rain pouring down, and his clothes moved like a green cloud dancing with the wind. The audience gaped at the scene.

Unexpectedly the drum stopped, and everyone in the audience became silent. After a long while, the people began whistling, stamping their feet and screaming in unison, "Neil! Neil! Neil!" At that moment Zhongyue recognized that the boy was Neil.

As Zhongyue watched Neil come down from the stage, he also spotted Dawa. He hadn't seen her for about three weeks, since school had begun. Pushing through the crowd, Zhongyue approached Dawa, who grasped Zhongyue's hand and repeatedly told him, "I've found it." He asked what she'd found. Dawa said he shouldn't have forgotten what he asked her to find. "It's Neil's hobby," she continued. "I know now. Neil had trouble listening to words, but had no problem with rhythms. The chief said he'd send Neil to the annual *powwow* contest for North American Indians in November." Zhongyue was very happy to hear about this. He told her that the DVD of the sign language dictionary he had ordered for them was in his car and that he'd give to them later.

While they chatted, Neil came over, riding on a man's shoulders. He held a soft drink in his left hand and a hot dog in his right, and his mouth was full of scarlet ketchup. The man was tall and well built, and his face was shiny. Not sure of his age, Zhongyue guessed he was Neil's father. Before Zhongyue had a chance to say hello, the man stretched out his hand, laughing out loud. "I'm Raymond, Neil's grandpa. Thanks for taking care of my boy."

Neil jumped down from his grandfather's shoulders. He gave Zhongyue a big toothy smile and pulled at Zhongyue's clothes. "K ... kite," he said.

Zhongyue patted Neil's head and spoke to him in sign language: "Sorry. I didn't bring the kite. How about next time?"

Then the loudspeaker announced, "Anybody who is interested in learning about the herbs on the mountain, please meet Dr. Raymond Maas in tent one."

Neil clapped his hands, calling, "Grandpa, Grandpa!" Dawa asked Zhongyue if he would come, saying that what she told him about herbs and healing was only a drop in the bucket. Neil's grandfather knew much more. Zhongyue followed the crowd of attendees into the tent and sat among them. Raymond gave everybody two gifts: a package of tobacco to honour Mother Earth, and a small bag of tea for peace of mind. He also introduced them to some brewing methods for Native teas, and mentioned safety issues about hiking on mountains. Then the group trekked onto the mountain.

After fifteen minutes, the noise from the *powwow* diminished; the woods gradually became darker, and the colours of flowers deepened. Raymond noticed a cluster of blooming purple flowers under a huge tree. Pushing the bushes aside with his wooden stick, he leaned over to pluck the plant. Suddenly a man and a woman jumped up from the ground, startling everyone in the group. The woman's blouse was unbuttoned, and her shoulder was partially exposed. Bits of grass were all over her clothes. A plastic sheet was spread on the ground, and a fur canteen and several wooden bowls were scattered on it.

Raymond hit his wooden stick so hard on the tree trunk that the stick broke into two parts. "You bastard! Joy! You dare to drink at this *powwow*? You've broken our ancestors' rules!"

Joy didn't reply. Instead, he picked up the fur canteen and walking away, leaving the woman standing there alone.

Everybody's high spirits were dampened, as if freezing rain had drenched them. Nobody spoke, but all eyes turned to Dawa. Pretending to see nothing, she squatted down with Neil and helped him to dig up an herb with sharp stones until only the root was left in the soil. Dawa dropped the stone and tried to pull the root up. But the thin root was very tough. No matter how hard she tried, she couldn't get it out. Trembling, she kept pulling. Zhongyue went over and cut off the herb. He picked the root and tossed it into Neil's basket. Then he helped Dawa stand up and said, "Let's go."

The three walked slowly and gradually fell behind the crowd. When the were some distance away, Zhongyue said hesitatingly, "Dawa, you could leave and bring Neil back to China."

Dawa's mouth pursed tightly, and her lips became thin and purple. She leaned against a tree. "Except for here, are there any places that can accommodate a child like Neil?"

Zhongyue was speechless.

Xiaoyue,

You said in your letter that Xiang will take you to Disneyland over the Christmas holiday. I've felt sad for a long time. Not only because I can't see you over the winter break, but also because as your father, I'm supposed to be with you. Xiang has taken away the chance for me to do so. You've asked me to take you to Disneyland for years, but I didn't do it because of my hectic life—I was busy writing my thesis, job-hunting, keeping my job, and getting a promotion. Things are always lining up in front of me, blocking my vision. I've forgotten that your childhood can't wait forever. Living in Sioux Lookout has helped me see many things in life. Every time I see that deaf child, Neil, I can't help but think of you, my dear daughter. Everybody can see Neil's misfortune, but few people notice his luck. Neil has a wonderful mom who always carries his dream. But I, your dad, am not the same. I can't carry your dream until I can forget my own. Neil's mom makes me feel guilty.

In early October, Zhongyue received a registered letter in a thick, large manila envelope. The unfamiliar name of a law firm on the envelope looked ominous. Inside were divorce papers.

Xiaoxiao Fan had initiated a separation, but she had also suggesting that spending a year apart might help them get back together again. After Zhongyue came to Sioux Outlook, the two had often talked on the phone, but their conversations were mostly about their daughter. Xiaoxiao had never mentioned divorce on the phone, not even a hint. Of course, Zhongyue should have guessed—separation was usually a necessary prelude to divorce—but he just didn't expect Xiaoxiao to act so quickly. He couldn't help but recall all the details of the relationship between Xiaoxiao and Xiang. Perhaps Xiang wasn't the result of the separation, but the cause of it. He felt like he had been walking in the dark and had had fallen into a trap without warning. His head spun. He picked up the phone to dial that familiar number.

The phone rang for a while before someone picked it up. It was Xiaoxiao. She was panting heavily, which made Zhongyue think about her in bed with Xiang. Holding his breath for a few seconds, Zhongyue faked a chuckle and said, "Xiaoxiao, I guess you just couldn't stop, right?" Xiaoxiao hung up right away. He dialled again, but no one answered. Sitting on the floor with the phone on his lap, Zhongyue was ready to keep calling throughout the night. Each time he punched the keys, he got angrier. Soon he felt anger exploding in his head. The receiver seemed to melt in his tight hand. About an hour later, when someone finally picked up the phone, Zhongyue felt as though his head had exploding into numerous fragments. His own howl almost knocked him down.

"Bring that Xiang in front of me if you dare. That man is a fucking asshole!"

The other end was deadly silent. After a long while, a trembling voice sounded: "Dad?" Zhongyue realized it was his daughter, Xiaoyue, who had answered the phone. He lowered his voice and said that he didn't know it was her. Xiaoyue said nothing, but she sighed weakly. It was gentle sigh, but it left a wound that would not heal. Zhongyue felt a pain in his heart.

"Don't sigh. You're only a kid. Sighing belongs to adults."

Xiaoyue protested that she wasn't a child anymore—she was

eleven. After a pause, she said, "In fact, you and Mom didn't live happily. Separation may be good. Don't worry about me. I'm okay. In the future, when you have a new home, I have two places to go, one home during the winter break, and another during the summer break. I have many friends who do this."

Her words touched Zhongyue's heart, but he was unsure whether he felt happy or sad. He found that children who grew up in foreign countries, compared to their peers in China, seemed immature in some aspects, but too mature in other aspects.

After the phone call, Zhongyue couldn't focus on the work he needed to prepare for the next day. He was lost in thought. Xiaoxiao and he always had thought that Xiaoyue was like a tomboy, rather carefree. He'd never thought that Xiaoyue had watched them and known about their unhappy marriage. Both of them had tried to hide their unhappiness from their daughter. His unhappiness was mainly due to Xiaoxiao's un-happiness, but he had been ignorant about his own feelings and about his daughter's.

Xiaoxiao had been among the elite, the flower of flowers. She'd been ahead of him in every major thing. She got her degree first, got promoted earlier, came to Canada six months earlier, and got a good job before him. Not to mention her salary was much higher than his. She was ahead of him, but unwilling to see that he had fallen permanently behind her. She always stepped forward first and then turned back to pull him towards her, until they were almost at the same level. That was Xiaoxiao's happiest time, but she couldn't indulge in it. She was used to plugging away, and she couldn't rest for long. She had to move forward and then come back for him. Even though he was always a few steps behind her, he eventually reached the goal she'd expected him to. What let her down wasn't that he didn't reached her goals, but that he did it at his own pace. She couldn't stand his laid-back lifestyle. He always felt like he was a thousand-year-old ox cart, each joint heavily rusted. If Xiaoxiao let go, he would immediately crash and break into pieces of useless wood.

The two of them continued in this lifestyle for several years, and gradually Xiaoxiao got tired of it. He was unaware of her unhappiness until it was too late. In fact, he could have done something, but, according Xiaoxiao, the problem was his personality: he was like a string when he was lifted, but like a heap when he was put down. At this point, he was unhappy simply because he saw that she was unhappy. His real unhappiness appeared much later.

Some years earlier, after having not seen him for eight years, his mother had arrived in Toronto to visit them.

His father had died young. As children, he and his two brothers had relied on the meagre wages of his mother, who worked in a shoe factory. She had only gone to elementary school, and she could only read a little. She did the dirtiest minimum-wage job at the factory: cutting rubber patterns. Her daily duty was to get hot rubber from the rollers and cut soles according to the prototype. His mother had asked for this type of work because the workers at the rubber workshop could get four extra *yuan* a month as compensation for working on the toxic raw rubber.

The raw rubber shed its colour. When Zhongyue's mother came home from work, her neck and her hands were black. When she smiled, the wrinkles on her forehead looked dark, too. Every evening, she washed her face and hands again and again, pouring out several basins of inky water. Then she cooked supper for her family. The meal was very simple—it rarely had meat —but she made a few dishes and a soup. After the meal, she cleaned up the dishes too. Then she sat down and began to knit. She could knit a variety of patterns: flat stitches, stacked stitches, plum blossom, and gold pin shape. She knitted woollen sweaters for others, but, when she knitted for herself, she used yarn reclaimed from old cotton gloves. Her sweater looked half yellow and half white, but it fitted her well. She made two *yuan* from each sweater. When knitting smaller sized ones with simple patterns, she could knit five or six sweaters a month—of course, she had to knit all evening, without any breaks.

Zhongyue was born during hard times. Food was rationed. Even in that southern area that was supposed to have fertile farmland and many rivers, people had to eat a certain amount other grains like corn meal and sweet potato flour. The three boys grew bigger and ate a lot. The shortage of rationed foods made the situation worse. Zhongyue's mother paid the higher price for the other grains that other people didn't want in order to have extra food for her children. At each meal, she always let her sons eat first. By the time she took off her apron and sat down to eat, the rice pot was often already empty. Buns made of sweet potato flour were very dry, even with some vegetable oil drops, and tasted like sawdust. Zhongyue's mother would chew one of these for a long time, but she had trouble swallowing it. As she tried to take in the food, the veins on her forehead would protrude. Zhongyue felt his heart tighten when he saw his mother eat the buns. However, at the next meal, he still couldn't resist the temptation of rice.

Due to years of malnutrition and overwork, Zhongyue's mother's health gradually deteriorated.

One night, when the three children were doing homework around the dinner table, she suddenly asked why the electricity was cut. Zhongyue said that the light was on, and his mother said nothing for a while. Then Zhongyue heard her crying—she had suddenly become blind.

After she lost her sight, Zhongyue's mother couldn't cut shoe soles any more. She was transferred to the packing workshop, which didn't require her to see. She could no longer knit either. After she lost her monthly compensation and additional income from knitting, the family lived a harder life. The three children learned to take responsibility. After homework every day, they worked on making matchboxes. They could make one *fen* from making two matchboxes. They made a hundred before going to bed. The children handed in some money they had made to their mother and used the rest to buy cod liver oil for her.

Zhongyue's mother's sight was better sometimes and worse at other times, but at least she wasn't totally blind.

Later, all three children grew up and started their own families. After graduating from university, Zhongyue lived in the provincial capital. His mother had lived alone since her children had left home because she didn't want to depend on any of them. Zhongyue was the youngest, and he was his mother's favourite. When he invited her to come to Toronto to visit them, she hesitated for a while, but finally came.

His mother had always conserved everything no matter where she lived. In Zhongyue's home, she didn't want to use the washing machine or dryer, so she washed her clothes by hand and hung them in the bathroom to dry. The clothes looked like flags and banners from different countries; water from the wet clothes dripped onto the floor. Xiaoxiao mentioned that the floor tiles might get damaged, and that the clothes that hung in the bathroom would embarrass visitors. Xiaoxiao repeated this many times, and Zhongyue's mother eventually started washing clothes after they went to work and putting them away before they came back home. She couldn't see the trace of water on the floor, and she assumed that others couldn't see it either. But when Xiaoxiao noticed it, she screwed up her face.

Zhongyue's mother used to work hard, and, in her son's home, her old habits died hard. Every day, her priorities were cooking a big meal and waiting for her son and daughter-in-law to come back from work. She still practised her way of cooking, stir-frying dishes in highly heated oil with all kinds of spices: ginger, onion, garlic, star-anise, and red and green chillies. Often, smoke would fill the kitchen and the smoke detector would ring loudly. Even after a whole night, the smell from the cooking of a meal wouldn't go away. After a while, the furniture and walls were covered with a layer of sticky grease.

Xiaoxiao asked her to lower the heat. Zhongyue told her to boil more and stir-fry less. His mother answered back, telling them that their way wasn't called cooking. Zhongyue's mother would comply for a few days, then resume her old ways..

Then Xiaoxiao began to take Xiaoyue out to meals, bringing back some food for Zhongyue and his mother. The problem was solved. But now that she had no meals to cook, Zhongyue's mother felt empty in her heart. She didn't understand English and even had trouble speaking standard Chinese, so she didn't like reading, watching TV, or going out. Every day she sat at home, waiting for her son to come back. When Zhongyue came home and saw his mother sitting motionlessly in the lightless living room, her eyes flashing like a cat's, he sighed and told his mother that electricity was inexpensive and keeping a light on didn't cost much money.

Lately, his mother had learned to smoke. She saved on everything except for her cigarettes, which she had brought with her from China. She had brought two large suitcases, and cigarettes had filled half of one. Zhongyue's mother only smoked a particular kind of cigarette produced in Yunnan because it was strong. She loved smoking while walking around in the house, and the ash from her cigarettes fell onto the carpet. Because of her poor eyesight, she walked over the fallen ash, leaving traces on the carpet. Xiaoxiao bought seven ashtrays and placed one in each room, but his mother always forgot to use them. Her teeth had yellow stains all over, and whenever she smiled, her blackened gums were visible. The cups, towels, pillows, and bedding that she used had a strong odour of smoke.

Zhongyue's mother had dreamed about having a daughter, but instead she had three sons. Her eldest son and second son had sons, too. Only the youngest son, Zhongyue, had a daughter. Zhongyue's mother was very fond of Xiaoyue, her granddaughter. Whenever she saw her, she wanted to hug and kiss her, but Xiaoyue bent herself like a porcupine and asked her grandma not to touch her. Xiaoyue spoke English. Zhongyue's mother didn't understand her, but she knew that Xiaoyue's body language meant she was avoiding her. Her extended hands hung in the air. Raising his eyebrows, Zhongyue told his daughter that he had been held by her grandma when he was a child. Why did she become a princess, and untouchable? Xiaoxiao didn't look at Zhongyue, but told his mother, because she had never lived with a smoker, Xiaoyue wasn't used to smoke. Hearing that, Zhongyue's mother was speechless. She did not dare to touch Xiaoyue after that.

Zhongyue's mother's visa was for six months, but after two months she said she wanted to leave. In fact, she hoped her son would ask her to stay. But Xiaoxiao didn't say anything, so Zhongyue kept silent. Despite her poor eyesight, Zhongyue's mother could see clearly that in her son's home, her daughter-in-law ruled the roost.

Zhongyue's mother had arrived after the Chinese New Year, and she left in the spring. Her flight was in the early morning. It was cold. Xiaoxiao and Xiaoyue were still in bed. Alone, Zhongyue drove his mother to the airport. Along the way, Zhongyue felt like he couldn't breathe, as if something was blocking his throat. Every breath sounded like a sigh.

After parking the car, they still had a lot of time. Zhongyue took his mother to a restaurant at the airport for breakfast. It was very expensive, and the food was foreign to her. Zhongyue's orders filled a table, but his mother hadn't gotten used to Canadian food. She only touched a little and then asked Zhongyue to pack everything up. Not wanting to waste the tea, she drank it up. Finally, she stretched her shaky hand over the table to grasp Zhongyue's. His mother's hand was very dry; the back of it was covered with blue veins that looked like earthworms. There was soil under her nails—it had come from the backyard when she had swept up the leftover leaves the day before.

"My baby, listen to her and follow her. When I was young, your dad followed me, too," said Zhongyue's mother.

She had become pregnant with Zhongyue at the age of forty. She'd never called his name; she just called him Baby. The word, baby, was like a stone that broke his heart; his tears welled up silently. He ran to a washroom and sat on the toilet. He stuck a tissue over his mouth and wept violently.

Back at the table, he took an envelope out of his pocket and placed it in his mother's pocket.

Two thousand U.S. dollars. "Five hundred for each brother. You keep a thousand," he said to her.

Then Zhongyue accompanied his mother in the long line for the security check. The mother and son didn't speak. Before his mother crossed the gate, Zhongyue said hesitatingly, "When my brothers write or call, don't mention anything about the money."

After seeing his mother off, Zhongyue left the airport. It was a chilly spring day. The morning sun was like cold water; the wind made new branches quiver. Zhongyue looked in his pocket for a tissue to blow his nose, but instead he felt the envelope with the money—his mother had put it back in his pocket.

That day, Zhongyue sat in the car and started the engine. For a long time he didn't move the car, and it puffed like a person panting. White smoke rose in the window, gathered together, and gradually dissipated. His vision suddenly became clear. At that moment, he realized his own unhappiness, an unhappiness that was separate from Xiaoxiao's.

So, two months later, when Xiaoxiao proposed the separation, he didn't object, although he was reluctant.

Xiaoyue,

The aurora is the luminous phenomenon of the earth's upper atmosphere in high latitudes. It's a result of the interaction between the solar wind and Earth's magnetic field. The solar wind is a stream of charged particles ejected from the sun. When it blows over the earth, it is trapped in Earth's magnetic field, which is in the shape of a funnel. Its leading edges face Earth's north and south magnetic poles, so charged particles from the sun move through the magnetic funnel into the earth's polar regions. The upper atmosphere in the two poles ejects light when it is bombarded by the solar wind. The light occurring in the northern hemisphere is called the northern lights, and in the southern hemisphere, the southern lights. One of my reasons for coming to Sioux Lookout was to see the northern lights, but I haven't yet gotten my chance. It's said that every year young people come from all over the world to have their weddings on the night when the aurora occurs. They believe that if their marriages and pregnancies take place under the northern lights, it will bring them the most intelligent children in the world.

For nearly two months after the *powwow*, Zhongyue hadn't seen Dawa, but he saw Neil from time to time. Once a week, he went to the Whitefish Elementary School to train teachers. After each training session, he would give Neil individual help to strengthen his sign language and his lip-reading ability. But one week, Neil wasn't at the school. The teacher said that Neil's mother had brought him to the Thunder Bay Hospital for an annual check-up; because he had been entered into the hospital's database for premature children, he went through a complicated follow-up examination each year.

That day, Zhongyue had come home from work and was about to cook supper when he saw dark clouds out the window, clouds that almost touched the ground. He suddenly remembered that he had a washed bed sheet and hung it up on the balcony—people here didn't like to use dryer, and every household had a clothesline. He rushed out to collect the sheet. As soon as he had pulled off the line, rain poured down. In the distance, it looked like shining white curtains, but near Zhongyue it looked more like sticks dropping into

Penguin Lake, making numerous holes. The lake was churned like boiling water.

Before he could shut the door, it was pushed open. Two completely soaked people, Dawa and Neil, rushed in. Their clothes were like thin silk on their bodies, and their teeth were chattering, making loud sounds. The water from their heads and bodies dropped onto the floor and formed muddy circles.

Zhongyue quickly took out two large bath towels, one for each of his visitors and sent them into the bathroom. Then he found a sweater and a pair of sweatpants in the closet and placed them near the bathroom door for Dawa to wear. He rummaged through his clothes, but he couldn't find a suitable garment for Neil, so he pulled out a blanket from the bed and put it near the door.

Neil came out first. He was tightly wrapped in the blanket. Only his face was exposed, small like the palm of Zhongyue's hand and red from the hot water. His little feet moved quickly, carrying his body in the blanket, like a wound up electric toy. His ugly face could have softened even the hardest of hearts. Zhongyue lifted Neil onto the sofa and used a small hair dryer to blow his hair dry. Before long, Neil fell asleep on his lap. His light breathing made Zhongyue's leg itch, and his saliva dripped onto Zhongyue's pants.

Dawa spent more time in the bathroom. Eventually she came out, already wearing Zhongyue's sweater. The sleeves were rolled up, but the hem reached her knees. In such a large garment, Dawa looked thin and small, like a girl who hadn't yet reached adulthood. Dawa sat near Neil's feet and unwound her braids to dry her hair. Zhongyue hadn't ever seen such long hair; it was like shred of clouds moving in the wind. After it was dried, she coiled it up into a big bun on the back of her head and Dawa's steam-covered face was revealed. It was pretty.

Dawa bent over to shake Neil, who sat up, but didn't know where he was. Dawa tapped Neil's face, saying that he had forgotten what he wanted to tell Dr. Chen. Neil suddenly woke up and opened his mouth, giggling.

"I, excellent." Neil gave Zhongyue a thumbs up, pointing to his own head.

Dawa couldn't help but chuckle, and her laughter was like a marble rolling all the way down a smooth glass surface. If no one blocked it off, it wouldn't stop. She laughed until tears welled out of her eyes. Zhongyue took an old newspaper, rolled it, and playfully tapped the back of her head with it.

After she'd stopped laughing, Dawa finally told Zhongyue that Neil's IQ, which had been tested in the Thunder Bay Hospital, was at the normal level. His only problem was his ability to communicate verbally.

"It means you're a big bucket full of water," Zhongyue said to Neil. "The tap is broken, so the water can't come out. Let me repair your faucet."

As Zhongyue spoke, he rubbed Neil's hair, which looked like a chick's nest. As Neil shouted "repair," he jumped off the sofa and fell on the floor. His blanket dropped off, exposing his naked body. His numerous ribs were like piles of stones; his penis was like a string bean swinging back and forth. Dawa picked up the blanket and chased her son. Catching him, she covered the blanket over Neil and then scolded him: "Don't you feel ashamed? You're old enough." Like a fish in a net, Neil struggled inside the blanket and finally managed to stretch out one hand.

Pointing to Zhongyue, he said, "He has, too."

Dawa stifled a laugh and turned her eyes away from Zhongyue. She asked if he had eaten. He said not yet. Dawa took out a package from her basket and said that they could roast two pounds of beef ribs that she had bought from the Old John's. There was a fire pit in front of the house that he probably hadn't used. Dawa said that they could dry their clothes with the fire as well. From Zhongyue's kitchen, she got knives, forks, and an iron rack. The three of them put more warm clothes on and moved a bench closer to the fire pit. Then they cleaned the pit, got wood, and made a fire.

The wood was wet from the rain. Zhongyue and Dawa added more woodchips to start the fire, but only smoke billowed around. Zhongyue's tears and runny nose made Dawa chuckle. "This is the way First Nations people smoke porcupines. You're like a foolish porcupine. Do you have to sit facing the smoke?" Zhongyue changed his sitting position and felt much better.

The moisture in the wood gradually disappeared, and the fire picked up. Near the fire, Zhongyue formed a frame with several branches and hung Dawa's and Neil's wet clothes on them. Dawa began to barbecue the ribs. The blue flame licked the iron rack; the fat dripped down and made crackling noises. The air was immediately filled with the savoury aroma of the roasted meat.

Dawa grilled a piece of meat and threw it to Zhongyue. Then she got another piece ready and tossed it to Neil. He refused to eat his own piece—instead he wanted to grab the piece in Zhongyue's hand. The meat was hot. Zhongyue stood up, tossing the piece of meat from hand to hand while he blew on it to cool it off. He nibbled on the rib little by little. Out of reach, Neil stomped his feet and shouted. Curving her mouth into a smile, Dawa said, "You're a rare one, you know." Zhongyue asked why. Dawa just laughed, but after a while she said that Zhongyue was the only person who treated Neil like a normal person and never spoiled him.

Zhongyue's hands and mouth were full of grease. He tore off a piece of bread to clean his finger, and then put it into his mouth. "How can I? It's better to treat him in a normal way. He'll learn how to fight through his life and how to develop this ability so he can rely on it."

Dawa cooked another sparerib, and, holding it with a metal rod, she handed it to Zhongyue. He didn't manage catch it; the meat dropped. They both tried to retrieve it, and in doing so, Zhongyue touched Dawa's arm. Dawa cried out and used her hand to shield her arm. Zhongyue thought Dawa had been burned by the fire, so he tried to open her hand. He rolled up her sleeve, and saw a bunch of injuries—small dots, side by side, huddled together like weathered flowers. They were new injuries, and the scabs had just formed. A thin, soft, pink layer was scratched and bleeding.

Zhongyue threw the rib into the fire pit dislodging the metal rack and sending sparks flying wildly around like moths. Dawa and Neil were startled.

"They are cigarette burns, right?"

Dawa looked up and saw Zhongyue's eyes crack open. His face was twisted, and his hair was standing up like steel pins. She reached her shaky hand to his head and patted his hair. Zhongyue pushed her arm away, and Dawa stumbled to sit on the ground. Neil went to his mother and snuggled sheepishly on her knees. Dawa cuddled her son tightly. Both were as silent as stones. The fire weakened. The burned meat stank. Gradually the dark night fell, and the stars illuminated the hill range, the disturbed forest, and the dying fire in the pit.

Suddenly, lights appeared over the mountains, which were blurred by the night. The lights cast a long beam and it was hard to tell where it began and where it ended. Because it was quiet and peaceful, the lights as though they had been there a thousand years, even though they had just appeared, so unexpectedly. Neil jumped up and shouted, "Northern, northern, lights!"

Zhongyue placed his finger on his lips, and Neil became quiet. The aurora borealis gradually widened and brightened. All the colours on the earth were swallowed by that light, leaving only a blue-green haze that filled the sky. Under the aurora borealis, everything suddenly became small: mountains turned into hills; lakes changed into droplets of water; the woods were only grass.

How about people? Zhongyue thought. *In the eyes of this*

light, people are just crickets and ants. Any worries that people may seem to be unmovable boulders in human eyes, but, in the view of the light, they are just a fine dust, smaller than an ant or cricket. Zhongyue was shocked by his own thoughts; his body actually quivered.

The wind picked up, and a loud crackling sound rose up from the forest. After a while, Zhongyue understood that it was the footsteps of the light, which soon changed and became a colourful ribbon. First it was red, then yellow, and then orange and purple. As Zhongyue watched, the ribbon transformed and then became intertwined, dancing across the sky. Sometimes it moved; sometimes it rested. When it was quiet, the aurora borealis was at peace and harmony, like at the beginning of the universe. When it moved, it looked like a colourful skirt waving in the wind.

The northern lights came and went very quickly. In as long as it took to smoke a cigarette, it all dissipated. The starry night was the same. It was like a wonderful opera that started and ended unexpectedly. It seemed as though the audience had just got enough time to follow the plot before the curtain was closed. Nothing more appeared—only silence.

Neil had fallen asleep on Dawa, who carried him into the house and then came out to pick up the clothes from the branches. They were almost dry, so Dawa folded and placed them into the basket. Zhongyue watched her fingers as they moved. Her two black eyes were deep and empty, and all the emotions behind them had become still and silent.

"Ten years ago, I met a monk at Qinghai Lake," Dawa said. "He said my life was too hard. He said that men of paper or flesh couldn't repress me. Only an iron man would conquer me."

Dawa sighed and whispered, "Joy's the iron man. Joy and Neil are my debt in this life. I owe them, and I can only pay them back slowly.

Zhongyue searched for some words to comfort her, but he found nothing to say. He could only walk over to Dawa and gently hold her in his arms. Her scarf fell down, and he smelled the last rays of sunlight from the petals of the chrysanthemum in her hair. In this boundless world, he and she had met on this vast northern land. She had her injuries, and so did he. He couldn't cure her, and she couldn't cure him. He watched closely as she climbed on a piece of decaying wood towards a bottomless abyss, but he couldn't save her.

Then a dark figure jumped off the roof. As the shadow dropped onto the ground, it sprained one of its feet, and its movement was slowed. When the shadow finally struggled to its feet, Zhongyue saw a shiny stick in the figure's hands.

It was a hunting rifle.

Before Zhongyue had a chance to speak, he heard a bang. The trees shook; birds were startled out of their nests and covered half of the night sky. His shoulder felt numb, and something warm gurgled out. He wanted to cry, but his voice couldn't reach his throat.

"Joy!" Dawa, like a lioness, growled wildly and jumped toward the figure. She grabbed him tightly, and the two struggled fiercely. Zhongyue heard another loud sound. After a moment, Dawa fell silent in his arms. Zhongyue wanted to help Dawa sit up, but she was soft and boneless. He stared around in the dark, a kind of endless blackness without beginning or end. He felt himself falling into the abyss. No rope could pull him out of that darkness—he knew that he'd lost his sight.

In the pitch darkness, he heard some rustling. Then he was able to make out Joy's boots stumbling through the woods. The sound of his footsteps was slow and hesitant, and then it stopped altogether. The world seemed to hold its breath; everything quieted down, becoming as silent as the ancient rocks. Suddenly there was another bang, and Joy fell heavily on the grass.

When Zhongyue was finally able to pull himself up,, he looked over at Dawa, who was lying on his leg. A bullet had passed through her neck and come out from her back. He was spattered with blood; it was thick like tomato sauce. He couldn't tell whether it was her blood or his. Her eyes were cloudy. Before mist completely covered her eyes, he saw something in them, something like a corner of starry sky.

"Neil ... is ... the child ... of the northern lights," Dawa said.

Xiaoyue,

    I was discharged from the hospital today. My world was swept by the hurricane; only debris was left behind. I need to clean up the debris little by little and to see if I can remake the world into its original shape. I must do this myself. Nobody can help me.

When Neil brought Zhongyue to the cemetery, the first snow in winter had fallen. The snow in the northern area was very dry and light, like fine dust floating in the sky. Without warning, it had already covered the entire town.

Zhongyue and Neil walked along a shovelled path and entered the cemetery. Snow had blanketed all the tombstones. There were snow banks of different heights. Some corners of the crosses were slightly exposed. Birds that looked for food flew from one mound to another, the rustling sound they made accompanied the falling snow triggered by their wings. Under each snow bank was a totally different story, but the heavy snow erased all the differences. Neil stood in the middle, and suddenly he lost his way.

An old cemetery keeper came and led them to the end of the row of holly trees. He shovelled out a narrow path. He told them that the tomb they were looking for may be the third or fourth one, and that they could find it by themselves.

Zhongyue bent over and dug into the snow bank with his hand. It wasn't difficult since the snow was very loose. But it was chilly, even though his hands were in thick leather gloves; they couldn't protect him from the fierce coldness of the north.

Finally he scraped the snow off a tiny tombstone that had a little angel with wings was on top. The inscription was:

John Harrison
2001-2004
The way to Heaven is led by a child.

Zhongyue knew it wasn't the right tomb. He took off his gloves and inserted his hands into his down-filled jacket to get warm. Then he began to scoop the snow on the next bank. As he worked, he wondered how that three-year-old child had died. *Car accident? Disease? Unexpected disaster? Keeping company with such a young child must be her preference. In her life, there were too many people coming and going. Now she just needs peace and quiet.*

The tombstone was slightly higher and easier to work on, but his hands felt frozen, so he had to take off his gloves more frequently to warm them. After many scoops and a few pauses, his fingers were almost completely numb by the time he reached the surface of the stone tablet. It was his first time seeing the tombstone, but he remembered the inscription—he had written it in Chinese.

Cher Dawa
1968-2005
Born in a place where the cosmos blooms.
Died on her journey to climb mountains.

Zhongyue's fingers caressed the carved inscription. Even though it had been under the snow for a night, the tombstone felt slightly warm to the touch, as if it had felt sunlight, meadows, golden bumblebees, and cosmos all over the mountains.

Zhongyue stood up, and, facing the tomb, he slowly made some signs. He didn't turn his head, but he knew that Neil was weeping.

Xiaoyue,

I have decided to apply to the social welfare department to adopt that deaf and orphaned child.

Translated by Zoë S. Roy.

"Toward the North" was originally published in Harvest, No 1, 2006.

[1]The lyrics originate from a Miao folk song. Quoted from Zejia Hu's *Dreaming of Guizhou Mountains* in *Harvest* No.1 (2006).

Contributor Notes

Yuanzhi Cai (pen name Yuanzhi) was born in Jinjiang of Fujian province, China. In 1988, she came to Vancouver to join her husband who was studying for a graduate degree. She now lives in Toronto and teaches Chinese at local high schools. Yuanzhi's writing career began in 1999 and she has since written a novel, numerous short stories, and essays. She has been awarded top prizes in writing contests by *The World Journal* (1999 and 2001) and *The People's Daily* (Overseas edition, 1999). She is now the vice president of The Chinese Pen Society of Canada, a Chinese-Canadian writers' association based on Toronto.

Daisy Chang was born in Shanghai and grew up in Taiwan. She was an acclaimed journalist, novelist, and television host in Taiwan. She moved to Canada in 1969 and retained a professional designation in accountancy in 1981 while continuing her commitment to public service as a community leader. She served the community at local, provincial, national, and global levels in activities ranging from advising on multiculturalism to helping restructure the taxation system in projects sponsored by the United Nations and the Government of China. She has published six novels, one novella, two short story collections, three humorous prose collections, one professional book on

Canadian immigration, and one professional book on Canadian tax planning. She was a recipient of the Governor General of Canada's 125 Commemorative Medal for "significant contribution to Compatriots, Community and to Canada" on May 24, 1994.

Xiaowei Chen (pen name Chen He) was born in Wenzhou of Zhejiang province of China. He was in the Chinese army when he was young and then worked in the transportation business. He went to Albania in 1994, where he was engaged in the trade of medicine for five years. Since he immigrated to Canada, he has lived in Toronto. He is currently a freelance writer. His major publications include novels *The War in Sarawak*, *A Clothe Doll*, and *A Fatal Long Journey*, stories "The City in a Black and White Film," "River Credit," "West Nile Virus," "I Am A Tiny Little Bird," "Night Patrol," and "The Night of Yibao." He has won several major literary prizes, including the first Café Literary Award for Short Fiction (2009), the Yu Dafu Literary Award for Novellas (2010), and the fourteenth *Fiction Monthly* Baihua Award (2011).

Yafang Shi (pen names Yafang and Eryuelan) lived in Hangzhou and Jinhua of Zhejiang province, China in her childhood. She went to Hangzhou University to study journalism. In 1992, she left China for London, England where she studied at the London School of Economics and Political Science, before coming to Canada in 1994. In 2002, she returned to London where she studied for her M.A. degree in sociology. Between 2003 and 2006 she worked in Shanghai, China. She immigrated to Canada in 2006 and currently lives in Markham, Ontario. She has worked for some Chinese-language media and CBC Radio. She is now the editor-in-chief of www.lovingsisters. com. Yafang was a columnist for a Toronto Chinese-language newspaper and her prose and poetry works appear in some local Chinese-language newspapers.

Bo Sun was born in Shanghai, China. He received his B.A. degree from Shanghai Normal University and taught there before he came to Canada as a visiting scholar at the University of Waterloo in 1990. He has worked for *The World Journal* and *Sing Tao Daily* in Toronto. He is now the editor-in-chief of 365netTV.com. Sun began his writing career in 1997 and has since published more than ten books. including novels and prose writings. He also edited three collections of stories and two collections of prose essays. He co-wrote and published, with Xiaowen Zeng, a twenty-episode TV drama which won a Chinese Writers Erduosi Literature Award and a Zhongshan Cup Overseas Chinese Literature Award in 2011. He is now the president of The Chinese Pen Society of Canada.

Tao Yang was born in Xi'an of Shaanxi province, China. He immigrated to Canada from Shanghai in 1998 and lived in Toronto for many years. He is now living in Vancouver and working as a real estate agent and writer of TV drama series. Yang started creative writing in 1993 and has produced two novels, as well as many short stories, TV dramas, and TV documentaries.

Xi Yu was born in Shanghai, China. He immigrated to Canada in 1996 and has lived in Toronto since. He is now a journalist for *Ming bao* (Toronto), a major Chinese-language newspaper based in Hong Kong and circulating in Canada and the US. Yu started writing creatively in the 1980s, and he was already a published writer before he came to Canada. After immigration, he has continued his literary pursuit and has published many novels, stories, and prose writings in *Harvest*, *Dangdai*, *Zhongshan*, and other famous literary journals in China. His stories have been selected and republished by the influential *Fiction Monthly*.

Xiaowen Zeng was born in Heilongjiang province, China. She began writing fiction in 1991, immediately after earning an M.A. in Literature from Nankai University, and continues to pursue her passion. She moved to the U.S. in 1994, and studied and worked there for nine years. In 2003, she immigrated to Canada, and since then she has been living in Toronto and working as an IT professional. She has published three novels: *The Day Time Floating Journey*, *The Night is Still Young*, and *The Immigrant Years*. She has also published three novellas, more than twenty short stories, and a collection of prose, *Turn Your Back to the Moon*. She won a Central Daily News literature award in 1996, and a United Daily Literature Award in 2004. Her short story "The Kilt and Clover" was ranked in the 2009 Top 10 by the China Fiction Association. She co-wrote and published, with Sun Bo, a twenty-episode TV drama which won a Chinese Writers Erduosi Literature Award and a Zhongshan Cup Overseas Chinese Literature Award in 2011.

Ling Zhang lived the first twenty-two years of her life in Wenzhou, a small town in the southeastern part of China, which has later become the setting of many of her stories. She worked as a lathe operator and substitute teacher in Wenzhou until 1979 when she left home to attend Fudan University in Shanghai, where she obtained her B.A. in English in 1983. Upon graduation, she was employed by China's Ministry of Coal Industry in Beijing as an English translator. In 1986, she came to Canada to pursue her M.A. degree in English Literature at the University of Calgary, and then, in 1993, she obtained another M.A. degree in Communication Disorders at University of Cincinnati. Having travelled extensively and tried many different career paths, she eventually settled in Toronto. She started to write and publish her fictional works in Chinese language in the late 1990s. In the course of over ten years, she has published eight novels and several collections of novellas and short stories. Her writings have won her several important literary awards in China.

TOWARD THE NORTH

Canada Council for the Arts **Conseil des Arts du Canada** 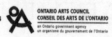 **Canadä**

We gratefully acknowledge the support of the Canada Council for the Arts and the Ontario Arts Council for our publishing program. We also acknowledge the financial support of the Government of Canada.

Cover design: Val Fullard

Library and Archives Canada Cataloguing in Publication

Toward the North : stories by Chinese Canadian authors / Hua Laura Wu, Xueqing Xu, and Corinne Bieman Davis, editors.

(Inanna poetry & fiction series)
Some stories translated from the Chinese.
Issued in print and electronic formats.
ISBN 978-1-77133-565-2 (softcover).-- ISBN 978-1-77133-566-9 (epub).--
ISBN 978-1-77133-567-6 (Kindle).-- ISBN 978-1-77133-568-3 (pdf)

1. Chinese Canadians—Fiction. 2. Immigrants—Canada—Fiction. 3. Chinese—Canada—Fiction. 4. Canada—Emigration and immigration—Fiction. 5. Canadian prose literature (English)—Chinese Canadian authors. 6. Canadian prose literature (English)—21st century. 7. Short stories, Canadian (English). I. Wu, Hua Laura, 1952–, editor II. Xu, Xueqing, 1957–, editor III. Davies, Cory Bieman, 1948–, editor IV. Series: Inanna poetry and fiction series

PS8323.C5T69 2018   C813'.01088951   C2018-904378-4
                                                    C2018-904379-2

Printed and bound in Canada
Inanna Publications and Education Inc.
210 Founders College, York University
4700 Keele Street, Toronto, Ontario M3J 1P3 Canada
Telephone: (416) 736-5356 Fax (416) 736-5765
Email: inanna.publications@inanna.ca Website: www.inanna.ca

FSC www.fsc.org MIX Paper from responsible sources FSC® C004071